Praise for

Singing with the Top Down

"*Singing with the Top Down* has everything I love in a novel: a colorful cast of characters with the most appealing heroine since Scout Finch; a rollicking plot that kept me up late turning pages; and a story that's tender, heart-warming, and wise."   —Cassandra King, author of *The Same Sweet Girls*

"With Sout' . . . . el is a delight."   —Dayna Dunbar, author of *The Wings That Fly Us Home*

"A feast for the heart. Wise, witty, and tender, this wonderful novel brims with expertly crafted characters and sparkling dialogue. A true pleasure!"   —Karin Gillespie, author of the Bottom Dollar Girls novels

"Debrah Williamson weaves tragedy and humor into a powerful coming-of-age story. Pauly Mahoney is a shining star, and the story of her journey through a tough adolescence and the American heartland is a winner. Take the trip with Pauly, Buddy, Aunt Nora, Tyb, and Puppy—and savor the pleasures of Williamson's masterful storytelling."

—Carolyn Haines, author of *Judas Burning*
and the Mississippi Delta mystery series

"With writing that sparkles, a story that shines, and a narrator who's nothing if not spunky, *Singing* is a story you can fall into and believe until the journey's end."

—Lisa Wingate, author of *Tending Roses* and *A Thousand Voices*

continued . . .

"This is the delightful story of the westward journey that parallels the pioneer tradition, complete with outlaws, Indians, and fellow travelers of various sorts. So put the top down on the convertible and join Pauly, Buddy, Aunt Nora, Tyb, and Puppy for high adventure. But watch out—there may be a mummy in the trunk!"

—Ann B. Ross, author of the Miss Julia series

"A coming-of-age charmer... Graceful and witty, Pauly's courageous voice is this bighearted novel's greatest strength." —*Publishers Weekly*

"Williamson invests Pauly's narrative voice with an authentic charm."

—*Booklist*

Paper Hearts

Debrah Williamson

 New American Library

New American Library
Published by New American Library, a division of
Penguin Group (USA) Inc., 375 Hudson Street,
New York, New York 10014, USA
Penguin Group (Canada), 90 Eglinton Avenue East, Suite 700, Toronto,
Ontario M4P 2Y3, Canada (a division of Pearson Penguin Canada Inc.)
Penguin Books Ltd., 80 Strand, London WC2R 0RL, England
Penguin Ireland, 25 St. Stephen's Green, Dublin 2,
Ireland (a division of Penguin Books Ltd.)
Penguin Group (Australia), 250 Camberwell Road, Camberwell, Victoria 3124,
Australia (a division of Pearson Australia Group Pty. Ltd.)
Penguin Books India Pvt. Ltd., 11 Community Centre, Panchsheel Park,
New Delhi - 110 017, India
Penguin Group (NZ), 67 Apollo Drive, Rosedale, North Shore 0745,
Auckland, New Zealand (a division of Pearson New Zealand Ltd.)
Penguin Books (South Africa) (Pty.) Ltd., 24 Sturdee Avenue,
Rosebank, Johannesburg 2196, South Africa

Penguin Books Ltd., Registered Offices:
80 Strand, London WC2R 0RL, England

First published by New American Library,
a division of Penguin Group (USA) Inc.

First Printing, August 2007
10 9 8 7 6 5 4 3 2 1

 REGISTERED TRADEMARK—MARCA REGISTRADA

LIBRARY OF CONGRESS CATALOGING-IN-PUBLICATION DATA:

Williamson, Debrah.
   Paper hearts/Debrah Williamson.
      p.   cm.
   ISBN: 978-0-451-22142-1
   1. Runaways—Fiction.   2. Teenage girls—Fiction.   3. Older men—Fiction.   4. Oklahoma—Fiction.
   I. Title.
   PS3623. I5674P37 2007
   813'.6—dc22   2007004621

Set in Centaur MT
Designed by Elke Sigal

Printed in the United States of America

For lost children everywhere—
may you find the home in your heart.

Chapter 1

The storm struck with take-no-prisoners fury. Sparking thunderheads swallowed the milk-thin sun and turned the uneasy dawn back into night. Cold wind chased a lone girl down the dark, empty streets. She hunched into her denim jacket and ducked beneath the awning of a store that would not open for hours. Overhead a hanging signboard groaned. The air was heavy with the threat of rain. Like any wild creature caught out in the open in unfamiliar territory, Chancy Deel was desperate for shelter.

She was new to the Midwest's violent rites of spring and had seen twisters only in movies. Given her current location and recent run of bad luck, she could not rule out the possibility of flying cows. The heavy sky rumbled and cracked, beading her face with the first cold-flung drops, spreading chilly panic to her gut. She hadn't become a juvenile in need of supervision because she'd made *good* choices, but hitching across the country to shiver in the rain with no plan B in her pocket might be her all-time worst.

The town she'd landed in was small and surrounded by cropland and wide, flat pastures. Cows, though potentially aerodynamic, could not mow lawns into neat green squares or wheel hippo-sized trash bins to the curb. So where were the people? Deserted downtown Wenonah, Oklahoma, could be the setting for a bad end-of-the-world movie with a weird rural twist.

Alien death rays vaporize all human life-forms. Nothing left standing but livestock and one idiot girl.

An orange neon OPEN sign flickered to life at the far end of the block. Chancy's heart surged. Open meant a dry hole with a door to keep out the rain. Clutching her backpack's wide straps, she ran through the downpour toward the warmth and was soaked by the time she blew into the Tip-Top Café. The door swung open with a friendly tinkle, then slammed shut in the wind. She stood blinking in the fluorescent glare, intoxicated by the aroma of coffee and frying bacon.

Country music warbled from a mini boom box next to the cash register. A string bean in overalls was seated at the counter. He glanced up from a plate of runny eggs, and with no change of expression, forked in another bite. The sixty-something waitress filled his coffee mug and turned to set the pot on the warmer. Her T-shirt, the same color as the yolks, sported the Tip-Top logo—a teetering stack of cups and saucers.

"We don't have a hostess or a smoking section, hon," she called over her shoulder. "Pick a spot. I'll be with you directly."

"I think she's lookin' for the drowned-rat section, Corl," the farmer said in an everyday, matter-of-fact voice.

The woman scolded him with a friendly shoulder shove. "You hush, Elman."

Shifting the heavy backpack higher on her shoulder, Chancy dripped and squished past the long counter and escaped into the public restroom. Drowned rat was right. She could handle being stranded, alone, hungry. But smelling like a wet dog violated even her low standards.

She yanked a handful of brown paper towels from the wall dispenser and wiped her face. A pale, big-eyed stranger peered out of the grainy mirror. All cheekbones and hollows and sharp chin. Dark hair plastered to her skull like a drowned corpse. Too much time between showers had left her moldy in places that didn't show, grimy in places that did. *No wonder the farmer had stared. Probably didn't get too many scary-looking ghost girls around here.*

She swayed on her feet and white-knuckled the lavatory. What was she doing, trying to lose herself in a place where cows outnumbered people? Her chest turned to stone. Breath jammed in her throat. The floor tilted. *Panic attack.* Chancy had believed the choking, out-of-body moments were minirehearsals for death until a ruddy-faced therapist in Pittsburgh had set her straight. Panic was only unreasonable fear. Imagined terror. Not the real thing.

Take control. Find the stillness. Breathe.

Chancy grabbed another wad of towels and blotted the rain from her hair. She'd figure out something. She always did. The road-worn girl in the mirror glared back, a mocking reminder of how badly she'd screwed up. Because she expected too much and asked for too little, the only person within a thousand miles who knew her name was speeding away as fast as his rusty old Civic could take him.

Alone was what happened when leaving was more important than arriving. Chancy trembled. Not from the cold. Or from the shame of being dumped like litter in the middle of Nowhere, America. She was angry. With B.J. for being the kind of mother she had to escape. With people who wouldn't leave her alone, and with Kenny Ray Kane for leaving her behind. Mostly she was mad at herself, for hoping that things could ever be different. Hot grease vapors fogged under the door and her stomach twisted. It had been more than eight hours since she'd jacked a snack cake and stick of jerky from a truck stop in Arkansas. Food first. Decisions later. She fished out the crumpled guilt money Kenny Ray had stuffed in her jacket pocket. Two fives, a ten, three singles. All he could spare and more cash than she'd seen in a while.

Chancy used the toilet and tried to scrub off the visible grime. She brushed her hair into a limp ponytail, shrugged off her denim jacket and changed into a dry shirt. When she returned to the dining room, Egg Man was gone, the eight stools at the counter vacant.

She angled herself into a booth near the door. Main Street was a field of water. Only a few big-wheeled pickup trucks were brave enough to plow its length. Bucketing rain sluiced off the dark green canvas awning. Pea-size hailstones pinged like buckshot against the glass and bounced on the sidewalk into the gutter. On the radio, a weatherman interrupted the country crooner's love-hurt-me-bad song to issue a county-wide severe storm warning.

"Coffee?" The smiling waitress set ice water and a laminated menu on the table. Bright pink lipstick bled into the lines around her mouth. She was too blond for her age and too cheerful for six o'clock in the morning.

"Thanks." Chancy's hand trembled as she turned over the thick white mug. Diner coffee smelled better than it tasted, but she would drink it anyway.

"Hoo-boy, it's really pelting down out there." The woman stood by the table, hip cocked, coffee carafe in hand. "Good news is, storm should blow over in a couple of hours."

"Okay." Chancy never encouraged conversation. But Chatty didn't seem to need any encouragement.

"Chilly for May, though. Predicted high of seventy-eight. Course, you know what we say about Oklahoma."

Chancy's shrug said it all. What mattered was how far Oklahoma was from Pennsylvania.

"If you don't like the weather, stick around a minute." The waitress laughed and paused as though expecting Chancy to laugh too. "I'm Corliss, by the way. You ready to order, or do you need a second?"

Chancy glanced at the menu. Her mouth watered at the prospect of eating food that was cooked, not mummified. Served on a plate, not wrapped in plastic. Purchased instead of pilfered. She couldn't choose. She wanted everything. Eggs and ham and bacon. Biscuits drowned in sausage gravy. A three-egg western omelet with extra cheese and hash browns on the side. Buckwheat pancakes and strawberry waffles and thick French toast drowned in syrup and sprinkled with powdery sugar.

She blinked away the satisfying images, searching for the least expensive item. "English muffin, please. Toasted." If she piled on jelly from the tiny tubs in the condiment basket, her hollow belly might be tricked into fullness.

Corliss tucked the menu under her arm and scoffed in her extra-hearty way. "Girl, chiggers on a hunger strike eat more than that. How about you try our, uh, Rainy-Day-Early-Bird Special?"

"What's that?"

"Two eggs, two sausage patties, two biscuits. Coffee included, for"— she looked up and pulled a number off the ceiling—"two bucks. What do you say?"

Chancy hadn't noticed a special on the menu but could already taste promise in the words. "Okay."

"How do you want your eggs?"

"Scrambled."

"Coming right up."

The waitress slid the order pad into her change apron and squeaked away in white Keds. Chancy marveled at the engineering skill required to pack a backside that broad into granny-waist jeans that tight.

Corliss slapped down the ticket at the pass station. "Order in!"

The cook's round black face filled the window, and his voice rumbled over the sound of sizzling grease. "Since when we got a Rainy-Day-Early-Bird Special?"

"Since you started minding your own business, Tyree."

"You know, Cat Lady," he groused with a head-shaking half grin, "you keep feedin' strays, they don't ever move on."

Chancy concentrated on the rain music beating on the glass until Corliss swung by to warm up her coffee and leave a folded newspaper. "Thought you might want to read the Sunday *Sentinel* while you wait."

"Thanks." Chancy avoided the woman's eyes. *Look down. Don't challenge. Never give anyone reason to remember.* Wary of kindness, she didn't know what to make of someone who couldn't possibly expect a tip and was nice anyway.

Back in St. Louis, when Kenny Ray offered to let Chancy ride along as far as Wenonah, he said she would be safe in the country town. She'd taken him at his word. Not because she believed safe places existed, but because she had ripped through her options. She needed to disappear for real, and riding to the west edge of nowhere had become another why-not decision.

Kenny Ray Kane, almost-friend and nineteen-year-old dropout dreamer, minded his own business. He didn't ask questions or offer advice and knew more song lyrics than regular words. The music in his head crowded out everything else. His tin-can car had zipped down the highway vibrating with bass, and Kenny Ray had stared at the yellow line, drumming crazy rhythms on the steering wheel to stay awake. Behind schedule and arriving in Wenonah in the deepest part of the night, he'd loaded up his impatient girlfriend, her tattooed brother, their instruments and three bulky amps. Kenny Ray and the Kane Raisers were headed south to the Austin music scene, and since Chancy couldn't sing a note, play a chord, or even hum on key, there'd been no place for her. Not in the band, and not in the overstuffed Civic.

Chancy sipped the strong coffee and thumbed through the *Wenonah Sentinel*. Today was Mother's Day. Definitely not a good sign. Opening the Trend section, she scanned an article about local mothers and daughters. Successful catering business partners. Two third-grade teachers at the same elementary school. Study buddies set to graduate from Wenonah State College next week. Best friends. Heart connections. Love and devotion. The newsprint blurred and Chancy's hands shook as she refolded the paper. She'd believed in mother love once. Tooth fairies and unicorns too.

At eleven she'd given up on Mother's Day for good and ever. A social worker with onion breath had agreed to take her to visit B.J. in the state hospital where she'd landed after choking down all her pills at once. Upstairs on the dead-end ward, a few listless, frowzy-haired women shuffled around the dayroom with tissue-paper corsages pinned to their sweatshirts. Others sat on plastic couches, their eyes glued to the door as though hoping some of their own abandoned, abused, or unaborted offspring might make the trip.

Chancy shouldn't have asked to go, but back then she'd had trouble separating the real B.J. from the capital M Mom who lived in her longing. She should have stayed at the shelter and eaten stale cookies with other unwanted kids. At least helpers were paid to pretend they cared. That day, Onion Breath had urged her over to the corner where her mother slumped on a folding chair, sedated and staring at the floor. When B.J. reached out a cold hand, Chancy flung down the crayoned card and ran from the room. Too late she had realized that being motherless was not always a bad thing.

Bucking for Waitperson of the Year, Corliss slid a workman-size platter of food onto the table. "I had Tyree throw on some gravy and grits. No extra charge. You like grits, hon?"

"I don't know."

"Don't they have grits where you come from?"

Chancy shook her head and swallowed a rush of anticipation. She picked up her fork and fell into the food, afraid to surface until she'd filled the black hole that was her stomach. She stole a glance at the waitress behind the counter. Corliss would be a capital M kind of Mom whose grown children would drop by later with hugs and pretty cards. Chancy imagined a younger Corliss placing good-luck notes in her kids' lunch sacks on test day and adding candy sprinkles to cupcakes baked for school parties. Now that they were older, she probably handed over tips to make a son's overdue car payment and gave good advice to a daughter with man trouble.

The rain pounded down, and Chancy lingered in the booth long after her plate had been whisked away. A few customers drifted in and out, trucker-looking men in advertising caps, wowing about the storm, joking with Corliss, sopping up gravy and guzzling coffee. When heads swiveled in Chancy's direction, she wrapped herself in stillness. Thanks to B.J., she knew how to disappear. She'd learned early that when there was no way out and no chance to fight, the only refuge was the one deep inside.

Maxwell Boyle stood in the doorway of his enclosed back porch and watched the storm lash new leaves off the yard oaks. Mother Nature knew how to pitch a proper fit. Beside him, his aging retriever whined at the hammering deluge. Alfie hated getting his head wet even more than he hated thunder.

"Don't blame you, boy. Too damp for ducks this morning."

Bad weather had blown down from the north, dumping hard rain like gangbusters for the last couple of hours. Standing water pooled in the pitted driveway and turned the yard into a rice paddy. Lightning sizzled across the horizon, followed by a crash of ear-cracking thunder.

Alfie backed away from the door and gave Max his sky-is-falling frown. Not all dogs could frown. Or smile. Alfie could do both. He might be right about the sky. Looked like the whole world was fixing to blow away. *Good riddance.* Last Max looked, it was going to hell anyway.

Alfie whined again.

"No walk this morning, buddy. Maybe later." Max was eighty-three, and the romance had gone out of rainy-day strolls. Alfie was holding his water. If he didn't act fast, the dog would whimper and fret until his obedient bladder burst. If ever an animal was too well trained, Alfie was it. Max stooped past the early morning crick in his back and spread old newspapers on the floor. Alfie sniffed and backed away.

"Best I can do. Take your pick. Pee on the paper or start building a boat."

Alfie nudged the door with his nose. Not to go out; just to see if the downpour had stopped. Dogs had no concept of meteorology.

Max opened the door. "Weather bad. Paper good. You gotta go, so go!"

Alfie didn't like Max's tone and barked back.

Whoever heard of a dog with privacy issues? "Oh, for Pete's sake. If it bothers you so danged much, I won't watch."

Max lumbered into the kitchen to brew a pot of coffee. When he reached for the filters, his hand was stilled by the thought that shuddered through him each time he performed the simple task or drew a breath or felt his heart trip.

I miss you, Hanna.

Hard to believe she was gone. Nine years his junior and fit as any fifty-year-old, she wasn't supposed to die first. He was the one with the bum ticker and a medical chart as thick as *War and Peace.* Always healthy and strong, Hanna had stood by him through illnesses ranging from the merely annoying to the truly life threatening. Any bookie with a brain would have stacked the odds against *him,* not her. She should have been a merry widow, blowing the insurance money on a summer in Venice with some Italian lothario. But then the cancer had grown. Rot Blossom, she'd called it with the cheerful sarcasm that had made her a favorite with hospice nurses.

He often wondered if Hanna had known she would go first. That would explain the certainty with which she'd brought Alfie into their lives. Eight years ago, when their nearly new coffeepot mysteriously shorted out, they'd headed to the shopping center for a replacement. The local animal shelter had set up cages of barking dogs in the center court in an outreach adoption program. Hanna had barreled past the cute, the ugly, and the peppy to zero in on a dignified golden retriever. A quiet observer in a pack of frenzied woofers. Most people wanted puppies and turned their backs on an old-timer with a faded muzzle, but not Hanna. With the oversureness that had been her best quality and worst flaw, she had chosen her canine soul mate.

Max's hand shook as he measured premium blend into the basket. He'd tried to talk her out of the impetuous act, reminding her that they'd agreed not to get another dog after Bunsen died. She hadn't listened. She'd declared Alfie special and deserving of more than a crate on doggy death row. Then she'd nudged Max in the ribs.

Old things can be devoted, as an ancient love machine like you should know.

While Max blustered, Hanna sealed the deal, claiming it was no coincidence that the coffeepot had gone kaput on Adopt-a-Pal day.

Some things are just meant to be, Professor.

God, I miss you, Hanna.

He missed her bossiness and her outspoken opinions and her need to always be right in arguments, both big and small. He missed her calling him an absentminded professor who'd lose his head if it weren't stapled on, and the annoying way she read newspaper articles aloud. It had been just the two of them for half a century. Two bowls of oatmeal on the breakfast table. Two yellow mugs on the cup tree. Two toothbrushes in a glass. How would he get used to seeing only one of everything? After six months, he still listened for her off-key humming in the morning and plumped her pillow at night. When he walked into a room and caught the faint, familiar scent of White Shoulders, his chest tightened. He thought he might be losing his mind, but his mind was of a piece. It was his heart that was broken.

He gazed out the window and watched rain pound Hanna's derelict flower garden. She'd made him promise not to let weeds reclaim the plot she'd lovingly nurtured through hot, dry summers and frigid winters. He had never cared about the yard, preferring to stay inside with his books, planting ideas instead of seeds. He'd let her down. Grief, as pervasive as strangling weeds, had kept him out of her haven. Max turned away from the window but could not escape regret. Summer was on the way, but his own cold winter was just beginning.

He laced his cup of strong coffee with real sugar and thick cream. None of that fake stuff. Hanna had nagged him about the triple threat of caffeine and calories and artery-clogging cholesterol. No matter. Cardiac valve disease would probably fast-pitch him out of the game at the bottom of the ninth anyway. He sat at the kitchen table, and Alfie trotted in to place a comforting paw on his thigh. "Poor old fella. You're lost without her too, aren't you?"

Hanna had claimed Alfie was an old soul who'd finally found his way home. During her last days, the old soul had slept on the floor beside her bed, summoning Max whenever she stirred. If not for Alfie's gentle alert on that last dark night, Max would have been dozing in the chair when she slipped away instead of holding her hand. He would have missed his chance to say good-bye.

He glanced at the business card stuck to the refrigerator under Hanna's BEAR WITH ME; I'M ON A DIET magnet. SHEVAUN WOOTEN, MSW. ADULT PROTECTIVE SERVICES. Social worker by profession, zealot by nature. The young woman had stormed onto the scene a few weeks ago and had been stirring up trouble ever since. Max wrapped the blood-pressure cuff around his upper arm as he did every morning, pumped the bulb and waited for the digital readout.

High, and no wonder. Wooten's well-intentioned interference was enough to make him blow a new stroke gasket or spring another leaky valve. Do-gooders! Thought they knew what was best for everyone. When she had called on Friday, he'd told her plain and simple he wasn't interested in assisted living, but he might as well have been speaking Martian for all she'd listened. Insisted on dropping by first thing Monday morning to "chat" about elder-care options.

Since when had a long walk off a short pier become an option?

The storm's turmoil matched the tempest brewing inside Max since Ms. Wooten's call. In a dim kitchen illuminated only by lightning and a bulb over the stove, he sipped coffee, ate toast, and chewed on the problem. A man hadn't ought to sweat bullets to convince some dynamo agency girl he could take care of his own damn self. In less than twenty-four hours, hardworking Shevaun Wooten would loom onto his doorstep. She thought she could back him into a corner and force him to make decisions about his future, but she had no idea who she was dealing with.

He wouldn't leave this house. It stood to prove the last fifty years had happened. That Hanna had existed. Max wanted no part of the new life Ms. Wooten promised. A crate on codger death row.

A flash of lightning silhouetted the bear cub salt and pepper shakers in the window. Hanna had toted them home from Yellowstone in 1967. She'd parked the silly things on the sill over the sink, and there they had remained, never once containing a grain of salt or flake of pepper.

Not everything has to be practical, Professor. Some things exist only to make us smile.

Max hoped he had made Hanna half as happy as she'd made him.

Her rack of useless souvenir spoons recalled summer travels. Sightseeing in the sun, making love in musty motor courts. No need to read the place-names. Max knew them by heart. Glacier National Park. Carlsbad Caverns. Royal Gorge. Mount Rushmore. Pikes Peak. The mementos were tarnished, but the memories were as clear as the endless snapshots they'd taken.

Max swallowed an extra blood-pressure pill in honor of Ms. Wooten's visit. The storm would blow over, but Adult Protective Services would not go away. He needed a plan but couldn't think about the future in a house so full of the past. Hanna had warned him about sitting too long in one place.

Dwelling is bad for minds and arthritic joints.

When the rain stopped Max pulled on his galoshes and clipped Alfie's leash to his collar. The dog picked his way gingerly down the driveway and nosed onto the sidewalk leading to the park. Across the street, Max's neighbor stooped to retrieve the plastic-wrapped Sunday paper in her yard. She shook the sodden bundle and the scattered drops sparkled in a stray ray of sunlight.

"Quite a storm, Dr. Boyle," she called.

He waved and nodded. Few people called him *doctor* these days. When he retired from the college, he'd gone back to being plain old *mister. Old* being the operative word.

Mrs. What's-Her-Name edged down to the curb and waited. For him to do what? Converse? They'd spoken before. She'd certainly introduced herself, but damned if he could recall her name. Alfie strained toward the young woman, ever ready to make a new friend, but Max waved without slowing down. He knew what Hanna would say.

At least the dog has manners.

Social graces be damned. He'd earned the right to be crotchety. Max shortened the leash and kept walking, leaving Mrs. Neighbor in her yard.

Marrowless old chickenshit.

He wasn't afraid. He was cautious. Shevaun Wooten was gunning for him, and he wasn't about to give her ammunition. He'd rather Mrs. Neighbor think him antisocial than reveal how rusty he was at talking. Speech therapy after the stroke had helped, but without Hanna, he had no reason to practice.

He was not a coward. At twelve, he'd run away from the orphanage. He'd ridden the Depression rails as a lean, hungry boy, and had walked into enemy fire in Italy before he was twenty. He'd dodged every bullet bearing his name. Made a good marriage. Led an honorable life in academia. Buried four tiny children and the woman he loved. He woke up every morning knowing he was alone except for an ancient dog whose own days were numbered, and he climbed out of bed anyway.

Let a coward do that.

Max stepped around a heavy limb that had fallen in the storm. Every big wind that blew through life left broken boughs and flattened flowers. Max had weathered many squalls, but Hurricane Shevaun might be the force that finally uprooted him for good.

They neared their destination and Max gripped the leash, huffing along at the dog's hurry-up pace. "Slow down, boy. You know I creak after it rains."

Alfie obeyed, but didn't stop to sniff every bush and hydrant as usual. Instead, he pointed his relentless nose toward the park as though he had an appointment he couldn't miss.

Chapter 2

The rain had stopped suddenly, like someone turned off a giant faucet in the sky. Wind-tattered clouds gave way to sunshine. Chancy lingered in the Tip-Top, needing to move on but undecided. She could gamble on luck and hike back to the highway. Climb into another car with another scary stranger. End up in another place she didn't know. Or she could stay in Wenonah and watch for a sign. No one in Pittsburgh would think to look for her in the middle of America. And a town where waitresses didn't expect tips and gave free grits to strays might be worth checking out.

Chancy unzipped her backpack and removed one of the small paper hearts she'd woven during the long car trip. The heart was made of scavenged strips of glossy newspaper ads. Not her best work. The shape was wrong, but the colors were pretty. Watery blues and greens. A mermaid's heart. She placed the token on top of the napkin dispenser where Corliss was sure to find it, then shouldered her backpack and stepped to the register.

"Everything all right?" Corliss rang up the ticket.

"Huh?" Panic iced through Chancy. Nothing was ever right.

"Food okay?"

"Oh. Yes."

"Even the grits?"

"Especially the grits." Curiosity made her break the no-conversation rule. "What are grits anyway?"

"Ground hominy."

"Hominy." Chancy had no idea what hominy was, but she liked the way the word rolled off her tongue. *Hominy. Harmony.* Something she'd always wanted. Now she had tasted the next best thing.

"I can tell you're not from around here." Corliss grinned. "Your accent."

"*I* have an accent?" Pretty funny considering the woman's every word was rolled in cornmeal and deep fat fried.

"You sure do. New in town?"

"Yeah." Chancy handed Corliss three ones and waited for the change. Twenty dollars left. If she spent two bucks a day on food, she could eat for ten days. If she ate every other day, the money would last twenty. Then what? She didn't want to go back to taking stuff from stores and paying with bartered hearts, but she would if she had to. There were worse crimes than stealing.

"Here ya go, hon." Corliss winked and dropped coins into Chancy's outstretched hand. "Y'all come back."

Y'all. She'd traveled so far even the language had changed. Maybe she should look around and wait for a feeling to find her. "How do I get to the public library?"

"East on Main, north on Windom. Big brick building. Can't miss it."

"Is it very far?"

"Five or six blocks." Corliss closed the cash drawer with her hip and winked. "Don't be a stranger. Come back tomorrow for our Danged-If-It-Ain't-Monday-Again Special."

Chancy liked Corliss and the Tip-Top's greasy ambience. She even liked harmony grits. But she wouldn't risk coming back. She turned away from the woman's big grin and slipped out the door. Viewed through the sun's prism, the tearstained world looked clean. Fresh. Real spring rain smelled better than the same-name deodorizer used to mask the stink of desperation and fear at the shelter. When Chancy had disappeared from the group home in Pittsburgh, the state had probably declared her a runaway. But running wasn't her style. She'd quietly waited for the right moment and had simply walked away from the confusion.

She crossed the street. Thirty-nine days and a thousand miles later, and here she was, walking again. Walking cleared away confusion and warmed her when she was cold. Walking helped her earn points by out-guessing the universe. How many paces to the next corner? To that big tree? To the gas station ahead? Lucky numbers earned points. Three. Six. Nine. Three white cars parked in a row. Nine birds on a wire. A building with six windows; three over three. Double points if she predicted the ac-tions of others. Which way would the guy on the green bike turn? Points could be traded for cosmic favors. Fifty for a safe night place. Twenty for something to eat.

Nothing was free.

Everything had to be earned.

Chancy had learned the rules of walking by making mistakes. Glanc-ing at passersby was okay; making eye contact was not. Wanderers and stumblers attracted bad attention. She was a blender and sliced cleanly through space, careful not to rattle too many molecules or leave a memory of herself behind. The town was larger than she had first thought, maybe even big enough to disappear in. Friendlier in the sunshine than in the storm. On Wenonah's downtown streets, purple pansy faces nodded from sidewalk planters. Green awnings shaded pretty window displays. Old-fashioned lampposts arched over each corner.

She paused outside a restaurant and read the chalkboard message in the window. SPECIAL MOTHER'S DAY LUNCHEON. 10 TO 2. FREE ROSE FOR EV-ERY MOTHER. A peek inside revealed a dim interior with flickering candles. Servers in crisp white shirts moved efficiently among upholstered booths and linen-covered tables. The well-dressed diners were mostly family groups. Treating Mom to a nice meal after church.

Chancy stepped into the awning's shadow as two people climbed out of a minivan parked at the curb. A tall woman and a coltish boy. The woman's hair was dark, and the boy's an unruly blond mess, but they had the same smile, and Chancy knew they were mother and son. She imagined herself in their circle, belonging. Knowing what to say and when to laugh. The pair leaned together, safe in real-mother warmth. The grinning boy held the door. The woman smiled back, proud of him, and swept inside. A lucky kid with a good mom who deserved a special lunch and a free rose.

On the next block, Chancy passed a two-story structure housing an antique store. The facade resembled a Victorian house like the dollhouse Chancy had played with in therapy when she was five. She'd placed the silent doll family in the rooms. She didn't have the words, real or imagined, to make them speak. The therapist had hovered in the background, watching, taking notes, prompting. *Then what happens?*

The day Chancy stuffed the mother doll inside a grinning Jack-in-the-box and slammed down the trapdoor, the lady set aside her pad and asked questions Chancy could not answer. After that B.J. moved them to a new place and play therapy ended, but Chancy never forgot the dolls or their perfect little house. Whenever she needed to hide, she made herself small enough to fit inside. She became sister doll, gliding from room to room, feet never touching the floor, floating up the stairs to find the quiet.

Then what happens?

The display in a furniture store window caught her eye. Soft couch, patterned rug. A fireplace with a flickering electric flame. A thick book lay upside down on an easy chair, the reading interrupted by a knock on an imaginary door. Chancy squeezed through the glass and into the room, as she'd once slipped into the dollhouse. She picked up the book and nestled in the chair, listening to the heavy *tock-tock-tock* of the mantel clock. Like the dollhouse, the window's welcoming room was perfect. The way real life should be. Then she blinked and was back on the sidewalk where she belonged. Outside the dream, looking in. Someday she would live in this room. She would own more than she could carry on her back. If she evaded B.J.'s destructive grasp, she wouldn't always be rootless and wingless, grubbing in the dark.

Wenonah, peaceful and promising, seemed familiar. The doll family might have lived in the old-fashioned Toyville town erected in Chancy's imagination, one daydream at a time. She stared at the traffic light dangling over the street. If she reached the corner before the light changed, something good would happen. She would learn why the pansies smiled, and the magic trembling in puddles would be more than a shimmer of imagination.

She beat the light.

The library didn't open until one o'clock. Chancy crossed the street to a park as manicured as a magazine ad. She zeroed in on the tallest tree. There would be a bench beneath it where she would wait for the universe to deliver. Wind ruffled Chancy's hair. She lay on the bench and looked up at a sky the electric crayon blue of drawings taped to art therapy room walls. Instead of being abandoned, maybe she had been left behind like a paper heart. A gift for someone to find. Warmed by the sun and exhausted from a sleepless night, she curled on her side with her backpack under her head and slept until the nightmare images unreeled and made her whimper.

"Excuse me, miss. Are you all right?"

The words barely reached her in the half world between oblivion and wakefulness. Someone tapped her shoulder. She recoiled and tried to slip from the dream's grasp.

"Miss?" The word was punctuated by a deep-throated woof.

Chancy threw off sleep like a heavy blanket. She opened her eyes and gasped at the old man leaning over her. "I'm okay. Really." She sat up and hugged the backpack to her chest.

"You were crying in your sleep." His words were slow and slurry, the way B.J. talked when she took too much medication. He clutched a red leash attached to a big golden dog.

"I do that sometimes." She rubbed her eyes. "Bad habit."

"World is full of mischief. It's not safe to sleep in public."

If he only knew. "Sorry."

"Don't apologize to me. I'm not in charge. Of anything." The man's wrinkled cheeks were reddened by a recent razor scrape. "Sure you're okay?"

"Yeah." For a moment, Chancy had forgotten where she was. The dream had consumed her, blurring the line between real and not real. According to former bunkmates, she babbled in her sleep, but she must not have said anything too weird this time. If she had, the old man would have avoided her, as she avoided street people who carried on conversations with themselves.

The dog extended a paw, offering a chance to change the subject. "What's his name?"

"Alfie."

"Funny name."

"He's an amusing fellow." The man's words were slow. Deliberate. She imagined him walking the same way, taking each step in his mind before he lifted his feet. Not a stumbler or a wanderer or a blender. A thinker.

She stroked the dog's white muzzle. "Is he old?"

"As Methuselah."

"Who?"

Blue eyes, faded as old denim, peered from beneath brushy brows. When the man smiled, only one side of his mouth moved up. "Fifteen."

"That *is* old." Over a hundred in dog years.

"About your age?"

Chancy's arms tensed around her backpack. Geezer Guy was good. She usually passed for older. "He's nice."

"He has to rest before we head home. May we join you?"

"Free country." Chancy scooted down the bench to make room.

"Used to be a free country. Back in the day." He settled with a low groan. His thin back curved like a question mark. "Nothing's free now."

Chancy relaxed a little. They agreed on something. A good sign. Normally she stuck to a no-conversation policy, but her head was a lonesome place to live, and the old man seemed harmless.

"Maxwell Boyle." He extended his left hand.

"Hi." Chancy kept her eyes and hand on the dog. Talking was one thing, touching another. She didn't pet anything without fur. Alfie's mouth stretched in a goofy dog grin and his plumed tail thwacked happily against the bench.

"It's common to offer one's name in a social exchange."

"I think the rule is, Don't talk to strangers."

He chuckled. "Touché, chickadee."

Two small boys ran into the park and headed for the colorful playground equipment. They took turns swooping down the slide, and Chancy escaped the man's scrutiny by thinking up names for them. Cody and Shane. A man and woman followed, pushing a stroller that held a baby in a pink sweater. Emily. Chubby little Shane rocketed down the slide too fast and the woman stepped forward to stop his momentum. A good mom doing her job. Catching her kid before he hit the ground.

"Nothing pleases the soul like the laughter of a happy child."

The old man's comment severed Chancy's imaginary connection with the playground people. "Is that a famous quote?"

"Not yet. It's an original Boyle."

She gave him a sidelong glance from her end of the bench. He seemed to expect her to offer her name. "Guess you're not really a stranger anymore."

"I believe we just met. Miss . . ."

"Chancy."

"Interesting moniker."

"It's dumb." She'd once asked B.J. why she didn't have a proper name. Katie. Stephanie. Jennifer. She would never forget her mother's reply.

Those are the names of girls who deserve something.

"Chancy. A name fraught with possibilities."

The old man seemed nice, but he was crazy if he thought that. The dog's head turned from side to side, entranced by their small talk. Chancy skated her hand along his back. "What kind of dog is he?"

"Part golden retriever. Part philosopher." Talking was hard work for him. Too many words and he had to rest. "He likes you."

"He does?" She scratched under his chin, and Alfie sighed like a person who had guided another's fingers to a middle-of-the-back itch.

"Oh, yes. Alfie's an excellent judge of character. Only takes up with exemplary people."

Chancy's eyes narrowed. "Is exemplary good?"

"It's exemplary."

She shook her head, an almost-smile playing at her lips. There wasn't much to do while lying low in libraries. She fooled around with computers. Looked at magazines. Tried to read poetry. She collected words she would never use and stockpiled them like crumbs to drop and follow out of the dark.

"Are you a teacher?"

His wide smile revealed perfect white teeth. Dentures. But his hair was real. The color of summer clouds, thick and brushed back from a tall forehead.

"Am I so obvious?"

"You talk like a teacher." Not like the burnouts who had taught the emotionally disturbed class. The good kind. She saw Mr. Boyle in a big room with dusty chalkboards. Marking tardies and assigning too much homework.

"What a perspicacious observer. Max is my name. Chemistry's my game."

"So, I'm right?"

"You are indeed."

A half grin formed without intent, giving unexpected meaning to Chancy's day. "I thought so."

"Wenonah State College. Dean Boyle. Retired now."

"Cool." A professor. Chancy had once dreamed of going to college and proving to B.J. and the State of Pennsylvania that she was smart, not slow.

"Don't be impressed by old news. And you, Miss Chancy? Do you attend Wenonah High?"

And just like that, the door that had creaked open between her wary world and his slammed shut. Chancy gripped her backpack in both hands to control the panic.

Breathe. Breathe. Breathe.

Everyone asked questions. *Who are you? Where do you come from? Where do you live? Why aren't you in school? Where are your parents?* If they would stop demanding the truth, she could stop running. All she'd asked of the universe was a moment to sit in the sun and have a normal conversation with someone who didn't care who she was.

"I gotta go." Chancy knelt to give Alfie a quick hug, and the big dog licked her cheek. Dogs weren't like people. They didn't lie or make promises they couldn't keep. They had teeth you could see. And avoid. They had real hearts. She hoisted her backpack and took off for the library.

Halfway across the park, she slowed her steps and cast a reluctant glance back at the bench. Mr. Boyle sat with his cap in his lap and his dog by his side. He smiled crookedly and waved his good hand, then reached down and waved Alfie's paw.

The need to be known dragged at Chancy's feet. Her chest ached, not from panic, but from regret. She expected the worst and usually got it, but Wenonah had offered something new. Out-of-the-blue kindness from two strangers had given her a glimpse of a world she could never inhabit. Offered her a tempting, bittersweet taste of what she might have been.

Chancy turned and ran, filled with inexplicable sorrow over an odd old man and a smiling dog she would never see again.

Chapter 3

Max knew all about running for your life. The girl wasn't just afraid. She had fled with the desperation of a GI zigzagging through a minefield. He'd seen that hopeless look before, in the eyes of combat-weary soldiers.

Alfie stood alert, his big body quivering. Max calmed him with a pat. "Settle down, boy. We can't save the world." Couldn't even save himself. He stroked the dog's silky fur and found something tucked behind his collar. "What's this?" His arthritic fingers pulled out a piece of paper, which he held in his palm. A heart made of woven paper strips. The scrap art was awkward and simple, with generous sweetness in the effort.

"Wearing your heart on your sleeve now, are you, Alfie?"

The dog yipped and danced in impatient circles, eager to follow the little heart maker. Max held fast to the leash. "Sit! We're too old to chase females." Especially lost angels.

Alfie finally obeyed Max's command but continued to stare in the direction Chancy had disappeared, as though seeing something Max could not. When had she slipped the heart under Alfie's collar? And why? What did it mean? He stared at the small token until he heard its unspoken message.

Don't forget me.

Max's troubles and impending showdown with Ms. Wooten suddenly seemed insignificant compared to the misfortune that had put so much sadness in a slip of a girl. Why was Chancy in Wenonah? From the ragged look of her and the clipped sound of those bitten-off vowels, he guessed she'd traveled a long way. It had been months since he'd worried about another person, and his chest ached at the notion that maybe what he needed was something—or someone—to care about.

Following Alfie's gaze, Max squinted across the park hoping for another glimpse of the girl. No sign of her. She had truly disappeared. He should have done more. Said more. Offered her something. Money for a meal. A few kind words. Hope. But hope was in short supply, and Maxwell Boyle had nothing left to give. Nothing a frightened young girl would want.

Anchored by the weight of a disconnected life, Max remained on the bench as his mind wandered. An hour slipped away, as quick as a moment. He cupped Chancy's homemade heart lightly in his hand like a baby bird whose bones his clumsy grasp might crush.

The old alarm clock on the night table ticked a steady reminder that time was running out. Max laid out clothes to make the right impression. A new shirt saved for a special occasion, blue enough to tone down the rheumy eyes of a restless night. Slacks pressed to a knife crease. Good socks. Leather belt. Wingtips, spit-shined and ready to march. Before the siege began at ten o'clock, he would slick his hair, shave his jowls, and douse himself with cologne. He might be a codger on the cusp, but he would be battle ready.

His old drill sergeant had taught him that a good soldier always prepared for the worst. Basic training. Camp Gruber. 'Forty-two. Funny how a man's memory worked. Max couldn't remember where he'd left the book he was reading, but he hadn't forgotten Sgt. Alvin Butts. The bigmouthed, hard-nosed, redneck son of a bitch's tough training had saved a lot of boys' lives overseas, including Max's own. Too bad he didn't have artillery support this time. He was a platoon of one with an impossible mission. He had to look young for his age, capable of taking care of himself and able to solve his own problems.

If he failed to convince Wooten he was sharp in body *and* mind, she would never sign off on his independence. Good-bye, Poplar Avenue; hello, Codgerville.

The little paper heart on the dresser drew his thoughts back to the mysterious girl from the park. She had haunted his dreams, and even when he was wide-awake and pressed for time, her pale face kept him company.

Don't forget me.

Later, Max stepped out of the tub and cursed. *Damn!* He'd left the bath mat in the dryer downstairs. Why hadn't he noticed before he climbed in? He pulled a towel off the ceramic bar and wrapped it around his waist. A glance at the wristwatch on the vanity told him he had time to trim his Nosferatu toenails. *And yes, Hanna, I will pick up the clippings.* How come they grew so fast these days? Nose hair, too. What was it about aging that sped up the growth processes of things a man didn't need more of? Old guys thin on the pate were brushy in the ears and nostrils, as if the hair grew in, instead of out.

Where were the damned clippers? He rifled the vanity drawer, then remembered he'd used them to snip tags off his new shirt. He'd left them on the dresser. Annoyed at so much forgetting, he reached for the door-knob and stepped into a puddle of water pooled on the uneven octagonal tiles. In the split second before his feet slid out from under him, Max knew exactly what would happen.

Timber!

He was going down and there wasn't a damn thing he could do. A frantic grab for the towel bar was foiled by his weakened right hand. He struggled for footing and managed a half turn before falling face-first like a ton of stroke-impaired bricks. His forehead struck the side of the com-mode, and a giant pain hammer slugged him between the eyes. The room exploded in a quick red flash, then faded to black.

What on earth are you doing, Professor? Hanna's reassuring voice prodded him back to consciousness. *Wake up. Don't make me come down there and kick your scrawny ass.*

Let me stay with you, Hanna.

You don't belong here, Max. Go home. You have an important job to do.

. . .

When he came to, all Max could see were blue flowers, but his cheek was pressed against something hard. The floor. He'd wanted to update the bathroom years ago, but Hanna had loved the mosaic flower tile from the thirties. *Hanna.* He'd felt her presence. Recalled her voice, if not her words. Had she spoken to him? Or had he heard another echo from the past?

Outside the bathroom, Alfie was barking up holy Ned. Downstairs, directly beneath the open window, someone banged on the front door. The fog was lifting. When Max tried to leverage himself to stand, he collapsed again. *Well, hell.* He'd fallen into a codger's worst nightmare and couldn't get up.

"Mr. Boyle! If you can hear me, open the door!"

Shevaun Wooten, Supergirl Social Worker. She was pathologically punctual, so it had to be after ten. He'd been out for over an hour. LOC. *Loss of consciousness.* That was what the doctor had called his blackout after the burglar had knocked him down the porch steps.

"Mr. Boyle!" Ms. Wooten called again. "Hang on. I'm trying to open the door with a credit card."

He was in a fine fix. The tile was cold and his ass was bare and the ever-resourceful Ms. Wooten was about to break and enter. If he didn't find that damn towel, she'd think Hanna had married him for his money. He groped the floor, came up empty and groaned in helpless frustration. No wowing with wit today. He was naked on the floor, like one of Hanna's garden slugs, waiting for Adult Protective Services to breach the door and start pouring salt.

Private! On yer feet!

He'd get up. Walk twenty miles in the rain. On an empty stomach. With trench foot and a boot full of blood. He wouldn't be a burden or let his country down. But first, a little shut-eye.

What have you done to yourself this time, tough guy?

Comforted by Hanna's faraway voice, Max slipped down the hole again.

Don't worry. I'll stay with you until that girl gets the door open.

. . .

"Mr. Boyle! Oh, my God!"

Max's eyes drifted open. Shevaun Wooten rushed to his side and knelt on the floor. As unobtrusively as possible, she tugged the wayward towel over his midsection.

"Are you hurt?"

"No." Talking in his head was easy. With his mouth, not so much. Once the first word unstuck itself, others stumbled out at their customary snail's pace. "Slipped. Trick I learned. From Chico Marx. Help me up."

"No, no. Don't move." Ms. Wooten barked orders into a cell phone. "I need an ambulance at 639 Poplar Avenue. Hurry."

"No!" Max groaned. He couldn't go to the hospital. "No ambulance!"

Wooten snapped her phone shut. "Mr. Boyle, you need medical attention. No argument." The young black woman wasn't much older than his college students had been, but she had a commanding air and the makings of a fine bureaucrat. When Max tried to sit up, she stilled him with firm pressure.

"Wait for the paramedics. You may have broken something." She fetched a cotton blanket from the linen closet and draped it over him from chin to unclipped toenails.

What a sorry sight he must be. Stringy old rooster on a spit. "Nothing's broken." He'd know if there were. He'd had a few fractures in his day.

"Better safe than sorry. If your hip's involved, moving will only make things worse. Stay calm. Won't be long now." The young woman leaned over and frowned in his face.

"What's wrong?" he asked.

"You have a nasty-looking goose egg on your forehead."

"I'm collecting those. Black eye?"

"Maybe." She grimaced. "Probably."

A lump on the noggin. Ammunition in Wooten's arsenal. If he wasn't careful, she'd kick him into an old folks' home before God could get the news.

She'd first become involved in his "case" after the burglary, when a nosy discharge nurse at the hospital had blown the whistle on him. Who knew it was against the law for old people to live alone in this town? He never should have called the cops. The thief hadn't actually stolen anything. Alfie had awakened Max in the middle of the night, and he'd found someone downstairs trying to make off with Hanna's silver. He'd chased the culprit, they'd scuffled, and Max had fallen off the porch. The biggest shock had come when he recognized the would-be thief. Eva's teenage son, Ricky. That night Max had lost not only a good housekeeper but also a considerable chunk of his faith in mankind.

He had hired Eva Dimas to clean house when Hanna got sick, and they had never had a problem. Unfortunately, her boy didn't share his mother's regard for honest work. Mortified by Ricky's subsequent arrest, poor Eva had up and quit. She wouldn't come back, even after Max promised not to press charges. Last he heard, she had moved her errant boy to El Paso. Max was unwilling to open the door to another stranger, and the housekeeper position remained unfilled.

"You may have a concussion," Ms. Wooten said matter-of-factly. "Your eye is starting to turn purple."

"You should see the other guy." Max squeezed back a tear. Humiliation. Fine reward for living honestly and eating his damn bran every day. Bette Davis had been right: Old age was definitely not for sissies.

"Don't worry." Ms. Wooten was better at giving orders than offering comfort. "You'll be fine."

"Get my clothes. Don't let 'em haul me out like this."

"Moving you could cause more damage."

Max sighed. Were hip sockets more important than dignity? He'd come full circle. Arriving in the world butt-naked, maybe leaving it the same way.

"At least put my clothes in a bag," he said. "For later. Can't walk out of the hospital like a plucked jaybird."

"The hospital will provide a gown."

"What will I wear home?"

"You may not come home. Today."

Oh, yes, he would come home. *Today.* "Clean clothes. Laid out on the bed. Bag in the hall closet. Humor an old man, huh?"

Ms. Wooten slipped into his room and returned with the canvas tote. "Shoes, too?" he asked.

"Shoes, too."

Despite protests that he wasn't injured and didn't need a second opinion, when the paramedics arrived they checked his vitals and inserted an oxygen cannula in his nose. They strapped him on a gurney and hauled him downstairs to the waiting ambulance. Talk about zealots. Damn fools had careened into the neighborhood with sirens screaming and lights flashing. Wouldn't want anyone to miss the show.

"I'll follow in my car." Ms. Wooten set his bag at the end of the gurney. "I can handle the paperwork. Admitting will have all your info in the computer."

The perks of frequent flying.

"Dr. Boyle, is there anything I can do?"

He looked up into Mrs. Neighbor's concerned face.

"Remember me? Jenny Hamilton? From across the street."

Of course that was her name. She had moved in with her husband and twelve-year-old son a couple of weeks before Hanna's death. Max had spoken to her in the yard a few times. Friendly in the distracted way of busy people, she had volunteered to sit with Hanna so Max could go out, but he'd declined. They had hospice. Hanna had continued to fail, and Max had stopped leaving the house altogether.

Jenny had brought him a foil pan of lasagna after the memorial service, but he had been too busy grieving to chat. Or to eat. The pasta had gone untouched, just as Jenny's friendly overture had gone unacknowledged. A few weeks ago, a contractor's crew had swarmed over the Hamilton house like ants on a dropped Ho Ho. He figured she was knee-deep in renovations, because lately he'd seen her only from a coming-and-going distance. She seemed nice enough, but it galled him to ask an almost perfect stranger for a favor.

"I hate to shut my dog up in the house alone. Would you see to him? In case I don't get home . . . right away."

"Yes. Of course." Jenny patted his blanketed shoulder. Did she know how risky it was to get involved in the problems of casual acquaintances?

"What's your dog's name again?" she asked.

"Alfie."

"Right. Don't worry about a thing."

"Key under the mat. Dog food in the pantry. Leash by the back door."

"I'll find everything. I'll take Alfie home with me and lock up the house. Adam can walk him after school."

Adam. The skateboarding gee-whiz kid in baggy pants who'd turned Poplar Avenue into a speed course. "Your boy like dogs?"

"Loves them. Save your breath. Don't try to talk."

Max had to talk, even if it was with the halting cadence of a village idiot. Talking was what he did. What he'd always done. Talk had gotten him out of tight spots and helped him over rough patches. Made up for the charm he'd lacked. Teaching was talk. Talk was teaching. He'd talked and taught for forty years. On their first anniversary, Hanna had admitted she'd accepted his marriage proposal because she couldn't imagine not talking to him for the rest of her life.

Now he was swaddled like a baby and strapped to a damned gurney. He couldn't stand up like a man or go down swinging. Talking was all he could do. If he couldn't talk, he might as well be dead.

"If I don't come back—"

"Don't say that," Jenny said. "Of course you'll be back."

"If I don't come back," he repeated firmly, "will you find Alfie a good home?"

"I suppose I could take him."

"Would you?" He'd placed her in an awkward position. Good people did the right thing, even when it went against their better judgment.

"Adam's been asking for a dog. Sure, okay. We'll take care of Alfie for you. But just until you get home."

"Thank you." Asking a stranger for help was awkward, but not nearly as awkward as discussing his pending demise. "If I don't come home . . . contact my lawyer. Pete Marshall. He's in the book."

"Pete Marshall. Of course." Jenny's smile was uneasy but bright. "Don't worry, Dr. Boyle. Nothing bad is going to happen."

Max sighed. Only the healthy under-forty crowd had that much faith.

He was living on borrowed time and had racked up the medical history to prove it.

The paramedics were all business as they folded the gurney into the back of the ambulance. Jenny handed Max a simple white card from her purse. "Here's my number, if you want to call and check on your dog. Everything will be fine. You'll be home before you know it."

The EMT slammed the door, and the driver took off for the hospital. Land of miracles and lost causes. Province of Saint Jude. Where the sick and injured went in and never came out. Hanna had begged Max not to let her die in the hospital. He didn't want to die there either. And he didn't want to face the inevitable music. He'd ignored the cardiologist's recommendation for treatment. Canceled subsequent appointments. He was being rushed into a trap.

Max fought the panic that threatened to turn his guts to water. He wasn't alone. He had someone. A kindhearted, lasagna-baking, card-carrying stranger. Jenny Hamilton. He wouldn't forget her name again.

The driver used the radio to alert the emergency room of their ETA. "Eighty-three-year-old male. S and F. Alert, following brief LOC in the home. Vitals stable." He rattled off blood pressure and pulse rates.

A female medic sat beside the stretcher with a clipboard, intently recording vitals on a form. She seemed to know what she was doing but looked about twenty. Everyone was so young these days. When had adults abdicated running the world to children? Pete had taken on a junior partner who looked like she should be selling Girl Scout cookies instead of practicing law. Over at the college, he'd once mistaken the assistant dean of the chemistry department for a grad student. Hell, the manager of Max's favorite restaurant wore braces.

"I know what LOC means." *Been there, done that.* "What about S and F? Scrawny and feeble? Screwy and fading fast?"

"No, sir." The young woman checked the serious-looking equipment. Monitors. Oxygen tanks. Cardiac jumper cables. "S and F means slip and fall."

"I see." The emergency room at Hospital High would be full of teenage doctors insistent on running tests and taking X-rays and helping

Shevaun Wooten make a case against him. Well, he had news for the well-meaning medics of the world. If they thought they could pack Max Boyle in mothballs without a fight, they had another group think coming.

"Young lady?"

"Yes, sir?" The medic leaned close.

"SOL is an old military term. You know what that means, don't you?" She raised a brow, but kept a straight face. "Yes, sir, I believe I do."

"Good. SOL is what I am now." *Shit outta luck.* "Write that down on your chart, why don't you?"

Chapter 4

I t was five o'clock before the ER doc cut Max loose. After running all the tests and taking all the X-rays he could justify to Medicare, the Eagle Scout in charge determined that not only were Max's hips intact, so were the rest of his fossilized bones. His skull was not fractured or concussed, and he was not the proud owner of a brand-new hematoma. He wasn't dehydrated or malnourished and hadn't suffered a stroke. He had, at some point in the recent past, experienced a mild cardiac infarction.

"Apparently, you hit your head when you fell." The doctor hadn't racked up a quarter mil of medical school debt for nothing. He consulted Max's chart. "You must have a pretty hard skull, Mr. Boyle. The extent of your injuries seems to be a major-league shiner."

"Looks like you went a few rounds with Oscar de la Hoya." The male nurse, a middle-aged hippie with a ponytail, handed Max his empty tote bag and started tidying up the exam room.

Wanting to escape before the doctor dug too deeply into his medical secrets, Max perched on the hard chair, clutching the bag to his chest. He hated the way the young doctor towered over him. Like *he* was the kid. "I told you people I was fine."

"We like to be careful." The doctor scribbled a few more notes and handed Max a sheet of discharge instructions. "You need to follow up with your primary-care physician as soon as possible."

"Why? No damage done. I eat my Wheaties."

The doctor frowned. "You haven't scheduled your heart surgery yet?"

"Haven't gotten around to it."

"Given the nature of your valve problems, I'm surprised you're in such good shape."

"Sorry to disappoint you." Max rose and hitched up his trousers. Wooten, the nitpicker, had forgotten to pack his belt.

"You should call your cardiologist as soon as possible."

"Can I go home now?"

"Is someone waiting to drive you?"

Max hadn't considered transportation. No way would he phone Wooten. Might as well open the door and whistle in the wolves. "Last I heard, that's what cabs are for."

"We prefer a family member drive you, sir." The doctor subtly shifted his weight, blocking the exit. He looked at Max differently now. Like maybe he was the winner of the Dementia Derby.

Family member? Sorry. Fresh out of those. Outliving your whole generation had its drawbacks. "Don't have any. I'm the last of my breed."

Dr. Whippersnapper probably shared Ms. Wooten's opinion that isolated seniors were a major burden on society. An old guy alone was a prime candidate for long-term care and could expect to be shipped to the nearest nursing home without passing go.

"Seriously, you need to get in to see a cardiac surgeon as soon as you can. Maybe I should contact your social worker." The doctor rifled through the chart, looking for her name. "I'll make sure she sets up a consultation and accompanies you to the appointment."

"No! Don't bother." *His* social worker. Made it sound like he couldn't cross the street without supervision.

The three minutes allotted for each patient was over, and the doctor was growing impatient. "Do you have a friend we can phone?"

"Sure, I have a friend! What do you think I am? A misanthrope?" Would a senile man know *that* word?

"Give the nurse the number and he'll make the call."

Caught in a lie, humble pie. Max didn't really have a friend, but he had something that would let him wiggle off the hook. He reached for the homemade card he'd tucked into his shirt pocket for safekeeping once pockets had been restored.

"Here you go. Jenny Hamilton is my friend." *Liar, liar, pants afire.* "Tell her I'm the old guy across the street," Max called after the departing nurse. "The one with the dog."

Max hid his relief when his neighbor actually showed up in her minivan at the emergency room entrance to drive him home. The doctor was long gone, but Nurse Hippie didn't need to know that Jenny Hamilton's concerned-friend act was just that—an act. He offered a brief explanation on the drive home and did not object when Jenny insisted on holding his arm and helping him up the front steps like some shaky old pensioner. He was dead on his feet from seven hours of being poked and prodded by everyone on the hospital staff, including the window washer. He was in no position to argue, even with fake concern.

Once she had Max settled on the sofa, Jenny hurried across the street and returned with Alfie. "He missed you," she said. "Adam tried to play with him, but he sat by the door and whimpered the whole time you were gone. I think he sensed something was wrong."

"He's smart that way. Would have called nine-one-one if he could have reached the phone."

Jenny laughed, even though the joke was as weak as Max felt. She looked around uneasily and offered to prepare a bite of supper.

"Thanks, but I'm not hungry."

"You must be. After what you've been through today? At least let me heat some soup. Won't take a minute."

"Well, if it's no trouble."

"No trouble at all. You relax. I'll make myself at home. It'll be a pleasure to work in an intact kitchen for a change."

Satisfied that his master had returned in one piece, Alfie settled on the floor and rested his snout on Max's foot. Max leaned back against the couch cushions and considered his next move. He was soul-deep weary. He'd had the stuffing shaken out of him today, but the worst thing was feeling helpless while others took control.

No, the worst thing was being alone.

In the past, he hadn't worried about being weak or losing control. Hanna had always been there to take care of him. He couldn't see after his cataract surgery. Couldn't walk after his hip replacement. He couldn't talk after the stroke, but none of that had mattered. Hanna could see for him. Talk for him. He'd gotten better. For her. Because of her.

He still had a ruptured eardrum that wouldn't mend, and a ticker that required electronic assistance and leaked anyway. No wonder he was feeling less than himself, what with all the bits he'd lost over the years. Gallbladder, appendix, moles, tonsils, adenoids, and a pinkie toe tip. Amazing how many body parts a man could live without, but with Hanna gone what was the point? He was losing control of the parts he had left. His prostate was enlarged, his bladder was the size of a crowder pea and he'd developed gastric reflux. He needed new valves in his heart, but artificial replacements wouldn't solve the real problem.

Maybe death was the only reliable cure for old age. Max wasn't afraid to die. He'd glimpsed the reaper before. Caught him out of the corner of a jaundiced eye, skulking in the shadows of the sickroom and flying across the battlefield. He'd beaten death as a child, surviving influenza, diphtheria and scarlet fever. He'd outrun it as a young man dodging German bullets and bombs. He'd lived through the sinking of a troopship and had jumped out of planes behind enemy lines. He'd walked away from three serious accidents, two automobile and one train, none of which had been his fault.

He had led a charmed life. He was a fighter, not a whiner, but he couldn't battle time, couldn't outrun the inevitable. His heart wasn't just leaking. It was broken. Why didn't it just do him a favor and stop? As movie mogul Samuel Goldwyn once said, *If I could drop dead right now, I'd be the happiest man alive.*

The phone rang, but before Max could stumble to his feet to answer, Jenny picked up the cordless receiver from the unit on the sideboard.

"Boyle residence. Yes, he is. One moment." She covered the mouthpiece. "It's Ms. Wooten. Are you up to speaking to her?"

Max groaned. *Shoot me now.* If he didn't take her call, she would assume the day had done him in. He nodded and Jenny handed him the phone before ducking back into the kitchen.

A few minutes later, she returned and set a tray on the coffee table. "You seem to be out of saltines, so I made a grilled cheese sandwich."

"Thank you." Hanna had always said melted cheese was good for whatever ailed you.

"You need to keep up your strength."

Right. He lifted the tray onto his lap. "She's coming."

"Who?"

"Wooten the Relentless. Tomorrow. She wants to have the talk we missed this morning."

"Is that a bad thing?" Jenny glanced out the window at her house across the street, as though reassuring herself that all was well. "You told me a little about your situation on the way home, but . . ."

"She's trying to force me out of my house. Push me into a *facility.*" He explained how the social worker had turned him into a case. A crusade. "She thinks she's looking after my interests, but she's a kid. What does she know?"

"Maybe she just wants to discuss your options."

"Folks my age don't have options." The words slipped out before Max realized how pathetic he sounded. Twin shiners didn't make him pitiful enough; he had to whine too. He envied cronies whose minds had failed before their bodies. Unawareness was the upside of senility.

Jenny's forehead creased in concern and she fingered the small silver heart at her throat.

"Nice locket," he said.

"Adam gave it to me for Mother's Day." She smiled. "Picked it out himself and paid for it with his allowance. He put a tiny picture of himself inside."

"Adam sounds like a good, thoughtful son." A boy's character was evident in his relationship with his mother. Max had been so young when his own mother died, he had no memories of her now.

"Yes, he is."

"You're close?"

"Very. Maybe because Tom never had much time for anything but work."

"You've had to take up the slack?"

"I try." Jenny changed the subject by offering to keep Max company while he ate. She sat in his recliner. "Is there anything else I can do to help?"

Max ate a bite. Chicken noodle, his favorite. Maybe he *was* hungry. "Thanks, but needing help is what got me into this mess in the first place."

"I take it you don't have any family in town?"

"No family period."

"I'm sorry. No one should be alone."

"Hanna was an only child, and my siblings are long gone. We had no children of our own."

None who had survived. Denying Hanna a child to love had been the cruelest of fate's tricks. She'd accepted loss after loss, saying the Lord had chosen for them, but Max was not a religious man. He often thought of the four little Boyles who had never played in the yard or dangled from tire swings or biked down the quiet street. Two boys who never tinkered with cars in the driveway. Two girls who never baked cookies in the old-fashioned kitchen. Ghost children. If Hanna's womb could have held them, they would be here now, filling the empty rooms, breaking the stretching silence. Keeping hope alive. Max tried to imagine his miscarried and stillborn offspring as they would be today, middle-aged with children of their own, but the picture was as blurred and dark as an old negative. He couldn't see them because they were never meant to be.

Max looked up from the tray. "If something—anything—happens to me, would you be willing to take care of Alfie?"

The dog glanced at Jenny and whimpered. Max often conversed with Alfie. He was a willing listener and seemed to understand every word, but they didn't always agree.

"Of course. He's a sweet old thing. Don't worry."

Well-intentioned advice, but worrying was the province of those unwilling to act. "I know we just met, Jenny, but can I ask you something?"

"Anything." She leaned forward with an encouraging smile.

Max didn't need his neighbor's endorsement, but his biggest fear was not thinking straight and failing to realize it. "Do you think I'm wrong?"

"About what?"

"To want to stay here? Pete says the house is too much for me. Thinks I should lighten my load. Get out from under the responsibility."

Jenny stole another uneasy look at her own home. "People can *live* anywhere. But they don't always feel alive when they're in the wrong place. Sometimes responsibility is what keeps us going."

Max stared into his bowl and poked at a piece of chicken. How was it a stranger understood his feelings so well and a longtime friend could not?

"What if you had help?" she asked. "Someone to cook and clean?"

"It's not easy to find a reliable person." Max explained how things had gone downhill after his former housekeeper's son had bungled a burglary. "I'd need live-in help to satisfy APS. Which would mean more than one person to cover the clock."

"Some cities have social programs designed to help elders stay in their homes."

He glanced up, afraid to be too hopeful. "Ms. Wooten never mentioned anything like that."

"Wenonah may be too small to support an aging-in-place program. Having moved from Oklahoma City, I don't really know what services are offered here," Jenny said.

Aging in place. A great idea but probably not available. Max had come to town after the war to attend college on the GI Bill. He'd fallen in love. Not only with Wenonah, a quiet throwback to another era, but also with Hanna. Over the years, the insular community had grown to a population of twenty thousand and offered the conveniences of a larger city while retaining a small-town attitude. No doubt in a few years, aging in place would come to Wenonah. Problem was, he didn't have that kind of time.

Jenny stood and patted his shoulder. "You may not have any family left, but you have a friend."

"You sure? I'm pretty high-maintenance. You have no idea what you're getting into."

"I'll take my chances." She smiled. "Just remember: You're not alone."

"Okay."

"Eat your supper before it gets cold. I'll tidy up the kitchen."

Max bit off a corner of the sandwich. Jenny grilled a mean cheese. It would take more than tidying to put the kitchen to rights. Like a hazmat crew. He hadn't bothered to put the dirty dishes in the washer for at least a week. Maybe longer. When had he last mopped the floor? Cleaned out the fridge? Emptied the trash? He couldn't recall. Details seemed to get away from him these days.

He took a hard look at his home through a stranger's eyes. Jenny didn't see Maxwell Boyle, war hero turned lover-boy professor and jitterbug champion. All she saw was a decrepit old man whose quality control was shot to hell. Since he couldn't reach the cobwebs or wipe the grime off windows, maybe he *should* be in a nursing home under strict surveillance.

Jenny was smiling when she returned a half hour later. "I'd forgotten how nice a sink with running water can be. We're using paper plates and plastic forks these days, so I actually enjoyed washing your dishes."

"I can save 'em up for you, if you feel deprived."

She glanced around like maybe the rug needed sweeping too. Or burning. "Anything else I can do before I go?"

"Thanks. I appreciate your help, but don't trouble yourself."

Jenny had said she wanted to be his friend, but she didn't know him. Or that he'd spent so much time buried in books, writing papers, expanding his mind, that he'd never developed a flair for domestic chores. Her family was intact. She couldn't understand that without Hanna, a clean house didn't matter.

She scooped up a haphazard stack of newspapers from the floor. "Adam's school is conducting a paper drive. Mind if I take these off your hands?"

"Be my guest. I was planning to recycle them. Never got around to it."

She hugged the papers to her chest. "I haven't been a very good neighbor, Dr. Boyle. Seems like we're just too busy these days to slow down and . . . care about one another the way we should. I know how much a house can mean to a person, and this is a great house. I'm sorry you're being pressured to give it up. And I'm really sorry you got hurt."

Max hadn't intended to let anyone else get close enough to care. "Don't let these shiners fool you. I'm tougher than I look."

"I've been . . . self-absorbed," she went on. "I'm dealing with some, uh, problems at home right now."

Jenny's face crumpled and Max feared she might cry. He had no idea how to comfort a kind stranger. "You're a fine neighbor. Haven't had to call the cops once on loud beer parties."

"Don't pretend all the trucks and hammering and power tools haven't disturbed the neighborhood's peace."

He tapped his ear. "Not mine. Hearing loss. Advantage of old age."

"You're just being nice. And I appreciate it."

"What's going on over there anyway? You installing an indoor skating rink or something?"

She laughed. "Nothing that simple. We're renovating the kitchen."

"You have my condolences." Talk about disaster areas. Max knew that old Mrs. Brandt, the former owner of Jenny's house, hadn't updated the place in fifty years. Probably hadn't changed the shelf paper in all that time either.

"We're demo'd down to the studs. I have no range and no sink. In fact, the only running water downstairs is in the utility room. We're kind of camping out, since the microwave and refrigerator are in the dining room. You wouldn't believe the mess."

"You get a lot of dust when you knock down plaster-and-lath walls."

Jenny stacked papers by the front door. "Dust in my eyes. Up my nose. Even between my teeth. The stuff works its way into your skin, like sand at the seashore."

"Evil dust demons tend to colonize every corner of a house," Max said. "But you're making progress, right?"

"Depends on your definition of progress. We paid Mr. Matiska's clock-watching crew an obscene amount of money to deliver the kind of devastation I could have achieved myself with a homemade bomb."

"Russ Matiska? Good contractor, sour human being. Ol' Russ likes to do things his own way. In his own time."

"Tell me about it. 'Overtime' and 'overrun' are his two favorite words."

"When you start tearing into old houses, you never know what monsters you're letting loose on the world." Hanna had painted and redecorated their home from time to time, but they'd never felt the urge to make major improvements. What was the point of living in an old house if you replaced character with convenience? Might as well build new.

"We've freed our share of those monsters," she said with a frown. "Mr. Matiska had to call in a special crew to handle the asbestos-laced acoustic ceilings that some enterprising homeowner added in the 1960s."

"We resisted that impulse, as you can see." Max glanced up at the twelve-foot-high ceilings. Original crown molding still in place.

"Smart move. They've also had to pull and replace bad pipes, and because the dated electrical system couldn't support new appliances, the whole downstairs had to be rewired."

"You bit off a big chunk of the biscuit," he agreed.

"But it'll all be worth it." Jenny's reassurance seemed more for herself than for Max. "Easy to forget when I'm wading through sawdust. I have to remind myself to look beyond the here and now and focus on what will be."

"The here and now can be a killer," Max said.

"I know. Things are taking longer than planned, but according to Mr. Matiska, 'Deconstruction comes before reconstruction, ma'am. Gotta walk before we run, ya know.'" Jenny cocked her head to one side and pretended to spit a stream of tobacco.

Max chuckled. "Sounds like Russ, all right." A few hours ago he'd had no reason to smile. Now Jenny's pitch-perfect impression of the tobacco-chewing contractor had made him laugh out loud. Felt good to laugh again. Especially at the expense of a blowhard like Russ Matiska.

"Adam thinks he'll be in college before he gets another home-cooked meal." She glanced at her watch. "I should probably get home. I hate to leave Adam alone too long. Tom's illness has been pretty upsetting to him."

"I'm sorry. I didn't realize your husband was sick."

She lowered her voice a notch. "I think he might be . . . well, depressed. I've tried to get him to go to the doctor, but he's being stubborn."

"We men hate to admit our weaknesses," Max said with a sigh.

"Tom thinks he can snap out of it on his own if he rests. He's always worked hard, but he hasn't gone into the office for over a week now. Can barely get out of bed. Says he's just tired. Depression is harder to cure than an infection, but I think he needs medication."

"Harder to accept, too." Max had been caught in depression's claws for months. Once spirits got low enough, it was nearly impossible to raise them. Pete had suggested Max see a doctor when the joy went out of his life, but like Tom Hamilton, he had refused. He'd been avoiding Pete lately. Letting the answering machine pick up his calls.

Happiness was no longer important to Max, but Tom had reason to get well—a family who needed him. That was the trouble with young men. They thought they had forever. Didn't seem to understand that time ran out and there were no second chances.

Despite their proximity, Max knew little about his neighbors. He'd been turned too far inward to get involved. Except for Adam racing around the neighborhood, the Hamiltons kept to themselves. Tom, a hardworking land developer who drove a big black SUV and wore expensive suits, was the busy wheeler-dealer type who worked long hours and was rarely home. That was another problem with young men. They didn't always appreciate their wives.

Jenny was a handsome woman. She didn't have an ounce of extra weight on her but lacked the brown, sinewy look of women who jogged in the park. Attractive in dark slacks and a pink shirt, she had to be pushing forty but appeared younger. Pale skin. Soft and feminine. Her brown hair was as thick and curly as Hanna's had been at that age. Her blue eyes reminded him of Hanna too. In fact, Jenny Hamilton resembled his late wife so much, she could have been the daughter he never had.

"I'm glad we had a chance to get acquainted, Dr. Boyle."

"Same here." Who knew reconnecting with the world would feel so good?

"I confess I was feeling a little sorry for myself today," she admitted. "I've been worried about my family. Thank you for giving me some perspective."

"No matter how bad things are, somebody's always worse off, right?" A family with problems was better than no family at all. "Hanna used to say, if we all hung our troubles out on the line, you'd take yours and I'd take mine."

"I wish I'd had a chance to know her. She was a very wise lady."

"Indeed."

"Well, I need to stop yakking so you can rest." Jenny gathered up the papers. "I'll see you again soon. I promise."

"Thank you for making time for an old man with no one left to fuss over him." Max remained on the couch, but gentleman Alfie walked Jenny to the door. There was more he should say, but he didn't know what. All he could think about was how he would feel once she was gone and he was alone again.

"You have my number, Dr. Boyle. Phone if you need anything."

"Call me Max."

She smiled then, and he realized Jenny Hamilton looked nothing like Hanna. Any imagined resemblance had been wishful thinking and the longing of an old man's heart.

In the alley behind the Tip-Top Café, Chancy crouched next to a parked car and waited for the waitress's shift to end. She didn't mind waiting. Rushing caused problems. Waiting almost never did. On Sunday she had waited until the library lady was busy shelving returns before she slipped into a study carrel. She'd been rewarded with two uninterrupted hours of dreamless sleep. When the library closed, she'd returned to the park bench. The old man and dog were long gone, the park deserted.

She had waited for darkness. When no eyes were watching, she'd ducked into the public ladies' room for the night. The floor was hard and her blanket thin, but a folded jacket made a good pillow. She curled up in a corner of the refrigerator-cool concrete building, her red-alert warning system switched on high, in case anyone approached. No one did. Wenonah probably had a shelter for people without houses and beds, but Chancy avoided such places. A kid on her own raised too many questions. She had spent two uneventful nights in the park, all the universe allowed since staying longer would be asking for trouble; tonight she would find a new place to sleep.

An engine backfired on the street, startling Chancy back to her purpose. She couldn't stop thinking about Corliss's kindness. She'd sorted through her memories of her first rainy morning in Wenonah, searching for the ulterior motive that propped up most good deeds. Finding none, she had reached the only possible conclusion: Corliss possessed a special power that was even better than X-ray vision, because it allowed her to see past an outside layer of bad to the tightly wrapped good inside.

When the farmer at the counter had looked at Chancy, he'd seen a drowned rat. The cook had seen a stray. Corliss had seen someone who deserved a friendly smile and discount eggs. Chancy wasn't invisible to the older woman, just as she hadn't been invisible to the professor and his dog. That meant something. Staying in Wenonah was the right thing to do.

Chancy mentally replayed the scene in the diner so many times, adding tidbits here and there, that she could no longer separate reality from embellishment. Maybe Corliss wasn't real, but just another kindness she had imagined. So she'd returned to the Tip-Top to make sure. In her mind, she had practiced walking through the tinkling door, sitting at the counter, ordering coffee. She had even imagined the words she would share with the chatty waitress. But she'd done none of those things, because being noticed was dangerous. Instead, she would see without being seen. She would wait.

The back door of the diner swung open and Corliss stepped out, lugging two overstuffed trash bags. She was dressed the same as before: yellow Tip-Top T-shirt, tight-legged jeans and sneakers. Today a stretchy white headband held back her bleached hair, revealing faded gray roots and a forehead crisscrossed by wrinkles. The imagined Corliss had loomed large in Chancy's mind, but the real woman was too short to see over the top of the Dumpster.

Corliss set down the trash and flung back the heavy lid. She grasped the first bag and tossed it up and over the side, grunting like an Olympic weight lifter on TV. She heaved in the second bag, but this time she coughed. And coughed and coughed. That didn't stop her. Chancy admired people who were good at what they did. People with skill and strength and gumption who kept jobs and worked hard and didn't think the world owed them anything. People who accepted responsibility and didn't take the easy way out.

Corliss ambled back into the diner, and Chancy released a pent-up breath. She had not dreamed those memories. The kindness and harmony grits were real. Chancy could keep Corliss as a faraway friend without feeling like B.J.'s loony daughter.

Corliss returned a few minutes later carrying a white foam cup. Looking up and down the alley, she called, "Here, kitty, kitty. Where are you? I know you're starvin', Marvin, so come on out." She dumped a clump of scrambled eggs in an aluminum pie plate on the ground. "Okay, I get it. You won't show yourself while I'm here. Fine by me. But come and get it before some alley mutt gobbles up your lunch." She *tsk-tsk*ed and here-kitty-kittied again before disappearing inside.

The door had barely closed when Chancy spotted a small shadow slinking down the alley. The shadow materialized into a skinny gray cat, no longer a kitten but far from grown. Too young to be on its own. Long legs, visible ribs. Whiskers too long for its pointy face. The smoky fur, barred with dark stripes, was sleek. Despite living on the dodge, Starvin' Marvin was staying out of harm's way. Taking care of himself. Making the right friends.

From her hiding place, Chancy watched the cat devour the food, ravenous and delicate at the same time. It finished eating and turned back into smoke. Disappeared. She knew that trick and imagined the cat cozy-curled in a secret hiding place with a belly full of contentment. Safe.

She was about to move on when Corliss stepped out again. She dug through the contents of the big white purse hanging off her shoulder and came up with a jangling ring of keys. She picked her way down the alley, walking like her feet hurt, to a parking lot behind a tire store. She unlocked a battered old car, punched up the flowered seat cushion, and climbed in. The ignition turned over with a greasy roar and the car backed into the street. Chancy ran around the Tip-Top and watched it chug past.

Taking her cue from the other stray, she clung to the shadows as she committed the vehicle to memory. Mismatched hubcaps. Blue paint peeling off the roof. A bobble-head baseball player in the back window. Strings of colorful beads swinging from the rearview mirror. Chancy gasped with a mix of thrill and dread. The paper heart! Only a brief glimpse, but she was certain she'd seen her heart swinging from the car's rearview mirror. Corliss had received the message.

Then what happens?

Chancy pressed her back against the bricks. Now she had a real connection with another person in Wenonah. If she spotted the old Ford parked in front of a house, she would know where Corliss lived. She could add real-time details like house color to the scenes in her head and imagine Corliss moving around inside.

Even if she didn't dare knock.

Chancy spent the next couple of hours walking around town, collecting points and looking for a place to spend the night. Pausing at street corners, she waited for a feeling to tell her which way to turn. Her confidence grew with every solid sign. It was creepy how well the game worked in Wenonah. Here she could move around without looking over her shoulder. No one bothered her or asked her to explain herself. Not once had she wanted to disappear.

Since her arrival, Chancy had purchased just enough food to stop her growling stomach, but her funds had dwindled quickly. She'd bought apples and cartons of milk. Crackers and cheese. She'd splurged on toothpaste and feminine hygiene because she didn't feel right about swapping hearts when she had cash in her pocket. She'd spent today's food money in a thrift store, buying a pair of used socks and a new old shirt. Clothes washed with hand soap in restroom sinks and stuffed in her backpack while still damp didn't smell good. She owed it to Wenonah to look her best.

Her stomach rumbled as she passed a convenience store, which she interpreted as a clear sign to step inside. A tired-looking clerk sat on a stool behind the counter thumbing a handheld video game.

Don't mind me. I'm nobody.

The clerk didn't look up. Chancy surveyed long shelves stocked with bags and boxes of high-calorie, prepackaged food. Favorite items called out to her, and her stomach cramped a reply. She stopped at the magazine rack and pretended interest in the colorful high-glam user guides meant for girls who had nothing to worry about but shiny hair and zit-free skin. Invisible to the clerk, she moved back into the food aisle. He continued to squint into the tiny screen as his thumbs pummeled the controls.

That's right. Enjoy your game. I'm not even here.

Anticipation made her stumble. The clerk set the game on the counter and glanced her way. She reassured him with a fake smile. "Do you have a water fountain, sir?"

He pointed. "Help yourself."

There it was. The invitation she'd waited for. She preferred to pay, but the clerk had given her permission. She wouldn't have to part with money this time. She could save it for another, less providing day. After quenching her thirst, Chancy plucked a tuna-salad kit from a plastic hook strip and slipped it inside her jacket. Her salivary glands pumped like crazy when she thought about mixing little packets of mayonnaise and pickle relish into the pouch of fish.

From her pocket she pulled a red heart that she'd fashioned from a flyer blowing around the park. She offered silent thanks and set the token on the shelf, but something didn't feel right. She still had a few dollars left, and taking the tuna felt more like a crime than a trade. Maybe the rules were different in Wenonah. She hesitated, waiting for the clerk to notice. He didn't.

Experience overcame guilt, and Chancy pushed out the door, nearly colliding with another customer. She drew in a startled breath when she recognized the same good mom who'd taken her son out for Mother's Day lunch. She wore her long hair pulled back today, but the smile was unmistakable. A silver heart dangled from a chain around her neck. A sign.

"Sorry, dear." The woman held the door for Chancy. "I wasn't paying attention."

Maybe, like Corliss and the professor, Heart Mom could see her too. Chancy lingered by the window while the woman made her purchases. Diet soda and a tiny box of mints. Before she came out, Chancy hurried away, hugging the weight of the tuna pouch. She felt rumbly but wouldn't eat yet. She would have control over something, even if it was just an impulse.

All business as usual, Ms. Wooten pulled a folder from her briefcase. "You look terrible today."

"Thanks for noticing." Max's tone was sullen and sarcastic, but Ms. Wooten couldn't seem to get past the black eyes and unshaved face.

"Let's get down to it," she said. "Because the doctor decided to discharge you, my job will be a little harder."

Max didn't like the sound of that. Who considered good health a complication? "What do you mean?"

"Had you required hospitalization, I could have gotten you admitted to a skilled nursing facility upon discharge. Since you were released directly from the ER, we're limited to looking at assisted living and an inevitable delay."

"Who's looking at assisted living?" Max bristled at the woman's misguided assumptions.

"I thought we agreed."

"We didn't agree on anything. Don't try to snooker me, young lady. My brain's intact. I passed that so-called neurological exam." Some exam. Start with one hundred and subtract by sevens.

"Your health status has been established. We're talking about living arrangements."

"You're talking," he said. "I'm being forced to listen."

Serious Shevaun didn't get the joke.

She launched into the speech she probably dreaded as much as Max did. The house was too big. The stairs too dangerous. If he fell again and broke his hip, he might not recover. She glanced around the room festooned with cobwebs and grimaced at yesterday's supper tray that he'd absentmindedly left on the coffee table. Clearly, he needed someone to clean the house. Cook hot meals. There had been several break-ins in the area, and seniors were particularly vulnerable to financial scams and crime. How would he defend himself against another attacker?

Apparently her question was rhetorical, because she did not give him a chance to stick a word in sideways.

"Falling in the tub is proof that you can't manage on your own."

"All it's proof of," he insisted, "is leaving the bath mat downstairs." For want of a nail, a kingdom was lost.

"It's my job to consider what's best for you."

"I can take care of myself."

"Clearly you need assistance." Ms. Wooten, no-nonsense and plus-sized, made an imposing adversary when wrapped in authority. "Someone to oversee your nutritional needs and make sure you take your medication on time."

"I slipped in a puddle of water." Max dared to breathe a little easier. No mention of valvular regurgitation. Maybe that Eagle Scout of an ER doctor hadn't gotten around to ratting him out after all. "Accidents happen. My little tumble hardly heralds the end of the world."

She checked her watch. "Tell you what. I need to step into the next room and make a few phone calls. Then we can talk."

Ganging up on him was what she was doing. Calling for backup. Who would it be this time? Men in white coats? The Octogenarian Protection League? Resentment ballooned in Max's craw. He wanted to break something, anything, but two things kept him from shoving Wooten out the door: old-fashioned manners and niggling doubt. What if she was right about the house being too much for him? Its current state of disarray raised the possibility. And he couldn't deny occasional memory lapses. Had he fed Alfie yet? Was Monday the day the trash men came?

He couldn't even think the A-word. His mind was his most cherished possession. He'd survived on wits and willpower more than once but couldn't bluff his way out of senility. According to a pamphlet he'd read at the hospital, half of all Americans over eighty developed Alzheimer's—a crappy-ass reward for persevering. Mother Nature was a stickup artist. *Give me your brain and everyone gets hurt.* He fought the urge to pick up the forgotten supper tray and hurl it across the room. He still had plenty of brain cells. A quick run-through of the periodic table held fear at bay. He was one of the lucky fifty percent.

Wooten reappeared and sat across from him. She wore a tight, professional happy face. "I spoke to the director of the assisted-living center. We need to get you on the waiting list as soon as possible. They require a deposit, which will be applied to your move-in fee. And the good news is, there are only three names on the list ahead of you."

Who knew out-to-pasture was such a popular place to be? "What does a place like that cost?"

"Rent depends on the level of care required." She consulted a brochure in her briefcase for the rates.

The cost was staggering. Not just the move-in, but the monthly fees. "I own a mortgage-free, four-bedroom house for which I pay only annual taxes and utilities. Do I understand you correctly? You think it's a good idea for me to spend several thousand dollars a month for a little apartment in a facility?"

"You're paying for *care*." Her patience was clearly wearing thin. Nothing was more exasperating than good, old-fashioned logic. "And the fee includes meals and housekeeping."

"What happens when I run out of money?" Seemed a reasonable question, but she frowned.

"If that happens, the state will pick up the cost of nursing home care."

"So after I blow all my money on the fancy place, I get a free ride at the not-so-fancy place?" Max wasn't trying to be difficult. Or maybe he was.

"That probably won't happen."

No. He probably wouldn't outlive his resources. Max did not take the colorful Grayson House brochure she offered. "Ms. Wooten, I'm tired. I have to ask you to go now. I'm afraid there's nothing to discuss."

"I'm sorry you feel that way." She clutched her briefcase in her lap. "I also spoke to my supervisor. She agrees I should recommend you be placed under court protection. In your best interests, you need to move into an appropriate setting where you can be cared for properly, but if you are not willing to go the assisted-living route, a nursing home is the next step."

Court protection? Nursing home? Real fear chilled Max's crustiness. Could things go that far? He hadn't taken Wooten seriously because she was young and eager and inexperienced, a kid in the first quarter of her life, but she had the power to decide how he would live out his days. Like a fool, he had overlooked the fact that her position gave her authority.

Max had once possessed authority. During his heyday, he'd wielded make-'em-or-break-'em power over students. Students had called him Old

Hard Boyle, but the serious ones had jockeyed for a place in his classes. He had been a fine teacher with a reputation for fairness.

As the nuns at the orphanage had often pointed out, life wasn't fair.

Ms. Wooten stepped into the silence his wandering thoughts presented. "Grayson House is a nice facility. You'll have your own apartment and can bring furniture and belongings from home. There's no kitchen, because you'll take your meals in the dining room, but each apartment is equipped with a small fridge and microwave for snacks."

Ms. Wooten added a bright tag to her sales pitch. "You can even keep your dog. Won't that be nice?"

Alfie looked up and whined. He had good reason to be nervous. When the old lady who was his previous owner had died, her heirs had dumped him at the animal shelter.

Ms. Wooten drove home the hard sell. "You can remain independent. And yet help will be there if and when you need it."

"*This* is my home." He hated the desperate crack in his voice. "I've lived here half a century. Can you understand that?"

The woman was startled by his intensity. She nodded but had no concept of fifty years. She'd been alive only half that long. "It's dangerous for you to live here alone. You've been involved in two incidents in less than sixty days: an attempted burglary and a serious fall. My job is to protect elders, and I wouldn't be doing that job if I allowed you to remain here."

Max gathered breath and strength. Time to entrench. Do or die. "I won't move. This is where I live."

"I understand. But time marches on. Things change. Now that your wife is gone, you've entered a different life stage."

A different life stage. Decrepitude. No dignity required. "You know what Inuits used to do with old people, Ms. Wooten?"

"No, sir." She closed her briefcase with a resolute zip. Her frustration made it clear that Inuits were out of her jurisdiction and not her concern.

"They placed their elderly on ice floes when they became helpless and unable to contribute. Set them adrift in a frigid sea."

"How barbaric." She had been schooled in political correctness and modern social work ethic, so her shock was genuine.

"No. A viable, *humane* solution. Quick and painless."

"Mr. Boyle. I'm aware that members of your generation often harbor misconceptions about long-term care."

He snorted agreement.

"Standards of the industry haven't always been high," she went on. "However, today all levels of care needs can be met. Facilities like Grayson House offer increased opportunities for recreation and socialization. Studies show that people with friends and strong ties to the community live longer and report a higher degree of satisfaction with their lives than those who live in isolation."

"Maybe I like being alone. Ever think of that?"

"No human being thrives in isolation."

The young woman had done her homework. She walked the walk and talked the talk. Her briefcase was zipped. Her decision made. "Long-term care may be good in theory," he admitted, "but it falls short in practice. I've seen what happens when people are forced into rest homes. They give up on life. Waiting for death is colder than an icy sea."

"I assure you, the situation is not as grim as all that."

Max sighed. "How do you know what I consider grim?"

She stiffened, and her next words underlined the futility of trying to reason with a made-up mind. "I'm sorry we don't agree. But I have a job to do. People are living longer, thanks to advances in medical technology. Long-term care has become an unavoidable necessity."

"I like a good steak now and then. I know slaughterhouses are an *unavoidable necessity*. I don't expect steers walking up the ramp to agree."

"Mr. Boyle, I've handled several cases like yours." She made no attempt to conceal her mounting impatience. "The resistance you feel now will fade once you settle into a good facility. Statistics prove that the cared-for elderly live longer."

"They don't really live longer," he muttered. "It just seems like it."

She chuckled then and patted his hand, a technique she'd probably learned in Intro to Relating to Codgers. She'd also completed the master course in professional detachment. "You just need time to get used to the idea."

Of course. Once he accepted that he was *elderly* and had a chance to embrace the notion that life no longer had meaning and nothing he'd accomplished in eighty-three years meant a damn thing, he would be fine.

"You have every right to feel the way you do."

So what if he had a right to his feelings? He wasn't entitled to act on them. Democracy didn't extend to the fogy end of the food chain. He could order Ms. Wooten out, barricade the door and refuse to be disenfranchised, but she'd call in the SWAT team to drag him out. If he tried to fight, he'd be pronounced combative and prescribed something calming that would make him forget.

He'd be told when to get up, when to eat. When to have a bowel movement. Before he knew it, someone would consider walking a dangerous activity and he'd be installed in a wheelchair, parked in front of a widescreen TV. Forcibly tucked in for the night by seven. A flock of estate vultures would pick over the belongings he and Hanna had accumulated during their fifty years together, and their treasures would be carted off by strangers. With their lives scattered to the wind, nothing would remain to prove that Max and Hanna Boyle had ever lived and loved.

The humor-impaired Ms. Wooten didn't see the irony, but there it was. Proceeds from the sale of everything he'd worked for would be used to fund his residence in Wheelchair City. He'd once visited a former colleague in such a place. An old bachelor academic with three degrees and a small fortune whose roommate was a dead-broke alcoholic on public assistance. Maybe the Skid Row residents had it right. What was the point of working hard to build a life if everyone wound up in the same place anyway?

Ms. Wooten's mind was made up, but Max did not have to roll over and take such a fate. There had to be a way out. Some loophole that even a stiff-jointed old fool could wiggle through. A whispering breeze wafted the scent of White Shoulders into the room. Hanna was near. He was wide-awake, in full possession of his consciousness, and yet he saw her clearly: standing at the bottom of the stairs, dressed in dungarees and a straw hat, her trusty transplanter in hand.

Hanna was saving him a place. Before she became too ill to talk, she'd ordered him not to grieve too long. To remember all the happiness they'd shared. She'd apologized for getting cancer. For failing him. She'd promised to wait for him on the other side, assuring him that the end was really the beginning and they would spend eternity together.

What was he waiting for? Why should he stay behind while his favorite girl settled into a better place? Doubt faded, along with fear, and Max knew exactly what he had to do. All he needed was a few days to tie up loose ends and put his plan into action.

"Mr. Boyle?" Ms. Wooten's gaze followed his, but she saw nothing. Knew nothing. Felt nothing. Maxwell Boyle was just another case to be resolved.

"On second thought, you may be right." He chose words that would make a wary Adult Protective Services representative drop her guard and postpone seeking that court order. "Maybe it is time I stopped trying to manage alone."

"Really?" Skepticism etched wrinkles on her coffee-colored forehead.

"I'm a reasonable man. I respect your position."

"You do?" Her face brightened. Apparently she'd braced herself for a difficult conversion.

The wind chimes Hanna had hung outside the window tinkled, and in their music, Max heard the words she'd spoken so often. *I love you more than sunshine.* A sense of peace settled over him.

"Make an appointment," he said, "to tour the rest home."

"*Assisted living,*" she emphasized. "Grayson House isn't a nursing home like Dogwood Manor, which is also a fine facility. At Grayson, you can enjoy a sense of independence."

A sense of independence. The perfect substitute for those who couldn't handle the real thing.

"I'm pleased by your decision, Mr. Boyle. Believe me, this is the best solution." She credited her powers of persuasion for his change of heart. "How about tomorrow?"

Eager beaver, weren't we? "Friday. I need to meet with my lawyer. Make financial arrangements."

"I understand. You'll have time to finalize things once we get you on the waiting list and you pay the deposit. In the meantime, I will keep you on my caseload and check on you when I can. Perhaps your nice neighbor would be willing to look in on you once in a while?"

"Sure." He would never burden Jenny like that. "How long do you think the wait will be?"

"There's no way to predict when a room will become available."

"Ah. Someone has to kick the bucket, huh?" Now *he* was a vulture, circling for the next road-killed senior.

She stiffened. "Nothing is ever certain with the geriatric population."

Well, one thing was.

"Could be a week," she said. "Or several months. You just never know."

Max slumped in disappointment as Hanna's image faded into the magnolia-patterned wallpaper. He waved a white-flag smile to convince the social worker she'd won.

Gloating a tad too much, Ms. Wooten made another phone call, and Max agreed to the time set for the visit. She didn't realize it yet, but the House of Doom tour would never happen.

He would rather die first.

Dusk settled on Chancy's third day in Wenonah. She tingled with anticipation. She'd done everything right. She had been careful, paid attention, earned points. She hadn't taken good things for granted. She'd stepped outside herself and risked reaching for connections. She hadn't been greedy and had left hearts to express her gratitude. Today she had even let herself feel something. *Lucky.* She'd stood outside the convenience store and watched the woman with the heart necklace drive away. When she looked down, she had spotted a shiny penny on the sidewalk. The woman had dropped it there, a message for Chancy to find. That was when she knew she'd find a safe place to spend the night.

She paused at the corner of Poplar Avenue and Oak Street. Which way? Poplar sounded like *popular*, a good thing. Oak. *Broke.* No one wanted that. The quiet voice spoke: *Poplar. Turn left.*

The houses lining the street were old, but not run-down and neglected like the crowded buildings in her other life. Dim apartments where hope escaped through broken windows and three locks on the door couldn't keep out desperation. Now that she'd had a taste of Wenonah's peace, she couldn't go back to a dangerous, clamoring world where chained dogs barked and music blared and babies cried. Where men beat women, and women slapped children. The air in that world was ripe with the stink of cooking meth, the night torn apart by sirens and flashing lights. Even when

B.J. was around, she never really was. Chancy had huddled alone within walls too weak to keep out the world and created a safe mind alternative. A place that felt like home.

Poplar Avenue could be that place. The houses were solid despite weather and time. They had bright windows like welcoming eyes. Wide, grinning porches. Flowers. Grass. Trees. On this quiet evening, there were no people sounds. Just birds and humming insects. Rustling leaves. At the end of the block, Chancy discovered the place she had visited in her imagination and the breath winged out of her.

A real-life version of the doll family's house with every full-size de-tail. A shady veranda wrapped around one side. Elaborate trim flanked the porch supports and swirled into curlicues at the eaves. Lacy curtains hung in the windows. The dollhouse had been white with blue shutters and this house was yellow with green shutters, but the difference in color didn't matter. Not with all her lucky numbers tacked next to the door: 6. 3. 9.

Signs were rarely that obvious. Chancy had to look at them from all angles, like a puzzle piece that wouldn't fit. Other times she had to spin them, or bend the edge of truth to get the message right. But this time the green doormat spelled everything out: WELCOME.

The house sat squarely on a large corner lot. In the backyard, vines and leafy tendrils from an overgrown garden spilled over the white picket fence that enclosed it. The grass in front of the house needed mowing, and scraggly weeds poked among the shrubs. Yet the house was perfect, just as she had imagined. Inside there would be a staircase with a shiny banister. Shelves with books and lamps to light the pages. Even without the sun, the house would never be dark.

Clouds gathered and the wind carried the scent of rain, making it more urgent to find a sleeping place for the night. When she was sure no one was watching, Chancy walked a few steps up the driveway and paused in front of a big yellow outbuilding. A garage. The wide front door was locked, but she eased the gate open and found a regular door on the yard side. She closed her eyes, murmured a hopeful request, and turned the knob. Locked. *Nothing free. Nothing easy.* She dug in her backpack for the piece of metal she'd fashioned into a pick for the times when B.J. locked her out of the apartment.

Wishing as she worked, Chancy poked and pried until the lock tumblers clicked. She slipped inside and set her backpack on the floor, closing the door behind her. In a moment her eyes adjusted to the waning light that seeped through the streaked windows. A solitary cricket greeted her. *Come in. I've been waiting for you.* Roaches and spiders and ants had earned permanent slots on her ick list, but Chancy had made her peace with crickets. Their friendly *chirp, chirp, chirp* had often kept her company at night. They sounded happy, like they knew where they belonged and were satisfied with their place in the world.

On one side of the garage a workbench stood under a wall-mounted pegboard hung with hammers and screwdrivers and wrenches. Rusty paint cans lined a shelf and musty boxes filled one corner. No surprise that the garage contained a car, but Chancy had not expected a big silver land yacht with whitewall tires, wire wheels, vinyl roof, and powder blue interior. Dust on the garage floor was undisturbed, so the car, which was from an era when gasoline had cost a dollar a gallon, had not been driven recently.

Grand in shiny excess, the car looked forlorn, as though it missed the sun and wind of the open road. She read the name above the wide grille: *Lincoln.* Her hand closed around the pocketed penny she'd found on the street. Lincoln. Definitely a good sign. Penny for your thoughts. Lucky penny. Lucky Lincoln. She'd let herself feel lucky today and now she was.

Outside the sun had set and the garage grew dark as night closed in. A light rain pattered against the window. The world was wet, but she had a safe place. Chancy hoisted her backpack and placed her left hand on the back door handle. It would not be locked. She was supposed to be here. The universe had led her to this dusty, crickety place where she could sleep surrounded by the smell of old leather and serenaded by a happy bug. She applied a calculated amount of pressure and the latch released with a metallic groan. One tug and the door swung open.

Welcome. The house meant what the mat said. She crawled onto a backseat as wide and soft as a mattress. Movie stars and royalty rode in cars like this. The musky scent of old tobacco clung to the velvety roof liner. Chancy didn't mind the lingering smell. She imagined a princess smoking skinny cigarettes clipped in a ruby-encrusted holder. The cricket chirped again. *You're not alone. I'm here.*

She pulled the packet of tuna from her backpack and quietly, ravenously, ate her bartered supper. When she finished, she curled on her side under the worn blanket. At dawn she would sneak out, but for now she could sleep without worry. Before she dozed off, she sorted and stored the hope Wenonah had provided. Kind, hardworking Corliss. The professor who loved his dog, and the heart-wearing mom who loved her son. Even the shadow cat was a gift, proof that strays mattered to some people.

Whatever tomorrow brought, for a few hours the magic coach belonged to her. Even if the nightmare stalked her tonight, its cold fingers could not squeeze the good things from her heart.

Still, B.J. taunted from the shadows.

You'll never be safe, dummy. People like us are cockroaches, scurrying around, living in holes, waiting for the big shoe to come down. Hard. You think you're better than me. You're not. Get down on your knees and thank God you have me for a mother and not some perverted bitch like mine. When I was twelve, my old lady, may she rot in hell, sold me at a truck stop for drug money. Have I ever done anything half that bad? No. I watch out for my kid.

Didn't I run that creep off with a knife when he tried to get funny with you? That's what good mothers do. Stop hugging me. Let go. Why are you always hanging on me? Look at me! Stop staring through me like I'm not here. That's how she looked at me. Dammit! You made me do that! You're trying to make me feel bad, aren't you? I gotta go out. Get lucky. Find somebody who can see me. Shut up. You'll be all right. Don't talk back! Stop looking at me like I'm nothing.

Don't ever forget. You are nothing too.

The dream startled Chancy to wakefulness, and her heart pounded in the dark. Not real. B.J. was far away. Her words weren't true. Falling back into a deep sleep untroubled by lies, Chancy settled into the car's plush upholstery and pulled the blanket up to her chin. B.J. was wrong. Someday Chancy would be something.

The cricket seemed to agree.

Chirp. Chirp. Chirp.

When Max awoke the day after Shevaun Wooten's visit, optimism had replaced uneasy dread. He would give Shevaun Wooten one less soul for the warehouse. He'd made his decision and worked out the details. Nothing could stop a man with a plan. He bent to pull up the bedspread, then straightened. To hell with making the bed. Hanna had exempted him from household duties on his birthday. Why should he do chores on his death day?

After he was gone, Pete would call in estate professionals to rid the house of all traces of geezer debris. A buyer with no sense of history would breeze in and renovate the life and spirit out of the place. Like well-intentioned Jenny Hamilton, the new owner would tear out the cabinets. Trash the appliances. Replace the blue flowered tile in the bathroom with sand-colored squares. An unmade bed didn't amount to a hill of beans when everything he valued would soon be lost to the highest bidder.

Max shuffled downstairs in his slippers. Screw the wingtips. The left one pinched his big toe, and not even John Wayne had died with his boots on. Patient Alfie followed him into the kitchen. He never dreamed the old dog would outlive him, but that was the difference between man and beast. God's little creatures fought for survival, while those made in His image could choose to heave it aside.

Max considered taking Alfie with him. The dog hated being left behind and loved car rides even more than walks. It was only right for them to travel to the afterlife together. Alfie stood at the back door, watching Max with patient eyes. *Are we going for a ride or what?* The dog's trust made him discard his selfish plan. He might be free to choose, but he didn't have the right to make that final choice for a friend.

Ignoring his empty stomach, Max elected to skip the whole last-meal thing. A man on a mission couldn't stop to fry bacon. A cup of hot coffee was all he needed. Caffeine courage to steady his nerves when the real thing failed. He filled the pot and set it to drip, then ambled into the room where Hanna had spent her last days.

Won't be long now, Hanna.

When she had become too weak to climb the stairs, she'd requested her hospital bed be placed in the glass-enclosed sunroom, and the hospice people had obliged. She'd wanted a view of the garden, though there hadn't been much to see. Winter brown grass. Leafless trees. Shrubs that needed pruning.

The garden struggled to survive. The first warm spring days had tempted herbs and perennials to surprising life. Laden with buds, azaleas and lilacs fought for their share of the sun. Sweeping yellow forsythia boughs arched like a bridge to summer. Hanna had called them God's messengers, sent to reassure the earth that winter was truly over. With no one to care, the bright, careless flowers didn't stand a chance. Like Hanna, they would die.

Don't be sad, Max; I'm not. The growing season is over. I'm going dormant in this life, but I'll bloom again in another garden. Don't grieve when I'm gone. I'll always be with you.

And she was. When strangers came to clear the house, they would wonder why the crazy old man had kept two-year-old magazines. The last ones Hanna had read. They would think he was too senile to empty her tissues out of the wastebasket beside her recliner.

Hanna. No one had loved life as much as she had. Why hadn't she listened when he'd begged her to quit?

Smoking is my only vice, Maxie. I don't drink. I don't gamble. I don't fill the closet with shoes I'll never wear. I don't lie or break promises. If I didn't have one bad habit, I'd have to apply for sainthood, and I hear the paperwork is a bitch.

They would be together again soon. Max shuffled back into the kitchen. Last night he'd phoned Pete and asked him to stop by later in the evening. When Max didn't answer the door, his old friend would let himself in with the spare key. He'd look around and wonder. Then he'd find the envelope with his name on it and his questions would be answered. Reading Max's last words, Pete would sink into a chair. Feeling what? Pity? Grief? Or secret relief that Max had saved himself from the final indignity?

He had already laid the foundation for his grand exit. He'd revised his will after Hanna died, appointing Pete executor with instructions to mix their ashes and bury them together in the pre-need plot he'd purchased. Pete would liquidate the estate and use the proceeds to create the Hanna McLean Boyle Scholarship Fund at Wenonah State College. Leah Perkins, Pete's new junior partner, would oversee the trust, invest the funds wisely, and award an annual scholarship to a deserving young woman. A smart cookie like Hanna. A girl with a good heart and a strong desire to make something of herself.

Overcome by the enormity of what he was about to do, Max eased into a kitchen chair. The black cat clock ticked loudly, measuring the rest of his life in minutes. Alfie pushed his head under Max's hand, demanding attention.

"Don't worry, boy. You won't be alone for long."

Even though he didn't know Jenny well, Max trusted her to honor his last request. He'd left Pete instructions to provide a monthly stipend for the dog's food and grooming and veterinary expenses. Max wouldn't be a burden on society, and his dog wouldn't be a burden on his new family.

Max ruffled the dog's ears. "You'll be fine with young Adam. Give the kid a chance. Maybe he wears funny pants, but time is on his side, and he still has a good stick-throwing arm."

Alfie's sharp bark was a reminder that fetching wasn't high on his to-do list. Max filled the water bowl and dumped dry food in the dish, then unlatched the doggy door so Alfie could get out to do his business. The dog paced near the back door, his nails *click, click, click*ing on the linoleum. Then he howled as he had the morning the funeral home attendants had wheeled Hanna out of the house. Could animals sense coming events? Earthquakes, maybe. Tsunamis. He'd read about dogs that alerted their owners to impending seizures. But insignificant deaths that barely registered on anyone's emotional Richter scale?

Alfie was upset about being alone. Max pressed a fist against the tightness in his chest. As convenient as a massive coronary would be right now, the clenching heartsickness wasn't angina but plain fear and old grief made new. The coffeemaker gurgled, and Max breathed in the familiar aroma. If he really were ready to give up on life, could something as simple as a cup of coffee give him pleasure? Maybe he had deluded himself into thinking he was taking control, when what he was really doing was giving up. Quitting. He wasn't afraid of dying, or of the unknown, or even of going to hell. What he couldn't bear was being a coward.

He filled a cup. Memories slipped back like a stack of old snapshots tossed on a table. July 1943. The invasion of Sicily. They'd chased the enemy from Catania to Messina, paying in sweat and blood for every mile gained. Pushing across the Rapido River under constant fire. Breaking out of an artillery smoke screen and charging onto a battlefield already littered with the bodies of men who'd been closer to him than his own brothers.

Unbidden, the face of little Jimmy Tucker wavered in the gray light. A kid who'd traded his razor blades to other guys for Hershey bars because he had to shave only once a week. A boy so crushed by surviving a battle that wiped out most of the platoon that he'd cried for his mother before putting his own sidearm to his head. Later, some wiseacre had joked that maybe he would "Tucker out" too and save the Third Reich the trouble. Another had said Jimmy had taken the coward's way because it took more guts to live than to die.

Max knew better. Dying was never easy. Inertia seeped under his defenses, eroding his confidence. Maybe he should stand his ground against Shevaun Wooten. Fight like a man. Hell, the least he could do was ask his lawyer if he had any real options. Then he recalled Pete's last visit. His friend had suggested that since Max was facing another surgery without Hanna, it might be time to consider other arrangements. Max had seen the uneasy look in Pete's eyes. Nothing scared a man of sixty-five like glimpsing his own mortality in an eighty-three-year-old face. Pete would consider Grayson House a good idea. He knew Max was circling the drain.

The doorbell jangled, and Max was surprised to find Jenny Hamilton on the porch. Her son slumped in the front seat of the minivan parked at the curb.

"Oh, good, you're up," she said. "I hate to bother you so early, but I plan to stop at the market after dropping Adam at school. I thought you might need something from the store?"

Her bright smile knocked him out of the dark place his thoughts had led him. "Thank you, but no. I don't need anything."

"Are you sure? Wouldn't be any trouble. In fact, if you give me a list, I'd be happy to pick up necessities for you from now on. Or, if you prefer to do your own shopping, you're welcome to come along."

"That's okay. I have everything I need." Except courage. Jenny's unexpected arrival reminded him he wasn't alone, made him waver.

"If you'd like, I can stop by later and help tidy up." Jenny glanced back at the van. "I don't mind."

"Thanks for the offer, but not today." A man with less than an hour left on earth didn't worry about dust. "You'd better get that boy of yours to school."

"Yes, I'd hate to make him tardy. You'll let me know if there's anything I can do to help, right?"

"Right." Max was touched by the offer. Jenny had her own problems and yet was willing to lend a helping hand. She was a good person and would take care of Alfie. "I have things worked out now."

"Oh. So you're going to assisted living?"

Before Max could answer, Adam tapped the car horn as an urgent reminder of the time. "You'd better get going."

"I'll check in with you later." She ran lightly down the steps, and Max watched the van until it disappeared.

He returned to the kitchen and sank into a chair at the table. A solemn-looking Alfie lay on the floor at the back door as though guarding the exit. A friendly neighbor's offer to pick up a loaf of bread didn't change a thing in the big scheme. Today was the day he would Tucker out and save Shevaun Wooten the paperwork. A shrill ringing tore into the silence and nearly startled Max out of his chair. Now what? As soon as he said hello, the social worker, whom his doubts had conjured, launched another attack.

"Mr. Boyle. Good news. A room at Grayson House opened up this morning."

Another one bites the dust. He didn't respond. What could he say?

"That means there're only two names on the waiting list now."

She knew how to make a man's day.

Ms. Wooten was too pleased to notice his silence. "I think we should take that tour this afternoon. Why put off until Friday what we can do today? The director tells me there's a chance you can get in much sooner than we originally expected. Wouldn't want to miss a great opportunity."

Finally, something they agreed on. Opportunities were meant to be seized. No more Mr. Wishy-Washy. Like the candy Hanna had made every Christmas, Max's determination finally reached the hardball stage. "Maybe tomorrow," he said. "I'm not up to a tour today."

"Oh." A single syllable, freighted with disappointment. "Tomorrow is fine." Ms. Wooten set a time to pick him up the next day. "You won't regret your decision."

Right again. In fact, he couldn't wait. He set the phone on the base. Returning to the kitchen, he glanced at the envelope propped against the sugar bowl. Last instructions and official suicide note. Pete deserved the words, and documentation would help the cops rule out foul play. Next to the envelope lay the small paper heart. Max scooped it up and pushed it deep into his pocket. He thought of the little heart maker and hoped someday, someone would love her the way he had loved Hanna.

He reviewed his plan. First, he'd squirt caulk around the garage windows to seal out any fresh air that might seep in to revive him. Carbon monoxide poisoning was supposed to be painless. Like going to sleep. *Nighty-night and sweet dreams.* Even with current gasoline prices, the whole damn process would cost less than the fee to have a pet euthanized. He would crank up the Lincoln and check the battery. God forbid the sixteen-year-old Town Car died before he did.

He realized there wasn't enough gas in the tank to finish the job, just enough to get to the nearest pump. Max had given up his license after his last heart surgery, but today he would flout the rules and drive his illegal self three blocks to the Jiffy Mart. After Hanna died, he had considered selling the car she had loved. She'd put thirty miles a week on the odometer, tooling around to club meetings and the beauty shop. Nothing had struck fear into Max's heart like watching her parallel park. No curb was too high, no space too tight. She'd run that car hard and put it up wet.

When Pete had asked why he kept the extravagant automobile, Max had been unable to explain.

Now he knew.

His final purpose. The car's final purpose. He would ride to heaven in style. His knees creaked, but his step was light. Alfie followed him to the door. Max looked around and said good-bye to a life well lived. He swigged the last of his coffee, and, instead of setting the cup in the sink, he wound up like a pitcher on the mound and threw it as hard as he could against the wall. The heavy ceramic shattered with satisfying finality. Max dusted his hands. One less knickknack for the estate-sale rat bastards.

The crash set Alfie off.

"Stay! No walk today. We'll meet on the other side."

Alfie barked. Once. Twice. Three times.

"Calm down. I'm not planning to break every dish in the house. Just one." He stooped and gave the old dog a hug. "Go find your spot and take a nap. Pete will be by later to deliver you to Adam."

Uncharacteristically argumentative, Alfie barked again.

"Stay!"

Alfie went down on his haunches, striking his best good-dog pose. Max slipped out the door, knowing he would not enter it again. Alfie whined softly, but did not disobey. Patting his pocket to make sure he had gas money, Max banged out the back porch door and headed for the garage and the great unknown.

Chapter 7

The car engine sputtered, turned over and backfired with a roar that startled Chancy out of a deep, drowning sleep. Flooded with panic, she popped up in the Lincoln's backseat and gasped. She wasn't alone.

The old man behind the wheel swiveled in the driver's seat, looking as startled as she felt. The bruises around his eyes were a shocking purple. He squawked and clutched his chest. Chancy tried to untangle herself from her blanket and scrambled on the floor for her backpack. The engine coughed and died. Several beats of tense silence stretched between them.

"Chancy?" he said finally. "Good God, girl. That you?"

She fumbled for the door handle and froze at the sound of her name. Who knew her in Wenonah? No one. Sleep had held her fast, long after dawn. She couldn't get away. She would have to explain her actions. Lie. This was what happened when she got too comfortable, felt too warm.

He spoke before she could wrestle the back door open. "What in heaven's name are you doing here?"

Finally recognizing the halting speech, Chancy rubbed sleep from her eyes and really looked at the intruder. No. *She* was the intruder. He belonged here.

"Chancy, right?" he repeated. "From the park?"

The professor. What had happened to his face? She felt cornered and confused, couldn't remember his name. Alfie. No, that was the dog. An exemplary soul.

"I'll go now." She reached for the door handle, and he pushed a button that lowered the lock.

"Hold your horses, young lady."

Red alert. Her heart pounded a warning. Threatened a panic attack. She might throw up if she didn't make it to the small, quiet place in time. She focused on breathing. In. Out. Would the old man call the cops? That was what straight arrows did. Turned problems over to the authorities. The police would demand answers. They'd ship her back to Pittsburgh. She couldn't return to the shelter and those horrible girls. Couldn't risk being sent back to B.J.

"Are you all right?"

The old man was concerned, as he'd been in the park. The tightness released, and Chancy's pulse slowed to a normal rhythm. "I didn't take anything. I promise."

"What are you doing here?"

"Just sleeping."

"Why?"

"I was tired."

The old man's frown softened. "Why *here*?"

She hugged her backpack. "The numbers. On your house. Six, three, nine. Lucky. Like pennies. Lincoln. Get it? The signs said it'd be all right to sleep here."

He sighed. "You're not making sense, child. You trying to confuse me?"

"No."

"How'd you get in? That door was locked."

"I picked the lock." Her stomach clenched with guilt. Wanting to be safe wasn't a crime, but breaking and entering *was*.

"You some kind of cat burglar? Car thief? What?"

"No! I just wanted to sleep without worrying someone would find me in the dark."

His look was long and hard. "So what's wrong with your home?"

How could she explain she didn't have one? Why should she? She didn't owe the old guy anything. Who *was* he? What was his name? Why couldn't she remember? A picture of a bubbling pot crowded her thoughts. Boil. No, Boyle!

"I'm sort of on my own."

His bruised eyes widened. "Little young to be a vagabond, aren't you? You a runaway? Homeless?"

"It's complicated."

"Ain't life always?" He sighed, unlocked the back door and removed the key from the ignition. He climbed out and gestured for her to follow. "C'mon."

"Why? You calling the cops?"

"Do I need to?" He frowned again. "Are you dangerous?"

"No."

"Got a three-fifty-seven Magnum in that knapsack of yours?"

"No."

"Think you could take me down? In hand-to-hand combat?"

"No." Any humor evoked by the image was lost to indignation. "Looks like somebody already did."

He smiled and waved his hand dismissively. "These? Earned 'em. The hard way. You don't look like a threat." He seemed more tired than angry. "A stiff breeze would blow you away. Grab your stuff and come with me."

"I can leave now. I won't be back." A hard promise to keep. She hated to abandon the silver chariot and the dollhouse with the magic numbers because the universe had steered her here. But it was time to disappear. Snagged on indecision, she waited for the old man to say the go-away words.

"Where are you headed?" He shuffled to the garage door, his house slippers *scritch-scritch-scritch*ing on the concrete.

"I don't know. What do you care?"

He shrugged. "Thought we were friends."

She froze. Only she had believed that. "Since when?"

"Since the park."

"Why do you want to be my friend?"

"You look like you need one." He stooped and examined the door lock. "You bust this lock?"

"No."

"Good." He stepped outside, and when she had joined him, relocked and checked the door. "Still works. You might be a cat burglar after all."

"Burglars steal things." Chancy didn't. She bartered for food and always left a heart behind.

He walked to the house like he expected her to follow. "You hungry?"

"No." Her stomach twisted against the lie. Eating regularly was a habit she couldn't break no matter how hard she tried to deny the need.

"Too bad," he said matter-of-factly. "I'm feeling a little wolfish myself. Don't you eat breakfast?"

The word made her mouth water. "Sometimes."

Clutching the wooden railing, Mr. Boyle eased up the steps to the enclosed back porch and pulled a key from his pocket. He stepped inside and was greeted by joyous barking. Alfie danced circles around him, as happy to see him as if he'd been gone for months.

"Settle down, boy! You're gonna trip me. Don't get your hopes up. I haven't been to the Jiffy Mart, but that don't mean I won't still go." He turned to Chancy. "What're you waiting for? Don't just stand there and let the flies in."

What *was* she waiting for? Every screaming cell urged her to run, but a quiet voice whispered, *Stay. Stay.* Now that she was almost inside, she wanted to see the rest of the house more than she wanted anything. She longed to climb the stairs, just one time, and trail her hand along the smooth wood of the banister. She needed to touch the lace curtains and hear the floorboards creak as she walked from room to room. Desperate to discover if a dream could be real, she couldn't take a single step in the right direction.

Alfie trotted out on the porch and urged her in with a welcoming bark. Dogs seemed to communicate with different sounds. Beneath his soft fur, Alfie's ribs expanded with each panting breath, and he wore a silly dog grin on his face. Nothing bad could happen in a house where a happy dog lived.

Mr. Boyle called from deep inside the kitchen, "Get in or get out. Makes no difference to me."

She stepped onto the porch as he pulled a skillet from a drawer beneath the oven. Three more steps to the threshold. Still close enough to the door to run if necessary.

"You like eggs?" he asked over his shoulder. He wore wrinkled khakis, a plaid shirt and blue slippers.

"Yes."

"Over easy or sunny-side up?"

"Fried eggs are fried eggs."

"Chef's choice, then." He padded to the refrigerator for a stick of margarine, which he placed on the counter, and went back for eggs, carrying two in each gnarled hand. After dropping two slices of dark bread into an old-fashioned toaster, he made another slow trip to the refrigerator. He turned around with a bottle of orange juice in one hand and a jug of milk in the other.

"You drink coffee?" he asked.

She nodded.

"Help yourself." He set a mug on the counter. "Reheat it in the microwave."

She slipped into the room and noticed crockery shards on the floor. The same yellow stoneware as the proffered cup.

Mr. Boyle followed her gaze. "Had a little accident this morning. Guess I'll have to clean up my mess after all."

"I can do it."

"Guests don't clean."

"Is that how you got hurt?"

"Huh? No. Not that kind of accident. I'm not hurt, just sporting bruises."

Chancy understood the difference. "You've been to all these places?" She read the names off tiny spoons in a rack by the door. Some she'd heard of; most she hadn't.

"Yes. Heat your coffee and sit down."

When the microwave dinged, she removed the cup and carried it to a breakfast table covered with blue-checked vinyl. She eased into a chair, holding her backpack on her lap.

"You got Mayan treasure in that bag?"

"No."

"Smuggled diamonds? Counterfeit loot?"

"No."

"Then for heaven's sake, put it down somewhere. Nobody's gonna make off with your worldly goods." He dropped a chunk of margarine into the skillet to sizzle and hiss.

Chancy tucked the backpack under her chair and clamped a foot down firmly on the strap. The house smelled old. Not bad old, like the piled-up trash and rotten fruit and leftover beer vomit in B.J.'s apartment. Good old. Memories of food and ghosts of flowers. A jumbled stack of unwashed dishes filled the sink. A greasy layer of dust clung to the flower plates on the wall and the doodads that cluttered a shelf. Gremlin balls of dog fur had rolled across the brick-patterned linoleum to stack up in corners.

The ceiling was tall. So were the cream-painted, glass-fronted cupboards. The copper-colored appliances were twice as old as Chancy, including a wheezy refrigerator set in a niche on the other side of the room. Blue cotton curtains hung limply from café rods in the bay window. Folded brown grocery bags bulged from the space between the microwave cart and wall.

An electronic blood-pressure monitor rested atop a TV tray, along with an open notebook filled with spidery dates and numbers. A row of medicine bottles lined up just so in the middle of the table. A large envelope slanted between a basket of beaded fruit and a china sugar bowl.

When Mr. Boyle caught her looking at the envelope, he slipped it into a drawer. He pulled something out of his pocket and laid it on the table before going back to his cooking. Her breath caught somewhere between hope and fear. He'd saved the lopsided heart she'd left in the dog's collar.

Without turning around he said, "I want to thank you for that."

"You're welcome." She hadn't expected appreciation, just the usual questions. *Why hearts? What do they mean?* Maybe the old man was different. He didn't demand answers, just concentrated on turning eggs. Acted like it was no big deal to feed a trespasser found squatting in his garage. A black cat clock ticked on the wall, its long tail and big eyes swaying as the seconds passed.

Chancy jumped when the toast popped up.

"Name your poison." Mr. Boyle didn't turn around. "Margarine or jam?"

"Whatever you have."

"Agreeable, aren't you?" When she didn't respond, he added, "Guess you don't talk much."

She shrugged, even though his back was to her. Talking was dangerous. B.J. had used Chancy's words to justify the smacks, starting when she was a toddler learning to talk. *Quit your yammering, dammit; you're driving me nuts!* Her mother always blamed Chancy for everything that went wrong. *Don't be a smart-ass! Are you trying to piss me off or are you naturally stupid? What did I ever do to deserve being stuck with a worthless retard like you?*

Bully girls at the shelter had made Chancy's life miserable by turning her words against her. *What are you looking at, dorkwad? Get outta my way, freak! What do you mean, you're sorry? I'll show you sorry.* Even the adults in charge, watchers and helpers and teachers, had pegged her wrong. Called her oppositional. Passive-aggressive. Emotionally disturbed. Chancy didn't believe the labels. She didn't know what she was, but she was none of those things.

"Here you go." Mr. Boyle set a plate with two fried eggs and two pieces of toast in front of her.

"Thanks." One thing the town of Wenonah had provided was food.

"Welcome." He sat opposite with his own plate. "You the religious type? Want to bless anything?"

"No."

"Me either." He picked up a fork. "Nothing to be thankful for these days."

Wrong. He had a smart dog. A big house. A shiny car. A quiet life. Not only did he own the roof over his head; he could sleep when he was tired, eat when he was hungry. Bathe whenever he wanted. He lived on a nice street in a nice town, far from the apathy of state care. He was an adult and could make his own decisions. He wasn't at the mercy of a bad mother who forgot all about him until he got in the way of her doing something self-destructive. Mr. Boyle had to be senile to think he had nothing to be thankful for.

They ate in silence, and the cat clock timed each bite.

• • •

Max didn't know what to make of the girl sitting across his breakfast table. Her unexpected appearance this morning had thrown a monkey wrench in his plans, but curiosity had made him take a rain check on the grand exit. Thinking about somebody else's problems for a change made him feel a little less useless. Last he'd heard, there was no deadline on dying.

He toyed with his eggs and nibbled on toast. He didn't have much appetite, but the girl ate as if she were on a timer and out to set a record. Her cuticles formed dark crescents of ground-in grime. Her shaky right hand hovered close to the plate, unconsciously guarding the contents. With her left, she mopped up egg yolk with a toast corner and stuffed the bread in her mouth. Southpaw. Dealing with a backward world.

He rose and toasted two more slices of bread. When he set them in front of her, she nodded and devoured the toast without missing a beat.

"If you're still hungry, I've got plenty of eggs." He wouldn't be around long enough to eat the dozen in the refrigerator. Someone might as well.

"No, thanks." She washed down the last bite with a gulp of coffee. "I'm good."

She was in any shape but good. Small for her age, nipped in the bud like a stunted rose. Her serious face was thin and wan, her deep-set eyes smudged with the dusky shadows of a recovering invalid. Lank hair hadn't been washed in recent memory. Neither had the rest of her, for that matter. Dirt stained the neck of her T-shirt, and a sour, unwashed smell drifted across the table.

Max slid aside his unfinished plate. Wenonah didn't have a lot of street people. The town was too far off the beaten path to attract transients, and its citizens took care of their own. He'd lived on the road in another lifetime. For all that the world had changed, some things never did. Larger cities teemed with an underground population of homeless who lived under bridges and scavenged in Dumpsters. The disillusioned. The penniless. The mentally ill. Where did this kid fit into the picture? Steamy pain radiated from her like heat from a stove. Lord only knew what kind of hell she'd been through. Where were her parents?

Max understood childhood misery. He was just six when his mother died after a long bout with tuberculosis. She'd spent her last year in a sanitarium, far from home. Max had lost her twice, first when she went away to convalesce, and again when she didn't return. His father, an unsuccessful and unhappy farmer, was already old and tired of parenting by the time his youngest child was born. He had relinquished Max's care to his teenage daughter until she escaped the drudgery by running off and marrying the first man who asked. His three older brothers hated farm work and had soon scattered to the wind. Influenza had claimed his silent father when Max was ten.

Having been one himself, Max knew what happened to unwanted children, both in the orphanage and on the road. Life had been sink-or-swim during the Depression, but urchinhood in the 1930s was probably a Disney movie compared to life on the street now. In those days, society had simply been down on its luck. Now the world had gone a little crazy.

He broke the silence. "You want a banana?"

"No, thanks."

"Should eat a banana every day. Keeps the doctor away."

"I thought that was apples."

"Apples, schmapples. Fruit's good for you. No matter what kind." Max kept his guard up. The girl didn't look dangerous, but neither had Ricky Dimas, and that kid had given him a concussion.

"Okay." She nodded. "I could eat a banana."

"You're younger than me. Help yourself."

She rose and carefully separated a banana from the bunch suspended from Hanna's wooden hanger. "You want one?"

"Don't mind if I do."

They sat at the table, quietly peeling and eating. "Tell me again," Max said, "about the lucky numbers."

She eyed him to size up genuine interest. Finally, she swallowed. "We have special numbers. Three, six and nine are mine. Same as your address."

"How do you know?"

Her dark brows drew down in confusion. "Your house numbers are nailed right over the door."

"No, I mean, how do you know what's lucky? For you?"

"I just do." She stood. "I need to go."

"You got an appointment? Someplace you need to be?"

"No."

"Sit down then." She did. He'd expected defiance. Maybe an angry tirade launched with an F-bomb. Words he didn't allow himself to *think* as a youngster spewed carelessly from the mouths of young people today. Kids younger than this one belonged to gangs. Carried weapons to school. Attacked teachers. Hijacked cars. Used drugs. Bore babies they didn't want. Max had longed for children most of his adult life. Now he was a little afraid of them.

But he didn't fear the quiet, broken girl in front of him. She was a puzzle, and he'd always been a sucker for a challenge. Hard to believe she'd found her way here. How many times had he thought of her since that day in the park? How often had he wished he'd helped her or taken away some of her sadness? Had his thoughts drawn her? He didn't buy her lucky-number rigmarole, but her presence gave him a second chance he hadn't expected.

In light of the teen violence statistics he'd seen on an episode of *60 Minutes*, the girl's resigned compliance surprised him. Maybe she was accustomed to doing as she was told. Guarding her plate and eating without speaking were evidence of something. Reform school? The nuns at the orphanage had demanded obedience. The kids who survived were not the vocal fighters, but the crafty loners. Survivors kept their mouths shut, their eyes down and their backs to the wall.

Max didn't know a damn thing about teenage girls, but he understood survivors. They didn't like questions. Never revealed too much of themselves. Wouldn't give trust easily.

Still, he had to try. "You got a last name, Chancy?"

Her glance darted around, lighting everywhere but on him. "Sure. Doesn't everybody?"

"You going to tell me?"

"Rather not."

"Fair enough. You're not from around here, are you?"

She shook her head. "You can tell by my accent?"

"Dead giveaway." Hard consonants and crisp syllables told him she came from north of the Mason-Dixon line, but even if she'd been mute, he would have known she wasn't local. Wenonah had too many social programs for a child to go unnoticed and unprotected on the streets for as long as it had taken that much dirt to accumulate.

"Can I go now?"

"If you want. This isn't a hostage situation." Max leaned back. "Door's still in the same place."

She shouldered her knapsack, and Alfie whined a rebuke. Couldn't believe his master would let a guest go so easily. Chancy ducked her head and hurried to the door. Instead of disappearing as Max fully expected her to do, she stopped and slowly turned around.

"Thanks for the food. Professor."

He was startled by the word that dropped unexpectedly from her lips. Except for Hanna, no one had called him that in years. His wife had used *Professor* both as a term of endearment and as a sarcastic poke in the ribs when he said something particularly stupid. An uneasy feeling niggled him. Could there be a connection between Hanna and this walking angel? Or was he just wishfully thinking again?

"Wait! You said something led you here. What was it?"

She bit her lip. Worried or afraid.

"I'm old. Heard it all. Nothing you say can surprise me."

"Signs. I listened for the voice to tell me where to go. 'Turn here. Now here. Stop.'"

"You hear voices?"

"Not the bad kind," she said in an earnest rush, "good ones."

"You mean intuition?" That he understood. He was experiencing some serious intuition right now. "Gut feelings."

"When I saw this place, I knew the voices had led me to my dream house."

Max sucked in a sharp breath. *Dream house.* That was what Hanna had called the drafty old Victorian, and nothing had ever changed her opinion. Not the tree roots that encroached on ancient sewer lines, not the faulty, outdated wiring, or the leaky roof. Frustrated by a long-ago termite infestation that threatened to bring the house down around them, Max had cursed the house as a money-sucking sinkhole. Hanna had laughed and said, *This too shall pass.* No trouble was ever bad enough to shake her belief in 639 Poplar Avenue.

Unreasonable hope unfurled inside Max. According to Chancy, a "voice" had led her here. *Hanna.* He'd heard her when he was hovering on the brink of unconsciousness. She'd told him he had something important to do. Maybe she had guided Chancy's footsteps. He couldn't let the girl leave until he knew for sure, but she was edging closer to the back door, ready to run the minefield.

The phone rang, and they both jumped. "Don't leave yet," he said.

"I gotta go."

The phone rang again. "Say you'll wait. Please."

"Okay."

Max groaned when Shevaun Wooten spoke. "Mr. Boyle? I wanted to let you know something's come up in my schedule. I need to bump our tour of Grayson House up to one o'clock tomorrow. Is that time convenient for you?"

Max glanced in the kitchen. Chancy stood by the window, staring at the bear cub shakers like she'd found two long-lost friends. "No, it's not. I need to cancel that tour."

"What? I don't understand. I thought we had an agreement."

"I'll get back to you." He pressed the disconnect button and left the receiver off the base.

"Those are from Yellowstone."

Chancy jumped sideways like a startled cat. "I didn't touch anything. I was just looking."

"Go right ahead. No charge to look."

She almost smiled. "They're cute. Is Yellowstone a place?"

"A park."

"Like Disneyland?"

"Not exactly. A national park. A famous natural wonder known for thermodynamic activity. And bears."

"Oh." The single syllable seemed to carry myriad meanings in her vocabulary. "I like bears."

"Me too. My wife and I vacationed there. Remind me to tell you about the geysers sometime."

"You have a wife?"

"Had. Lost her. A few months back."

"You live here by yourself?"

The girl's incredulous tone reinforced Shevaun Wooten's opinion that he was just taking up space. "I have since Hanna passed."

"How'd she die?"

Some things never changed, like kids and curiosity. "Lung cancer."

"Oh."

"You smoke?"

"No!"

"Good. Don't start. Habit's not worth a life."

Chancy nodded, as though familiar with the concept. "Do you still want to know my last name?"

"Only if you care to tell me."

She let out a long breath. "Deel."

"Deal, then." Max had made stranger bargains and waited for the big revelation.

"No, not deal. Deel," she repeated. "D-E-E-L. Chancy Deel. You know, like a sticky situation."

Risky business. Iffy proposition. Dicey undertaking. Max smiled. Her name was an apt description for the plan crystallizing in his mind. A plan that just might save them both. Or at the very least, buy them a little time.

Thank you, Hanna. For looking out for me.

Max leaned against the kitchen counter for support. "Tell me something, Miss Chancy. Do you suppose I could interest you...in a D-E-A-L?"

Chapter 8

Chancy backed into the door and tightened her grip on the knob. If the next words out of the old guy's mouth were *sex slave*, she would lay rubber and disappear. This time for good. "What kind of deal?"

"Let's adjourn to the sunroom." Mr. Boyle heaved himself away from the counter with a groan. "What I propose may take some explaining, and my backside is too bony for kitchen chairs."

Chancy waited for the red alert. Trusting girls who didn't listen to internal warnings ended up in basements, chained to the plumbing. The thought of Mr. Boyle being dangerous almost made her laugh, but she couldn't be too careful. The most successful serial killers were those who looked least threatening. A few more moments ticked by, and the inner siren remained silent. It didn't scream, "Run!" like it had that cold night in St. Louis. The professor was old, practically feeble. She was no black belt, but if he tried anything, she *could* take him down in hand-to-hand combat.

"Shall we?" He raised a bushy eyebrow and waited.

What was her problem? He'd shown her nothing but kindness. Why not hear him out? She'd been in tighter places. Escaped skankier propositions than anything a white-haired old gramps could think up.

Mr. Boyle led Chancy through the living room. *Parlor* was what actors in long dresses and stiff coats would call the room if it were in a movie. Stuffy in style and temperature, the high-ceilinged room was heavy with outdated furniture, dark with wine-colored floral wallpaper. Rooms should breathe, but this one was choking on the clutter of dusty knickknacks and magazines and books. She wanted to throw open the windows and let in fresh, new air.

The sunroom at the back of the house was a pleasant surprise. Wide windows fitted with tightly rolled bamboo shades overlooked the backyard and an enclosed flower garden that had grown wild and tangled. It was more weeds than flowers, but even an eye accustomed to concrete and bricks could see the landscape's neglected beauty.

Someone who loved nature had brought the outdoors into the room. Dark, terra-cotta floor tiles contrasted with walls painted the pale yellow-green of tender shoots. Bright cushions bloomed on white wicker furniture. On a side table, a bowl of delicate seashells tempted Chancy to press her ear against the rim in hopes of hearing a whisper from the ocean. A ceiling fan rotated lazily overhead, one wobbly blade groaning like night wind on each turn.

"This is my favorite spot in the house," Mr. Boyle said. "It was Hanna's favorite place, too."

"It's nice." The room was more than that, but Chancy didn't dare admit it out loud. She eased into a wicker rocker and opened herself to the room. Spaces were like people. Some had hearts and some didn't. She could feel safe in a space, or threatened, depending on how it embraced her. Mr. Boyle's sunroom was safe, but sad. Unhappiness had crept in, crowding out the light and leaving a dark chill that pressed down on her like a heavy hand.

Mr. Boyle settled on the wicker settee, and Alfie stretched out on the floor in a puddle of sunlight. "First things first. You on the lam from the law?"

"What?"

"Are you wanted by the police?"

She wasn't wanted. Not by anyone. "No."

"So you're not an escaped fugitive?"

"I walked out of a group home. I doubt they want me back."

"I can't be a party to kidnapping. Are your parents looking for you?"

She could answer that one truthfully. "No." B.J. was probably in no shape to look. Yet.

"Okay, then." The old man cleared his throat, as though trying not to choke on the words he was about to say. "I need your help."

"What?" Chancy couldn't help anyone. Her mother had never missed an opportunity to remind her how useless she was.

"Long story. Probably not very interesting to a young person. Will you hear me out?"

Chancy nodded. She loved stories. Her best childhood moments had been spent sitting cross-legged on smelly carpet squares listening to a teacher read. She'd been swept away by the adventures unfolding on the turning pages. They had offered her another way to disappear by carrying her out of reality and into worlds where endings were happy and children were never alone.

"After Hanna died, I guess I lost my grip," Mr. Boyle said. "You would have liked her, by the way. I know she would have liked you."

Hanna. Hanna. Hanna. Chancy tried out the name in her head, pleased by the sound and how it made her feel. The sunroom had belonged to Hanna. It carried her happiness and held her sadness. The garden must have been hers too. That was why it was untended. Like Mr. Boyle, the plants had struggled to get along without her, and neither knew which way to grow next.

Mr. Boyle explained how his former housekeeper's son had tried to rob him, and how Adult Protective Services had blazed onto the scene. He stressed that Ms. Wooten would not give up until he was out of sight and out of mind in a retirement home somewhere.

"Now I'm a *case*." There was a surprising fire in his eye, and the word was something disgusting he had to spit out. "I'm not a case. I'm a man. But I know when I'm licked. I'm no match for a whole agency full of do-gooders."

Chancy wasn't sure how she fit into the picture, but she understood Mr. Boyle's problem. Helpers ganged up on people. They had judges on their side. Court orders and official-looking papers. Authority.

"Much as I hate to admit it," he said, "Wooten the Relentless might be right. As you can see, I own a lot of house. It's hard to maintain, and I'm not as spry as I used to be."

"Have you been sick?" The shuffling walk, the labored speech, the way he favored his right hand. Something bad had happened to him.

"Ministrokes. TIAs, the doctor called them." He flexed his neck, revealing pale scars on either side. "I had surgery to ream out my arteries and haven't had one since. Knock on wood."

TIA was a pretty name for such an ugly thing. "What happened to your face?" She tried not to stare at the dark bruises rimming his eyes like a mask.

"You mean my Rocky Raccoon look?" He shrugged. "Barroom brawl."

"Really?"

"No. Of course not. I fell and conked my head. Don't worry," he said. "I look worse than I feel."

"You look pretty bad."

"So they say. I spend too much time alone. Alfie's a good sport, but a rotten conversationalist. I could use some practice talking."

And breathing. He had trouble taking in air and speaking at the same time.

"All of a sudden things are going to twelve kinds of hell around here." Alfie's head popped up to whimper disagreement with that assessment. "Can you see," the professor said, "why I need your help?"

All Chancy could see was an old man slipping into frailty who thought she could defend him against Adult Protection Services. If they were anything like Child Welfare, he was out of luck. Social workers had swooped into her life many times, but she'd never considered them the enemy. They had given her food and toys and clothes that fit. Attention too, for a while, until a hungrier kid with a bigger bruise or more broken bones came along.

They had a tough job. Sometimes they messed up and put kids in places that weren't safe. With people who were just as bad as the ones at home. They forgot to go back and check. There were too many hurting people in too much need. They never had enough time. She'd once overheard a helper say, *There isn't enough compassion to go around.* Authority was absolute, but it didn't always listen, especially to people who couldn't speak loud enough. Children without words. Old people whose voices had grown weak.

"Sorry. I can't help you." She was insignificant. Invisible.

"But you can. You might just be the answer to my prayers. That is, if I were still a praying man. Which I'm not."

"What can I do?"

"Save me from the old-age home."

"I can't do that." She wavered on the edge of panic, trying not to fall, but her breath knotted in her throat. She'd run away to escape a mother who'd needed too much saving.

"Are you okay, dear?" he asked.

"I should go."

"Wait! Hear me out." Desperation put a sharp point on his words, and they poked at her resistance. "Do you know what symbiosis is?"

"No." Chancy's mind raced. She didn't know anything. That was what B.J. said. Helpless too. Was it a hole in the ozone? A disease? A pimp-worthy perversion? "Does symbi-whatsis involve leather and whips?"

Mr. Boyle stared at her for a long moment. "Oh, dear God. No!" Startled laughter gave way to coughing, and he carried on so long, Chancy worried he needed 911. Alfie rose from his spot on the floor and sat at the old man's feet. The dog kept looking from his master to her, as though entreating her to do something, but she couldn't save Mr. Boyle. Not from a wheezing attack. Not from a helper with a court order.

"So what is it then?" she asked when he had finally collected himself.

"Symbiosis is when two dissimilar organisms live together. In a mutually beneficial relationship."

"Ooookay."

"I need live-in assistance. You need a place to stay. That's where the mutually beneficial part comes in."

"You want *me* to take care of you?" Mr. Boyle had to be crazy to think she could fool a social worker into thinking she was qualified for that job.

"Wooten's busy," he said. "She's looking for a way to dump me from her caseload. You can cook. Clean. Run errands. If I had a personal assistant, I could convince Wooten I don't need assisted living."

She could never do that. She set the rocker into anxious motion. He didn't know that her only experience was being a disappointment, a burden.

Mr. Boyle leaned forward, his elbows on his knees. "What do you say, Chancy Deel? You're a cagey customer. Are you game to outfox the APS?"

Chancy's throat tightened. She couldn't daydream herself into a new life, no matter how hard she tried. "I can't cook."

"Can you open a can?"

"I think so."

"Then we'll stock up on Campbell's and Dinty Moore."

"I'm"—she hated to admit she was worthless, but he shouldn't find out the hard, painful way—"not smart enough."

"All you need for this job are eager hands and a willing heart."

"I *can* clean!" Housekeeping had never been a priority for B.J., but every group home and shelter had been big on organization. *Make your bed. Sweep the floor. Hide your pitiful pile of clothes in your assigned drawer. Brush your teeth. Wash your hands.* She knew the basics of neatness and cleanliness, even if she hadn't had the opportunity to practice lately.

She glanced around. Dusty balls of lint and fur had gathered in the corners of the sunroom too. Months' worth of grime streaked the windows. Despite neglect, the old house was still beautiful; it just needed cheering up.

Chancy fisted her hands in her lap to hide the grubby nails. Her own hygiene had suffered on the road, but she could do better. If she worked hard and tackled one room at a time, maybe she could help Mr. Boyle put a fresh face on 639 Poplar Avenue.

"What you don't know," he said, "you can learn as you go. Fair enough?"

She squirmed with guilt. She didn't dare point out how unfair such an arrangement would be to him. Life had dropped few windfalls in her lap. She couldn't blow this one. Mr. Boyle was willing to let her live in his house, and all she had to do was take care of it. That wasn't a job. It was a waking dream.

"I need housekeeping. Laundry. Dog walking. Errands. Shopping. I'm old, not helpless. You won't have to follow me into the toilet, if that worries you."

She kept her eyes on her hands to hide her relief. Good to know she wouldn't have to get too close.

"For all that, I'll provide you with room and board. And a salary."

Chancy glanced up sharply. Too much good luck could not be real. Wages? If she had money, she would pay him to live here. She was either sleeping or making up stories in her head again.

"Does two hundred a week sound . . . reasonable?"

"Two hundred?" she croaked. "Dollars?"

"Well, pesos don't spend around here." He grinned, in case she missed the joke.

"You mean I can live here *and* you'll pay me?"

"It's not a handout. You'll earn every penny. I can be a hard task-master."

"Two hundred dollars." She was not yet used to the idea.

"Well, there is one more thing I will expect you to do. Something you might not like."

She knew it. *Right. One more thing.* Hope deflated.

"I hate to put you in a delicate position, but you will be required to lie."

"What?"

"We can't tell the truth. To anybody. Wooten's smart. To fool her, we'll have to make up a believable story."

"A story?"

"Something to explain your presence here. The truth won't cut it."

"You want me to make up a story?"

"That's the only way the arrangement will work. Think you can do that?"

When things seemed too good to be true, they usually were. Chancy's thoughts tangled in emotion. *Say yes. No, run. Take what you can get. Don't risk it. Why not? Because.* As much as she feared staying in one place too long, this had to be a sign. Making up stories was the only thing she had ever been good at. She called it putting a good face on the truth.

"I need to think."

"Take your time. I gotta go to the john." Mr. Boyle limped across the room, pausing at the doorway. "You gonna sneak off? Disappear on me?"

She shook her head. She couldn't disappear. Not when she had a chance to live a real pretend life, if only for a while. She usually didn't spend more than two nights in one place, but this was 639 Poplar Avenue, and something told her she'd be safe here for much longer.

"I'll be right back." He made a face. "On second thought, I might be a while. Damned prostate."

Out in the hallway, the downstairs bathroom door clicked shut. Silence settled around Chancy, and she closed her eyes, waiting. The red alert never let her down. It had appeared when she was little to help her steer clear of B.J.'s boyfriends' grabby hands. It had told her to lock herself in the bathroom when B.J. drank too much or took the wrong pills. The red alert had helped her avoid dangerous playground bullies. Not just trippers and hair pullers, but mean-mouthed girls who made fun of her clothes and called her names. Thanks to the red alert, she'd known which teachers cared and which helpers could be trusted. If she paid attention to the voices, she could tell the difference between people who had hearts and those with an empty hole at their core.

The red alert had led her to Oklahoma. Last winter, desperate to get out of Pittsburgh, she'd hitched west. She had landed in St. Louis when a ride with a middle-aged drug lady ran out. Not a dealer, the woman had clarified with a practiced grin, a sales rep. She peddled medicine and had a big black suitcase on wheels full of anti-everything. Antidepressants. Anticoagulants. Anticholinergics. Chancy hadn't understood a word she said.

The woman gabbed nonstop about her horrible divorce and asshole ex who tried to make *her* pay *him* alimony since she earned more money. Men were like Slinkys, she said: fun to play with, but once things got tangled up, they were impossible to straighten out. Ms. Chatty had pressed a twenty-dollar bill into Chancy's hand before letting her out of the car on the grimy side of the Mississippi River.

That night the chill air had been heavy. A cold witch moon, silent and watchful, reminded Chancy she was alone in a strange, dark world. Freezing water lapped the riverbank, inviting her in for a quiet silver sleep. Why not? She had nothing. No one. She was more lost than she'd ever been. No one would care if she died. She had been tempted to release the slender thread that she'd clung to for so long. Staring at the frigid waves, she'd lost her fear. Death wouldn't be so bad. Life was worse. She would rather die than go back to B.J.

Without warning, the murky clouds had dropped a load of snow. Stinging fingers of ice had driven Chancy away from the river's edge. She didn't want to die. She just wanted a reason to live. Prowling for warmth, she had stumbled into a grunge hangout that stank of sweat, weed and beer. She'd stood shivering just inside the door until a scary-looking guy noticed her. He introduced himself as Shaggy Dave with elaborate good manners that were creepily charming. He stuck out a big, dark hand and steered her to a table in the corner, where he looked her over as if he were measuring her for a coffin.

You a skinny thing, but nothin' a little chicken and dumplin's won't cure. You stick with Shaggy, baby; he gonna make you rich.

The red alert had gonged like a three-alarm fire bell. All Shaggy Dave would make her was dead. She had to escape, even if she didn't know where to run. When the pimp swaggered to the bar for a beer, Chancy slipped into the night. Running blind, she pounded down sidewalks blanketed with slush until her chest filled with liquid fire. Shoes soaked, jeans wet to the knees. Icy needles stung her face. She finally stumbled onto a parking lot awash in the yellow glow of snow-shrouded streetlights. Shivering, she hid in the shadows and watched families go in and out of a pizza joint. Mama Mia's. When the alarm bells stopped clanging and she could breathe again, she ducked inside.

She sat in the back and ordered a single slice. The boy in charge didn't make her pay, so she ended up eating four. That was how she met Kenny Ray. When the storm turned the world white, customers stopped coming. With a couple of hours left on his shift, Kenny Ray Kane had sat at her table and talked. He told her she reminded him of his little sister who lived with his mother in Arkansas. She nodded. Didn't say much.

He talked about music and how he was saving money to get his band back together. At closing time, he offered to let Chancy sleep on his couch. No red alert warned her away, and she snapped at the chance to get off the street and away from dangerous men like Shaggy Dave.

Kenny Ray's place was a dingy, furnished studio apartment over some old lady's garage. Compared to Chancy's rock-bottom slot on the food chain, wannabe musician Kenny Ray Kane's lifestyle was practically MTV. She had fully expected to "pay" for his hospitality, but he never touched her. She was his good deed for the month. He said helping others earned him points with the Big Guy. Chancy wasn't sure she believed in God, but she understood the point system. Kenny Ray had the twitchy look of the chronically self-medicated, but he had a good heart. He also had a girl in Oklahoma and a dream in Texas. All he ever talked about was how Kenny Ray and the Kane Raisers would be the next big thing.

Chancy stayed because she had nowhere else to go. She cleaned his apartment while he was at work and ate the pizza he brought home. At the end of the month when his lease was up, he said he was leaving and wouldn't mind company. He offered to let her ride along as far as Wenonah, Oklahoma.

She accepted. Oklahoma was west of Missouri. Farther away from B.J., and at that moment, disappearing was all that mattered.

With Alfie at her feet, Chancy rocked and waited. When the old man returned, he patted her shoulder as he walked by.

"So what's the verdict, young lady?"

She shrank from his touch. She wouldn't let him get close. She wouldn't care about him. Wouldn't trust him with secrets. She would knock down his cobwebs and eat his eggs and make up a story for the social worker. She would do her best not to screw up. "Okay. I guess."

"Not exactly the enthusiastic endorsement I'd hoped for, but I'll take it."

What did she have to lose? Eventually he would realize she didn't deserve his kindness. That she was as worthless as B.J. always said. As emotionally disturbed as the girl in the state's reports. If she got scared, she would run and be no worse off than before.

"Are the terms acceptable?" he asked.

Two hundred dollars a week and a place to live? Free food? Hot showers? What wasn't acceptable about riches beyond her wildest dreams? She wasn't smart enough to beat the system. Couldn't help Mr. Boyle keep his house for long, but the temptation to sleep under a roof, even for one night, overshadowed the fear of failure. "They're all right."

"Good." He leaned back with a sigh. "Glad that's settled."

"Mr. Boyle?"

"You can't keep calling me that." He concentrated. "Let's see now. You can call me Uncle Max." He shrugged like he didn't care. "I never had a niece or a daughter or a grandchild. I'd like to hear the words before I die."

"Uncle Max." Chancy had never had a father or uncle or grandfather. She would like to *say* the words. "I don't know if I can do what you want."

"I believe you can." He smiled. "I have faith in you."

She blinked away sudden tears before he could see them. No one had ever expected anything good from her. Maybe the universe really had led her here. To Max Boyle and his too-good-to-be-true kindness. He had offered her something no one had: a chance to prove her life was worth something. If she didn't fail, didn't disappoint, she might yet earn an old man's desperate trust.

"I'll try," she promised softly.

His lopsided grin transformed him. He looked a little bigger. Straighter. More certain. Like the weight of the world had been knocked off his shoulders. Like a man with newfound hope. Had she given him that hope?

"That's all I need to know, Chancy Deel. Trying is all I'll ever ask of you."

Chancy didn't know what to make of her new "uncle." She would do her best not to make him regret giving her an opportunity, but she wouldn't let herself care.

She could never give him her real heart.

Chapter 9

"What should I do first? Wash the dishes?" The girl shot from her chair like a missile fired from a rocket launcher. Once she made up her mind, she didn't waste any time. Max admired her level of commitment, but since when had youngsters become so enamored of chores?

"Hold your horses," he said. "Plenty of time for that. I need to show you your room first."

She froze. "I can have my own room?"

"I thought about making you sleep on the hearth. Like Cinderella. But there's no fireplace in the kitchen. A bedroom will have to do."

Her brows drew down, twin dark slashes joined in the struggle to determine whether he was serious or not.

"I'm kidding. Please forgive my rusty jokes, dear. My sense of humor is as creaky as the rest of me."

"Oh," she said after a moment. "You were teasing."

"Trying to."

She shrugged, impassive. "You weren't making fun of me?"

"No."

"Okay."

As they passed through the kitchen, she hoisted her bulging knapsack. No telling what she had in that thing. Leading the way upstairs, Max paused on the landing like he needed to catch his breath. What he really needed was a moment with Hanna. Reassurance. He nodded at the framed sepia-toned portrait that had long been his favorite.

"Chancy, meet Hanna."

The girl studied the picture as though it were a painting in a gallery. "She looks like a person who would be interesting to know."

"She was." Max approved of the girl's insight. Hanna would have preferred being called interesting over beautiful any day. By movie-star standards, she was no glamour girl, but she had been a stunner just the same. Tall and full of unrestrained energy, she had possessed the angular figure of a young Katharine Hepburn. She had also shared the star's chestnut hair and outspoken manner. The aristocratic actress had appealed more to a man's intellect than to his libido, but Hanna had appealed to both. He'd expected her to be shy on their wedding night. He couldn't have been more wrong.

"How did you meet her?" Chancy asked.

"She was in the first class I taught as an assistant professor." He'd stood before the roomful of freshmen like a man facing a firing squad, wanting nothing more than to get the whole thing over with.

"She was your student?"

"Yes. That's why I had to wait four long years before I could ask her for a date." The wait had nearly killed him, but he wouldn't violate the school's no-fraternization policy. Compelled by a sense of honor sharpened in the service, he'd tried to ignore the attraction he felt for the pretty coed.

"What was she like?"

"Sat in the front row. I still remember what she was wearing. White blouse with a lace collar. Pleated skirt. Bobby socks and saddle shoes." He had to explain those fashion statements. "She had a lot of confidence for a nineteen-year-old." He laughed. "More than me, and I was twenty-eight."

"You were nervous?"

"Scared spitless." He explained how he'd studied chemistry on the GI Bill after the war. He'd found a niche and turned an interest into a career. "Thought I knew it all, but I didn't know what real chemistry was until I met Hanna McLean."

"It was love at first sight?"

"Not first sight. I didn't fall in love until halfway through the period. Hanna caught my eye and gave me a thumbs-up. After class she stopped by my desk. I was stuffing lecture notes in my bag. I never forgot what she said."

"What?"

The girl's interest seemed sincere. " 'Don't be so nervous next time, Professor. You're going to be a fine teacher.' Hanna gave me a lot to live up to."

Chancy continued to stare at the portrait, her head tilted to one side. "She was right, wasn't she?"

"About what?"

"You are a fine teacher."

"Was. Hanna knew more than I ever will." She'd been wise, even at eighteen when she sat for this photo.

"She's wearing a pretty dress."

"It was her high school party formal." An off-the-shoulder miracle of pale, ruched chiffon. The photographer had captured her in a rare serious moment, her face in profile, posed on the edge of a chaise, with the gown's carefully arranged skirt drifting like early snow. Her hair fell in loose waves around her shoulders. She'd believed no woman's scalp should be tortured by hairpins.

"You miss her."

"Every moment of every day. But I treasure the time we had together." Max turned from the portrait. Hanna was gone, but she was only a memory away. At the top of the stairs, he pointed out the bathroom before opening a door at the end of the hall.

"This used to be the guest room. It's musty now. Haven't had visitors for years." He opened the linen closet and pulled out fresh sheets. "Help yourself to towels and washcloths."

Now that Chancy was no longer a flight risk, Max wasn't sure what to do with her. He needed to trust the geriatric lapse of good judgment that had made him invite the grubby girl into his home. Apparently, his unfortunate experience with Ricky Dimas had not instilled a lick of caution.

Hanna had loved to point out that the definition of insanity was doing the same thing over and over and expecting a different result. He hoped she was wrong.

This morning in the garage when Chancy had popped up in the Lincoln's backseat, she'd looked small and scared and alone. Her pinched face and hungry eyes posed no threat. Despite rough edges and her unkempt appearance, she did not exude danger. Her uncommonly quiet composure made her a person *he* wanted to know. She was a kitten caught in a bear trap, and he felt compelled to prove there was still goodwill in the world. He wanted to make her smile, because it went against nature for a child to be without mirth.

At first, he intended to feed her breakfast and send her packing so he could get back to his grand exit. By giving her his ready cash, less gas money, he planned to make Little Miss Lonely Heart his last unselfish act on earth. Surely a man who skidded through the Pearly Gates with the stink of a good deed still on him would impress the hell out of Saint Peter. Maybe even undo the damage of the whole taking-his-oswn-life, mortal-sin thing.

Then something unexpected had happened. Between the first batch of toast and the second, Max had realized with blinding clarity that he wasn't ready to die. Maybe that was what Hanna was trying to tell him when she whispered in his dreams. Chancy had sat at his table, quiet and cautious. Waiting. He dared to hope that maybe she was waiting for him to show her what her life could be.

On that long-ago day when Hanna had insisted on adopting Alfie, she'd said, *We can give him a home, but he will give us so much more.* When she died, Max's sense of calm and peace had died too, but today, for the first time in months, he had felt sure about something.

Some things are just meant to be, Professor. You don't always get to choose. Sometimes fate chooses for you.

He could give Chancy a home, but she would give him more. He hoped fighting the system with the help of a frightened wisp-child wasn't another sign of slowly advancing dementia.

Chancy set her stained pack on the red oak floor and turned slowly, taking in the room. Max remembered painting the walls on a distant Saturday when all he'd wanted was to watch a televised football game. Hanna had come home lugging shopping bags full of linens and a can of paint. Buttercream yellow, she'd called it. When was that? 'Eighty-four? 'Eighty-six?

She'd been caught up in another brainstorm. A brain fart, he'd muttered as the football game went on without him. She wanted to fix up a room and offer cheap board to a deserving student who couldn't afford to live in the dorm. He'd groaned at having a kid, possibly one with little support and lots of needs, mucking up their quiet house. In the end, he'd gone along because no one stood a chance in the face of Hanna's determination.

When they finished redecorating, the room was bright with her optimism. The ad she placed in the campus paper attracted a few takers, but none stayed long. Young people wanted to party and entertain friends. They wanted to come and go on their own schedule. Even the promise of low rent, meals included, could not overcome the liability of living with two old people set in their ways.

Now the paint was as faded as Hanna's hope had been. The French provincial furniture wasn't antique, just dated. The ruffles on the royal blue dotted Swiss curtains and bedspread drooped. Even the daisies in the print over the bed, once a symbol of his wife's joie de vivre, seemed to mock.

"Make yourself at home," he said. "I know it's not much, but you can fix it up to suit your taste."

"I like the room just the way it is." Chancy's words were soft and sure. "I don't want to change anything."

He opened the closet door. "There are plenty of hangers in here. Let me know if you need more."

"I won't need more."

Max glanced at the knapsack containing everything she owned. *Right.* He knew about traveling light. When he was Chancy's age, he'd jumped freight cars and huddled over tin-can fires with other vagrants, traveling from Oklahoma to California and back again. To a kid tasting life for the first time, riding the rails had seemed more like an adventure than end-of-the-rope desperation. He'd seen the country and learned to read and heed the scratched hobo symbols on trees and fence posts.

Good woman lives here.

Beware mean dog.

Man with shotgun.

Max had begged for handouts at back doors from Amarillo to Sacramento. He'd been run off the premises with a pitchfork. Welcomed in and fed cold fried chicken. He'd been cursed and blessed and prayed over. He'd slept under bridges and in barns and in back pews of wayside churches. One lady had given him her dead son's coat after showing Max the boy's coffin picture. In a vacant building outside Reno, a wild-eyed bum had tried to stab him in the neck with a sharpened spoon handle.

There were all kinds of people in the world. Good, mean, indifferent. Those footloose days had taught Max how to read intent in a man's eyes. The importance of owning his own place. The value of belonging. Of standing for something. And having someone to come home to. Life had shown him the difference between letting go and giving up. He'd done a few things on the damnation list, but he knew how cold it was at the bottom of the well. He would offer a helping hand when he could.

"Wait here," he said. "I'll be right back."

Max lumbered down the hall to the master bedroom and slid open the closet doors. His meager collection of trousers and shirts and two good suits had been pushed to one end of the rod to make room for her colorful wardrobe. Hanna had loved tailored pants. Crisp jewel-toned shirts. Long scarves and silver jewelry. He hadn't had the heart to dispose of her things. On sad days he held the garments close to breathe in her faint presence. He shuffled through items folded on shelves until he found what he was looking for, then returned to Chancy.

"Here. You might as well have these." He thrust a pair of flannel pajamas and a long pink chenille robe into the startled girl's arms. "Don't worry. They're new. Hanna was saving them for her next trip . . . to the hospital. She didn't get a chance to wear them."

Max wasn't sure what reaction he had expected, but when her face stiffened into an unreadable mask, he knew he'd done something wrong. A young girl wouldn't want an old lady's clothes. Flannel! What was he thinking? Feeling like a fool, he tried to take back the rejected clothing, but Chancy's arms tightened around them.

"Thank you." Her chin quivered; her eyes filled. "These are the nicest things I ever owned."

Her glistening eyes ushered in the first real smile he'd seen from her. She didn't have to say anything else. He knew. He had made the right decision. His whole life had pointed him to this moment.

"Here's my thinking." Max sat at the table while Chancy put away the dishes from a late soup-and-sandwich lunch. "First thing we have to do is cook up a good story."

"We can say I answered your ad," she suggested. "You know, like 'help wanted'?"

"You're too young for that. Don't want to let on that you're . . . on your own. That'd raise too many questions. We need a good reason for you to be here."

"I'm your great-niece from New York?"

"Nope. Wooten knows I'm fresh out of relatives. Family's good, though." Max smacked his palm on the table. "I know! You're my godson's daughter."

"You have a godson?" She hung the striped dish towel on the hook by the sink and smoothed it with a lingering touch.

"No, but Wooten doesn't know that. Who's to say I'm not a godfather?"

Chancy frowned. "Isn't a godfather some kind of gangster?"

"Only in the movies." Max laughed. "A godfather is a man who sponsors a child at baptism. Backup guardian, in case something happens to the parents."

"Like when the vice president runs the country if the president can't?"

"Right. We'll say your parents are academics traveling on sabbatical."

"What's that?"

"When professors take a semester off. To study or conduct research. Or write a book."

"And I couldn't go. So I'm staying with you."

"Might work." With the basic shape of the lie-to-end-all-lies hammered out, they might have a snowflake's chance in Haiti of pulling off the ruse.

Chancy looked down at her stained shirt and ragged nails. "Think the social worker will believe I'm a teacher's kid?"

The privileged daughter of loving parents? No way. The girl looked like she'd been living under the porch and had the social skills of a feral cat. "We can fake that part." At a loss to put his question delicately, he said, "Would you like to take a hot shower?"

"Oh, yes." She sighed as though she thought he'd never ask. "Please."

"Use the upstairs bathroom. Help yourself to the Prell." *Hint, hint.* "While you're cleaning up, I'll jot down some notes. Important thing is this: We get our story straight and stick to it. Don't want to trip each other up."

"Can I, uh, use the washing machine?" She squeaked the request as if asking for the moon and a neighboring constellation.

He resisted the urge to correct her grammar. All kids were sloppy with *may* and *can* these days. "Sure, dear. Anytime."

After she left, Max found a yellow legal pad and pen in a drawer where he spotted the big envelope addressed to Pete Marshall. *Lord.* His official last wishes had come back to bite him. The packet looked old. An ancient artifact from a bygone era. He slipped it under Hanna's embroidered towels. A few hours had changed everything. In a blink, life was worth living again.

He couldn't have Pete over now. The wily lawyer could ferret out a phony alibi with his eyes closed. Max dialed the law office and learned Pete was in court. He asked the receptionist to cancel their meeting, saying he wasn't up to company after all. Lying to a friend was another tangled web he'd have to unkink later. He hated doing it but had no choice. Necessity was the mother of invention, and a mean mother too.

Alfie whined at the door, and Max let him out, then sat at the table trying to fill in the blanks of his imaginary godson's family. Half an hour later, Chancy slipped back into the room. She had to be the quietest kid he'd ever met. Nothing like Adam Hamilton, always pumping up and down the sidewalk on his skateboard, feet like pistons. Blasting music from an open window, bouncing a basketball in the drive. The boy was as rackety as a box of ducks, but Chancy crept about like a sad little specter.

She returned with her laundry. Her dirty wardrobe, wrapped in a threadbare green blanket, made a small bundle. Steam from the shower had put spots of high color in her cheeks. Her wet, slicked-back hair gleamed darkly against her pale skin. Like a child playing dress-up, she wore the pink robe with sleeves folded back, the belt cinched around her waist. The robe was too long for her and pooled in a pink puddle around her feet.

"Detergent's on the shelf. Dryer sheets, too."

"When I'm finished, I can do your laundry." She bargained for favors, like everything had a price.

"No need. I'm good." Max owned more than three changes of clothes.

"What do you want me to clean first?" She'd tucked a worn but freshly laundered gray shirt neatly into equally worn jeans. Her holey sneakers would not have survived a trip through the washer and were still as grungy as before. Max's sense of smell wasn't what it used to be, but even his fossilized nostrils rebelled at the odoriferous footgear.

"You can start your official duties tomorrow." Max had filled only half a page with lies. He was no Hemingway, and writing fiction was hard work. "We'll call today . . . orientation."

"What do I have to do?"

"Get acquainted. Learn the ropes. Get our story straight. Here's what I have so far." He read aloud. "Your folks teach at the University of Oklahoma."

"Won't work."

He looked up. "Why not?"

"I don't sound like I'm from Oklahoma, remember?"

"Good point."

"And that would be easy to check."

"Right again." Wooten was the determined type. She would definitely check. Chancy was shaping up to be an excellent prevaricator. Something to remember. "So where do you come from?"

She hesitated, weighing her words. Finally the scale tipped. "Say they teach at the University of Pennsylvania."

"Farther away."

"Harder to check."

She let in Alfie, and Max made another note. When the doorbell rang, he glanced out the dining room window and spotted a familiar tan car parked in the side drive.

"Damn! It's her!"

"Who?"

"Doggedness personified. Shevaun Wooten, MSW."

"The social worker?"

Chancy's wide eyes and panicked tone reminded Max of single-reel comedies in which the Keystone Kops caught melodramatic burglars in the act. *Cheese it! The coppers!* Instead of dread, an unlikely thrill of anticipation raced through him. How long since he'd laid anything on the line? Taken a chance? Had some fun?

"What's she doing here?"

"Trying to catch me with my pants down. Probably shouldn't have hung up on her."

"What will we do?"

"We have no choice. It's time to get our show on the road."

"Wait! We haven't worked out the story yet."

"We have to improvise, like all good actors."

"Think we can fool her?"

Not in a million years. Max heard the clang of the long-term-care door slamming shut behind him. "Why not? We have youthful innocence *and* aged wisdom on our side."

His imminent undoing pressed the doorbell again. Shevaun Wooten was soon perched on the sofa, stiff and unyielding, her dark eyes shuttered with doubt. "I don't understand." She glanced from Max to Chancy, who hadn't uttered a word so far. The girl sat with gaze downcast, hands clenched in her lap, clearly crumbling under the weight of the impossible charade.

"Simple," Max managed breezily. "Due to unforeseen events, Chancy, my godson's daughter, will be spending the summer here."

"And this all came up—"

"Unexpectedly."

"You say they're on sabbatical?"

"That's right."

"Aren't sabbaticals usually planned well in advance?"

Checkmate. Skepticism rolled off the young social worker. She wasn't buying it. Oliver Hardy's classic words to Stan Laurel echoed in Max's mind.

Well, here's another nice mess you've gotten me into.

Moments ticked by. Max maintained eye contact, challenging Ms. Wooten to blink first. *Aged wisdom, where art thou?*

"Oh, everything *was* planned." Chancy looked up, her face transformed. Gone was the wary expression, replaced by a preternaturally animated smile. "I was set to spend the summer traveling with my best friend's family. We were going to Glacier National Park. The Royal Gorge. Yellowstone Park."

Nice itinerary. Hot off Hanna's souvenir spoon rack.

"The details had been worked out for *months!* My friend's father"—Chancy's gaze shifted out the window and back to Ms. Wooten—"Mr. Gardener, said we needed to get away from televisions and computers and see what makes America great. Natural wonders and all that."

"Uh-huh." Ms. Wooten relaxed a little. Hard not to be sucked in by Chancy's fake enthusiasm. She was the natural wonder. Either a born storyteller or a pathological liar.

"Well, um, then something bad happened."

"Bad?" Ms. Wooten's interest level shot up. Chancy knew how to increase suspense. Misfortune was always more engaging than happiness.

"Really bad." Chancy's gaze flitted to the lace curtains before plunging on. "Lacy—she's been my best friend since fifth grade—her grandmother started having . . . TIAs. She'd already had that operation, you know the one where they clean out your arteries? Anyway, she was doing fine; then when everyone least expected it"—she paused, swallowed, reached for the drama—"she had a stroke."

"Oh, my. I hope she's all right," Ms. Wooten said. "Your friend Lacy's grandmother."

"The doctors are sure she'll recover. Thank goodness."

"That's good." Ms. Wooten, guardian of the elderly and corporate caregiver, was relieved by the news.

Chancy sighed. "Of course, the Gardeners canceled the vacation."

"Of course," Ms. Wooten agreed.

"Of course." Max nodded. Stories should have happy endings.

"They all flew to, uh . . ." Chancy's gaze wandered again, subtly looking for clues. She zeroed in on the magnolia-patterned wallpaper behind Ms. Wooten's head. "Walla Walla. To be with Grandma Blossom."

Max coughed. Lucky Grandma had her whole devoted family with her.

"Since I couldn't go, Daddy called Uncle Max and asked if I could spend the summer here."

"Oh?"

"It was really my idea. I love visiting Uncle Max. I haven't been back for a while and was afraid Alfie would forget me. But guess what? He didn't."

Right on cue, Alfie rose and propped his muzzle on Chancy's thigh. "See? We're still buddies, aren't we, Alfie boy?"

Alfie barked once in agreement. *You bet.*

Ms. Wooten looked to Max for corroboration. Still in shock over the ebullient details frothing out of Chancy, he could only nod in sage wisdom. He hoped Chancy had simply taken improvisation to a whole new level and was not the practiced liar she seemed. Otherwise, how could he ever believe a word she said?

"Mom agreed a summer in Wenonah was just what I needed." Chancy executed a perfect teenage eye roll. "Hellooooo. Safer than an archaeo-logical dig in the Middle East? Yah!"

"The Middle East?" Ms. Wooten asked.

"I *know*. Crazy, right? What with all the bombs and stuff. I can't even call them. Cell phones don't work where they are."

"Sounds remote. And risky."

"If you knew my folks, you'd understand. They're looking for proof to support the book they're writing. Pretty boring stuff, if you ask me, but my parents are nuts over"—she scanned the cover of a *National Geographic* stacked beside her chair—"ancient Sumerian kings the way I'm nuts over Orlando Bloom. They're such nerds. But I love them." She stopped, breathless, and threw an urgent sideways plea in Max's direction.

His cue. Enter stage right. "My godson and his wife are scholars. The dig site is on the Euphrates. I tried to talk them out of going to such a hot spot, but they wouldn't listen. You know how dedicated scientists can be."

"Yes, I suppose so. But the Middle East?"

Chancy dispelled the shadow of doubt cast by Ms. Wooten's words. "Their work is really important, and they're not in an area where there's any fighting, so I try not to worry."

"Good. I see why they would prefer you stay here."

And everyone lived happily ever after. Ms. Wooten was smiling now.

"I've been on digs before." Chancy's exaggerated groan was convinc-ing. "Borrrring! And hot. Nothing to do but count ants in the sand, which gets old after a while."

"I can imagine."

"We're going to have a great time. Right, Uncle Max?"

He nodded. "Right."

"Right." Ms. Wooten echoed the word in a tone that said she still wasn't convinced. "Mr. Boyle, are you sure you're up to caring for a child all summer?"

Before he could speak, Chancy popped onto the arm of his chair to insert appropriate emotion into the story. She leaned down and pretended to hug him. The embrace was all for show, as false as her story, as devoid of reality.

"I'm not two years old, you know," Chancy said with a disarming grin. "I can take care of myself. In fact, before you arrived, we were talking about all the things we plan to do together, right, Uncle Max?"

"Uh, yes," he agreed. "We have compiled quite an agenda."

"Oh, like what?" Ms. Wooten leaned forward, curious now.

Good question. What would a broken-down codger and a vagabond teen put on an agenda, if they had one? *Think, man. Throw the woman a bone. A tiny metacarpal will suffice.*

"The first thing we're going to do," Chancy gushed, "is clean up this place. Things piled up after Aunt Hanna died."

Aunt Hanna. How she would have loved the sound of that.

Ms. Wooten glanced around at the clutter. "Good plan. Then, when you get ready to sell, much of the work will be done."

"Exactly!" The pushy social worker could think he was getting the place ready for prospective buyers if that would get her off his back.

"So can I assume," she said, "that your plans haven't really *changed*. They've merely been placed on hold?"

"Temporarily."

Ms. Wooten shifted in her chair. Reached for her briefcase. "Uh-huh. So by the end of the summer . . ."

"I will be ready and willing to take that tour." Hell would also be completely frozen over, and pigs would be running their own flight school, but she didn't need to know that.

He had tossed her a bone of Brontosaurus-size proportions, one that relieved her of the burden that was Maxwell Boyle, at least for the time being. She could leave now. Her job was done. Her conscience clear.

Max had a new spring in his step as he walked the social worker to the door. Using Chancy's tall tales as currency, he had just bought himself a priceless gift.

One summer.

Three months in which to live the rest of his life.

Chapter 10

Once the social worker left, Chancy could breathe again. She stood at the window and watched the woman back her car out of the drive, turn left and disappear around the corner. Safe. Again. For now. Ms. Wooten had looked relieved when she said she was glad Max had someone to stay with him while he waited for his name to move up the list. *Lucky how that worked out.* She'd promised—really more of a threat in disguise—to stop by in a couple of weeks to see how they were doing.

No way would Chancy stay that long. The two-nights-in-one-spot rule applied only when she had to sleep on the street, but the old man would soon realize that asking her for help had been a mistake. Then she'd be out. Alone. She'd known Max for only for a few hours. Why did the thought of leaving his house twist her stomach into knots? She turned from the window.

Uncle Max eased into his recliner and propped up his feet. "Miss Gulch gone?"

"Who?"

"Miss Gulch." He raised his voice to a familiar witchy pitch. "I'll get you, my pretty, and your little dog too!"

Alfie looked up and whined. Chancy smiled when he tucked a paw over his eyes. "Yes. She's gone."

"Thank God. I thought she was onto us there for a minute. Nothing like a close call to set a man's heart to racing."

"Are you okay?" she asked.

"Better than okay. Exhilarated."

Chancy wasn't sure what that meant, but it sounded good. Several long moments ticked by. She'd never been an employee before and had no idea what her next move should be. "What do you want me to do now?"

"Sit down," he said. "We need to talk."

The knots in her stomach tightened as Chancy eased onto the edge of a straight-backed chair. Nothing good ever came of people saying that. They just wanted to tell you what they thought was wrong with you. She stared at her feet. The hole in the toe of her left sneaker was bigger today.

Uncle Max cleared his throat. "Well, that was quite an entertaining development. Who the heck *are* you, young lady? Sarah Bernhardt reincarnated?"

Sarah Bernhardt? Wasn't she the girl who killed her parents with an ax and forty whacks? No. That was Lizzie somebody. Chancy came up blank. She had no memories or pictures linked to the name Sarah. "I'm sorry. I didn't mean to say anything wrong."

She wasn't convinced the words had even come from her. They'd appeared out of thin air, manifested by sleight of hand, like the cards and flowers conjured by the amateur magician who'd entertained the shelter inmates with his tricks. At six, she'd sat on the floor, hypnotized by the young man's clumsy moves and awkward banter. The older kids had hooted with the bad kind of laughter, making him so jittery he started dropping things.

Tricked too often by life, the throwaway children around Chancy were propelled to their feet by sneering accusations.

"You pulled that out of your pocket!"

"It's not the same card!"

"The coin was in your other hand the whole time!"

"You suck!"

"Faker!"

"Loser!"

The magician lost control of his audience but gamely finished his performance. If Chancy had been able to find her voice, she would have yelled at the disbelievers, *Sit down. Shut up. Let him pretend. Let me.* Why did they have to ruin the make-believe? She wanted the magician to wave his wand and make *her* disappear. Drowning in the waves of restless energy, she'd gone still, floating on the noise like a leaf on the surface of a puddle. She'd willed herself to grow smaller and smaller, until poof! The magic worked, and she was tiny enough to live under the magician's silky red square of distraction.

Gradually the children's noise faded to a numb roar and the room dimmed. Chancy slipped into the quiet place where she was never hungry and always clean. Where she could speak without fear and feel something that didn't hurt. Beside her, a boy yelled, "Hey, she's doing it again!" and that was all she remembered until she awoke in her bunk, kid-sized and covered by a rough blanket instead of a silky scarf. The sheet beneath her was cold and damp, her punishment to endure.

That night, she had finally understood that some people would never believe in magic. They wanted everything to be real so they could tear it apart and step on the pieces. She had hoped Uncle Max would believe. If he did, she could pretend he really was her uncle, that the yellow room really belonged to her. She could be herself and wouldn't have to disappear again.

But as always, words had ruined everything. She blinked away hot tears. She'd only wanted to stay a little while.

"I'm sorry," she said. "I'll go now. I didn't mean to do anything bad."

"Bad?" The word rolled off his tongue like a foreign phrase he didn't understand. "No need to be sorry. What in heaven's name are you talking about?"

She wiped her sleeve across her eyes to erase evidence of her weakness. For years she'd locked her tears in a soul-deep dungeon, but since meeting Uncle Max, they'd lived too near the surface. "I don't?"

"Oh, child! That was a high-caliber performance. Got me right here."

He smacked his thin chest. "Grandma Blossom? Genius touch. Sarah Bernhardt would be proud."

"Who *is* Sarah Bernhardt?"

"Only one of the greatest stage actresses of all time. A little before your day, of course." He laughed. "Heck, even before *mine!*"

Understanding dawned slowly. "So you're not mad at me?"

"Mad? Why would I be? I was stammering like Ned at his first recital, but you! Why, you grabbed the bull by the horns. That was some song and dance."

Chancy faltered, distracted by all the visual images in his words and unable to follow his meaning.

"We agreed to make up a story we could stick to." He slapped his thigh. "In terms of fish tales, that was a whopper!"

Fish? Bulls? Right. Fish-and-bull story. No, cock-and-bull story. She'd heard that. Somewhere. Clancy hadn't planned to tell a story. Wouldn't have tried, even if she'd had the courage. She'd simply stared at a faraway place until the words shimmered before her like a heat mirage in the road. They had floated up, clung together, shaped themselves into sentences.

He released the recliner's footrest, and the chair bolted upright with a mechanical clank. "How'd you do that?"

"Do what?"

"Transform like that. I was afraid you weren't going to say anything, and then bam! You hit your mark and the show was on!"

"I borrowed the voice. From someone I knew once." A girl at the shelter who had talked too much to hide her fear that maybe this time she had pushed her parents too far.

"I spent over forty years surrounded by young people," he said. "All those sighs and groans and eye rolls were spot-on."

Chancy had picked up those from bunkmates and fellow inmates. She hadn't known the gestures were hers to use until she needed them.

"Brava, young lady. You are an amazing mimic."

"So what I did was okay?"

"Better than okay. Warms my heart to think we might actually pull off our little charade." He looked pointedly at the wallpaper. "Blossom. Walla Walla. Where do you put wallpaper?" he asked rhetorically before answering his own question. "On the walla, of course. Chancy Deel, you have proved the old adage that still waters do indeed run deep."

"Is that good?" Everything in the world could be divided into two piles. Good. Bad. All Chancy had ever wanted was to escape the bad pile.

He laughed, and the fear that had flooded her newfound security slowly receded, taking the sludge of doubt with it. She hadn't done a bad thing. For once her words would not be turned against her or earn her a hard smack in the mouth. She wouldn't fall asleep tonight tasting blood, wishing she could take back the words and bury them in a box at the bottom of a hole. She could stay in the yellow room. Sleep in her own bed. Rest without worry. For now.

"Sumerian kings!" Uncle Max's chuckles turned into gales. The desire to laugh with him streaked through Chancy like hot lightning. She giggled, finding release in a moment of complete and pure happiness. He laughed harder, and once they started, they couldn't stop. Soon her eyes filled with tears of merriment. Tears she didn't have to hide.

"Oh, my, my, my. This old house has been silent too long." He pulled out a handkerchief, dabbed his eyes, and waved it like a flag of surrender. "Thank you for the most fun I've had in ages."

At that moment, Chancy felt he really could be her Uncle Max. She longed to hug him for real. To feel the press of his thin bones and smell the sharp scent of his shaving lotion. Because of him, she'd tasted a moment of joy. He had given her possibilities.

"Whew, I needed that. A belly laugh is better than a bitter pill any day." Uncle Max turned thoughtful. "They say laughter is the best medicine. If ever I had doubts, that little act you just put on has made a believer out of me."

A believer.

She was one too.

He crossed the room and opened the lid of an old-fashioned cabinet.

"What's that?" she asked over his shoulder.

"An outdated anachronism."

"A what?"

"A record player." He slid open the console door, selected one of the records inside and pulled a vinyl LP from the sleeve. "We called these platters. Back in caveman days this was how my generation listened to music."

"I like music," she said.

"Me too. Haven't wanted to listen to anything upbeat lately, but I have a sudden itch to hear Duke Ellington." Uncle Max dropped the needle on the record and a swingy instrumental spun out. His toe tapped the rhythm.

"What's it called?" The happy sound turned bad memories into smoke.

"'Don't Get Around Much Anymore.' That's been my theme song lately, but maybe we can change that."

She peeked into the cabinet. "You have a lot of records."

"I used to live in the music. Hanna loved to dance. She called me a dancing fool, but she was no slouch. Boy, could we jitterbug."

Chancy had seen a jitterbug routine in a movie once and tried to imagine creaky old Uncle Max tossing the girl in the portrait around a dance floor.

"Doubting Thomas," he said as though reading her mind. "I wasn't always old, you know. I took Hanna dancing on our first date. I always said she stepped into my arms and into my heart. She was a perfect dance partner, and I knew with absolute certainty that I would marry her because I couldn't imagine not being her partner forever. We danced our way through life." He had a faraway look in his eyes. As if he were dancing in his mind. Or holding Hanna.

"When swing gave way to jive and rock and roll, we learned all the new steps. Nothing was too complicated for us. Lindy hop, stroll, the twist. My technique was all right, but Hanna had *It*. Stage presence. Showmanship. She's the reason we won contests. Do you need to see the trophies?"

"Nope. I believe you."

The song ended, and Uncle Max changed the record. A trio of female vocalists harmonized upbeat lyrics about a boogie-woogie bugle boy.

"No one even saw me when we danced that one." He was far away again, staring out the window. "Every eye in the place was on her. Watching her made a man glad to be alive. Remind me to tell you more about that someday."

"Okay." Just like the music's tempo, Chancy's heart beat faster at the thought of having a someday with Uncle Max.

"I have a question for you," he said over the song's ending flourish.

Questions usually made her stomach ache, but this time the music had made her feel warm. "Okay."

"Who exactly is this Orlando Bloom fellow you told Ms. Wooten about?"

Chancy went to the bookcase, pulled down the volume she'd spotted earlier.

"Lord of the Rings." He stroked the faded cover. "I read this a long time ago, but I don't understand the wizard and elf connection."

"Orlando Bloom is the actor who played Legolas in the movie. He's in all the teen magazines." Shelter girls who'd given up on real love had plastered his smiling image on the walls over their beds.

"Which makes him, what? A sex symbol?"

"More of a heartthrob, according to the magazines."

"That's what I love about life," he said with a sagely wise nod. "If you pay attention and aren't too smart for your own good, life teaches you something new every day."

As the lively music slid into a song about sitting under the apple tree, Alfie rose from his resting place and stood patiently at the door. Uncle Max chuckled as he switched off the record player. "And then there's the same old, same old. Hang on, buddy, I know you need to go out for a walk."

"I'll do it." Chancy was eager to show her willingness to work hard, but so far he hadn't asked her to do anything. "You said dog walking was my job."

"That's right. I did. And there'll be plenty of days when I'll be glad to hand you the leash. But you know what? I feel so good today, I think I could boogie down the street. Beat me, Daddy, eight to the bar. C'mon. How about we take a turn around the block together?"

He plucked the leash from the hook in the kitchen. She closed the door, and the old man and old dog eased down the steps.

"When we get back," Uncle Max said as Alfie led the way, "we'll fix ourselves a bite of supper."

"Together?"

"How else?"

Together was a whole new concept to Chancy, but she liked the sound of it.

She broke free of the murky darkness, gasping for breath, her chest tight with ice. The monster stalked her across the nightmare landscape of her dreams. Reaching. Grasping. Feeding on hope. Moon-slicked light poured through parted curtains and spilled on the bed where she lay. She sat up and opened her eyes wide so brightness could flush black images from her mind.

The room swam into focus, but Chancy couldn't breathe. What was she doing in a strange bed in a room she didn't recognize? Sleep was a thief, and this time the dream had stolen too much. She kicked off the cold, thin sheets and scrambled to her feet. She needed to move. Get out. Run. She yanked open the door. With one hand clutching the knob, and the other fisted against her thawing, thumping heart, she fought to put herself in this place.

Framed pictures on the wall. Uncle Max. Hanna. A dusty trophy from a long-ago dance competition stood on the dresser. He'd pulled it from a box in the downstairs closet. Proof of the past. An unlikely connection. Blood pounded recall into her head. The dream was over. This was real. She was in Wenonah, safe in a house with magic numbers. She wasn't trespassing. The old man had invited her. *Make yourself at home.* She didn't have to disappear. She could stay. Faint light leaked out of the bathroom and threw her lonely shadow against the wall. The plastic lamb night-light was real. The monsters weren't. Chancy rubbed her arms beneath the flannel pajama sleeves, smoothing the badness. She'd been sucked under the dream again, but everything was all right now.

Move. Breathe. Shake off the cringing dread.

Down the hall, Uncle Max had left his bedroom door open. For the dog. As though answering a whistled thought, Alfie materialized in the doorway. He didn't threaten or wag his tail. More like a dog statue than a flesh-and-blood animal, he stood motionless between her and his master.

It's okay, boy. Don't worry. It's just me.

The heavy sound of the old man's sleep rumbled down the silent corridor, rhythmic and predictable, like someone rolling marbles across a wooden floor. One, two, roll, three, wait, wait, roll. A comforting white noise that insulated the house from the world. Peaceful. Not like the gulping, sobbing, squeaking, screaming, cursing night sounds that had surrounded her in the shelter.

Without stopping for shoes, Chancy tiptoed down the stairs and through the house. She turned the dead bolt on the back door and stepped onto the porch. Spotting rubber boots by the door, she tugged them on and lifted the screen door's hook. The door's hinges screeched like a night bird. It was hours before dawn, and the moon was still high. Chancy had no destination in mind. She just needed to move. To get out of the box and feel the cool air on her face. Most of all she needed to walk away from the dream and the scary feeling that someday she might not wake up and would be trapped in the dark forever.

She crossed the dew-damp grass to the garden she'd glimpsed earlier. The flower garden was set apart from the rest of the yard, enclosed by a chest-high wooden fence draped with vines. Last year's bare woody runners poked through new foliage like accusing fingers. Chancy walked around the fence until she found a gate with a metal latch. It opened easily. She pushed aside tendrils of paper-thin ivy and stepped inside.

The plot wasn't large, maybe forty by fifty feet, every inch bristling with unchecked growth. She didn't know much about plants, but assumed they were like people: Untended and unloved, even good ones turned into bullies. Blowsy shrubs. Trailing vines. Messy clumps of foliage. Overpowering the weak plants that withered and died from neglect. The night garden was dark and dense. Wooden birdhouses sat atop poles and empty feeders swayed in the breeze. A thick mossy scum coated the birdbath. Dangling wind chimes tinkled like mice dancing on piano keys. A gnome here. A plaster angel with a broken wing there. At the far end of the garden, under the tunneled shadows of three sheltering trees, a concrete bench glowed white as a bone, beckoning.

The night was quiet; even the insects were sleeping. She could think here, hidden from view by the vine-trussed fence. Outside the fence, the world grasped and asked for too much, but inside she was alone. And alone had always been the safest way to be. Chancy's rubber soles crunched on the winding gravel path. The bench was tomb-cold when she sat down, but the chill wasn't why she shivered in Hanna Boyle's flannel pajamas. The dream and dread fell away, and an unexpected realization slammed into her mind.

The forgotten garden was a sign as clear-cut as signs could ever be.

Unlike most children, Chancy had never looked forward to Christmas. She learned early not to attach sentiment to a holiday that made her mother come apart at the seams. Her only good Christmas memory was the year she was twelve. B.J. was hospitalized, and Chancy was in a juvenile shelter where a church group had delivered brightly wrapped packages. She hung back while other kids lined up for gifts, and by the time someone urged her to the front of the room, only one present was left.

We saved the best for last, the lady said. *For you.*

Chancy found a book inside the box. She read the slim volume many times over the years, and managed to hang on to it despite being shuffled from place to place. She didn't own much, but *The Secret Garden* was a treasured possession because it reminded her that endings could be happy. The story was set in a different place and a different time, but Chancy had understood the sour-faced orphan girl. Like Mary Lennox, she had never felt that she belonged to anyone. She was a poor kid from Pittsburgh but had learned many lessons from the little English aristocrat. She learned that girls alone had to be strong and keep their feelings inside. That it was all right to stare at her hands in her lap and to sit quietly doing nothing. She had learned that things were never what they seemed and that everyone had secrets to keep.

In the story, Mary had believed in the kind of magic that made invalid boys strong and turned sad people into a family. Chancy wanted to believe in that magic too but never expected real life to be like a book. Coming here was no accident. 639 Poplar Avenue was not Misselthwaite Manor, but the old man was sad because his wife died, just like Archibald Craven. This little garden was as forgotten and as full of promise as the one the children had brought back to life. Maybe she could be like Mary Lennox and make other people happy. Maybe.

Like the careful gardener who'd erected the garden fence to protect tender plants from predators, Chancy had walled off the last tender thing within her. She'd first built the wall to keep B.J. out. Mary Lennox's pretty mother had left her alone with servants, but Betty Jo Deel, an addict who couldn't see past her own need, had simply left Chancy alone. She didn't consider motherhood a responsibility. Just bad luck. She said being a mother was like drawing the joker in the game of life. A kid needed too much attention. Wasted too much of her time. According to B.J., children were an anchor that dragged women down until they drowned in a never-ending tide of shit and spit and puke and tears.

Chancy had tried not to be an anchor. Even when she was too young to understand her mother's words, she had thought being invisible would make her mother happy. If she was quiet and stayed in her own space, maybe bad attention wouldn't fall on her like acid rain. She'd first started disappearing when she was four. For a time, she and B.J. had lived in a rent-by-the-week motel room with a broken window and one bed. Chancy didn't want to sleep between her mother and whatever man she brought home, under blankets that smelled like cigarettes and sweat and something worse. She had made a place for herself on the floor of the narrow closet.

That was fine with B.J. Children should not be seen *or* heard anyway. Especially retard children who couldn't talk like they were supposed to. B.J. went out most nights and left Chancy alone. The tight space of the closet felt safer than the room with the broken window. One night she awakened to the familiar grunting and gasping noises that often filled the room. She didn't want to see what the man was doing to her mother, but she needed to use the bathroom. When she eased open the closet door, it squeaked, and the tattooed stranger sat up in bed. "What the hell? You got a kid?"

"If you want to call her that." B.J. had reached for a cigarette, but the naked, smelly man had loomed over Chancy.

"I don't need no audience," he said. "Get the fuck back in the closet."

Chancy couldn't tell him she had to use the bathroom, not because she didn't know the words, but because she was afraid. Sometimes she practiced talking when she was alone. Her teddy bear talked to her and she talked back. But she didn't dare speak to B.J. and had returned to her nest of dirty clothes on the closet floor. The man had propped a chair under the knob, turning her safe place into a prison.

Chancy didn't cry. She had to focus all her energy on not wetting herself. If she did, she'd get a bad slap and maybe worse. B.J. would make her wear the soiled panties for a hat. She didn't know what a bladder was, but she felt it aching deep inside. She imagined it as small as her thumb. Then as small as a fingernail. Then as small as the white half-moon on her pinkie finger. Smaller and smaller until it disappeared and stopped hurting. The man thought he had locked her in, but instead Chancy had locked him out.

A night bird called from a limb overhead. Chancy breathed deeply of the rich, grassy, living smell of the garden. She'd never had a real home. Had never felt loved. B.J. wasn't a good mother, and Chancy had never known her father. He was just some guy B.J. had met on a binge and had forgotten before she missed her period. Before she was even in kindergarten, Chancy had known she was a careless accident who never would have happened if the rubber hadn't broken.

A melody from Uncle Max's old-fashioned music drifted through her mind, filling her heart with hope. If she could stay here, for a little while, maybe she would learn how to live. Maybe she could help him regain his strength, just as Mary Lennox had made Colin strong. Mary had given the people around her a reason to change. More than anything, ever, Chancy wanted to be someone's reason.

A few years ago, she had overheard a counselor and teacher discussing her. The teacher was convinced Chancy had a learning problem, but the counselor had said, *Her brain is alive and well and working away in the dark. It's her heart that's dead.* He was wrong too. Chancy's heart wasn't dead. If it were, thinking about what she might yet become wouldn't hurt so much.

After that eavesdropped conversation, she'd started making hearts and giving them away. To let people know she wasn't dead inside—just afraid. The signs seemed to be telling her she could trust Maxwell Boyle, but could she give away her real heart?

Chapter 11

The next few mornings, Max rose early, his wakefulness due more to anxiety than habit. He didn't think Chancy would make off with the silver but was genuinely relieved when she turned up for breakfast, because he had half expected her to disappear while he was sleeping. Alfie had awakened him when she'd slipped out the house the first night. The dog had stood silently by the bedroom door as though admonishing Max to follow their unlikely guest. When he didn't, Alfie had finally settled down beside the bed with a sigh.

Too old to stumble into the darkness and knowing nothing of how to comfort a troubled girl, Max had pulled the blanket up to his chin. He'd stared at the ceiling, waiting. And feeling more alone than ever. Foolish too, to think he had anything left to offer a child. Why would a girl like Chancy want to stay in his musty old house when the wide world beckoned? His mind had taunted him through a painful whatever-were-you-thinking routine, until he'd finally heard her light steps in the hall. The closing of her door. Alfie had sighed again, and Max had closed his eyes, squeezing back tears.

Chancy didn't talk much, but he sensed some relief on her end too, as though she had been waiting for him to renege on their deal. They were uneasy with each other those first days, but soon learned how to share space and be in the house together. He had to bite down on questions that bubbled to the surface of their conversations. He wanted to know more about the past that had forced her out on her own, but it was too early for confidences. For now he was satisfied that she hadn't made any more midnight pilgrimages.

Chancy was sweeping up scattered dog kibble around Alfie's dish when someone knocked on the front door. Startled, she dropped the broom and the handle hit the linoleum like a gong. "Who's that?"

"Better not be Wooten," he grumbled. "It's only been three days since her last spy mission."

"Should I answer it?"

"Let me." He folded the newspaper. "Maybe you should stay out of sight for now." She nodded without a word. "Just until we see who it is." She went back to her sweeping. Max ignored the prickly guilt that accused him of doing something wrong. He was selfish enough not to want to hand Chancy over to inquiring authorities and was relieved to find Jenny Hamilton on the porch.

"Good morning, Max. I thought I'd stop by to see if you're ready to let me do a good deed yet."

"You feeling the urge, are you?" She got points for her straightforward manner. He liked a woman who didn't beat around the bush.

She held out a plastic-wrapped loaf. "I don't have an oven, so I unpacked my old bread machine. Thought you might like some raisin bread."

"How thoughtful. Thanks. This will taste good with my morning coffee."

She looked uncomfortable, and Max wondered if she expected to be invited in. When he didn't, she said, "I'm taking Tom to a doctor's appointment today. Do you need anything while I'm out?"

"Nope. But I appreciate you thinking of me." Jenny was trying. He hated brushing off her offers but couldn't let her get too close until he and Chancy had finessed their story. Or maybe he dreaded the inevitable lies. She deserved better from him. "How's your husband feeling?"

"He finally agreed to see someone. He's willing to admit he can't get over his depression on his own, so that's progress. Maybe if he gets on medication, he'll be better soon."

"I hope so. How's Adam?"

"Looking forward to the end of school."

"I'd be worried if he weren't."

"I should be going. You have my phone number. Call if I can help."

"I try not to take advantage."

"Nonsense." She grinned. "I'd invite you to dinner, but we're eating a lot of takeout these days. Tell you what. Once the kitchen is finished, if it ever is, I'll cook something special to christen it. You'll come, won't you?"

"Wouldn't miss it. Hang in there. Russ Matiska will have that kitchen whipped into shape in no time."

Her smile faded. "If we don't run out of money first." She waved and backed down the steps. "Next time I'll stay longer."

"You do that." *Great.* Lying to Shevaun Wooten was simple self-defense, but lying to Jenny was shameful. Max closed the door and leaned against it.

"So?" Chancy stepped from the kitchen, twisting a dishrag in her hands. "Are we in trouble?"

"No. That was my neighbor. Nice lady." He told her how Jenny had helped him the day he went to the hospital and how once school was out, Chancy would probably see her son, Adam, around.

"I don't like boys much."

"You'll like the Hamiltons."

"They sound nice."

"They have their share of problems right now, but who doesn't?"

Chancy was obviously no stranger to problems and nodded gravely, then turned back to the kitchen. Her squeaky rubber soles gave Max an idea.

"We need to go shopping. We can take a cab to town."

"What about your car?"

"No license." He didn't want to think about the Lincoln. His almost-weapon of minor destruction. Couldn't think about how close he'd come. "Come on. Girls like to shop, right?"

"I don't need anything."

He looked pointedly at her feet. "Oh, I think you do. Those things are falling apart." The old canvas sneakers with the star on the sides were the kind boys had worn on the basketball court in his day. They had probably been black at one time, but the color was hard to detect now, except on the rubber part, formerly white but now dark with grime. The little toe of her right foot peeked through a frayed hole, and the strings were broken and knotted in several places. Nothing looked more forlorn than a raggedy child, even a clean one.

"I can't afford new shoes."

"My treat." Max had plenty of money he could not take with him.

She shook her head, offering a glimpse of the quiet stubbornness she'd revealed more than once since moving into the room upstairs. "I want to pay for my own stuff."

"Okay, then. Consider new shoes a requirement. I plan to keep you busy, and you'll need firm footing to go about your duties safely. As your employer, I should supply all work-related necessities."

She gave him a skeptical look. "Is that normal?"

"Normal, schmormal." He dismissed her doubt. "We're a brand-new operation. Normal for us is whatever we want to do." Max grinned. "I like making up rules as we go, don't you?"

She nodded again, loath to waste a word when a movement would suffice.

"I say we hit the mall first, then the grocery store." He poked around the kitchen, checking the pantry. Just like Old Mother Hubbard's cupboards, his were mostly bare. The past few weeks he hadn't had much interest in cooking, even less in eating. Loss of appetite was an inevitable part of the aging process, but that ER doctor had ragged on him about a twelve-pound weight loss like he was wasting away to nothing. Now that he had a companion at the table who seemed to enjoy his stories, Max actually looked forward to mealtime. With his appetite off the missing list, he was wolfing food like a farmhand.

He set a pad and pen on the table. "We'll go to the market on the way home, but we should make a list. I suffer from a chronic case of CRS, you know."

She looked up, unduly alarmed. "What's that?"

"Can't remember squat." He laughed, but confusion still pinched her features. Communicating with his new boarder was an ongoing challenge, especially when he forgot how serious and literal she was. He'd expected more savvy and attitude from an edge-living kid, but Chancy was surprisingly unworldly. She was clearly a troubled teen with a questionable, undisclosed past, but what bothered him most was the fact that she didn't seem to know how to have fun. She floated around without making a lick of noise and was polite to the point of demureness. Had she just arrived in a time machine from a gentler past? Maybe in her world remoteness offered protection. She had finally shown signs of warming up to his jokes, but sarcasm and irony and exaggeration were still lost on her.

"You're out of orange juice," she said.

"Put that down. And cookies. There's an old cookie jar around here somewhere." After the funeral, he'd stashed the vintage jar on an out-of-the-way shelf because his heart broke every time he looked at the silly thing.

"Here it is!" He hesitated. What if his grip failed again? He didn't want to break Hanna's prized jar, but he was tired of feeling like a weakling. He grasped the colorful stoneware carefully and set it on the table.

"Little Red Riding Hood!"

"Hanna kept Red full of homemade cookies. For years, she baked twice a week, just like clockwork." He shared crowded memories with Chancy. The spicy warmth that had lured him to the kitchen when Hanna slid a batch of cinnamon-sprinkled snickerdoodles from the oven. The way she'd limited treats to one a day for fear of losing her figure. How she'd served him cookies and cold milk every night during the news. Funny how remembering didn't feel sad when it made someone smile.

Chancy tapped the pencil on the paper. "What's your favorite cookie?"

He didn't have to think. "Peanut butter."

"Really? Mine too!"

She seemed pleased that they had something in common. She started to write *cookies* on the grocery list, then stopped. "Why don't we make some from scratch?"

"I guess we could. Homemade tastes better than store-bought any day." Max opened a dog-eared cookbook and flipped through the pages until he found Hanna's recipe. "Here you go. Write down what we need."

Chancy's left arm curved over the paper in concentration as she copied the ingredients. A tremor of wonder passed through Max that left him shaken and surprised. Was it possible that only a few days ago, he'd been ready to throw in the towel for good, and now because a little girl had startled him with unexpected sweetness, he was once again excited about cookies?

Chancy looked up when she finished writing. "Can we bake today?"

"Why not? We have all the time in the world." And that was exactly how Max felt. Like he suddenly had all the time in the world.

Chancy couldn't remember the last time she'd had new shoes. She laced up the fancy trainers the salesman claimed all the kids were wearing. The leather was so white. So perfect. It smelled good. Uncle Max said new shoes were a work requirement, but they felt like a luxury. She'd suggested a cheaper alternative, but he'd insisted. *You get what you pay for.*

"You should get a pair, too," she said.

He looked at his shiny wingtips. "Why? I'm not slated to run any races."

"Those soles are slippery."

"She's right," the salesman said. "Athletic shoes aren't just for athletes these days. I sell a lot of them to seniors who need arch support and traction."

"Nah, these are fine." Max tapped one shoe, then the other on the floor, like an impromptu little dance. "Had 'em for years. Nothing more miserable than breaking in a new pair."

"I changed my mind." Instead of tying her new shoes, Chancy slipped them off and placed them back in the box. She borrowed Uncle Max's pointed look. "Nothing more miserable than breaking in a new pair."

Max sank onto the chair next to her and propped one leg across his knee. He examined the bottom of his leather shoe. "All right. Put 'em back on. You made your point. Maybe if I had some rubber under me,

I'd be steadier on my feet. Besides, these blasted things always pinch my toes."

Smelling another sale, the salesman urged Max to remove his shoes. He took the measurements and scurried off to find the right size.

"Satisfied?" he asked.

Chancy nodded.

He shot her a squinty look and muttered an exaggerated accusation. "Extortionist!"

She wasn't sure what the word meant, but this time she knew he was not really mad at her. Uncle Max liked to hide behind crabbiness the way she hid behind silence. "Your toes will thank me."

"We'll see. Except for *ouch*, my toes haven't had much to say for the last thirty years."

When the salesman returned, he hardly had to work at all to make the second sale.

Later at the grocery store, Chancy waited with the shopping cart while Uncle Max searched for the restroom. One thing she'd already learned about old people: When they had to go, they *really* had to go. He seemed to spend a lot of time in the bathroom at home. She watched him walk away down the soup aisle and smiled. He was definitely steadier on his feet in the black, thick-soled shoes. She'd had a good idea, and he had benefited from it. Because his fingers were gnarled and his joints stiff, she had suggested he get shoes that closed with sticky strips instead of laces. He admitted that not having to tie would save him several minutes a day. At his age, a man had to make every minute count.

Chancy watched other shoppers while waiting for Max to return. Making endless selections from the shelves seemed to be no big deal for most people. Boring even. She had no idea what it felt like to choose whatever she wanted, as much as she wanted, and pay for it at the register. Even when B.J. had food stamps, Chancy was never allowed to choose. A woman with a piled-high cart walked by. How many paper hearts would it take to trade for that much food?

In the next aisle, two women greeted each other with small talk.

Chancy perked up when she recognized a familiar voice. She eased to the end of the aisle near rows of canned beef stew.

"Hey, I hear Eddie's back in town," someone said.

"Been home since Mother's Day." Chancy's pulse pounded. She would know that drawl anywhere. Corliss. "He dropped out of thin air. Surprised the stuffin' outta me."

Holding her breath, Chancy eased the cart around an end display of saltines until she could see the women chatting in the middle of the aisle. Eavesdropping was wrong, but seeing Corliss again felt right. Chancy plucked a box of crackers off the shelf and pretended to read the label.

"It's been, what?" the other woman asked. "Six months since you heard from him?"

"Thanksgiving." Corliss's back was to Chancy, so she didn't have to worry about being seen. Corliss must have just gotten off work. She was wearing a yellow Tip-Top T-shirt. "I thought he might make it home for Christmas, but I ended up putting his presents in the closet."

"I drove by your trailer yesterday, but I didn't see Eddie's truck." The second woman wore a sweatshirt with a basket of puppies on the front. She was about Corliss's age, and her gray hair was poofed into a bubble on her head. Maybe she was hard of hearing. She talked a little too loudly.

"He doesn't have a truck anymore. He hitched home."

Corliss knew somebody who hitched? That had to be a sign. A voice on a loudspeaker announced a special on fabric softener, and Chancy strained to hear the rest of the conversation.

"So how's he doing?"

"Oh, you know. Pretty good. Considering."

"He still have that ... problem?" The puppy lady seemed reluctant to name whatever Eddie's problem was. She must have been a friend and not just a curious acquaintance, because Corliss opened up.

"You mean his drug problem?" Corliss's shoulders slumped. "Once an addict, always an addict. That's what they told us in family counseling when he went through rehab. Twice."

"You spent your life savings getting that boy help, Corl, and he slipped down both times."

"He claims he's quit for good and needs to stay with me for a little while until he gets back on his feet."

"Honey, you've heard all that before."

Corliss leaned on the cart's handle. "Don't remind me."

"You be careful and lock up your valuables. Don't forget what happened last time."

A mother pushed a cart with a wobbly wheel and crying toddler in the seat past Chancy, and the noise nearly drowned Corliss's reply.

"I got my Zenith back. Amos Simpkins at E-Z Loan called me at work. Said he gave Eddie sixty-five dollars. Claimed he was saving my television from a worser fate out of the goodness of his heart."

The puppy lady snorted. "I'm guessing his heart wasn't big enough to get that old tightwad to waive the interest charge."

"You got that right!" The women laughed together, even though the subject was serious. Chancy wondered if Uncle Max ever worried about her pawning his television. "Took me three months to bail that set out of hock. I missed half a season of *Law and Order*."

"So how long does Eddie plan to stick around this time?"

"I don't know, Ada Fay. I stopped looking gift horses in the mouth a long time ago. Now I just live day to day and hope for the best."

"Honey, are you sure you can go through this again?"

"I'm his mother. What else can I do?"

"Bless your heart. Nothing weighs heavier on a mama's soul than seeing her child hurting." The woman gave Corliss a hug, and Chancy longed to hug her faraway friend too. Corliss was a good mom, but it didn't sound like Eddie was the kind of son who brought her Hallmark cards.

"You remember that family support group I went to for a while?" Corliss asked. "The leader lady said addicts always tell you what you want to hear. She warned us against believing the lies. But I have to. I got nobody but Eddie. I was thirty-seven and had given up on babies when I had him. That boy's always meant the world to me."

"I just hate seeing him drag you down again, Corl."

"He claims he's off drugs for good. I think he means it. I never saw him look so beat down and scared as he did when he showed up at my door."

"What happened to him?"

"He won't say, but it must have been bad. Last time he came home, the group leader said I was enabling him. She told me to see the addict, not the child he used to be. She flat-out warned me against letting mother love blind me to the truth."

Chancy knew the damage drugs could do. She'd sat silently in group therapy as other children poured out their hearts. She also knew some drugs were good. B.J. was easier to live with when she took her medication.

"That sounds like good advice," Ada Fay said.

"You think it's hard to be a mother?" Corliss patted her friend's shoulder. "Try *not* to be one when your baby's crying on your couch and begging for another chance. Then you'll know what hard is."

"Eddie's twenty-five years old, Corl."

"He'll always be *my* baby. It's been three weeks since he used anything. I believe he can get clean."

"I hope it's not too late. Wonder what happened to make him change?"

"He won't tell me. All he says is one day he stopped wanting to live." Corliss unzipped her purse and pulled out a tissue and blew her nose. "I was so glad to see him. All these months I've been scared to death the next knock on my door would be the sheriff saying they'd found Eddie's body."

"He must have hit rock bottom." Ada Fay hugged Corliss again. "That's what it takes to make a drunk or an addict change his ways."

"I don't want to lose him."

"Course you don't. Thank God there's no rock bottom in a mother's heart."

Chancy jumped when Max spoke behind her. "Sorry I took so long. Had an unexpected development." He pushed the cart and talked about how regularity was a gift that young people would never appreciate. Chancy took one last, lingering look in Corliss's direction.

"What's next on our list?" he asked.

She helped him find the items they needed but couldn't stop thinking about the encounter. If Corliss's conversation hadn't been so personal, Chancy could have pretended to bump into her by accident. If Max hadn't returned when he did, the other woman might have gone on her way, and Chancy could have approached Corliss. Maybe they could have stood and chatted, just like old friends.

That idea chilled her. No. She could do those things only in her mind. Corliss knew she wasn't the girl she and Max had made up. She'd seen Chancy's drowned-rat reality. Talking to Corliss might get Uncle Max in trouble with Ms. Wooten. She didn't want to spoil things, but longed to be her real self with someone. Corliss, who could see past the bad things and still love her son, could be more than a faraway friend.

Chapter 12

"I can't get out of this appointment." Max had put Pete Marshall off twice since Chancy's arrival. If he didn't show up at the attorney's office and prove he was alive and kicking, his friend would take it upon himself to drop by. "I really don't want to do our Laurel-and-Hardy routine for Pete. He'd see through us in a flash-pan second."

"All right." Chancy removed a load of laundry from the washer. He'd offered to buy her new clothes at the mall, but she refused. She had only three or four threadbare outfits, jeans and long-sleeved shirts, mostly gray. Even her formerly white socks were gray. Ghost color.

"Do you know who Laurel and Hardy are?"

"No. Are they from the movies?"

He smiled. "Child, you haven't seen a comedy until you've seen one of theirs. I have some videotapes around somewhere. We'll watch them later. Together."

"I'd like that."

"I hate leaving you alone this morning." She'd agreed to keep a low profile to avoid arousing suspicion, but there was more to her reticence. Chancy was self-contained, her emotions truly closed off. It might be good for her to meet some more people.

"I don't mind. Really." She stuffed her wet clothes in the dryer and pushed the button. "I'm used to being by myself. I'll stay busy. Alfie will keep me company."

"I think he'd rather stay with you anyway." The old dog had not only accepted Chancy, he followed her around like a duckling imprinted on a scientist's boots. She had bonded easily with Alfie too, even though she admitted she'd never owned a dog. She carried treats in her pocket, and Max had caught her slipping them to Alfie when he'd done nothing to earn one, as though rewarding him just for being there.

In contrast to the eerie stillness that fell on her at times, Chancy seemed to need to move. She walked Alfie twice a day, and the old dog displayed surprising energy in her company. Sometimes Max tagged along on neighborhood circuits, but he didn't always feel up to the long rambles Chancy preferred. He knew she needed time away from the house. She said walking helped her think, so he stayed behind and watched until she and Alfie were out of sight. They shared close quarters, but she might as well be on the moon for all she revealed. He knew thoughts filled her mind; memories haunted her. She listened to his stories for hours on end, a rapt look on her face, but if he tried to ease into personal territory, she slammed shut like a cellar door.

Little Chancy Deel was a mystery and a worry. At first, Max had stewed the whole time she was gone. He didn't kid himself. Any day she could take Alfie out and keep on walking. Disappear for good, or slip away in the night. She was a child and she belonged somewhere. To someone. He had to remind himself that she was a runaway, not an angel sent to deliver him from sadness. She'd run before and could do so again. Or be taken away. Losing Alfie would hurt, but the thought of Chancy gone from his life caused Max pain he never could have foreseen. He didn't want to give her that much power, but even when he tried to guard his heart, he couldn't.

A knock at the door made him reach for his jacket. "There's Jenny." He'd broken down and asked her for a ride to Pete's office. She popped over daily and seemed to need to do something for him. Despite her own problems, she made time for him, and he owed her.

Max turned to Chancy. "You want to meet her?"

Chancy leaned against the counter, hugging her middle and clutching the ends of her sleeves in clenched fists. "I'm not ready."

"She won't bite. You might like her."

"I like things the way the are. For now."

"Don't forget: No man is an island."

"What?"

"Never mind. Take it easy while I'm gone. I'll be home in time to fix lunch."

"About that. When do I get to start making lunch?"

"Soon. I don't want you to feel overwhelmed."

"I've never been bewildered by grilled cheese."

Max paused at the door. "My goodness! Was that a joke?"

She just smiled.

Chancy peeked through the living room drapes. She wasn't ready to actually meet the neighbor, but curiosity made her want to see her.

A breeze whipped Jenny Hamilton's dark hair, and she reached up and tucked a strand behind her ear. She opened the car door and glanced back at the house as though looking for something. Chancy yanked the curtains shut. *Her!* Max's neighbor was the good mom with the silver heart necklace. Chancy had seen Jenny her first day in Wenonah. Then again the next day at the convenience store when she'd said, "Sorry, dear." That meant her tall, curly-haired son was Adam, the boy Max had mentioned. Had she earned enough points to keep the Hamiltons close? Was this twist another sign?

Chancy collapsed on the lumpy sofa. Alfie rested his head in her lap. She stroked his warm fur and tried to interpret the startling new message. Gradually her heart stopped racing, and a peaceful knowing settled over her. She understood what the universe wanted to tell her.

She was finally doing something right.

Chancy was still thinking about Jenny when she went into the kitchen. She lifted the top off Little Red Riding Hood and helped herself to a cookie. Uncle Max had supervised as she measured and stirred. He'd helped roll the chilled dough into balls, which they'd flattened with forks dipped in sugar. She had fought a panic attack when the first batch came out with black bottoms, but Uncle Max just laughed and said something about the blind leading the blind. He tipped the baking sheet over the trash can, and she held her breath as the burned cookies slid off. She tried to apologize, but he wouldn't let her. He adjusted the oven temperature, and she'd made the crisscrossed fork patterns perfect so the rest of the cookies would turn out right.

She'd asked for more work, but Uncle Max didn't seem to think she was capable of anything complicated. He cooked their simple meals. She washed the dishes. He swept. She held the dustpan. At the grocery store, he pushed the cart and she reached for items on low shelves. The peanuty taste of cookie success made her want to try her hand in the kitchen.

"Hey, you! Want to go outside?" she suddenly asked Alfie.

He sprang to life and beat her to the back door. She pulled off her new shoes and slipped on Uncle Max's galoshes, just as she had most afternoons while he was napping in his recliner. Yesterday, worn out by the shopping trip and cookie baking, he'd slept longer and harder than usual. It was five o'clock on the cat clock when she came in, but he hadn't stirred. She panicked, thinking something bad had happened to him. He was so old. She didn't know what to do if he got sick. Or died. While debating about 911, she noticed the steady rise and fall of his chest. When the blood stopped pounding in her ears, she could hear him snore.

She loved that comforting sound.

The first night she'd awakened in the dark, shaking from the dream, alone. Now after Uncle Max fell asleep down the hall, she opened her door and let in the wheezy noise that reassured her with each breath.

I'm here; I'm here.

I'm here.

Last night Alfie had padded into her room. With a small, snuffling sound, he curled up on the braided rug to let her know he was there too and she was not alone anymore.

The morning sun was bright, and a sweet scent drifted out of the garden. Chancy unlatched the gate and slipped inside. She hadn't told Uncle Max, but she spent at least an hour every day exploring Hanna's special place. She was safe there, hidden behind the fence like the children in her book. Just as Mary had felt more and more awake with each day spent at Misselthwaite, Chancy felt more alive since coming to 639 Poplar Avenue.

Yesterday she'd sat on the stone bench, scouring the book for clues that would help her tend the plants. But *The Secret Garden* wasn't written for would-be gardeners, and contained no practical advice. An Oklahoma backyard was very different from a nineteenth-century English garden, so she was on her own. Hanna had known, but she couldn't tell Chancy what needed to be done.

She pulled dried weeds to expose tiny nosegays of wild violets. Amidst a tangled plant that smelled like pizza, she found a small white plaster angel reclining with wings folded. She wiped the dirt from the angel's face. Growing in the same area were clumps of herbs with the scent of onions and lemons and sage. She nearly tripped over a cluster of starlike succulents spilling out of a broken, half-buried clay pot. Tiny new sprouts circled the bigger plant like a mother surrounded by children. Just as Mary Lennox had discovered small miracles hidden among the weeds and snarly vines, so did Chancy. She was living the book's dream.

There were no tame foxes or fey robins in Hanna's garden, but Chancy was not alone. A fat brown toad inhabited a small mushroom-shaped hut decorated with flowers. She imagined Hanna had painted *Mr. Toad's House* over the door. At night when the toad tenant came out to croak at the stars, she lay awake, listening to his throaty solo. She'd scrubbed out the bird-bath and refilled it with fresh water. Now dragonflies hovered over the surface, their wings glittering like jewels. A pair of sparrows were busy building a nest in one of the birdhouses. They flew out, searching for tid-bits of straw or dog hair or yarn, and took turns adding to their home. In another house, cheeping baby jays waited for parents to flutter in with a juicy insect for lunch.

Alfie put his nose to the ground and followed it to an exposed tree root at the back of the garden. Summoned by his loud *woof!* Chancy pushed aside a stand of weeds and found a fur-lined nest filled with tiny blind mice. They were the size and color of pencil erasers, curled together in a squeaky ball. Alfie backed off, unwilling to disturb the burrow, but what about marauding cats? Chancy covered the entrance with mounds of dead grass, certain the harried mama would appreciate her efforts when she returned.

Animals' instincts made them care gently for their young. They didn't have to study how to be good mothers. B.J. had never learned the lessons taught in court-mandated parenting classes, but the mouse mommy did her job just fine. Her tiny brain worked properly, bathed in maternal hormones. She gave birth and nursed her babies, washed them, kept them warm, and protected them until they were big enough to take care of themselves. The process seemed so simple. Natural. Why was motherhood difficult for some humans?

Chancy lost track of time in the warm bee-droning sunshine. She had knelt to pull weeds from the gravel path when Uncle Max startled her to awareness.

"What are you doing out here?" he asked. Not too sharp, but sharp enough.

"Nothing. Just . . . taking care of things." At least, that was what she thought she was doing. Uncle Max's frown deepened, so maybe she was trespassing in some way.

"Well, don't waste your time."

"Why not?"

"This plot's a wreck and a ruin. If you like pulling weeds, stick to the borders in the front yard."

"But it's nice out here. I think we should fix up this garden." Her words tasted like defiance. If Max, like the master of Misselthwaite, had a reason to abandon the garden, she would try to change his mind.

"Too much work. Trumpet vine has gone ballistic. You have to dig those shoot-'em-up runners out with a shovel. Backbreaking work. Trumpet's a fast-growing tyrant, set to take over the world. I told Hanna not to plant any."

"So why did she?"

"Hummingbirds love the nectar in the orange flowers."

"I don't see any flowers."

"They'll come later. In the summer." He opened the gate and stepped inside. "See that gray-green plant over there? That's wild rue. Hanna planted it for the monarch caterpillars. They'll eat it right down to the ground, but it always comes back."

"Is rue a tyrant?"

"Nope. A survivor."

Chancy asked about other plants, and Max's frown smoothed. He identified lemon verbena and catnip. He swept aside dead grass to reveal a clutch of monarda, which he said the settlers had called Oswego tea because they used it to replace real tea on the frontier. He explained that horehound could be made into a sore throat remedy, and that purple coneflowers, or echinacea, were used in cold medicine.

"We should definitely clean up out here," she said. "I'd like to learn more about the plants. Do you have any books?"

"Do witches have warts?" Uncle Max waited for her to follow him out of the garden and closed the gate.

"Is that sarcasm?" He'd explained that people used nonliteral language when they wanted to say something different from what they meant, but she didn't always understand.

"No. Sarcasm is irony meant to wound. That was a joke."

"Because witches have a lot of warts, and you have a lot of books, right?"

"Now you're cookin'," he said, even though she really wasn't. Maybe this was his nonliteral way of giving her permission to cook.

"I was thinking if I learned what all the plants are and how to take care of them, maybe I could make the garden happy again."

"Happy?"

"It's sad. We can bring it back to life."

Max shook his head. "Nope. We have enough work to do in the house without tackling this mess. This was Hanna's baby. We need to let it go."

"We can give it back to her."

He looked at her sharply. "Hanna's gone."

Then *he* was sad, and Chancy didn't have the words to explain how restoring the garden would give Hanna's memory a place to live.

His Adam's apple bobbed. "I think it's time I get someone in to knock down this fence and mow the whole thing over."

"You can't do that! What about the mice and toads and birds? They can't lose their homes." All Chancy knew of Hanna had come from Max's stories, but she was certain losing the garden would break Hanna's heart. Destroying it would break Max's, even if he didn't realize that yet. He kept Hanna's clothes in the closet. Her perfume and lotion in the bathroom. Her car in the garage. He should keep her garden for the same reason.

"Have you ever read *The Secret Garden*?" she asked. "It's a children's book. An old one."

"I'm old, but I don't recall the story. I was always on the move when I was a boy. Didn't have much time to read."

"Would you like to read it now?"

"You have it?"

She told him how she'd received it a long time ago for Christmas and had kept it through the years.

"I would be honored to read your book," he said. "But what's that got to do with this overgrown jungle?"

"You'll see when you read it." Chancy knew that if she made the garden beautiful again, Hanna's spirit could take wing. She could move on, knowing her work was done, leaving her memory behind in the garden. If Uncle Max could be content with memories, he wouldn't be sad. "I'll do all the work if you'll tell me which plants are weeds and which ones are flowers."

"That's a fine distinction." He must be thinking about Hanna, because his eyes filled with the moist, remembering look.

"Hanna always said a weed is just a flower growing in the wrong place." He looked at her for a long moment and smiled. "I think she was right about that."

Later, when Uncle Max settled in his recliner for a nap before supper, Chancy clipped Alfie's leash to his collar. Her favorite job wasn't really work. She loved dog walking. Choosing a different route each day allowed her to learn the lay of the land, and she now claimed bits of Wenonah as her own. She let herself in and out of the house, using the key attached to a First National Bank of Wenonah key chain that Uncle Max had given her. She reached in her pocket and touched it.

Real. The powerful token belonged to her. Owning a key that opened a door where nothing bad ever happened was the best kind of magic. Better than the book magic that had transformed Colin Craven from a sad, sickly boy to a happy, healthy one. She clutched the leash and Alfie led the way. When she was living on the street, late afternoon meant looking for a bolt-hole in which to spend the night. No more. She knew exactly where she would sleep: in a soft bed inside a buttercup-colored room beneath a painted field of daisies.

Alfie stopped to sniff a bush, and Chancy waited for him to read his pee-mail, as Max called the messages dogs left one another. She had time. She could spend an hour in the rocker on the porch, watching grass grow and listening to bees buzz in the lilac bush. Wenonah's gentle rhythm had calmed her desperate inner tides, just as Uncle Max's quiet routine had reshaped her days. She no longer had to sleep with one eye open or worry about danger around every corner. Unlike B.J., she could depend on Uncle Max. She never knew the world could feel so safe.

Alfie replied to the message and moved on, his tail swaying like a flag. When he stopped to drop plops, she recovered them in a plastic bag to dispose of later. Responsibility made her feel strong. After they made their rounds, it would be time to go home. *Home.* She was careful not to say the word out loud and tempt the universe to take away the gift, but she now knew what it meant.

Everything had been going so well that she decided to surprise Uncle Max by preparing their evening meal. She had searched Hanna's cookbook until she found a creased page splashed and stained from use. Apple-baked pork chops had to be one of Uncle Max's favorite dishes. It didn't seem complicated. All she had to do was follow the directions.

"Hey! Watch out!" A skinny boy on a skateboard whizzed by. Alfie tugged at the leash and barked. The boy braked abruptly a few feet ahead and flipped the board with his foot, catching it deftly in one hand. He knelt and playfully ruffled the dog's silky ears. "I know Alfie. Who are you?"

"Chancy Deel." She didn't have to ask his name.

"I'm Adam. I live down there." He pointed to the two-story house across the street. "Where do you live?"

"Right there."

"Since when? Mom said the old guy lives by himself."

"Not anymore."

"You're not from here, are you?"

"No."

The boy's pants were so baggy Chancy wondered how he kept them from slipping off his thin hips. He was years younger than her but four inches taller. His too-long blond hair swirled around his head in unruly curls. She grimaced at the angry red scrapes oozing on both elbows.

"I'm visiting Uncle Max. For the summer." Even though she hadn't tried the lie out on many people, it was easy in her mouth, like the truth.

"Do you skate?"

"No."

"Why not?"

"I don't want to move that fast on something that small."

He laughed and bent his arms, giving her a closer look at his scabby elbows. "It's not the speed that gets you. It's the stopping."

"You should wear a helmet." She made an egg-cracking gesture. "This is your brain on the sidewalk."

"You sound like my mom. Have you been talking to her?"

"No." The universe had made their paths cross several times, but they hadn't exactly carried on a conversation.

"She bought me knee pads and elbow protectors and a helmet. Won't let me out of the house without 'em."

"So where are they?"

He snorted. "In the garden shed. If the guys saw me in that stuff, they'd call me a wuss."

"Yeah. I can see how being called brain-damaged would be better."

He laughed again. "You sound *just* like my mom. It's creepy. I don't get why she makes such a big deal out of *safety gear*." He sneered the last two words in a momlike voice.

"Maybe she doesn't want to change your diapers again and feed you through a tube."

"Gross! What are you? The helmet police?"

"Just a bored bystander." Chancy tugged on the leash and started home.

"Wait! Where's the fire?" Adam skated alongside her, one foot rhythmically propelling the board.

"I got things to do."

"Like what?"

What a pest. "How old are you?" she asked.

"Twelve. And a half. How old are you?"

"Fifteen."

He waved hands afflicted with fake arthritis. "Oooh, Granny, you're ancient!"

"You're not."

"You wanna hang?"

"No way."

"Why not?"

"I need to fix dinner for Uncle Max."

"What are you cooking?"

"Apple-baked pork chops." She'd planned the rest of the menu during the walk. "Mashed potatoes and green beans."

"Yum. Can I come?"

"What?"

"Can I come to dinner? Never thought I'd say this, but I'm sick of takeout. In case you haven't noticed, we're remodeling."

"No kidding." Hard to miss the trucks and workmen and noise.

"Our kitchen looks like Yafet's Diner in downtown Beirut. So what time do we eat? Is it formal? Do I have to wear a suit and tie?"

His T-shirt was four sizes too big. The brat probably didn't own a tie. "Anyone ever tell you you're obnoxious?"

He considered. "Every day. But I'm good for a laugh. C'mon, give me a chance, *Chancy*. Pretty please."

This time he held his hands up to his chest like a dog begging for treats. His tongue lolled out in an exaggerated pant. He was impossible, but he made her smile. She stopped on the sidewalk in front of Max's house. Across the street, workers tramped in and out carrying debris that they tossed in a big construction Dumpster.

"C'mon! Only you can save me from an overdose of KFC," he pleaded. "If I have to look at one more extra-crispy strip, I'll jump off the Okalala Bridge."

Adam Hamilton was a show-off who used words like he rode the skateboard, with little regard for his own safety. She wasn't bored now. Part of her wanted to know more about teasing and joking and playing with words.

"Okay," she said. "You can come."

"Whoo-hoo! What time?"

"Six?"

"It's a date."

"It's definitely *not* a date. More a gesture of pity."

"Hey, whatever works," he called as he pistoned across the street.

Chancy watched Adam jump the curb and roll up the sidewalk. He ducked into the backyard, probably to retrieve the helmet he'd ditched. She shouldn't have let him fast-talk her. Cooking for Uncle Max was one thing, but a guest? What if she couldn't pull off the menu? What if she did? The cook at the Tip-Top had warned Corliss about feeding strays. If Chancy fed Adam, would she have trouble getting rid of him?

It didn't matter. He was just a silly boy. But what if he figured out the lie and told his mother? Chancy should have asked Uncle Max's permission first. It was his house. His food. He might be mad that she invited another person.

She started across the street to tell Adam she'd changed her mind, but halfway to the door, she turned and marched back. Alfie trotted amiably beside her. She didn't know what hostesses were supposed to do, but uninviting guests had to be a bad thing. This was Wenonah and Adam Hamilton was a neighbor. Asking him to dinner was the neighborly thing to do. He wasn't like the tenants in B.J.'s building, a gangbanger, meth dealer or registered sex offender. Adam was a harmless, cocky boy who seemed to need company more than pork chops.

Uncle Max was asleep in the recliner and didn't stir when Chancy slipped into the house. In the kitchen, she pulled out the cookbook and read the recipe again. *Serves four.* Plenty. Even with a guest. She scanned the unfamiliar cooking words.

Pare.

Sauté.

Baste.

She had a feeling she'd bitten off more hospitality than she could chew.

Chapter 13

What's burning? Max's dream was really a memory. Townies had set the vagrant camp on fire. He stumbled out of the flaming shack, choking and gasping for air. So much noise and smoke. He'd escaped the mob, more terrified by the hatred than the flames. He made it out alive, but one of the old men didn't. He stirred and sniffed the air. Something *was* on fire. Disoriented by remembered details of a seventy-year-old event, Max ejected himself from the recliner and followed the scent of incinerated meat into the kitchen.

Wearing bulky pot mitts on both hands, Chancy removed a smoking baking dish from the oven. She saw him, and her face collapsed. "I'm sorry! It's not supposed to look like this. I'm sorry!"

"What is it?" He peered into the pan and his stomach lurched. Smitty had been the old hobo's name. In what black brain hole had that memory been hiding all these years?

"Dinner."

"Maybe the question should be, What *was* it?"

"Apple-baked pork chops." Tears filled her eyes. "I'm sorry."

"Don't worry about it." More painful images blasted back, and before he knew it, tears filled his eyes too. He turned away quicky and waved a dish towel to dissipate the smoke.

"Are you mad?" Chancy slid the pan onto the top of the range.

"No." He grasped the counter with both hands to keep from collapsing.

He shouldn't have run out of the fire without Smitty. He'd been thirteen and strong. He should have saved the old fellow. He should have *tried*.

"Uncle Max? Are you all right?"

He would be. It wasn't fair for his mind to rewind the past when he was fast-forwarding his future. He peered into the pan. Carbon-based fossils under a cremated fruit shroud. Nothing like the succulent dish Hanna had served so often. "May be a bit . . . overcooked."

"I don't understand." Chancy flipped open the cookbook and scanned the page. "The recipe says to bake fifty minutes at three hundred and fifty degrees."

"And?"

"I was getting behind, so I turned the oven to five hundred degrees. But I cut the time down to twenty minutes. That doesn't work?"

"Apparently not."

"They're ruined."

"It doesn't matter."

"It does to me."

"Chancy." Max thumbed a tear from her cheek and she flinched. He'd forgotten the unspoken rule: *No touching allowed.* "Never cry over spilt milk."

"But there's no m—"

"Or charred chops. Okay?" When she didn't respond, he asked again: "Okay?"

She nodded.

He lifted the lid off a bubbling saucepan. "We'll eat this. Apple-sauce?"

"Mashed potatoes." She groaned over the pot of soupy glue. "I don't know what went wrong."

"Did you drain the water before you mashed the potatoes?"

"Was I supposed to?"

"Don't worry. Common mistake. Won't tip the planet off its axis." And neither would a bad dream. Even one that had really happened.

"Oh, no, the green beans!" She reached for a smaller pan sizzling on a back burner. Equally scorched. "They're stuck to the bottom."

Max made a mental note to check the battery in the surprisingly silent smoke alarm. He set the pan in the sink and filled it with water. "A little soak and the pot will be good as new."

"The beans won't."

The living room clock chimed. On the sixth note, the doorbell rang.

"Oh! That's Adam!"

"Hamilton?"

"I invited him." She glanced around at the devastation and slumped. "I'm sorry. I should have asked."

"The more the merrier." Max patted her shoulder and started for the door. The distraction should put him squarely back in the here and now. "Thoughtful of you to include the boy."

"I'm sorry. I wanted dinner to be a surprise."

"And it will be. Stop apologizing."

"What'll we do?"

"Improvise. We're old hands at ad-libbing."

"So what's this stuff called again?" Adam frowned as Max ladled a heaping scoop of meaty gravy over the crisp toast on his plate.

"You can call it SOS. However, the French phrase is shit on a shingle."

"Sweet. Hope it doesn't taste like it."

"A mess hall special. Don't knock it till you try it." Max filled his own plate. He'd managed to whip up a replacement supper in no time.

Chancy took a bite. "I've had this before. Isn't it creamed beef on toast?"

"That's the genteel granny name. Soldiers call 'em like they see 'em."

She took another bite. "Yours tastes different."

"Secret ingredient."

"Do I even want to know?" Adam's eyes widened in worried exaggeration. He'd made Max laugh as he recounted his meeting with Chancy and how he'd coerced a dinner invitation.

"Dash of Worcestershire."

"Not bad." Adam tried a bite. "Better than overbaked pork chops."

"*Oven*-baked," Chancy insisted.

"If you say so. Remember, I was one of the first on the crime scene." Adam forked in another bite. "We're talking waaaay *overbaked*."

"Think you could do better?"

"Hey, I'm a mathlete. I know twenty minutes at five hundred does not equal fifty minutes at three fifty."

Chancy had pulled the smoldering pan out of the oven expecting corporal punishment for an honest mistake. Max had tried to wipe her tears, and she'd flinched as from a blow.

He was pleased she'd taken initiative, because it showed she was starting to trust. Adam's good-natured teasing had finally enabled her to let go of defensiveness. Max listened to the children banter, ready to step in if the boy went too far. Chancy was fragile, ruled by doubt, but she was finally venturing out of her protective shell. Tonight she had not only indulged jokes at her own expense, she had even dished out a few tentative ones in return.

Like a pair of seasoned performers, he and Chancy had fed Adam the rehearsed story, and the boy had accepted it without a blink. Chancy's manufactured history had been very convincing. She was definitely a puzzle. A skilled liar who used dishonesty as a survival instinct to manipulate strangers. In general, lying had earned a bad rep, but playing fast and loose with the truth had paid off for Max this time. Dishonesty had made his life worth living again.

Part of him wanted desperately to know the truth of the girl who'd swept in and saved his life. Who was she? Where did she come from? How long before someone came looking for her? She must have a family who missed her. A mother who loved her. What perversity had thrust a sweet, lovely child on the mercy of an unkind world? What good fortune had crossed her path with his?

He grappled with the questions daily, but respected the limits she'd set. He was afraid to push too hard. If he didn't know Chancy Deel's real story, it was easier to believe the one they'd invented. If he didn't know who she was, she could remain what he wanted her to be: a gift he didn't deserve. Chancy believed in magic numbers and signs and the powers of the universe. Why shouldn't he?

Adam mopped up the last of his food and held out his plate. Adopting a wide-eyed Oliver-ish expression, he said, "Please, suh. May I have some more?"

With all the recent practice, speaking had become easier for Max. Adopting the role of indignant headmaster, he bellowed in his best thespian voice, "More? Who here dares to ask for *more*?"

Adam giggled over his second helping. Bewildered by the unfamiliar reference, Chancy looked from Max to Adam. "That was a joke, right?"

Max had spent two years in a drafty orphanage scraping the bottom of a paltry bowl and added real-life details as he explained *Oliver Twist* to her.

"So it's a story about children without parents?" Chancy asked.

"Orphans," Adam said, "who turn into pickpockets."

"They steal to survive?" She grasped the concept quickly.

"At first maybe. Then this creepy guy named Fagin takes over..." Adam left the rest to her imagination.

"Did one of the orphans write it?"

"No," Adam scoffed. "Some dead English dude."

"Charles Dickens," Max said. "*Oliver Twist* is a novel."

"I'd like to read that story," she said softly.

"Oh, no, you wouldn't," Adam said. "It's a honkin' big book. We had to read some of it last year in English. Rent the movie. At least it has music."

"No," she insisted. "Movies are good, but I like to see the words."

"I have the novel somewhere," Max told her. "We'll look for it tomorrow."

"And you'll read my book?" she asked.

"Sure. *The Secret Garden*."

Adam brightened. "I know that one! Mom took me to see the play. Man, what's up with so many orphans in England?"

Max laughed. "Adversity. The best fiction illuminates a character's struggle to discover his inner strength."

Adam nodded. "Yep, that's what my English teacher said."

"So not having parents makes a person strong?" Chancy considered her own question. "Like Oliver and Mary Lennox."

They continued to talk long after the food was gone. "So how's your father, Adam?" Max asked.

"What do you mean?" The boy's ready smile slid off his face.

"Your mom said he was seeing a doctor. Is he feeling better?"

"I don't know." Adam broke eye contact, fiddled with his fork. "He stays in his room most of the time. Sleeping."

"That must be hard on you."

Adam shrugged. "Not so different. He's always been gone most of the time. Only before, he was working."

Unfamiliar with the situation but sensitive to the stretching silence, Chancy stared at her plate.

"Maybe the medication will make him feel better soon," Max said.

Adam shrugged, a universal teenage sign that Max remembered from his teaching days. Could mean anything. *I don't know. I don't care. Leave me alone.*

"Oliver Twist didn't know how good he had it." Adam's fork clattered onto his plate and he picked at a tiny hole in the vinyl tablecloth. "Life would be so much simpler without parents."

Chancy looked up sharply at that, but didn't speak.

"Don't base your opinion on a Hollywood musical," Max warned. "I was an orphan. It's no great shakes."

"But they're both always there now," he insisted. "Dad's closed up in his room. I never see him, but I know he's behind the door. Not talking. Not working. Just *there*. Mom was happier when he was working. Since he's been home, she's up in my grille half the time. 'Do this. Wear that. Don't do that.'"

"Sounds like a mother loving her boy to me," Max said. A wife worrying about her husband, her family. Her marriage.

"She should have five kids instead of one. To water down the love. The full dose is too much for one guy."

An adolescent boy impatient for independence might feel smothered by a doting mother, especially an anxious one who overcompensated for an absentee father. *Anxious as a hen with one chick.* Max's own mother had used the expression many times, but his memories of her had faded. In a moment of panic, he realized he could no longer remember what she had looked like. Why could he recall poor dead Smitty's face but not his own mother's?

"It's weird. Having Dad around so much, I mean. Before we moved here, I hardly ever saw him. He left before I got up and didn't come home until after I went to bed."

"What kind of work does he do again?" Max really had forgotten.

"He's a land developer." Adam affected a deep baritone. " 'Son, do you know what you call a land developer who doesn't work twenty-four/seven? Bankrupt, that's what!' "

"No crime in working hard." As soon as he spoke the words, Max knew he'd touched a nerve. Adam's voice crumbled into something small and shaky.

"Is it a crime to miss all your kid's soccer games and school programs?"

"You play soccer?"

"I quit when I was nine. What's the point?"

"I'm sure your mother made the games."

Adam snorted. "Mrs. Soccer Mom Supreme? Oh, yeah. Never missed one."

That sounded like Jenny. Trying to do the job of two parents. Max hadn't realized how tense things were at the Hamilton house. And yet Jenny had taken time to check in on him regularly.

"Dad didn't want to move here. He liked living in Oklahoma City."

"What about you? Must have been hard to leave your friends."

Another dismissive shrug. *Never had that many.*

Budding teenage angst. Distant father. Overprotective mother. New kid in town. Things hadn't changed much since Oliver Twist's day. Lonely boys were still the same. "I take it Wenonah was your mom's idea?"

"Everything is always Mom's idea. Some kid brought a gun to my old school. She totally freaked! Next thing I know, here we are. No one was even shot or anything. Just a weird kid showing off. Mom called it 'potential gang activity'." His derisive spin revealed his disagreement with the interpretation.

"Gangs are bad," Chancy put in.

"Yeah. In east LA, maybe. But one suburban weirdo with a gun isn't exactly a turf war."

"Guns are bad too." Chancy looked at Max for confirmation. "They kill people."

"No," Adam said. "Don't you read bumper stickers? People kill people. Mom picked Wenonah because it reminded her of Mayberry. Whatever that is."

City people idealized small-town life. "I believe Barney Fife had a gun," Max said.

"Whatever." Adam pushed his plate aside, a clear signal that it was time to change the subject.

"Have you ever jumped out of a plane?" Max's question had the desired effect on Adam.

"Nooo. Have you?"

"Sure. Lots of times. The first time is the hardest, though." Max relayed a few adventures from his army days. Adam asked about his childhood. Since lighthearted boyhood memories were scarce, he told them about the time a group of older orphan boys pelted him and his friends with ripe persimmons.

"Sister Blessida, the history teacher, taught us how medieval armies used catapults to hurl stones over castle walls. That gave me a good idea."

Adam brightened. "You made a catapult?"

"A very primitive one. There was a stand of young saplings on the grounds. My gang hung out there. One day we lured those persimmon-pitching bullies into a trap."

"What kind of trap?" Chancy was curious too.

"We went out to the dairy cow pasture and gathered a wheelbarrow full of half-dried cow pies."

Adam chuckled. "You mean . . ."

"Yep. We bent the limber saplings down as far as they would go, balanced those little surprises just so, and on my count, we let go. Wham! Right in the kisser!"

"Now that's gang violence!" Adam laughed, but Chancy looked confused until Adam explained that a cow pie wasn't a beef-flavored pastry.

She still didn't get the joke. "Didn't that just make the bullies madder?"

"They left us alone after that," Max explained.

"Respect, man," Adam put in.

"So they didn't have knives or anything?" Chancy pushed.

"We were just kids."

"Kids can have knives," she insisted.

Adam was looking at Chancy differently. *Uh-oh.* Max step-ball-changed to a new topic and described the first time he'd hopped a freight train.

"How old were you?" Adam was quick with questions, but Chancy listened quietly. Maybe she was still thinking about bullies with knives.

"I went to California the first time when I was twelve."

"My age?" Adam's chin rested on his folded arms.

"Yep."

"By yourself?" A lot of doubt in two words.

"You're never really alone on the rails. I had plenty of other down-and-outers for company." Talking about good times helped Max rebury the bad.

"Mom won't even let me ride my board over to the high school by myself. I have to stay on Poplar Avenue. You went all the way across the country."

"Different time, different life." In good conscience, Max couldn't glorify the past. "Plenty of nights, when I was freezing in the back of a boxcar, or running from a railroad agent with a baseball bat, I wished I had a home and folks to take me in."

Adam grimaced. "Anytime you feel the need to have a thumb pressing down on you, you can borrow my mom!"

The boy tried to act grown-up but shifted from mood to mood like a child with few worries. Later, as they washed the dinner dishes, he jostled Chancy at the sink. "Hey, your sleeves are getting wet."

"That's okay. They'll dry."

"Seriously, dude, push 'em up. Here, I'll help you." Before she could protest, he lifted her arm from the soapy water and tugged up the damp fabric.

"No! Leave me alone!" Chancy jerked away. The plate she was scrubbing slipped from her hands and crashed to the floor.

"Cripes! What's your problem?" Adam stepped back, confused.

"Nothing. Just keep your hands off." Chancy stretched the sleeve over her forearm, but not before Max caught a glimpse of pale skin marked by welts and scars.

Adam backed away, too startled by her outburst to notice. "Sorreee. I was just trying to help. No need to throw plates."

"It's not that. I . . ." Her voice caught as she stooped to pick up the shards. "I'm sorry. I didn't mean to break anything."

Max removed the broom and dustpan from the closet and turned to Adam. "We'll finish cleaning up. Why don't you look in the hall closet and find a game for us to play?"

"Are you sure?" Like most males, the boy was at a loss when it came to female emotion. "I can help."

"We'll take care of it. The games are on the top shelf."

Adam left the room and Chancy pulled down her sleeves, catching the damp ends in white-knuckled fists. She folded her arms tightly around her middle and stared at the shattered plate like a dream she had forfeited.

"I'm sorry, Uncle Max. I'll pay you back for the plate."

"Don't be silly." Max swept the glittering china chips into a pile.

"Here, let me hold that." She knelt and angled the dustpan to collect the broken glass, which she then dumped in the wastebasket.

"I ruined everything." She choked on a sob. "I always do. You and Adam were having fun."

"Weren't you having fun?"

She looked up, her eyes full of tears and wonder. "Yes. I was." Her own words seemed to surprise her. "Until I messed up again."

"No such thing." Max wanted to embrace the girl but didn't dare risk doing more damage than good. She had so much to hide that Adam's innocent touch had driven her back into her frightened, lonely shell. "An accident. That's all. Don't give it another thought."

Easier said than done. Max could not get the image of those scars out of his mind. Some looked like cuts; others were round, like burns. Old wounds, fresh pain. No wonder she ran away if someone had hurt her like that.

"Hurry up, you guys!" Adam called. "I'm setting up the board."

Clancy searched Max's face. "Why don't you blame me for all the bad things I do?"

"Because you haven't done anything bad. Blame hurts everyone. Forgiveness takes away the hurt."

She was silent for a long moment. "Some things can't ever be forgiven."

"All things can be forgiven, Chancy."

"No." She shook her head stubbornly. "Not everything."

"Letting go of blame frees the heart for kinder things." Max avoided physical contact, consoling instead with soft words. "Let's put this moment behind us."

"You can do that?"

"I already have. Adam has. So can you. C'mon, let's see what game he chose for us to play."

"Adam's a kid. He thinks *everything* is a game."

Max smiled from the doorway. "When you get to be my age, you will understand what a comforting attitude that can be."

Chancy played Monopoly as she did most things, with quiet determination. While wheeler-dealers Max and Adam went noisily broke, she focused on purchasing utilities and railroads, accumulating property and adding houses and hotels. She soon controlled the board.

"You've played this game before," Max said. A Tommy Dorsey album spun on the console, the big band beat as lively as the game.

"Do your parents play games?" Adam asked. "Mine don't have time."

"Saturday is game night at our house." Chancy didn't falter over this new detail, and it occurred to Max that maybe her lies were really just wishful thinking. He knew all about that. "We sit around the kitchen table. Dad's really good at Scrabble, but I'm better at Memory."

"Man, I suck at that game," Adam admitted.

Max grinned. Probably because the boy had a fifteen-second

attention span. Chancy, on the other hand, was skilled at shutting out the world.

Adam had already shaken off the incident in the kitchen like Alfie shaking rain from his coat. He groaned when he landed on Chancy's Ventnor Avenue. Rocking back, he threw his hands in the air. "You're a slumlord!" He went bust counting the rent into her outstretched hand. "I'm tapped out."

Fleeting panic pinched her face. "Oh, sorry. Here. You can have some back. I didn't mean to take it all." She pushed the fake money into his hands.

Adam laughed. Because everything really was a joke to the boy, he didn't understand when others were serious. "Duh! Taking it all is kinda the object of the game."

"It's getting late." The last three hours had been an exhilarating reminder of how full little moments could be. It had been a long time since Max had dealt with youngsters' roller-coaster emotions. "Maybe we should call it a night."

Adam glanced at the clock. "Cripes! Mom's gonna kill me. She told me to be home by eight."

"You're late," Chancy pointed out.

"Ya think?" Adam started for the door, then paused to reveal his mother's gentle influence. "Thank you for inviting me, Chancy. And thank you for the, uh, SOS, Mr. Boyle. And the stories."

"Call me Uncle Max."

The boy's face brightened. "Really? Okay, cool! See you around the 'hood, Chancy."

Adam blew out the door like a spring storm. His arms flew up as he leaped off the top step and plunged across the dark street toward the beckoning porch light.

They stood in the doorway watching until he was safely inside.

"Well, that was fun." Max stretched. "Wore me plumb out. Talking to Adam is like chopping wood: hard work with a big warm payoff at the end."

Chancy continued to stare into the night. "Do you think his mother will be mad at him for being late?"

"I'm sure she'll forgive him."

Comprehension washed over her delicate features. "That's what mothers are supposed to do, right? Forgive?"

"Sometimes mothers are the ones who *need* forgiveness," he said.

Across the street, the porch light went out. When Chancy turned, the light had gone out of her eyes too.

Chapter 14

"**E**xcuse me! Are you Chancy?"

Chancy looked up from the clump of lilies she was weeding. Her heart leaped into her throat when she spotted Jenny Hamilton leaning over the garden gate, her silver heart necklace winking in the sun. She nodded, too startled to elaborate, and Alfie bounded over to greet the visitor.

"Hi, I'm Jenny, Adam's mom. I live across the street."

"I know." She looked young and pretty with her hair pulled up in a high ponytail. She wore tan cropped pants and a purple T-shirt and shoes with no backs, like a mom actress in a feed-your-kids-right TV commercial.

"I knocked but no one answered."

"Uncle Max is upstairs taking a nap." Chancy stood and wiped her hands on her jeans. Last night, Adam seemed to believe their story, but maybe not. Maybe he told his mother a weirdo girl was taking advantage of Mr. Boyle.

Jenny fumbled with the catch and pushed the gate open. She strolled in and looked around. "Wow, I didn't even know this garden was back here. It's kind of like the secret garden in the book."

Chancy dropped the garden fork. Jenny knew about *The Secret Garden*. Then she remembered that they'd talked about it last night. "Adam said you took him to the play."

"Did he? I'm surprised he remembers. He was only eight at the time. I was that age when I read the book. I loved it. Every time I see a robin, I think of Dickon's little pet."

Chancy's pulse pounded. Maybe Jenny Hamilton wasn't a threat after all. Loving Chancy's favorite book had to be a good sign. "Some birds built nests in the birdhouses, but they're not robins."

"I think robins build their nests out in the open. The eggs are such a pretty shade of blue. Check the shrubs. You might find one."

"Okay."

"Adam tells me you're Max's niece?"

"Not really." A drop of truth felt good before the lies started. "Uncle Max is my dad's godfather."

"I see. I'm surprised Max never mentioned you. So how long have you been in Wenonah?"

"Not long." More truth.

"Adam told me about your parents' trip and everything. How long do you plan to stay?"

Forever. And a day. "For the summer, I guess."

"That will be good for Max. And for Adam. He really had a great time last night. He talked about his visit all the way to school this morning. He hasn't been that chatty—or happy—for weeks."

Chancy didn't know what to say. Adam had seemed plenty happy to her.

"School will be out soon. I've been worried about him getting bored this summer. He usually goes to camp, but we've had some, uh, unexpected expenses, so we had to cut out a few luxuries. I hope he won't be a pest."

"Maybe he can help us fix things up around here."

Jenny flashed Adam's look-alike smile. "I'm sure he'd love to." She leaned close and her voice became conspiratorial. "I think he found a new idol in Max. He told me all about Max's stories and his record player and 'old-timey' music. Apparently Max has done a lot of 'neat stuff.' Even jumped out of airplanes."

"In the army. I saw his uniform in the closet." Chancy tapped the dirt off the gardening fork.

"He kept it?"

"And medals too. He has a lot of those. For being brave."

"I have no doubt." Jenny smiled. "Adam said he never knew old people could be so interesting."

That sounded like Adam, but made Chancy bristle. "Uncle Max is the most interesting person I've ever known." The best truth of all.

"I think he's delightful. I know Adam will enjoy visiting. But you let me know if he gets under your feet or causes problems."

"Okay."

"I'll tell Max to put him to work. That'll keep him busy. He hates all the construction noise, and I'd rather know he's over here than skating around the neighborhood. That board scares me to death."

"We always have plenty of things to do."

"I see that. What kind of daylilies are those?" Jenny pointed in the general direction of Chancy's weeding efforts.

She shrugged. "I don't know. Is there more than one kind?"

"Oh, hundreds. Growers are always coming up with new varieties." Jenny looked around at the various clumps of green spires poking out of the ground. "Looks like whoever planted this garden liked daylilies."

"This was Aunt Hanna's garden." Sometimes Chancy forgot that she had never really known Uncle Max's late wife. His stories had made her come alive, and Chancy felt her presence in the house, but stronger here, in the garden she had loved. "I'm trying to fix it up."

"You have your work cut out for you. It's pretty overgrown."

"I don't mind working."

"Adam says you've been helping Max clean house too."

"He got a little behind with that."

"I've offered to help, but he's so independent. I'm glad he has you to keep him company." Jenny snapped her fingers in sudden recollection. "Max told me he had worked something out with Ms. Wooten. I bet you're it."

"I am." She'd never been anyone's solution before, and the responsibility was scary. "Would you like something to drink? We have lemonade."

"I'd love some. It's getting warm out here. Aren't you hot in that shirt?"

Chancy smoothed her long sleeves. "No. I don't get hot."

"Oh, that's right. You're not from Oklahoma."

Uncle Max was still upstairs. Chancy fixed two glasses of lemonade and they carried the drinks to the shady front porch so they wouldn't disturb him.

"How's the remodeling coming along?" Chancy sipped lemonade.

Jenny grimaced. "What did Adam say? That I've ruined his life and wrecked his health by making him eat microwave dinners and carry-out?"

"Not exactly."

"Can I be honest with you?"

"Sure." Chancy stared into her glass and felt bad about not being honest with Jenny.

"Things are pretty tough for Adam right now. What with his dad sick and money tight. The house is a wreck. I'd really appreciate it if you were nice to him."

"Why wouldn't I be?" Did Jenny think she wasn't a nice person?

"Well, you're so much older. And he can be a pest. So many questions! But he thinks you're really cool."

"He does?"

"For a girl," Jenny qualified. "Believe me, that's high praise coming from a twelve-year-old boy."

"Does his dad have cancer or something?" Adam hadn't said why his father was sick, but Chancy imagined people with cancer slept a lot. According to Max, Hanna had spent her last days sleeping in the sunroom.

"No, no. Nothing like that. He's depressed. But he's on medication now, so we should be seeing some improvement soon."

"I know about depression."

"You do?"

"I knew somebody once who had it. Does your husband get too happy sometimes too?"

"No. He's not bipolar or anything. The doctor thinks he's just clinically depressed."

"His brain chemistry's out of balance."

"Right." Jenny seemed relieved not to have to explain. "You're a very bright girl. You know, it's kind of a relief to talk to someone about this. I don't know many people in Wenonah. I thought moving to a small town would be different. Instead, it's been isolating."

"I like Wenonah better than the city." Saying true things was like having a real conversation.

"Let's all have lunch sometime. You and Max, and me and Adam."

"What about your husband?"

"Tom's not ready to go out yet. But soon. You know, we should go to the Tip-Top Café. They have the best hamburgers in town. If you like hamburgers."

"You know about the Tip-Top?" Maybe she shouldn't have been so worried about talking to Jenny.

"Hey, I'm on intimate terms with every restaurant in town. My kitchen is a disaster area, remember?"

"Right. Do you know a waitress there named Corliss?"

"Corliss? Sure. She's a sweetie. How do you know her?"

"From eating there."

"What do you know—small world, isn't it?"

Chancy had always thought the world was big. Too big for her. Maybe she was wrong.

"It's a date then." Jenny set her empty glass on the wicker table between the two rockers. She stopped at the bottom of the steps and waved before heading across the street. "Don't forget. Some Saturday we'll go to lunch."

And just like that, Chancy made a real friend. Was it possible to want something so badly and still be afraid of it?

She was sitting on the porch when Max awoke from his nap and joined her. "I thought I heard voices out here," he said.

"You did. Jenny Hamilton just left."

"Oh, no." He sank into the twin rocker. "I was afraid she'd show up while I was dead to the world and trip us up. What happened?"

"Nothing." He didn't think he could trust her to talk to people alone. That explained why he'd been so agreeable about her avoiding Jenny.

"What do you mean, *nothing*?"

"We talked. Mostly she did. About Adam and daylilies and *The Secret Garden.*"

"Did she swallow the bait?" She gave him an exasperated look, and he clarified. "Do you think she believed the story?"

"Yes. Bits of it are true, you know." Chancy wanted to be as good at telling the truth as she was at lying. "She's nice."

Max seemed to relax. "I told you."

"You didn't really think she'd get us in trouble, did you?"

"You never know. A do-gooder is a do-gooder any way you wrap her."

"She invited us to go out to lunch some Saturday."

"I guess we could do that. Better yet, we should invite them here. They're probably tired of eating in restaurants. You can help cook."

Exciting and scary, like riding a roller coaster. "I'd better not. I might burn something."

"When you fall off a horse, you have to get back on. Oh, this is for you." He pulled an envelope from his shirt pocket. Her name was scrawled across it in shaky, slanted letters.

"What is it?" She made no move to take the offering and rubbed her forearms through the fabric of her shirt. She'd lain awake worrying last night that he'd seen the marks when Adam tugged on her sleeve. She was afraid he'd ask questions that she'd have to answer, but more afraid that the marks would scare him, like they had other people, and he would tell her to leave.

"Open it and find out." He waggled the envelope with an imperious shake. "What are you waiting for? Go on, take it. Payday."

"What?"

"Payday. Not the candy bar. The moola. I should withhold taxes. File IRS forms in triplicate and all that, but what's a little tax evasion to a couple of world-class evaders?"

"I don't understand." He was giving her money because he was too nice to send her back to the highway. He'd give her money for a bus.

"What's not to understand about cold, hard cash?"

She swallowed hard, choking on her words. "You want me to leave."

"What?" His bushy brows drew together. "Of course not. Why would you think that? I'm paying you for doing your job as we agreed."

"I can't take your money."

"We have a bargain. Two hundred a week. This is yours."

"I haven't earned that much money." Despite her efforts, the house was still cluttered and dusty. The windows were streaked and the weeds had grown taller. She'd made little progress in Hanna's garden. "You can't pay me for burning a meal and breaking a plate."

"Nonsense. You walk Alfie."

"That doesn't count. I like being with him."

"Job satisfaction is important."

"I haven't done enough."

"You've done plenty. You wash every dish we dirty. You even washed the one that broke. You took out the garbage. And you scrubbed the bathroom! My old tub hasn't looked that shiny in months. Do you know the secret to success in the workplace?"

"I never had a real job before."

"Always exceed expectations."

"Have I done that?"

"My dear, if what I expected from you was here"—he extended one hand at waist level—"what you've already done for me is here." He stretched the other hand far over his head.

"Really?"

"You betcha." He slapped the envelope into her hands with won't-take-no-for-an-answer finality. "Max Boyle does not welsh on a deal. You take this and don't give me any sass about it."

Two hundred dollars weighed less than Chancy expected. How could something so important to her future feel so insignificant in her hand? She pressed the envelope to her chest. She'd never had that much money before. Never thought she was worth so much. Her throat tightened, not from an incoming panic attack but some other emotion. Gratefulness. If Max had seen the marks, they didn't matter. He wasn't like the pickpocket Oliver. Max accepted what she could offer and didn't ask for more.

"When you're ready to tackle this hovel," he said, "we'll whip the place into shape together. If Wooten comes poking around, we'll knock her socks off."

Chancy nodded, happy to be a person who earned her way.

"Run upstairs and stash your wealth," he said. "One day soon, we'll ask Jenny Hamilton to drive us to the bank, and you can open a savings account."

"Thank you, Uncle Max."

"I'm the one who should thank you. Now hurry up and put your money away. We have work to do."

Chancy ran up the stairs, feeling as light and floaty as she had that first day in Wenonah. She'd never thought of herself as the kind of girl who had a savings account, but money in the bank meant security. Security was safety. The magic of the house's numbers had paid off again. She could forget everything that had happened before Wenonah. The past couldn't ruin what she had here. She could create her own future. One that did not include B.J.

A plan had started to form, but she hadn't dared believe until she held the money in her hand. Now she was sure.

She could be new, because everything had happened for a reason.

Fate had put her in the car with the lady drug rep who'd dumped her in St. Louis. Fate had sent Shaggy Dave to scare her into running through the snow to Mama Mia's, where she'd met Kenny Ray, the only person who could have driven her away from her stormy life and into one that was peaceful and sunny. She'd tried to rely on lucky pennies and birds on a wire, but luck did not exist. Just signs that led to what was meant to be if she paid attention.

Chancy slipped her new riches into the drawer of her night table. She noticed a scrap of paper on which she had doodled a teetering stack of coffee cups one night while spinning imaginary conversations with Corliss. Her heart beat faster. She could have real friends in Wenonah. First Uncle Max and then Adam and now Jenny.

Corliss was a sign too.

Chancy had no idea what role the stranger with the tired eyes and kind heart would play in her future, but she knew she hadn't landed in the Tip-Top Café that stormy Sunday morning by accident.

Corliss was important. She meant something in the universe's scheme of things. It was up to Chancy to find out what.

Chapter 15

A week later, Chancy stood outside the Tip-Top with Alfie's leash in one hand and a plastic bag containing her excuse in the other. She listened to the bell over the door tinkle each time a customer went in and out. She glanced in the window. The noon rush was over, but most of the booths were full and so were the stools. A heavy, red-haired waitress plodded behind the counter, filling coffee cups. Chancy didn't see Corliss. Maybe it was her day off.

Chancy had walked halfway to the diner twice this week, but had turned around both times, convinced she needed another sign before taking such a big step. The older woman knew Chancy's life was counterfeit, which made her a threat. Maybe she should stick to make-believe conversations. The nightmare didn't awaken Chancy as often as before, but when it did, she imagined Corliss sitting at the foot of her bed, offering comfort in her cheesy, cheery way.

The older woman had seen something good in a cold, shivering girl that first stormy morning. Without the encouragement of her kindness, Chancy might never have stayed in Wenonah. Would never have met Max or Adam or Jenny. Would never have known the blind devotion a dog could give. Corliss was important. She was a connection between Chancy's old life and the new.

A bridge to link the two worlds together.

This morning, for the first time, Uncle Max had fixed hominy grits for breakfast, and Chancy had known. Today was the day.

So where was Corliss? She tied Alfie's leash to a lamppost and ducked inside. A man slid off the stool closest to the door and Chancy took his place.

"What can I get for you?" The waitress pulled an order pad from her apron pocket. Her lipstick was the color of blood.

"I'm looking for Corliss."

"Just missed her. I come on when her shift ends. She's waiting for her ride out back, so if it ain't come yet, she may still be there."

"Thanks." Had she misread the signs? Since she'd been in Wenonah, sometimes she forgot to work for points with the universe.

Chancy retrieved Alfie and hurried around the building. When she heard Corliss talking to the rumble-voiced cook, she flattened herself against the wall and waited for him to leave. She stroked Alfie, whispering, "Quiet, boy," then peeked around the corner. Corliss stood in the alley, purse in hand. Was she smaller? She didn't even come up to the big cook's shoulder. He was dressed all in white, from his white knit cap to his white rubber-soled shoes.

Corliss sighed. "Another day, another dollar, Tyree."

"Sure was busy. Bet I fried a hundred burgers. You have a good day?"

"Fifty-eight bucks in tips. Not bad for a weekday, but Donald Trump probably makes that much while he's sneezing."

"Yeah, but you got better hair." Tyree looked around. "You afoot?"

"Eddie borrowed my car. He's looking for a job. Said he'd be done in plenty of time to drive me home."

"Good to hear he's job hunting. Tell him my cousin said they're hiring down at the quickie lube place."

"Thanks, I'll pass the word."

"So how's the old Tempo running these days?"

"I wouldn't put it in the NASCAR, if you know what I mean. It leaks oil and blows smoke, but if anything happened to it, I'd sure enough be up

Shit Creek without a ride. I don't know about you, but my end of Shit Creek's been under a flood advisory lately."

"I hear that." The cook's laugh rolled down the alley like a bowling ball. Corliss's laughter turned into a painful-sounding hack.

Tyree patted her back. "Girl, you need to see somebody about that cough. It's hung on you like a tick on a fat dog. You need to stop drinking Robitussin and get yourself to the clinic."

"Got no money to waste on doctors. I'll be fine. I've just been more tired than usual, that's all."

Tyree glanced down the alley. "Looks like ol' Eddie's running late."

"A little."

He looked pointedly at his flashy wristwatch. "More'n a little, I'd say. C'mon, you can't walk three miles home. Let me drive you."

"I'll wait for him. Last thing in the world I want to do is give Ramona Gill a chance to say, 'I told you so.' She's convinced Eddie's gonna take my car and disappear into the sunset. Or sell it for drugs."

"That redheaded busybody needs to mind her own damn business."

"She knows everything. Told me I was in for a world of hurt this time. She's wrong. Eddie's doing good." Corliss shifted her purse to the other shoulder. "He'll be along directly."

"Hell, don't listen to Ramona. If she knows so much and does everything right, how come she weighs two-forty and leaves the Tagalong Tavern alone every Saturday night?"

"Tyree! Delia let you go to the Tagalong?"

"Hell, no! I hear things, is all." He fished a key ring from the pocket of his cook's pants and dangled it in front of her. "I'll be glad to drop you off."

"Thanks, but no. Eddie'll show up."

"He grew a new dependable streak, did he?"

"He won't let me walk home."

"Well, okay now, if you're sure."

"I am. You go on. Tell Delia I said hey."

"I'll do that. She's fryin' up that mess of catfish we caught yestiddy evenin' over at Okalala Cove."

"Sounds good."

"Oh, they'll be good, all right. I sure like eatin' what I don't have to cook."

"If you ever need a fishing buddy, I wish you'd call Eddie. Be good for him to get some fresh air, and I like a crisp pan-fried fillet."

"Sure thing. Delia only goes to keep me comp'ny. She'd be glad for a chance to stay home. Tell him I'll give him a call sometime."

"You know what he said last night? He said coming home to me was the best move he ever made. Claims I'm better than rehab." She snorted. "Better be. Mother love's all I got to give him these days."

"He's lucky to have you, Corliss."

"You know," she said, like she just remembered something, "even after nineteen hours of hard labor, I didn't take any anesthetic. I wanted to do right by my baby and not let any drugs cross over to him."

"Nineteen hours?" Tyree blew a long, impressed whistle. "Whoo!"

"Yeah. Cosmic joke's on me, I reckon. See you in the morning."

"Bright-tailed and bushy-eyed." He snapped a little salute and walked backward down the alley. "You *sure* you don't need a ride?"

Corliss waved. "Go home to your wife!" Once the big black man drove away, her smile faded and she limped over to the steps behind the diner. She sat down with a tired huff and rested her head on her folded arms.

Chancy gathered her nerve and led Alfie around the corner. "Hello."

Corliss looked up and grinned. "Shoot! Hello, yourself."

"Remember me?" Chancy clutched the leash in one hand and the plastic grocery bag in the other.

"Sure do. Don't think you ever told me your name, though."

"Chancy."

"Pretty name. I'm—"

"Corliss. I remember."

"Corliss Briggs, that's me. And who's this old fella?" Corliss stretched out a hand to scratch the dog's ears.

"Alfie."

"Sweet thing." Corliss stroked his fur. "You're a lot less damp than the last time I saw you."

"I've been dry for a while now."

"You look like a whole different person. You lost that half-starved, up-to-my-hips-in-gators look. You must be in a better situation."

Chancy nodded.

"You haven't been back to the Tip-Top. I've been looking for you."

"You have?"

"I thought you must have moved on."

"No. I'm still here."

"Good. I want to thank you for leaving me that heart."

A wave of happiness broke against Chancy's barriers. "No need. It's just a scrap of paper."

"Meant a lot to me. Best tip I ever got. I wish you'd teach me how to make those little pretties. I'd like to whip out a batch for Meals on Wheels."

"What's that?"

"Volunteers take food trays to shut-ins and elderly folks in town. I'm busy working during mealtime, so I can't drive. But in my spare time I make favors to put on the trays. I call them pep-me-ups."

Corliss was a pep-me-up. Chancy felt better just talking to her. She didn't seem to be the question-asking type. "Hearts are easy. I can show you."

"Oh, I would like that."

"Maybe I could help you. Make some pep-me-ups, I mean." She used money now, not hearts. She hadn't made any since she'd been with Uncle Max, and was excited at the prospect of doing something to cheer up old folks.

"That's a fine idea." Corliss unzipped her purse, pulled out a pen and jotted two phone numbers on the back of a dollar-store register receipt. "Most mornings I'm working. Here's the number. This is my home phone. Give me a call and we'll set up a day to get together."

"Really?" Why was everything good prickly with scary feeling? Chancy pushed the receipt to the bottom of her front jeans pocket.

"Sure. I'll buy some pretty paper and, if you're willing, we can make hearts for the folks over at the nursing home too. To brighten up their rooms. In fact, you know what? If you have the time, maybe you'd like to go on visiting rounds with me."

"I don't know. What do you do?"

"I'm a professional visitor." Corliss pressed a fist against her lower back. "Some of them old people don't ever have any company. Once a week, I run over to Dogwood Manor and go room to room. I tell dumb jokes and make 'em laugh. One old lady with bad cataracts likes me to read to her. You look smart. I bet you enjoy reading."

"Yes." Chancy thought of all the times she'd sat in a circle as a little girl, listening to a story unfold. She wanted to give that pleasure to some old lady who couldn't see the words anymore.

"Some can't talk, so I just sit and hold their hands for a while. Just visit."

"I could do that." Maybe she wouldn't hold hands, but she could do the rest. Living with Uncle Max had taught her that old people had a lot to offer.

"You'd be a good visitor. All those folks need is someone willing to care a little. Mostly they need someone who's patient enough to listen. They enjoy seeing a new face. Especially a pretty one. I can't get over how good you look."

"Could Alfie come?"

"Why, you're just full of good ideas. I've heard of visiting dogs before, but they don't have one at Dogwood Manor. By all means, Alfie's in."

Alfie wagged his tail, like he understood that he'd just been invited to do something fun.

A car rounded the corner and Corliss looked up hopefully. When it drove on, she shrugged. "I'm waiting for my ride."

"You could take a taxi." That was how Uncle Max went places. He wanted to drive again and said losing his license was worse than losing his pinkie toe tip.

"Oh, no, cabs cost an arm and a leg."

"I have money, if you need some."

"Aren't you sweet? No, honey, Eddie won't let me down. Say, if you're here to eat, we got the best hamburgers in three counties right in there."

"No. I'm looking for the little gray cat that hangs around the alley."

"Oh, yeah." Corliss retied a loose shoelace and muttered how she couldn't wait to get home and put on her fuzzy house shoes. "I've been calling that gray kitten Marvin. He's so slippery, I didn't think he'd show himself for anyone but me."

"I noticed him . . . when I was here before."

"You know, come to think of it, I haven't seen him for a couple of days. Can't imagine where he's gotten off to."

"You don't think something bad happened to him, do you?" Chancy jiggled the grocery bag. "I brought cat food."

"Well, that was thoughtful of you. Probably nothing bad happened. He may have moved on or is eating somewhere else."

"Do you think he found a good place to live?"

Corliss shrugged. "Maybe. Hard to tell with strays. They never stay in one place very long. I think they're afraid to belong to anyone. If he was born wild and didn't get enough human holding and cuddling when he was young, he might never learn to trust people."

"I hope he found a home." Dogs and cars and people could hurt something so small.

"If you want, I'll keep that cat chow in the kitchen. I put out food for the little hungry guys. There's always some of them meowing around. I'm sure they'd like this better than cold eggs."

Chancy relinquished the bag. "If you see Marvin, will you let me know?"

"If you give me your phone number."

Chancy wasn't ready for that. Corliss might be a bridge, but for now she needed to keep her two lives separate. "I'll check back."

"Guess you're looking for a pet."

"Maybe. I hate to think of Marvin all alone."

"That cat's wild as a March hare. You want a kitten, best get one out of the paper. Cats born among humans and raised by a sweet old mama cat make better companions. Folks always got extras."

"That's okay. I don't want just any cat. I was worried about the gray one."

"In that case, I'll keep my eyes peeled."

"Thanks." Now that she'd used up her excuse to talk to Corliss, Chancy didn't know what to say. Corliss didn't mind silence. She petted Alfie again, and Chancy showed her how he could shake hands.

"You're living near here now," Corliss said. Not a question, more like a confirmation. The older woman didn't pry or push.

"Not too far."

"I'm over at the Mossy Glen Trailer Park." She heaved herself off the step. "Good three miles, so I'd better start hoofing it home."

"What about your ride?"

"Guess I been stood up. That boy probably lost track of time."

"Maybe he had car trouble." Chancy couldn't let her know she'd heard about Eddie in eavesdropped conversations. Corliss should have taken the ride Tyree offered. People dependent on chemicals, even the kind doctors prescribed, could be unreliable.

"Hey, maybe he's chasing a hot lead on an interview." Even fake cheer didn't seem fake coming from Corliss. "Wouldn't that be something?"

"He might have run out of gas."

"Or had a flat tire."

"Lots of things could have happened." He would have an excuse. B.J. always did. Unless she was so far gone she didn't care. A teacher had once given Chancy a pretty coat, one of the few nice things she'd ever owned. She'd been proud of that coat, even if it was secondhand. Then one snowy morning she got up to go to school and discovered B.J. had traded her coat for a carton of cigarettes. The betrayal had been colder than the icy wind. Chancy hoped, for Corliss's sake, that Eddie hadn't skipped town with her old car.

"I like walking," Chancy said. "Walking makes me feel good."

"You're lucky. Walking makes my bunions hurt," Corliss grumbled.

"I'll walk with you for a way."

"I'd like that. When I get home, I may have to dish my son up a piece of my mind. But not too big a piece," she added with a wink. "I need to hang on to what-all mind I have left."

"Maybe you could give him a heart instead."

Corliss shifted her heavy purse on her shoulder, like she dreaded the long trudge home. "Oh, honey, I done give that boy every little bit of my heart."

Before they reached the end of the block, a rusted-out blue car with Mardi Gras beads swinging from the mirror screeched to the curb. A young man with wavy brown hair leaned across the seat and called out the passenger-side window, "Jeez, Mom! Sorry I'm late. Long story."

He didn't look anything like Corliss. Chancy searched for the mother-and-son similarities she'd seen in Jenny and Adam but found none. Unlike Corliss's open expression, Eddie's was unreadable. He didn't set off the red alert, but was definitely the type who inspired caution. His mouth was unsmiling and the notch in his chin could have been carved out of his thin face with a knife.

"Better late than never. Eddie, this is my friend Chancy. And *her* friend Alfie."

Chancy had another friend. One who was no longer far away. They exchanged hellos. Alfie poked his nose in the open window and sniffed. Chancy noticed a box of fried chicken on the seat.

"Get in, Mom. I bought dinner, so you don't have to cook."

"Where'd you get the money?"

"Mom." Eddie wouldn't talk in front of a stranger. Chancy understood. She also recognized the jumpy look in his eyes. B.J. got it when she needed her medicine. "Never mind," he said. "Just get in."

"Chancy, do you and Alfie want a ride home?" Corliss asked.

"No!" She didn't want Eddie Briggs to know where she lived. "We like to walk, remember?"

Corliss opened the door and climbed in, holding the box of chicken on her lap. Alfie sniffed again.

"Eddie? Where are your manners?"

He looked up at Chancy through the open window. "Nice to meet you."

Chancy nodded and watched him merge into traffic and disappear. She was glad he had shown up, but Eddie wasn't the kind of son she'd imagined for Corliss. She deserved one who went to college and had a good job and paid her bills so she didn't have to wait tables. One who wouldn't be late and make his mother, who had a cough and shouldn't be working at all, walk after she had poured coffee for eight hours.

"C'mon, boy. Let's go home and see what Uncle Max is up to." She'd been gone a couple of hours. Maybe he was thinking about her, wondering what was keeping her. She had so many reasons to smile now, she didn't have to practice in her room at night. Wenonah had given her all these smiling things, but the biggest gift was someone who cared where she was. Chancy suddenly wanted to hear Uncle Max's voice. "Maybe we should call him."

Alfie barked to let her know calling was a good idea.

She found a phone in a kiosk outside a minimart. When she pulled coins out of her pocket, she found the receipt with Corliss's phone numbers. The woman who didn't have money for taxis had spent three dollars for a box of get-well cards at the dollar store to give to people who needed cheering up.

Chancy pictured Uncle Max in his chair, the newspaper open in his lap as she punched in the number. The phone rang and she could see him setting the paper aside. Flipping down the footrest. Rocking on the edge of the seat, one, two, three times before pushing himself up with a grunt. The phone rang again and she heard him call out, "Hold your horses, dang it. I'm coming." Another ring, as he ambled into the dining room and reached for the receiver.

"Hello?"

"Uncle Max?"

"Chancy, where are you? I've been worried."

"Alfie and I are walking. I wanted to call and tell you I'll be . . . home in a little while."

"You're a good girl for letting me know. How about chili for supper?"

"Sounds *bueno*."

"Is that a joke?" he asked.

"Yep."

His laugh crackled like static on the phone. "Okay, then. Hurry home."

"I will."

She would.

Chapter 16

By the time another week passed, not only did Max have trouble remembering why he'd ever wanted to drive to the big auto garage in the sky, but he couldn't imagine getting along without Chancy. She had dropped out of nowhere to give him a reason to get up in the morning. An excuse to remember the past without pain. She was the daughter Hanna had always wanted. The granddaughter they'd envied among their cronies. Sometimes the too-wise, too-tender girl did not seem real at all, but a perfect figment of his lonely imagination.

She was no spoiled, rebellious teen. She had suffered, but her spirit had somehow survived, and Max wanted to live long enough to see her blossom into the woman he knew she could be. Failing that, he willed his heart to continue beating until her emotional scars healed like those on her arms. Irony being ever-present, now that he had the desire to live, his body—and perhaps his mind—seemed to be failing fast.

One recent night Max had awakened in the dark hours before dawn. The painful urge to urinate pushed him toward the bathroom like a steam shovel. He swung his feet out of bed, careful not to step on Alfie. The dog wasn't sleeping on the rug, and Max's heart tripped and stumbled. He panicked for a moment, unable to shake off the confusion. Hanna was gone. Alfie was gone. He was alone. He didn't remember the old dog dying. Had he dreamed it? No, he'd dreamed of his father's funeral. The teaching sisters had swooped in to cart him off to the orphanage, just as Ms. Wooten wanted to force him into a court-ordered nursing home.

Increasingly frequent memory gaps could be bridged during daylight hours, or hidden. In the dark they stretched like a bottomless abyss waiting to suck him down, make him disappear. Thinking straight was as urgent as the need to pee. Max's chest tightened with fear as he stumbled into the bathroom, only to find reality in the night-light's glow. His hands shook with relief and he fumbled with his pajamas. The sink gleamed; the towels were fresh. Chancy had placed a lavender-scented deodorizer in the outlet. Because of her, everything was all right. Alfie was healthier than ever, fit from long walks he took with her, and wisely slept in her room now. He knew she needed his reassuring company more than Max did.

Because of Chancy, Jenny and Adam Hamilton dropped by most days. She had pried open Max's tough shell so others could get to the tender meat inside. Adam would never admit it, but he idolized the girl, like a younger brother idolized an older sister. In response to his questions about their trips to the park and around town, Chancy said they talked a little. Max suspected Adam did most of the talking. Chancy was better at listening.

He flushed the commode and washed his hands. The man in the mirror was so old. Hanna had made him feel invincible, but she was gone now and that was his mortality staring back at him. Each beat of his leaky heart swept him closer to the end. When he climbed back into bed, his frail body shivered under the covers.

The heart doctor's patient coordinator had called to chide him about missing the appointment the hospital had arranged. He'd forgotten about it. Or maybe he'd chosen to forget. He didn't want to have his eighty-three-year-old chest cracked open. Was that a sign of a failing brain? Maybe counting on a scarred and scared little girl to help him live his remaining days was proof of incompetence.

No. That was pure selfishness.

Max wasn't much help with heavy lifting and couldn't climb a stepladder, but Chancy's enthusiasm for housecleaning more than made up for his shortcomings. Late one afternoon, she was finishing up in the dining room. She'd washed the inside of the windows and wiped the sills. Knocked down cobwebs with the broom and swept the wood floors. Using the hose attachment on the old-fashioned vacuum cleaner, she'd sucked the dust off the heavy drapes, and between the two of them, they'd dragged the Persian rug out to the clothesline. Laughing and coughing at the same time, they'd beaten every speck of lung-clogging dirt out of it.

She'd climbed onto a chair to remove all one hundred and forty-eight dangling crystals from the chandelier over the table. Once the little jewels had soaked clean in the ammonia mixture he showed her how to prepare, she had dried and carefully rehung each one. Now they sparkled over the gleaming dining room table like gemstones.

"I love the smell." Chancy finished rubbing the sideboard with furniture polish and leaned over the surface, breathing deeply.

"That stuff?" Max looked up from the couch where he was stacking yellowed newspapers in a box. "Fake lemon."

"This is how clean is supposed to smell."

"You really made that sideboard shine. Hanna would be proud. It came down through her family, you know. Heirloom."

"I thought it looked old."

"Been around a hundred years or more."

She laid her cheek on the top and stretched her arms along the wide walnut expanse as though hoping to hear a whisper from the past. "I can feel its heart, but I can't hear its voice. Tell me the story."

Max stopped folding papers. The girl had a way of looking at things that made the old world seem fresh. "Well, let's see now. According to Hanna, her grandmother had that piece shipped to Indian territory—all the way from a German furniture maker's shop in Chicago. By train. Traveled from the railhead to Wenonah on a mule-drawn freight wagon. Must have cost a fortune in those days. Not the most practical thing Libby McLean ever bought."

"Beautiful things *are* practical," Chancy said. "People need pretty things like they need air."

"Miz Libby would agree with you. As the story goes, before the sideboard was even uncrated a rich cattleman offered her triple what she paid for it."

"And she said no."

Max chuckled. "According to family legend, what she actually said was, 'Sir, there is not enough tea in Shanghai to tear this artful piece from my hands!'"

"I don't know what a sideboard is used for, but I know that feeling."

"What feeling?"

"Furniture joy. I never had anything this . . . permanent. I always wanted to live in the rooms I saw in magazines and furniture store windows."

"I never took you for someone who cared about having a lot of things."

"Not a *lot* of things," she clarified. "Joyful things."

Max had never looked for joy in furniture, but what Chancy said made him think. Slabs of wood, unremarkable and ordinary, crafted into turned legs and doors adorned with carved leaves. Transformed. Something rough and plain made beautiful. There *was* joy in that. He'd been transformed too. A rough, self-taught orphan had been forged into a professor by education and the fire of life.

Chancy rubbed her hand over the gleaming wood. "Touching something that a long-ago lady loved is like reaching back through time. Almost like I know her."

"Maybe that's why antiques appeal to folks," he said.

"All memories don't have to be bad." The wonder of discovery often underscored Chancy's words. "Some can be good."

"Oh, memories should all be good. Better to forget the bad." Hanna had helped him do that. Maybe bad memories were coming back at night now because she was no longer there to keep them away.

"What did she look like?" Chancy asked.

"Who?"

"Libby."

"Ah, yes. The plucky Elizabeth Wheelwright McLean. Staunch champion of Oklahoma statehood. Tell you what. Once we're done in here, I'll dig out more pictures and you can see for yourself."

"I'd like that."

A little later Max stood in the arched doorway and surveyed their efforts. "We performed a minor miracle in here, but something still isn't right."

Chancy looked around. "Did I miss something?"

"What is your honest opinion of this wallpaper?" Though faded, the colors were still dark and dreary. Wine red paper splashed with overblown magnolia blossoms linked by twining green leaves. Monster flowers that belonged in a science-fiction movie about man-eating plants.

"It's okay, I guess."

"No, it's not. It's hideous. Hanna thought so too. But she ordered it from a small sample. We paid plenty to have it hung. Changing it would have taken too much effort, so we learned to live with the ugliness."

Chancy's shoulder lifted in a characteristic shrug. "After a while, you stop seeing what's really there and see only what you want it to be."

"Exactly!" He never ceased to be impressed by her insight. In some ways she was much older than her years. Or maybe she'd just lived through more than a child should have.

"Hmmm." She turned in a tight circle, assessing. "The wallpaper makes the room dark."

"Dark as a cave," he agreed. "Do you know about blind albino fish?"

"No."

"A rare species that lives in the deepest, darkest waters in the depths of caverns. Through years of evolution, they have lost their eyes and their color because they no longer need them."

"So, they swim around in the dark," she said, "thinking the light went out in the world."

"That's right." When had the light gone out in Chancy's world? What would it take to make it shine again? "I feel like a blind albino fish in here. We need to do something."

"Like what?"

Max worked up a corner of the paper with his thumb. He'd paid the paperhangers a premium price to prep the walls correctly, making the paper easy to remove. Until today he'd never felt the need to put their work to the test. When he'd loosed a sizable square, he grasped the edge in both hands and gave a firm jerk, yanking a long strip off the wall.

"Uncle Max! What are you doing?"

"Stepping into the light."

"You messed up the paper. We can't fix that."

"Good riddance. No going back now. I fear we have no choice but to pull down every last strip of this woebegone paper. I say we paint the walls a nice color. What do you suggest?"

"Green?"

"Ah, but what shade of green?" He pulled down another strip. "Lime, hunter, pine? Sea foam, mint, sage? Ours is a green planet and there are a staggering number of shades in the world."

"How about lighter than broccoli, but darker than celery."

He laughed at the image, already seeing another transformation. "Yes. I think you hit the nail on the head. Don't just stand there. Start ripping."

"The room will definitely look brighter." She grimaced and shot him a dicey look. "Okay, if you're sure." She loosened a strip and tugged it down.

"And less like the bottom of a cavern." He grunted and pulled beside her.

"It'll be a big change."

"I'm ready for a change, the bigger the better." Nothing stayed the same. Time couldn't stand still. Failure to adapt was death. Basic law of evolution. Clinging to the past left no opportunity to embrace the future.

Adam came over when school was out. "Yipes! What's going on in here?"

"Work." Chancy removed pictures from the wall and continued stripping paper.

Max directed her to fill the household bucket with warm water and grab sponges from the pantry. They would need to remove the sizing from the walls before painting. Adam climbed the stepladder and loosened strips near the ceiling. Working as a team, they soon made the monster flowers history. Adam and Chancy raced to see who could fill the most nail holes with spackling compound. They were ready to paint.

"Boy, did we make a mess." Adam voiced everyone's opinion.

"No problem. Cleaning is my specialty." Chancy proved her claim by pressing a black trash bag into Adam's hands. "You stripped it. You stuff it."

Once they'd gotten rid of the paper debris, she directed Adam to vacuum while she dusted.

Max pulled the telephone book from the sideboard and handed it to Chancy. "Look up painting contractors."

"Can't we paint it ourselves?" She seemed genuinely disappointed.

"It's a big job. Living room and dining room. I don't know if I'm up to that much painting."

"I'll do it." Chancy's quiet statement sounded more like a plea for confidence than an offer.

"I'll help." Adam jumped right in. "School's out soon and I'll have plenty of time."

Max returned the directory to the sideboard. "I hope you two aren't taking too big a bite off the biscuit." He grinned as comprehension washed over Chancy's pale face.

The children's energy lifted Max's spirits but soon exhausted him. Chancy insisted he go back to boxing old newspapers while they finished cleaning. She asked him to tell stories while he stacked, and he chose his favorite subject: Hanna. He'd waited four long years to ask her for a first date and then had taken her dancing to show off the jitterbug steps he'd learned in smoky USO clubs.

"Can you show me how to jitterbug?"

Adam's question made Max laugh. "Do you have nine-one-one on speed dial?"

Chancy baited the boy. "You? Dance? I'd like to see that."

Adam pushed back the rug with fake indignation and demonstrated some amazing moves he called break dancing. "Try that!"

Chancy refused the challenge. "No, thanks. I like my bones too much."

The give-and-take of her conversation had improved. Max could thank Adam's friendly boisterousness for that. The boy would be a fine man who would treat women with the same respect he showed his mother. How had a childless widower lucked into having two children in his life?

"Let's get some music going." Max suddenly had a yen for Glenn Miller. The needle dropped and the first stirring bars of "String of Pearls" crackled to life. The wailing saxophone filled him with that old toe-tapping urge, and he allowed himself to be coerced into demonstrating a few prizewinning steps.

"Uncle Max and Aunt Hanna won dance contests," Chancy told Adam.

"Cool! Let me try." Gawky but game, Adam stood alongside Max to copy his movements. "C'mon, Chancy."

Adam reached for her hand but she drew back and folded her arms. "I'd rather watch."

Adam had no such inhibitions and demonstrated what he'd learned.

"Not bad for a beginner," Max said. "Let me give you a piece of advice, son. Learn to dance and you'll have to fight off the girls with a stick."

"Especially spastic monkey girls who need a partner." Chancy's comment was serious but made everyone laugh anyway.

After Adam left, Chancy returned Hanna's silver tea service to the sideboard. Max had taught her to buff it with a polishing cloth, and she'd painstakingly removed every speck of tarnish as though scrubbing the silver so intensely would remove the blight from her life. Still dissatisfied with her little tabletop tableau, she placed a crystal vase at the opposite end. She fetched a framed wedding portrait from the bookcase in the living room.

"We'll have to cover everything before you paint."

"I know. I just want to see how things will look." She placed the picture in front of the vase. "You were handsome."

He chuckled. "A regular heartthrob." His looks had almost been a barrier between him and Hanna McLean. On their second date she had told him she wasn't sure she could date a man who was prettier than her. He'd laughed, but for the first time in his life he'd wished for bigger ears, a weaker chin, or a crooked nose. When she branded him "too good to be true," he'd told her not to worry. Once she got to know him, she'd realize how far he was from perfect.

The phonograph needle reached the end of the album, and Max lifted the arm. "How do you like the Andrews Sisters? Pretty tame compared to music today, huh?"

"Their happy music makes me feel like I'm full of fizzy bubbles inside," Chancy said.

"How about some Count Basie? I got Benny Goodman too. Enough music to make us feel good all day."

"One O'Clock Jump" spun out of the turning vinyl disk, and Max noticed Chancy swaying to the rhythm as she made a final adjustment to the sideboard arrangement. She stepped back to admire her work.

"How does it look?"

Max shoved the last box of discarded newspapers to the front door for pickup. Jenny had offered to haul the papers off to the recycling center since the school paper drive was over.

"You have an artist's eye," he told her. "The place feels alive again."

She went still as though feeling the room awaken around her. "It's breathing."

Chancy was right about beauty being oxygen for the soul. Max didn't want to think about tomorrow or next week. Today was enough. "I feel like I'm breathing again too."

Chancy was perched atop a ladder washing windows outside the house. They accomplished a lot in the last few days. She and Uncle Max had taxied to the home center and picked out paint. Dusty Laurel was the color of a new spring leaf. Uncle Max had deferred to her and she'd taken her time, determined to select the perfect color. Tomorrow was the last day of school, and she and Adam had made plans to start painting right away.

He hadn't been over to visit since the construction crew's trucks had pulled out a few days before. The big Dumpster was gone from the Hamiltons' driveway, and the house that had once vibrated with the shrill blast of nail guns and the mechanical buzz of drills had fallen oddly silent. She'd walked over earlier to see what was going on, but no one had answered. The muffled sound of raised voices upstairs made her stomach tighten in dread. Life with B.J. was one chaotic storm after another, and Chancy worried that Tom's illness was unraveling the Hamiltons' lives.

The old need to escape conflict had driven her back to Uncle Max's house, where the only conflict was what to have for lunch and the loudest noise was the ticking clock.

She moved to the next window and replayed the last time she'd seen Jenny. On Saturday they'd had Adam and his mother over for a spaghetti lunch. Uncle Max had had the bright idea to create an Italian trattoria atmosphere in the dining room. He'd explained what that meant as Chancy spread a red-and-white-checked cloth on the table. The old green wine bottle he found in the pantry was fat with ancient multicolored wax. A fresh candle had flickered throughout the meal. No one understood a word of the Italian folk songs playing softly on the turntable, but Uncle Max said that when the spaghetti sauce came out of a jar, the music had to be authentic. Once during the meal, Jenny had excused herself to go to the bathroom, and Chancy had glimpsed a sparkle of tears in her eyes.

When she came back to the table, she was her old self again. Happy and funny. Jenny's hidden tears made Chancy think maybe she also had a secret hurt she couldn't reveal.

Uncle Max insisted Jenny take a plate home for Tom, and they said good-bye on the porch.

"You two are so cute together," Jenny said. "I still can't believe how well everything worked out." When she gave Uncle Max a hug, Chancy pretended to play with Alfie. Jenny's next words splashed her with new fear. "Seems like such a lucky coincidence that your summer plans changed right when Max needed help most."

Jenny suspected something. Maybe she had cried because she was sorry she had to call Ms. Wooten back to investigate. Uncle Max said do-gooders always stuck together.

No. She'd been careful. No one knew. The old Chancy was a paper doll from which Uncle Max had helped her trim all the bad parts. She'd locked the bit of leftover goodness, the part Corliss had seen that day in the diner, safely inside an imaginary heart-shaped necklace like Jenny's.

"Oh, no. No luck about it." Uncle Max knew what was real, even if Chancy didn't always. She had relaxed, a little, when he said, "Hanna said coincidence is just the Lord's way of remaining anonymous."

The garage door slid up across the street. Adam walked out first and poked along in her direction. Normally, he did everything fast. Skated fast, moved fast, talked fast. He flitted from subject to subject like a drunken bee. Nothing about Adam was slow, but he was moping today. Jenny backed the van into the street, and Chancy tried to get a good look at the man slumped in the front seat. His head rested against the side window. The man with silver in his hair had to be Tom Hamilton.

Jenny called Adam to the driver's side and spoke to him before pulling away. She waved as she drove off, but Adam didn't wave back. He stared after the van, then kicked a small rock skittering into the gutter.

"Need any help?" he asked.

"We only have one ladder."

"Can I hang out till my mom gets home?"

"Sure. Is everything all right?"

"Dad's medicine made him sick, so Mom's taking him to the doctor. I'm gonna say hi to Uncle Max." He banged through the front door. Maybe Jenny had called him back to the van to remind him not to talk too much. To keep the family's troubles in the family. It was hard to keep secrets.

When Adam and Jenny were around, Chancy had to be on her guard every minute. She had to always be "on," Miss Normal Teen, monitoring words and actions for authenticity. Being a carefree girl staying with a beloved godfather for the summer was harder than stripping wallpaper or sorting through clutter. To keep their story straight, she'd started writing down the details and studying them like a script.

Whatever was wrong at the Hamilton house, Uncle Max would cheer Adam up. He liked learning about tools, and the two of them had spent a whole afternoon in the garage building a birdhouse for Jenny. Chancy had taken them a snack of cookies she'd baked and had stayed to listen to some of Uncle Max's war stories. Adam hadn't opened up about his father since the night they ate SOS. Mostly he jabbered about music and movies and video games. Chancy had never had a pesky younger brother, but Adam was qualified for the job.

She scrubbed the grimy windows as Uncle Max had shown her, avoiding streaks by using old newspaper. They had plenty of those. Jenny was trying to convince Adam to spend the summer in Texas with his grandparents, but he told Chancy there was no way he'd leave his mom. They would miss his constant racket, but life would be easier for her and Uncle Max if Adam were out of the picture. Lying to Ms. Wooten had been easy and necessary. Lying to a friend made her stomach hurt.

Adam was back, his hand shading his eyes as he looked up. Faint red stains quirked the corners of his mouth. He'd been hitting Uncle Max's fruit punch again.

"What happened to the construction guys?" she asked.

"Mom sent them away."

"So the kitchen is finished?"

"Nope. A bigger wreck than ever, like everything else."

"So why did they leave?"

"Mom wouldn't say. Man, the sun is bright. Aren't you hot?"

"No."

"What's up with you anyway? You always wear long sleeves and pants." Adam was dressed in his usual baggy shorts and too-big T-shirt. "You're so pale you make Dracula look like a lifeguard."

"I don't want to get sunburned. Ever hear of skin cancer?"

"Ever hear of sunscreen?" He glanced around. "Yard looks like crap."

He was right. When she wasn't working in the garden, she was helping

Max clean the house. They'd forgotten about the grass, but it had not forgotten to grow. "You gonna report us to the neighborhood watch?"

"I could mow it."

"Do you even know how?"

"It's grass. Not rocket scientry," he said in an exaggerated hillbilly accent. "Maybe if ah try reeeaaaallll hard, ah can figger it out."

"Probably." That was what she liked about Adam: He never stayed glum for long.

Uncle Max let Alfie out, and Adam ran around back to play. In a few minutes they returned, rolling in the overgrown grass together. He tossed a fetch stick, but the old dog just stared at him, bored by the concept.

He fetched the stick himself and waved it under the dog's nose. "Hello! Alfie, you're a retriever. Get it? Retriever? Stick? Chasey-chasey!"

Alfie gave her an entreating look to please explain to the short guy why he wouldn't get sucked into that game.

Whatever was going on at home with his father, Chancy thought, *at least Adam had Jenny.* Like all good moms, she'd make sure he didn't get hurt. He complained about her protectiveness, but his protests were those of a little boy stumbling toward manhood. He depended on his mother to clarify his feelings and reassure him that no matter what he did, she loved him anyway. He relied on her especially now that his father was ill. Chancy had seen her young friend angry, resentful, disappointed—spinning from one ragged emotion to another like a compass needle. His mother's love was the true north that always pointed him in the right direction.

Wenonah had shown Chancy what family could be, even when things didn't go right. Corliss hadn't lost faith in Eddie. Jenny gave Adam enough love for two parents. His wife was gone, but Uncle Max's memories fed his spirit, just as food nourished his body. Having a family meant never being alone.

Chancy felt a sense of accomplishment when she finished the front windows. She wasn't worthless. She could do things. Another gift Wenonah had given her. She climbed down the ladder, dumped the plastic pail of grimy water beneath the shrubs and refilled the bucket from the faucet.

Adam bounded up, then danced back to avoid getting his clunky shoes splashed. "So what do you think? Can I mow the yard?"

"I have to ask Uncle Max. Bring the bucket." She folded the ladder and dragged it around back. Adam followed.

"No problemo. I'll ask him myself." He plopped down the pail and clomped up the back steps.

A few minutes later, Chancy heard the lawn mower roar to life. Adam leaned into his work, cutting even swaths through the shade grass. Uncle Max must have given him the famous you-can-do-anything-you-set-your-mind-to speech. She had finished the sunroom windows by the time he killed the engine. He stood below the ladder, his blond curls damp against his scalp, a man-sized sweat stain V-ed across the back of his shirt. He grinned and waved a bill. "Check out the Jackson. Uncle Max paid me twenty big ones."

"Good for you."

"And hey, it's official. I'm the new lawn dude. Twenty dollars a week for twelve weeks. Wow, that's . . ." He paused, his forehead creased in con-centration.

"Some mathlete."

He smirked and kissed the bill. Even when problems arose, he could still have fun because he knew his mother would make things better. Only a child whose security was never in doubt could be so optimistic.

The front door opened and Uncle Max appeared with chilled cans of soda. "Thought you two could use a break."

Adam popped his drink and sprawled on the porch step next to Alfie.

"Yard looks fine, son," Uncle Max said. "All the rain we've had lately made the grass shoot right up. Glad you could mow before it got any taller."

"I couldn't get close to the fence." Adam tried to sound like an old landscaping pro. "Do you have a Weedwacker?"

"In the garage. Have you used one before?"

"No," he admitted with a sheepish grin. "Will you show me?"

"Finish your pop first."

While they drank, Adam told Uncle Max how his mom had hung the new birdhouse in a tree in the backyard. Chancy sat in the swaying wooden porch swing that Hanna had hung herself because she believed women should never rely on men for everything. She lost herself in the simple pleasure of warm sunshine on her face and cold cola bubbling down her throat. There was a special calm in freshly cut grass and chirping insects.

Why did good-hearted people die of horrible diseases while people without hearts lived on? Hanna should be with Max. It no longer seemed strange when he talked to the portrait on the landing. He wasn't crazy, just lonely. Their love was so strong, death had not diminished it. Maybe Chancy was meant to hold the gift of their love close, pressed into the imaginary locket with the good part of herself. Through her, their love would live on, even after Uncle Max was gone.

Chapter 17

C hancy paused at the bank window and frowned at the figures in her savings book.

"Something wrong?" the teller asked.

"I think you made a mistake." She slid the little brown folder across the counter. "You gave me too much money."

The teller punched a keyboard and scanned the computer screen. "No mistake. If you put a hundred and seventy-five dollars in the bank every week, it adds up pretty fast."

"What about this amount?" She pointed to the middle column.

"Oh, that's interest. It's end of the compound period. It's yours, all right. Thanks for banking with First National." She smiled around Chancy. "Next!"

Chancy stashed the bankbook in her new backpack. Four deposits. More than seven hundred dollars. In two more weeks she would be a thousandaire. She had no idea what having so much money would feel like, but she couldn't wait to find out.

"What do you mean, you can't cash this?" The man at the next window sounded surprised. His voice and his impatience were familiar. Eddie Briggs.

"I'm sorry, sir," the teller said pleasantly, "but you don't have an account with us."

"It's a paycheck. It won't bounce."

"Bank policy, sir. You can take it to the bank it's drawn on."

"I can't drive all the way to Oklahoma City. I earned this money. What the hell am I supposed to do?"

"I'm sorry. If you had a checking or savings account, we could honor the check. But otherwise . . ." She looked around him and gave the next customer in line a bear-with-me smile.

"That's bogus! C'mon, lady, give a break. It's no skin off your teeth."

"Sir"—she didn't sound so pleasant now—"that is bank policy. If you'd like to open an account—"

"Just screw it!" Eddie wheeled around and almost bumped into Chancy. She mumbled, "Sorry," and he peered into her face.

"Hey, don't I know you?"

"No. I know your mother."

"Yeah, I remember. Lacey, right?"

"Chancy."

"You look a little young to be one of Mom's friends." Eddie wore navy blue work clothes and new work boots. His shirt was pressed and his pants held a sharp crease. Chancy imagined Corliss standing over an ironing board, pressing out the wrinkles so her son would look nice on the job. "You're not in a nursing home, so how do you know her?"

"From the diner."

"I've seen you, though." Whiskers shadowed his thin face. He had not shaved today. "Are you the one she calls the little heart girl?"

"I might be." Unless Corliss knew more than one.

"You were supposed to teach Mom how to make paper hearts or something, right?"

"She told you?"

"What is it, some big secret?" As though he couldn't imagine his mother having a secret.

"No."

"You got her all excited. She said you didn't call." A fact he seemed to hold against Chancy.

"I've been busy." She and Adam had spent a few days painting the newly stripped walls and waxing the wood floor.

"Whatever!" Eddie slapped the check against his palm. "Can you believe this? Mom's been after me to work, so I get a job and finally earn a paycheck. Now I can't cash it." THE LUBE PLACE was embroidered over one shirt pocket, EDDIE over the other. The blue check he folded and stuffed into the EDDIE pocket was the color of the three little eggs in the robin's nest Chancy had discovered in the garden that morning.

"I have a savings account here," she said.

"So?"

"Maybe that would make a difference to the bank lady."

"Are you kidding me? You'd be willing to guarantee my check?"

"I don't know." *Guaranteeing* was a strong word. "What do I have to do?"

"Let's find out." Eddie stared at the floor while they waited for the teller to count a thick stack of bills for another customer. Her hands moved so fast they were a blur.

"May I help you?" Her smile faded when she looked up and saw that Eddie was back.

"She has an account here." Eddie jerked a thumb toward Chancy, and she slid her passbook toward the teller. "Is that good enough for you?"

The teller glanced uneasily from Eddie to Chancy and back again. "Do you know this man, honey?"

No, but she knew his mother had faith in him. Chancy smiled to inspire confidence. Her own. "Yes."

The teller scanned the figures in the book. "You know if his check isn't honored, the funds will be withdrawn from your account, right?"

"Withdrawn?"

"And you can't access the funds until the check clears. You have enough to cover it, but—"

"Jeez, she gets it." Eddie shifted his weight impatiently. "C'mon, will you? I don't have all day. I gotta get back to work."

"It's okay." Chancy trusted the message in the robins' eggs. The Lube Place wouldn't go bankrupt overnight.

Eddie got his cash, and they stepped out into the blinding sun.

"Wenonah feels hotter than Pittsburgh," Chancy said by way of small talk, "but Uncle Max says it's the humidity that gets you."

"Why'd you do that?" Eddie asked. "You don't know me from Adam."

"I didn't think you were Adam. He's a lot younger." Eddie's puzzled frown meant she'd said something wrong. She waited for her throat to clench with panic, but nothing happened.

"So what are you, a Good Samaritan or something?"

"Your mother was nice to me once."

"That's hard to believe."

"You don't think Corliss is nice?"

He laughed. "I *know* Corliss is nice. She'd give you the shoes off her feet. I mean it's hard to believe you'd do something for me because . . . Never mind." He sniffed and shook his head. "So, thanks, kid. I appreciate it. See you around, huh?" He walked a few steps and turned. "The check won't bounce. You can stop worrying."

"I'm not."

"Well, you look worried."

"No. That's just my regular face."

He finally smiled and his skeptical look softened to amusement. "What planet are you from?"

"Earth." Maybe his question was a joke, but she wasn't taking any chances.

"If you say so." He was still chuckling as he walked away.

The egg-colored check, a clear-as-day sign, wasn't the reason Chancy had helped Eddie. She'd made the offer because of Corliss, who was like the stress rock she'd seen on a counselor's desk once. When he needed to relax, he had rubbed the rock until the tension disappeared. He'd wanted Chancy to try, but no way was she touching his rock. Rocks didn't have magical powers, but some people did. Special people, like Corliss, who had little reason to be happy but were anyway.

Chancy unzipped her backpack and found the receipt with Corliss's phone numbers. She'd memorized them, but kept the paper because of all the threes and sixes and nines. The longer Chancy lied to Adam and to Jenny, two people who had become as close as real family, the more she needed to talk to someone with whom she didn't have to pretend. Someone who could handle the truth and accept who she really was. One more test. She would walk three blocks west. If she found a pay phone on one of those blocks, she would take it as a sign that she was supposed to call today.

She strolled down the street, staying in the shade when she could. She no longer followed the old walking rules to avoid notice. She could amble along, looking in shop windows like any other Wenonah resident. It felt strange not having Alfie trotting beside her, but he was home with Uncle Max, and she was free to do more than window-shop for a change.

She stood outside the kind of clothing store she never would have entered before. One with pouty white mannequins in the window and sales-clerks who wore trendy clothes and too much makeup. She shifted her backpack. Why not? She had money in the bank, cash in her bag. She could buy something if she wanted. No reason to be invisible. She rubbed her arms through the thin fabric. Frequent launderings had made her limited wardrobe clean, but threadbare. She swallowed hard and opened the door.

A skinny girl with a tiny rhinestone in her nose offered to help Chancy find something. When she said, "No, thanks, just looking," the girl went back to the counter and the fashion magazine she'd been flipping through. She seemed to think Chancy belonged in her store.

Chancy browsed the racks of clothing. Forty-five dollars for a shirt? She couldn't spend that much for a single item when she could find real bargains at the Nu 2 Yu thrift shop. When Chancy left the store without buying anything, the rhinestone-nose girl didn't seem surprised. Chancy wanted something nice; it didn't have to be new. By her shopping in secondhand stores operated by charity organizations her money helped people.

Chancy felt at home among Nu 2 Yu's crowded racks and jumbled shelves. Last time she was in the store, she'd reluctantly parted with a couple of Kenny Ray food dollars for socks. Now she had money to spend, and somewhere down the line, another person might benefit from her purchase. She sifted through a stack of jeans and wondered if the Kane Raisers had found their dream in Austin. She liked to think so, and imagined switching on Uncle Max's radio someday, just in time to hear her first benefactor belting out one of his crazy songs.

The friendly volunteer attendant helped Chancy put together several outfits. For less than the price of the fashion store shirt, she got three long-sleeved tops, a pink button-up shirt like Jenny's, a long print skirt, gray slacks, two pairs of jeans, and sandals. Maybe not what the models in *Vogue* were wearing this season, but she felt like an heiress. She would stuff the old gray shirts in Uncle Max's rag box and get rid of a few more reminders.

The old lady attendant wore a name tag. VONCILLE. She took Chancy's money and opened the register. Her fingers were knotted and blue veins ridged the backs of her hands. She wasn't fast like the bank teller, but she would have better stories to tell.

"You have lovely hair, dear." The lady smiled as she counted the change.

"Thank you." Had the bud of good inside her opened up like one of Hanna's dormant flowers, growing until it was visible to others?

Voncille patted her own white cotton candy hair. "Can you believe mine used to be the same color?"

"Yes." Chancy believed a lot of things now. Mostly she believed in possibilities. Before she could pocket the change, she noticed a homemade collection can on the counter. WON'T YOU PLEASE HELP? Amy Brown, Elmwood Elementary kindergartner, needed a bone-marrow transplant. The bald, bright-eyed child beamed from a photocopied picture taped to the side of the can. Not a weak wisp of a smile, but a gap-toothed hundred-watter, her little face full of hope.

Chancy slipped five dollars through the can's slot. Outside, she turned the corner and spotted a phone kiosk in front of the little grocery store across the street. The universe was paying off quickly these days.

"Hello?"

The single word was as flat as a forgotten balloon. Not bouncy with the good cheer Chancy expected from her previous conversations with Corliss. Maybe she'd dialed wrong.

"Hello!" The sagging word stretched thin. Tighter and tighter until the words finally popped. "Who *is* this? If you're looking for Eddie, he's not here. Just leave him alone!"

"It's me. Chancy."

"Who?"

"Chancy Deel."

"The little heart girl? Well, mercy me." At the other end of the line, the words puffed up to the bright, rounded shape of their imaginary talks.

"You gave me your number. Said I could call."

"I sure did. But, honey, I just about gave up on hearing from you."

"I'm sorry I took so long."

"Well, I'm happy you called."

"You are?"

"Sure as Sunday. Hey, I saw that gray cat again the other day."

The little cat's smoky image wound its way between what Chancy planned to say and what actually came out. "How did he look?"

"Fat and sassy. I tried to catch him, but he was too quick for my old legs. He's a wild thing. Living on his own made him spooky and extra slippery. He didn't want to get caught. Probably too late to tame him for a pet."

"Probably."

"I left some of the food you bought, and he scarfed it up, lickety-split."

"I'm glad." Good cat news was another sign that she'd been right to call. "Do you still want me to show you how to make the hearts?"

"Okay, hang on a minute." Corliss covered the mouthpiece, but Chancy heard her coughing. Deep and dusky, a jagged hack that sounded like it had been scraped out of her lungs with a fork. "Sorry. I've been aw-ful phlegmy lately. Can't seem to shake that summer cold. What'd you say again, honey?"

"The pep-me-ups?"

A silent moment ticked by. Chancy imagined Corliss shoving all the important things she had to worry about out of her mind in order to re-member that she had once been interested in weaving paper hearts.

"Oh, sure. I got you now. I was resting when you called. Takes me a spell to wake all the way up. My brain's just like the old gray mare. You

know, ain't what she used to be." She went on before Chancy could interpret. "You bet I'm interested. I bought paper and everything."

"You did?" A honking horn made Chancy lean into the kiosk.

"I didn't know what kind was best, but the clerk at the craft store
pointed me in the right direction. I got all kinds of pretties."

Chancy didn't have a word for how she felt. More than happy. Elated.
Corliss had taken her offer seriously. She had gone out of her way to get
the paper. Spent money. She'd patiently waited for Chancy to call. The
connection had been there all along, planted that first morning in the Tip-
Top. It had been growing quietly, without help, like the tiny, wild Johnny-
Jump-Ups that popped up in unexpected places.

"You still there?" Corliss asked.

"Yes, ma'am." At that moment, she couldn't imagine being anywhere
else. If her instincts about Corliss had been right, maybe she could depend
on other feelings too. And not have to wait for signs. "When do you want
me to teach you about hearts?"

Corliss cleared her throat. "No time like the present. What are you
doing right now?"

"Shopping. I'm on a pay phone in front of a grocery store."

She asked which one and Chancy read the name on the window. "Nu-
way Market."

"Lord, child, that's a hop-skip from here. If you walk down to the
light where Barnhart crosses Twelfth and turn right, it's just five blocks
to Mossy Glen."

"You want me to come now?"

"Why not? I'd offer to pick you up, but Eddie's got the car at work."

"I'll walk." She would tuck her new clothes in her backpack and get
rid of the shopping bag.

"Well, okay, great. I'll put the kettle on." Corliss paused. "I'm gonna
see you soon, ain't I, honey?"

"Soon as I can get there."

"You hurry up, then. I can't wait. You're the best thing that's happened
to me in a month of Sundays."

Chancy hung up and dialed Uncle Max to tell him she might be gone a couple of hours. He said in that case maybe he'd lie down for a while. He didn't ask about her plans, showing faith in her, like Corliss's faith in Eddie.

"Are you feeling all right?" Earlier she had caught him pressing his fist against his chest with a pained look. When she expressed concern, he said he just had a touch of heartburn.

"I'm fine. You have a good time."

Chancy smiled all the way to Mossy Glen Trailer Park. She'd never been on anyone's list of best things that could happen.

"Come on in here." Corliss held open the trailer door. "Make yourself at home. Oh, Lord, let me get that stuff out of your way." She scooped a pile of clean boy underwear off the couch. "Sorry the place is such a mess. Finally trained Eddie to do his own laundry. Folding is next on the lesson plan."

"I don't need much room."

"Since Eddie's been staying with me, I can't seem to keep up with things the way I once did. You get used to doing for yourself and then wham! There's another person to pick up after. I like to rest on my day off, but sitting puts me behind on chores."

Chancy sat on the couch. Corliss looked different. Her pale face was as gray as her roots. "Are you sure you have time to make hearts today?"

"Heck, hon, I got nothing *but* time." Corliss eased into a lumpy recliner. "And a trailer full of clocks that don't run."

Silent clocks covered almost every wall of the dark trailer. Chancy tried out something Adam might say. "I guess they prove time really can stand still."

"There ya go!" Corliss laughed herself into a coughing fit. "I got to where I didn't hear 'em anymore. They were just background noise to keep me company. Eddie hated the racket so he took all the batteries out."

"How'd you get so many?"

"Picked one up here and there. Garage sales and such. Finally had to stop 'cause I ran out of places to put 'em. Last winter when I turned sixty-two, I counted my clocks. Guess how many I have?"

"Sixty-two?" Most were cheap plastic with animals and cartoon characters on the faces. A small clock wreathed in gaudy orange blossoms sat on a shelf over the TV. With each tick a tiny fake hummingbird moved silently in and out of a flower.

"Right! You must be psychic."

"I never knew there were so many different kinds."

"Oh, yeah. That was the fun, you know. To see what I could find next. Before Eddie shut 'em up, they went off every hour on the hour. They sound like trains, foghorns, cats, birds, you name it. That one there plays 'It's a Small World.' Guess you're proof of that."

"Of what?"

"That it's a small world. Eddie called and said you helped him cash his first paycheck. Next thing I know, you're calling me. Small world. He was looking for a reason to quit, so thanks for helping him get his money. Maybe he'll stick with the job now."

"He doesn't like what he does?"

"Calls it grunt work. Eddie's no mechanic, but he's taking a stab at gainful employment. We don't know exactly what he is yet, but at least he's bringing home a paycheck to help with expenses."

"That's a start."

"When he was a little boy, he wanted to be a policeman, but he lost that dream somewhere." Corliss's smile was sad. "I keep telling him the Lube Place is a step in the right direction. He works the evening shift. Leaves when I get home from the diner; that way we're not under each other's feet all the time. We're sharing the car until he saves up for his own." Corliss clambered out of her chair. "Mercy, where are my manners? It's hot out there. You must be thirsty from your walk. Can I get you something to drink? Pepsi? Tea?"

"Water, please?"

"You'd think a career waitress would know to offer water." Corliss tut-tutted as she filled a tall glass of ice at the tap.

"The Tip-Top must be a nice place to work," Chancy said.

"As greasy spoons go, it ain't bad. I can still be a waitress there. Most places the job's been upgraded to *server*." She shrugged. "Describes the work better but sounds a little hoity. I like people, so slinging hash suits me."

"Have you always been a waitress?" Chancy thought the job was complicated. So much to remember and carry.

"Pretty much. I bet all the coffee I poured in my lifetime would fill Lake Okalala. Speaking of the lake, Eddie caught a nice mess of catfish the other day. Still got some in the freezer, if you can stay for supper."

"Maybe some other time."

Corliss sank back into her recliner and propped her thin white legs on the footrest. Her ankles were as swollen as the fat sausages Uncle Max cooked for breakfast. "Me in my housedress with no powder! You'll have to excuse me for looking such a fright."

Her pallor was more worrisome than frightful. "I think your housedress is pretty."

Corliss patted hair that had been flattened on one side by her nap. "Enough about the Bride of Frankenstein. Let's talk about you."

"Not much to tell." Eventually, maybe. Corliss was easy to talk to. So was Jenny, but in a different way. Jenny thought Chancy was a regular girl and talked to her about regular girl things. Corliss would understand troubles.

"I guess you've been keeping all right." Corliss smiled expectantly.

"Keeping what?"

"Yourself."

"I'm staying with Uncle Max."

"I didn't know you had relatives in town." Corliss pulled a crocheted afghan over her lap.

The swampy air conditioner gave Chancy a chill too. Wanting to tell the truth was a good goal, but breaking the living-a-lie habit took guts. And more trust than she had yet mustered. She made a deal with the universe: No lies this time in exchange for Eddie not quitting his job today. "Just Uncle Max."

"I've seen a lot in my day, honey, and can usually peg people pretty good. I would've sworn you were hitchin' that morning you blew into the Tip-Top. Looked like you'd been on the road a while."

"I had been."

"Reckon you got folks looking for you."

"No one misses me. I promise." Most of the time Chancy tried not to think about B.J., but sometimes late at night she wished she could be more than a black hole in her mother's mind. She'd tried so many times, so many ways to make things different between them. Nothing had worked.

"I wouldn't be too sure about that. Eddie was gone a long time and I missed him every day. If you're in trouble and there's anything I can do to help, just say the word."

"I've been on my own awhile. I'm not in trouble."

"I guess you're sure about that."

"Positive."

"Just about everybody has family."

"Uncle Max is my only real family." At least the kind that mattered. The kind who cared. It felt good to say the words aloud. She meant nothing to B.J. Never had. But she meant the world to Maxwell Boyle. He hadn't said so, but he didn't have to.

"I know a lot of folks in town." Corliss didn't press the way most people did. Instead she eased the door open a little more each time she spoke. "I might know your uncle if you told me his last name."

"Boyle."

"Max Boyle, you say?" Corliss mulled that over.

"He taught at the college for a long time."

"Oh, sure, the professor! That's him. Hanna was his wife."

"Yes."

"I was sorry to hear she passed. Read her obit in the paper. Such a nice lady. Always had a smile, even on her bad days. I clipped the piece out if you want to read it. Got it right here." She opened a drawer in the table beside her chair and sifted through the contents until she found a thick envelope.

"I cut out a lot of obits." She pulled a folded piece of newsprint from the stack and handed it to Chancy. "Some days it feels like everyone I know is dying."

"Thanks." She started to read, but when Corliss told her she could take it home and read it later, she placed it in her backpack. "You knew Hanna?"

"We met at the oncology clinic. I used to drive my little neighbor lady to chemo appointments. The procedure takes a few hours, so we'd all sit around and visit. Hanna was the cheerleader of the group. Always positive, keeping spirits up. She could tell a good joke, and she loved flowers. Only time I saw her get down was when she had to stop working outside. She was so worried about that garden. She said Max had a black thumb."

Chancy knew what that meant. Uncle Max had said it before. "I'm not a very good gardener either," she said, "but I've been trying to put the garden back the way it was before she got sick."

"She'd be proud to know that."

"Did you meet Uncle Max too?"

"Sure. He'd come with Hanna. Sit right there the whole time unless he was jumping up to do something for her. Sweet old couple. And funny as all get-out. Big kidders. You could just see the love shining out of both of them. My friend said I could drop her off and pick her up later, but I always stayed. Hanna had a way of making people feel good about themselves."

An old man's memories of his extraordinary wife had made Chancy feel good too, but she'd wondered if Hanna was really as amazing as Max thought. Now she knew.

Corliss eased into her next comment. "Honey, Hanna told me they didn't have any relatives. Said it was just her and Max. She fretted over how he'd get along without her. I'm sure she would have mentioned a niece."

Chancy hesitated, considered, admitted: "Max isn't my real uncle."

"More of an honorary title, then."

"We're . . . friends." They meant more to each other than the simple word implied, but Chancy was at a loss to explain. He'd once called their relationship symbiotic, but it had grown beyond being mutually beneficial. "He needed help, and I needed a place to stay, so I'm working for him."

"Like a home health aide?"

"Something like." That was easy. If Corliss accepted a little truth, she could handle more.

"You seem awful young to be working. You ought to be out having fun."

"I'm almost sixteen. Old enough to be responsible."

Corliss studied her for a moment. "Yes, I guess you are. I'm sure you're a big help to Max. Give him my regards."

"Do you want to make the hearts now?"

"Where is my head today? You didn't come out here to chew the fat. I put the supplies on the kitchen table. Paper and scissors and pencils and glue. I wasn't sure what all you needed."

Chancy sat at the small dinette and Corliss showed her the paper she'd purchased. In addition to colorful construction paper, she'd selected a variety of patterned parchment-type paper, marbled and swirled and watermarked and textured. Foil and matte and high-gloss finishes. Rainbow colors. Pastels. Dark jewel tones. Chancy had never seen such beautiful paper and knew she had to buy some too. She'd used construction paper when she had it, but mostly she'd made do with whatever scraps were available, recycling what others considered trash. She couldn't wait to create designs with Corliss's wondrous paper.

"First you make a template. Do you have any lightweight cardboard?"

"Would an index card do?"

"That'll work. We can tape two or more together if we want to make bigger hearts." Chancy drew a template with markings for the strips and showed Corliss how to cut two pieces of paper in different colors. Then she wove the strips together and secured the ends with a dot of glue. "If you want to hang them, you can punch a hole with a fat needle for string."

"I have yarn. And fishing line." Corliss didn't seem so tired now. "Oh, that's pretty. And they aren't hard to make at all. Where'd you learn?"

"In art . . . class." She'd almost said *therapy,* but that was part of Chancy's old life. Not this one. Creating hearts had been the first thing she'd ever done well. The only way she'd known how powerful it felt to please others.

"Let's use construction paper for tray favors," Corliss said. "We'll save the good paper for room decorations for the nursing home residents."

"Okay." Chancy traced around the small template, filling a sheet of purple construction paper with the design, and passed it to Corliss.

"We can't make all these today," she said. "To save time, how about you take half the paper home with you? When we get a sizable pile, we'll deliver them together."

"You'd trust me with your paper?"

"Why wouldn't I?"

"You don't know me. What if I . . . disappear with it?"

"And do what? Sell my construction paper on the black market?" Corliss laughed. "I know you won't let me down. Now, let me see what you're doing there. I've never been the crafty type, so I don't know how good I'll be at this. I'll give it a try." She made the first cautious cut.

Chancy remembered what Max had told her when she'd made the same promise. *Trying is all I'll ever ask of you.*

Chancy's fingers flew, cutting heart shapes in many colors. She imagined the faces of the unknown people her efforts would touch and felt their smiles warm her own heart as she bent to the task.

Chapter 18

After her visit with Corliss, Chancy knew it was time to bring her two worlds closer together. Corliss had seemed to understand the lies she and Uncle Max had told Ms. Wooten.

"Do what you gotta do, honey," she'd said. "You think that little gray cat we've been feeding would still be running free if he turned himself in down at the pound? No, he would not. Sometimes secrets need to be kept."

And Chancy was certain Corliss would keep hers. While they made hearts, she revealed more about her time with Uncle Max. Saying the words had been a profound relief, like the feeling when a bad headache finally went away. Chancy regretted that they had to keep lying to Jenny and Adam, but Corliss's easy acceptance made her think that maybe someday she could be herself with them too.

She showed Uncle Max the paper Corliss had given her and explained their project. He listened quietly, without speaking or smiling, and she was afraid she'd done something that hurt his feelings.

"How is it you know this woman again?"

Chancy told him Corliss was the first person she'd met in town and that the waitress's generosity and kindness had convinced her that Wenonah might be different.

"If it hadn't been for Corliss," she said, "I would have never met you."

His worried frown smoothed into a smile. "Then I probably need to send this lady a bouquet of thank-you flowers."

"She knows you too, from the oncology clinic. That was another sign it was okay to tell her things."

"She was a patient?"

"No. She drove a neighbor in for treatment."

"Sorry, but that time's a blur. Wait a minute. I remember now. Little woman, big laugh?"

"That's Corliss." And she wouldn't have to be a faraway friend anymore.

"Sure you don't mind staying alone, Uncle Max?" Chancy washed the lunch plates and put them away. "I don't have to go to the movie."

"Yes, you do. Adam needs a friend right now. Inviting you to a movie is his way of reaching out." Max longed for an antacid to relieve the weight in his chest, but if he opened the bottle before Chancy left, she would insist on changing her plans. "I'll get out another box of old pictures, and we can go through them later. That was a good idea you had about writing info on the back. Should have done that years ago."

Alfie settled at Max's feet and whimpered under his breath. Alfie was good at sensing when Max was under the weather. The old traitor was trying to squeal on him.

"Something wrong, boy?" Chancy didn't miss a trick. "Do you think he's feeling all right, Uncle Max? He didn't eat much this morning."

"He's fine." The dog was just big on melodrama. "Pretty shirt you're wearing. I'm glad you finally broke down and went shopping. I was going to ask Jenny to take you to the mall."

"I don't think she has time to shop these days."

"Haven't seen her much this week. What's going on over there?"

"The remodeling guys left a big mess. Jenny calls her kitchen 'the ruins of Pompeii,' whatever that is."

He explained. "So you and Adam have been helping clean up?"

"Just dust and debris. The kitchen's not really usable."

"Did she say why the crew quit?"

"Only that the remodeling plans were on hold." A horn honked in the driveway. Chancy draped the dish towel over the hook and hurried to the back door. She gave Alfie a quick pat and blew Max a kiss. Something new. Airborne kisses were a way for Chancy to express affection without physical contact. Even after so much time, she shied away from being touched.

Once she was gone, Max sighed heavily and shook his finger at Alfie. "You mind your own business, you hear?" He found his stash of antacids in the cupboard and chomped down three. Tinkling wind chimes drew him to the window, but when he looked out, there was no breeze. Hanna was calling him to the garden. She had to be pleased with all Chancy had accomplished. A fat robin flew out of the lilacs. Chancy had been excited about the nest she'd found. The robin perched on the edge of the birdbath, its head cocked to one side. The shallow water had evaporated in the sun. Chancy would fill it when she returned, but why make the little mother wait for a cooling bath?

With Alfie at his side, Max opened the garden gate. The crushing weight that bore down on him too often these days had lifted. He twisted the faucet and tugged on the hose Chancy kept neatly coiled in an empty whiskey barrel planter. He recalled how surprised Hanna had been the day he'd set up the birdbath. She had loved getting—and giving—unexpected gifts. The old hose leaked in several places and should be replaced. Max stared at the water dripping innocuously into the grass and pressed his hand to his heart. A little leakage was no big deal.

The robin was splashing happily when Max went inside to escape the heat. He picked up *The Secret Garden*, determined to finish reading it. He'd tackled it at bedtime but had always fallen asleep before getting very far. He wasn't sure why Chancy identified with a whey-faced English orphan girl, but she'd asked anxiously about his reading progress a few times. He looked forward to discussing the story as they had *Oliver Twist*.

He'd read four chapters in the slim volume when Jenny showed up.

"Chancy suggested I stop by and check out the new paint," she said with wide-eyed innocence.

More likely Chancy had asked Jenny to make sure he was still ticking. He played along and invited Jenny in. "What do you think?"

She oohed and aahed over the transformation in the living and dining rooms. "This looks wonderful, Max. Such a difference. Who picked the paint color?"

"Chancy."

"She has a great eye." Jenny adjusted the old drapes. The faded gold color no longer looked out of place. "Taking down the wallpaper made it so much brighter in here."

"So bright I can see how ratty this furniture is." Chancy, who knew a thing or two about camouflage, had tried to disguise the ugliness by draping an afghan here, tossing a pillow there. Max wasn't blind. The massive eighties tweed furniture looked as out of place as horse apples on velvet.

"You have some nice pieces," Jenny said. "The Stickley rocker. The Mission-style tables. Are those real Tiffany lamps?"

"Yes. Hanna won a bidding war at an estate auction to get those. Maybe Chancy and I will go to Bradley's and pick out a new sofa and chairs."

Jenny gave him a puzzled look, as though a man who was too old to buy green bananas probably shouldn't invest in new furniture. He offered her a cup of coffee and they sat at the table in the breakfast area. She noticed the boxes of vinyl tile stacked in the corner and asked what refurbishing task he planned to tackle next.

"Not me," he said. "Chancy. When we were at the home store, she talked me into tiling the kitchen. Big black-and-white squares. Peel and stick."

"You're going to do it yourselves?"

"We took a free class at the store, but this is Chancy's project. These knees force me into a strictly supervisory role."

"A class, huh? Chancy's parents have allowed her to be self-sufficient. I guess because of their careers and travel, she's had to grow up fast."

"I'm all for letting her take on big jobs. The more children do on their own, the more initiative they develop. My theory why thirty-year-old adults won't move out of the house? Their parents never let them stand on their own feet when they were young." Max gave Jenny his sagest look. Maybe she'd take the hint and loosen her hold on Adam a little. She meant well but did too much. If she didn't let the boy try his wings, he would never learn to fly.

"But laying down tile?"

"It's all about math, you know. Once you calculate the cuts and get the first one down, the rest is easy," Max said. "We could sure use Adam's help. He's a whiz at math."

"He could use the experience in case we have to learn to lay tile in our own kitchen."

"Chancy told me Matiska's crew pulled out. Creative differences?"

She stared into her cup. "I had to let them go."

"You weren't pleased with Russ's work?"

"Money issues. I don't know when Tom will be able to go back to work, and we have to tighten our belts. I'd hoped . . . His partner's keeping the pot boiling. For now. Our investment income will cover bare necessities for a while longer, but I needed to make serious budget cuts."

"Sorry to hear that. You know I have money put away—"

Jenny looked up, and her eyes filled with tears. "Maxwell Boyle, if you think I would consider taking your savings to pay for something as frivolous as granite countertops, you do not know me very well."

"A loan maybe?"

"No! We have enough trouble meeting our obligations already."

"Maybe compromise on the countertops?"

"Believe me, my expectations have been scaled way back. I'd settle for a stove and sink that work."

"That shouldn't be too expensive."

"The subfloor and new drywall are in. That's it. It'll still cost plenty, even for the no-bells-or-whistles version." She drew a sharp breath. "Silly me for thinking a dream kitchen would make everything right."

"So you're sacrificing the kitchen to punish yourself?" Max speculated.

"No. To save money. I don't know what else to do. Tom's always taken care of our finances. He's a good provider. All I ever wanted to do was to take care of my family. Now I've let them down."

"You do plenty. How's Tom feeling?"

"He had a bad reaction to some medication and refused to take it anymore." Her voice caught. "His depression got worse. I had to give him an ultimatum before he'd see the doctor again. At least he's on something new now. I hated destroying two hundred dollars' worth of medicine, but that just means we'll meet the insurance deductible sooner, I guess."

"Is the new drug working?"

"Too soon to tell. They can't treat mental illnesses like pneumonia. It's all trial and error. An expensive trial and too many errors, if you ask me. And in the meantime, everyone, especially the patient, suffers."

Max patted her hand. "I wish there were something I could do to help."

She plucked a paper napkin from the holder on the table and blew her nose. "Are you kidding? You've already done so much. Especially for Adam. I've been a basket case myself lately, trying to take care of Tom and acting like our family meltdown is just a big adventure. It's hard to hide the truth from Adam when it's right under his nose."

She sniffed. "You know why Adam loves playing Monopoly with you and Chancy? Because our game of Let's Pretend We're All Okay has become impossible to win."

"So why hide the truth? Sometimes things are rotten in Denmark. And in families. You cling and hope."

"I can't burden Adam with our financial problems. He's just a little boy."

"He's not so little. When I was his age I hopped a freight train to California. In the Middle Ages, twelve-year-olds carried swords into the Crusades."

She leaped at the chance to lead the conversation down a different path. "Adam loves your stories. Things would have been a lot harder for him this summer if he didn't have you and Chancy. He refers to you as his almost-grandpa, you know."

"I thought he had real grandparents."

"I lost my mother when I was in high school. She wore herself out trying to provide for the family because Dad didn't. He was never around for me, so I can hardly expect him to be there for my son. Tom's father pushed his boys to excel. Adam's tender heart couldn't take the pressure."

"He mentioned you wanted him to spend the summer in Texas."

"Last-ditch desperation. Tom's mother is okay—kind of a nonentity, as wives of domineering men can be—but his father would nitpick Adam to death. I changed my mind about the trip."

"Good. Adam's welcome here anytime."

"Thanks. You know why I insisted on moving to Wenonah?"

"Something about safety issues. A gun at school?"

"That was the excuse, not the reason. I grew up in apartments with cold white walls. No posters or pictures because my mother was afraid nail holes would cost us our security deposits. We never had grass. No pets allowed. My father was always moving us around. Looking for what, I never knew.

"It sounds dumb when I say it out loud, but I wanted to give Adam what I never had. A home that had stood for a hundred years and would stand for a hundred more. Permanence."

"Words of wisdom from an old man: Walls and roofs don't provide security. The people inside them do."

"I know." She covered her face with her hands and sobbed quietly. Max waited while she cried it out. "I thought Wenonah would be good for us. For our family. Tom wishes we'd never moved here. He wanted to stay in the city and build one of those hideous McMansions. I knew we had to move the day he showed me the plans. Ostentatious. Fake. Cold. I wanted a house with a history and a future. Something old and quietly grand."

"Well, you got the old part right."

Jenny laughed and wiped more tears. "That's what I love about you, Max. You always go right to the heart of the matter."

They drank coffee and talked, comparing fathers and how difficult it was for some parents to connect with their children. Max told Jenny about his old man's rejection. She told him how her selfish father had left the difficult part of living to her mother, who'd worked hard and died young.

They got around to Tom again, and Jenny revealed how her husband's desperate drive to earn his father's approval had cost him a chance to be a father to his own son.

"When Adam was small, Tom left his care to me. He worked hard to build something for our future. I believe he thought he'd have plenty of time later to be more involved. More emotionally invested in his son. But he never did, and now it's too late."

"It's never too late."

"Tom doesn't know how to talk to Adam. He won't admit it, but I think being home sick has shown him what he missed out on. The knowing is eating him up inside and making his depression worse."

"You try to be everything to Adam. Have you considered that maybe you're shortchanging Tom by not making him responsible for figuring out how to be a real father to his son?"

"Am I? God, I can't do anything right!"

"You're too hard on yourself, Jenny. Maybe moving to Wenonah was the end of life as you knew it, but also the beginning of a new life. If you'd stayed in the city in your fancy McMansion, Tom never would have slowed down enough to realize he'd missed the boat with Adam. Admitting our mistakes is the first step to rectifying them."

She smiled through tears. "You give me hope, Max. I don't want to get all mushy here, but you might as well know something. When I'm alone at night and feel like I'm drowning, I think of you."

"Me?"

"You're my rock."

"Well, you know, if you're drowning, a big old rock is the last thing you need."

She laughed. "There you go! Making me feel good again." She swept tears from her eyes. "I think of you and all you've accomplished. All the challenges you've faced. You and Hanna were so lucky to have each other. Even now, when she's gone, you keep going on. You don't give up. No matter what. You inspire me not to let my family down."

"I've done my share of giving up." What if he'd gone through with his good-bye-cruel-world routine? What would Jenny have thought of him then? Had he been a little demented that morning he found Chancy, *his* rock, in the garage? Because now that solution did not seem like a good idea, no matter how he twisted it.

Jenny's cell phone rang, and she checked the number. "It's Adam calling from Tom's phone." She listened, then said, "Okay, if you're sure. I don't mind picking you two up. All right. 'Bye."

"The movie's over but they want to get a Coke and walk home."

"Maybe Adam needs time to talk. Chancy's a good listener."

"I'm glad he has her. I know she's never dealt with things like this; she seems very sheltered, but—"

"Jenny, about that. I should tell you something." Max hated lying to his friend after she'd bared her soul and called him the Rock of Gibraltar. How would she react when she found out their whole relationship was based on deceit? His heart clutched again, this time with guilt. No. He had to talk to Chancy first. Spilling the beans to Jenny would betray Chancy's trust. Just as not spilling made a mockery of his friendship with Jenny. Pick your treason. Either way he was Benedict Arnold.

"Tell me what?"

"Never mind. Some other time." This time his phone rang. "My, aren't we popular today?" He excused himself with a grin, but as soon as he heard Shevaun Wooten's voice on the line, all the good feelings vanished. She'd called several times since her last visit, and he'd managed to delay another meeting. When she phoned, she sounded busy and pressed for time, as though Maxwell Boyle were just one more item to be checked off her to-do list.

"I'm following up on our previous conversations." She shuffled paper on the other end. "I see you missed the doctor's appointment we set up for you." Her tone was accusatory, insinuating that he'd probably done other things wrong too, and she would soon find out what.

"I rescheduled." He'd told the patient coordinator he would reschedule anyway.

"Not according to the office records. If transportation is a problem, I can arrange to accompany you—"

"Why are you doing this?" Everything was going so well. Chancy had blossomed. The house was clean. He had purpose again. Why couldn't the woman leave him alone?

"Why am I doing my job?" Ms. Wooten sounded genuinely surprised.

"Why are you nipping at my heels? I'm telling you I'm fine. I don't need help. Not from you. Or from your agency. I want you to mark my name off your list, because I am no longer your problem. I'm sure there are plenty of folks who do need help, but I'm not one of them."

Ms. Wooten sputtered something at the other end, and Max smacked the phone down on the base. When he returned to the kitchen, Jenny was leaning over the boxes of tile, pretending to read the label. He'd forgotten about her. How could he have forgotten he had company in the space of a few seconds? Obviously, Jenny had heard his end of the conversation.

She gave him a wary smile. "I was about to ask if there was anything I could do for you, but after that, I think I'll retract the offer."

"Wooten rides again. Think she'll take the hint?"

"I don't know. She seemed like the officious type." She carried her coffee cup to the sink.

"You catch more flies with honey," he muttered. He shouldn't have blown up that way. Wooten had probably written *argumentative* next to his name in her phone log. "You know how some people age like fine wine? I believe I have turned to vinegar."

"Nonsense. You made me feel better. Thanks for being a soft shoulder for me to cry on."

"I thought I was a rock."

"You're all three: a soft, vinegary rock." She dropped the cell phone into her handbag. "I should go check on Tom. He doesn't get hungry anymore and forgets to eat if I don't take him a tray. Thanks again, Max. I'm so glad I got to know the real you."

Insert knife in heart. Twist. Repeat. Maybe he could make up for all the lies by offering a little insight. "Look, Jenny, I know you're trying to protect Adam. But reality teaches us to be strong. Maybe you need to let Tom and Adam find their own way through this difficulty. Together."

Her face brightened as though he'd just revealed the fourth secret of the universe. "You're my hero, Max Boyle." She wrapped her arms around him. Hugged tight.

He hugged back. "Nah, you should probably go with Spider-Man for that."

. . .

"My favorite part was when the space alien captain's head blew up." Adam made the appropriately squishy, explosive sound effects.

"Yes, that was . . . colorful." Chancy squinted in the bright afternoon light. She'd almost be willing to watch the Martian's head blow up again if she didn't have to walk home in the sun-furnace.

"Man, I know how a steak feels." He danced backward ahead of her, sizzling now instead of squishing. Her confused look forced an explanation. "Like when you take a hunk of meat from the fridge and throw it in a hot pan?"

"Right."

"Sometimes I think *you're* an alien." He eyed her suspiciously. "Or maybe a pod person."

"No. I'm a regular person."

After a few blocks they ducked into a noisy fast-food joint for cold drinks. Adam also ordered two junior burgers and large fries. He paid, just as he'd insisted on paying for her movie ticket, since he had saved most of his lawn-mowing money.

"Isn't it a little early for dinner?" she asked.

"Dinner? Heck, this is a snack." He talked about the movie some more and Chancy listened, taking Uncle Max's advice to be a friend.

"Do you ever have . . . trouble with your dad?" he asked after he'd downed one burger.

"No." Hard to have trouble with someone she'd never met. When she was little, Chancy had made up stories about her missing father. He'd always been tall and handsome and hardworking. A fireman. Or a soldier. Dream Dad had wanted a little daughter more than anything in the world. Night after night in her imagination, he had swooped in to rescue her from B.J. He'd held her in imaginary arms, kissed her cheek with imaginary lips and told her he'd never let her go. Dream Dad had kept her company when she was alone. Then she'd grown up and realized that any man who would have a one-night stand with her crazy mother probably wasn't the gallant rescuer type.

"Mom treats me like a baby." Adam offered Chancy some of his fries. "She thinks I don't know anything."

"You know stuff," she said in his defense. "But your mom doesn't want to tell you things she thinks you don't *need* to know."

He considered. "Okay. I guess. I asked her if she and Dad are getting a divorce."

"Are they?" The Hamiltons' unsettled home life convinced Chancy that families were hard things to create. Even good people had trouble making them work.

"Mom said no, but I hear them yelling at each other. Mom tells Dad to keep his voice down, but he gets upset. He makes Mom sad."

"What does he make you?"

"I don't know. I want to hate him, but I can't."

"He's your dad."

"I used to think he could do anything. I don't know what happened."

"You grew up?"

He grinned. "Do you ever wish you could go back to being a dumb little kid forever?"

"No. I never want to go back. You can't live in the past."

"I just want my father to fix everything back the way it was before."

"Maybe he can't. People can't be anything but what they are."

"I don't know who he is, really."

Was that another of Adam's dumb jokes? "How can you live in the same house with someone and not know him?"

"Try living in my house for a while. You know my father has never been to any of my schools? He never watched me play soccer. That's why I quit. I had all these crappy little trophies, the kind everyone on the team gets. He promised he'd come to my tournament but he didn't. Mom made excuses for him, like she always does. 'Something came up at work.' That was my last game. I stuck a steak knife in my soccer ball and smashed those dumb trophies and threw them in the trash."

"You don't seem like the violent type." A serious observation.

"I'm not! I didn't stick the steak knife in my coach or anything. Sheesh."

"Sorry. I don't have any brothers, so I don't know how fathers and sons are supposed to act."

"My dad never takes me anywhere."

"What about all those places you've been?"

"With Mom. Even when Dad is with us, he isn't really. Seriously. One day, I looked through the photo albums and I only found him in *seven* pictures. Invisible Dad strikes again! Can you believe that?"

"Yes." The only picture she had of her and B.J. together was a strip of black-and-white shots from a photo booth. She'd been seven when her mother had taken her to an amusement park. They'd had fun at first, in a wary, uneasy way, until Chancy climbed out of a stupid caterpillar ride and realized her mother had disappeared. At the lost-and-found booth, a woman who never took the brown cigarette out of her mouth made a little-lost-girl announcement over the loudspeaker. Chancy had tried to tell the woman she was not the one who was lost. B.J. was.

Her mother had shown up half an hour later with a strange man in tow. Chancy was so relieved, because she was beginning to think maybe this was the time when B.J. wouldn't come back. She slid off the chair to run into her mother's arms, then stopped when she heard B.J. tell the cigarette lady, *Shit, I forgot I had the kid with me.*

Adam slurped his drink. "This morning Mom was yelling at Dad, asking how she was supposed to fix the kitchen if he didn't get well and go to work. He yelled at her and said maybe she should try working for a change if she wanted the damn kitchen fixed so bad."

"Will she?"

"I don't know. What would she do?"

"She said she went to college. She could get a job."

"She majored in psychology. You have to be like a doctor to be a shrink."

"She could do other things."

"You know what she told Dad? That she couldn't go off and leave me alone all day. She opened the bedroom door then, and I heard what Dad said, even though he wasn't yelling anymore. He said, 'What am I? Chopped liver?'"

Chancy didn't understand what Tom had meant, but she didn't dare ask Adam to explain. He looked too sad.

Chapter 19

"Maybe we should keep the old sofa and chairs." Chancy tensed with dread as she looked around Bradley's Fine Furniture Emporium. The shopping trip had seemed like a good idea when Uncle Max first suggested it, but she had changed her mind. If she couldn't bring herself to pay forty-five dollars for a shirt, how could she not be freaked out by four-digit price tags?

On her first day in Wenonah, she had pressed her nose to the glass of this very store and longed for a better life. Now real life, like the sprawling furniture store, offered a bewildering array of choices that she was not qualified to make.

"Too late," Uncle Max said. "I already paid a guy with a truck to haul that stuff to the landfill this afternoon. If we don't find something we like, we'll have to sit on the floor."

Chancy stuck close to him as they browsed the make-believe rooms. Every available inch of floor space was packed with color and texture and style. Luxurious fabrics. Polished wood. What did she know about nice things? The sofa and chairs destined for the dump were in better condition than anything in the furnished rooms and apartments she'd shared with B.J.

Her mother had said she didn't care about "materialistic crap" because it only weighed her down. But what if B.J. was wrong and meaningful objects were like ballast in the warships Uncle Max had told her about? Ballast prevented ships from capsizing in storms.

"So what do you have in mind?" An eager saleslady hovered nearby.

"Wish I knew," Uncle Max said. "Last time I picked out furniture Jimmy Carter was president."

The saleslady pitched the selling points of a massive leather sofa, but he shook his head. "Too many cows had to die to make that." He sat on one couch, testing. Then another. "Hanna always picked out things for the house. They all feel the same to me."

"Would you be interested in hiring our in-store decorator for an additional fee?"

"No. We need to do this ourselves, but I'm tone-deaf when it comes to style. Chancy, you'll have to help me choose."

"I can't. I don't know anything about making choices. Besides, it's not my furniture." Maybe the life she'd created with Uncle Max wasn't really hers either. Chancy Deel, regular girl, was as fake as the artificial fireplace in the store's window display. The residents of Wenonah looked at her differently now, but nothing about her was real. She had no ballast to prevent her from capsizing back into her old life.

B.J. had ruthlessly weeded their belongings each time they moved from place to dreary place. Chancy had been forced to leave her pathetic treasures behind. No room in the suitcases for the doll she wanted to love or the school papers with stars. *Take a mental picture*, her mother had said with vicious glee, *it'll last longer*. As Chancy got older, she'd learned to keep the things that mattered, like her tattered copy of *The Secret Garden*, close. She couldn't get attached to anything that wouldn't fit in her scruffy backpack, which could be grabbed at a moment's notice.

"Chancy? Are you okay?" Uncle Max drew her away from the saleslady. "You look a little pale."

"I'm fine. I want to go outside." She hadn't felt the urge to escape for weeks, but the jam-packed room made her dizzy.

"Okay. But I can't do this by myself," Uncle Max said gently. "I need your help. Now more than ever." She didn't think he was talking about furniture, but something else. The blood stopped pounding.

"All right. I'll help you."

"Good. I want you to pretend for a moment. If you could have anything in this whole big store, what would you choose?"

"Anything?"

"Anything your heart desires."

Chancy was good at imagining. She rubbed her forearms. She wanted to be real for Max. For the first time, she really looked at what the store had to offer. Surprising possibilities. Just like life.

An hour later, when Uncle Max wrote the check, Chancy had second thoughts about her careful selections. "You can't spend this much money. Maybe we should look for something cheaper."

"Oh, you don't want cheaper," the saleslady said, then waited while he scrawled his signature on the check. "You want something that will last."

The next morning the store delivered a tailored camel-colored sofa and two recliners. The transitional-style chairs, in a color the saleslady had called smoky cinnamon, did not look like recliners at all and would be easier for Uncle Max to get in and out of.

He surveyed the new room. "I gotta hand it to you, kiddo. These colors look really good with the paint. Where'd you pick up your decorating sense?"

"Magazines." She arranged a few select accessories on the polished tables. The stained-glass lamps shed a warm glow on the rug. The room did look like something in a picture.

"Hanna would be proud of what you've done for the house." Uncle Max swallowed hard and cleared his throat. "Thank you for sharing this." He pulled her worn copy of *The Secret Garden* from the end table drawer. "I finished reading last night and look forward to discussing the story over dinner tonight. But right now, I have a gift for you."

"You don't have to give me anything."

He pulled three slim volumes from the bookcase and placed them in her hands. "I want you to have these. When Hanna became too weak to work in her garden, she started writing about it. She'd sit in the sunroom, propped up on pillows, and scribble for hours. Said if she couldn't be out there"—he nodded toward the backyard—"she would grow a garden in here." He tapped the side of his head.

"She was imagining." Chancy already felt connected to Hanna's memory, but now she had more. Her words. She opened the cover of the first book and read the title printed in neat block letters.

A Time and a Season
Musings from the Porch

"She'd never shown any interest in writing before she got sick," Max said. "But suddenly she couldn't get her thoughts down fast enough."

"What's in here?"

"A little bit of everything. Planting notes. Observations of butterflies and life. Inspirational quotes. A few good jokes. Hanna always had a lot to say. She wrote every day, even when she was keelhauled by chemo. I asked why she was so desperate to record everything, but she didn't seem to know."

"Or maybe she couldn't explain." Chancy's finger traced the lines Hanna had written. Her handwriting had been bold at first but had grown shaky in the third book. "I think she wanted to share her knowledge before it was lost."

"I knew that someone who loved *The Secret Garden* would understand." Uncle Max sniffed. "As I read about Mary Lennox and Colin, I thought of you living in some dark place, wanting your own little piece of earth like the children in the book. I understand why restoring Hanna's garden is important to you."

"Do you think I can?"

"I'm sure of it. But you'll need Hanna's help, because Lord knows I have two black thumbs."

"Thank you, Uncle Max." For so much. The memories he'd given her could be recalled without pain. Chancy didn't yet know what the journals contained, but she understood what they meant. She didn't have to rely on gifts from the universe anymore.

She could count on people.

And she could believe in herself.

A few days later, Max joined Chancy in the living room. The light rain pattering against the window had driven her out of the garden, and she sat in one of the new chairs reading Hanna's journals, her legs draped over the side, barefoot because she'd kicked off her muddy old shoes on the porch. The Carpenters crooned from the console about rainy days and Mondays.

Chancy studied Hanna's notes as though preparing for the bar exam. She'd drawn planting diagrams and devised schedules for fertilizing and pruning. The fire to succeed, once ignited, was hard to put out. Max had seen her determination the day she and Adam laid the new kitchen tile. Adam had relied on mathematics. Not Chancy. Instinct was her guide in all things. Jenny had been so impressed by their work, she had recruited the children to help her put down the same black-and-white tiles in her own kitchen.

Max settled in the other chair with the newspaper and a cup of coffee. He'd had good days and bad days this week. So far today had been good.

Chancy looked up from her reading and laughed. "Hanna said God made rainy days to give gardeners a chance to clean house."

"So why are we reading instead of cleaning? The hall closet won't straighten itself, you know."

"Just a few more minutes, please?"

To satisfy her insatiable curiosity, Max had given her books and charts from Hanna's master gardener classes. She'd memorized the names and growing conditions of all the plants in the garden, including those that had succumbed to neglect. Hanna would approve of Chancy's zeal. When they'd discussed disposal of their estate, Hanna had suggested establishing a scholarship fund in Max's name to honor his contribution to the college. He'd finally convinced her that he preferred to be remembered in the hearts and minds of his students, and a scholarship in her name was the way to go. She'd agreed but had been very specific about potential recipients.

A bright girl who has nothing but a wish to be something.

A girl like Chancy. Earlier, Max had leaned over the garden gate, amazed by all she'd accomplished since he'd given her the journals. Untended for two previous growing seasons, the garden's bones were visible once again. He'd watched Chancy divide a clump of daylilies using the two-fork method Hanna had favored. She'd made the cuts like an old pro. Grinning self-consciously, she'd told him how she planned to replant the divisions to fill in designated bare spots, and how several plants that had died would need to be replaced. Otherwise it wouldn't really be Hanna's garden.

Max had pretended interest in a bright yellow butterfly. Plants could be replaced, but not people. He'd not had the heart to tell Chancy the truth: No matter how hard she worked, the garden would never be the same.

"Did you know plants catch powdery mildew from a fungus spore in the air?" she asked.

Max lowered the newspaper. "Don't believe I need to know that."

"But it's interesting. How about this? 'Place a layer of crushed eggshells in the bottom of a planting hole to add calcium and improve drainage for all plants except those that prefer acid soil.' Now that's smart. Reading what Hanna wrote is the next-best thing to knowing her. It's like she's talking to me and will help me make the garden right."

"Astute observation."

"Astute is a good thing, right? I think I understand why Hanna wrote everything down." She spoke quietly, without looking up. "She hoped someone would come along and bring the garden back to life after she was gone."

Max's throat tightened. "Maybe."

"Do you think she knew it would be me?"

"I believe she did." The paper lay forgotten in his lap. The day before she died, Hanna had perked up a little. Max had wanted to celebrate, but the hospice nurse had warned him that patients often rallied just before the end. Hanna hadn't eaten much for a few days, but that morning she'd asked for one of his special fried eggs. After he fed it to her, she'd sat up and stared out the window into the garden.

"What is it, honey?" The plants were dormant, the invading weeds brown. "What do you see?"

"The angel."

Max's heart had slammed into his chest. Hanna had laughed weakly. "Don't worry, Professor. I'm not seeing celestial visions. There." She pointed out the small stone statue. It had been overturned and was half-hidden in the Bermuda grass that had crept under the fence. "The angel's wing is broken."

"I'll get you a new one," he'd promised, willing to give her the moon and all the stars, if only she would stay a little longer.

"Don't you dare." Hanna had collapsed lightly on the pillow. "I like broken angels. They're the best kind."

Chancy chuckled. "Listen to this, Uncle Max. 'Old gardeners never die. They just spade away.'"

Once when he'd done something particularly geezerish—he couldn't remember what—Hanna had spouted off at him.

Old chemists never die; they just stop reacting.

He'd come back with the gardener crack and the game was launched.

Old deans never die; they just lose their faculties.

Old redheads never fade; they just dye away.

They had laughed like children who believed they were immortal, until Hanna had flung a zinger he couldn't top.

Old fishermen never die; they just smell that way.

At the time, Max had enjoyed their one-upmanship, but now he knew the truth. No one was immortal. Everyone died. The trick was making your time count by spending it with the right people.

"I don't know if you noticed, but I'm up on ladders and step stools a lot." Chancy poked her head in the hall closet and pulled out another box. "What's in here anyway?" The contents of the packed closet resembled a cross-section of the earth she'd once seen in a science book. Only instead of geological eras, the junk was marked by decades.

Utility bills from the 1970s secured by rotting gum bands. Canceled checks from the 1980s on which the ink had faded like ghost writing.

Folders filled with newspaper clippings from the 1990s. Old chemistry journals and calendars. Boxes of Christmas cards the Boyles had received, carefully labeled by year. Candle stubs. Pens that didn't work. Scraps of wrapping paper too small to save but too good to throw out.

When they'd first started cleaning, Chancy had shared an idea she'd seen in a magazine article. They'd used the system ever since. Three labeled boxes waited. *SAVE. TOSS. DONATE.* Uncle Max's job was to decide the fate of items she separated from the molten tangle, but he had trouble with the concept and spent more time relating the history of worthless stuff than filling boxes.

They worked in silence until he asked out of the blue, "Do you know how to drive?"

"No."

"Maybe it's time you learned. You'll be sixteen soon." He rescued a driver's manual from the toss box. "My license lapsed after my heart attack and they gave me this in rehab. Said I'd have to study for the written test to get my license back. Then Hanna got sick, and I never got around to it."

Chancy flipped the colorful pages containing diagrams of road signs and lane changes. The rules of passing and parking. "Looks complicated."

"Government makes everything complicated. Know how I learned to drive? I was in Italy in 1943. A captain threw me a set of keys and ordered me to drive a jeep. So I did. Didn't get a license until I came stateside."

"Things are different now."

"Shouldn't be. Too many rules."

"Without rules, wouldn't there be more accidents?"

"Rules of the road are the same as always. Don't go too fast. Don't hit anything. Don't get hit. How about I teach you how to handle the Lincoln? Then, when you're old enough, you can get a license and make it legal."

"I don't think so." She climbed down from the stool and set a box of old papers on the floor.

"Afraid to live dangerously?" Uncle Max poked in a shoe box full of junk.

She dumped the contents of the shoe box into the toss box. "Remember, we agreed. If you haven't used something in this century, throw it away."

There was a pause; then she said, "I can't get a license."

"Not right now."

"Not ever."

"Why not?"

"I don't have identification. No birth certificate. No Social Security card." She didn't exist, not officially anyway. "You have to prove you're in school and have taken driver's education. Or that you graduated." She knew that much. Driving was another word for independence, a hot topic among shelter inmates. Even if she had ID, she didn't dare present it anywhere and risk being yanked out of the best thing that had ever happened to her.

"Unless you were found under a cabbage leaf, we can get copies of your identification."

"Too dangerous." Who knew what kind of lists her name was on? What databases she was in? She'd checked a Web site for missing and exploited children on a library computer once. She had found hundreds of children's pictures, but not her own. Apparently, to make the cut, someone had to care if you were missing or exploited. The state wouldn't look too hard, but if her name started showing up, they might contact local authorities.

"I guess things have changed more than I realized," he said.

"I don't know the law here, but you can't waltz in and get a driver's license just anywhere these days."

"Which means no more driving because someone throws you a set of keys."

"Exactly."

Uncle Max frowned. "We might have to break the law. You up for that?"

"No! We could get in trouble, you know." Driving was part of growing up, and Chancy wanted to feel like a normal teenager, but she wasn't about to flirt with serious lawbreaking. She couldn't go back. Not to the streets. Not to the shelter. And especially not to B.J.

"C'mon, we'll be careful and stay off the thoroughfares." Uncle Max

gave her a sly look. Was it still considered peer pressure when the one ex-
erting the pressure was nearly seventy years older?

"If the police catch us driving without a license between us, they
might arrest us." Max still wasn't convinced, so she added a more dire
warning. "Ms. Wooten has been checking up on you. She would use an
arrest to prove you're incompetent. Then where would you be?"

"Assisted living."

"You wish. Try jail."

"I see your point." Mentioning the social worker's name had a bogey-
man effect on Uncle Max, cooling his enthusiasm. "But it's a shame to
have a nice car and not be able to go anywhere."

"Maybe you should get *your* license reinstated." Max was the one who
needed to drive. Chancy had other ways of feeling normal.

"There's a fantasy for you." His laugh was bitter. "No telling what
kind of restrictions they have against senile old farts driving."

"Call and find out," she challenged.

"What's the use? Cards are stacked against both of us."

She nagged off and on for an hour, her wheedling words chipping
away at his resistance. Finally he cracked, and she stood by for moral
support while he dialed the number on the driver's manual. According to
the officer who answered, since Max's license had been expired for more
than three years, he had to take the written test and driving test, as well
as pass a vision exam. He relayed the information with a that's-the-end-
of-that sigh.

Chancy wouldn't let him off so easily. "Guess you'd better start studying, huh? If I can memorize the Latin names of plants and learn to recognize them by sight, you can learn how to park on a hill."

"I *know* how to park on a hill." He turned away with a loud sniff and
picked up the save box, dumping the contents into the one labeled TOSS.
"I don't need any of this stuff. Don't need to drive either. Where would
I go?"

"Giving up?"

He flung another box of papers into the trash. "Being realistic. You
saw the manual. Said yourself it's complicated. I'm old. Had a stroke.

That's shorthand for brain damage, you know. Probably forgotten everything in the manual, plus stuff that isn't."

"You're a professor," she said quietly.

"*Was.* Now I'm just an old fool. With a bum hand."

"Your hand is almost back to normal." For exercise, they'd lined up a row of canned goods on the table and he'd moved them to the opposite side as fast as he could. Working around the house and in the yard had put more strength into his grip.

"Okay, so I don't have a bum hand. Just a bum head."

Uncle Max hid his fear behind anger. He didn't think he could pass the tests. He didn't want to fail or admit that the people who had decided he wasn't good enough were right. Chancy had felt the same way many times. Not about driving, but about everything else. Maybe when he thought about relearning the driving rules, he felt as overwhelmed as she had in the furniture store.

"I want you to pretend for a moment." She mimicked his words from the day they picked out the furniture. "If you could climb behind the wheel of the Lincoln and put the pedal to the metal and drive anywhere in this whole big world, where would you go?"

"Anywhere?" he asked, willing to play along.

"Anywhere your heart desires."

"No place in particular. Not like I want to take a road trip or anything. I just get tired of calling for rides. You know, I could've bought and paid for my own cab by now."

"So where would you go?"

"I just like knowing that if I need something, I can go to the store without having to plan ahead like the logistician for Patton's army."

"What else?"

"And if I feel like taking Alfie for a ride in the country, we can hop in and feel the wind in our faces."

"Sounds good." She didn't have to say much. He was convincing himself.

"Driving is freedom." He dumped another box of junk. "Taking away that right robs a man of more than his mobility."

Uncle Max had given her so much and asked for little in return. She wanted to help him regain something important.

"I'll study with you," she offered.

"I'm too far gone to study." His sagging shoulders had already given up on the idea.

Chancy placed her hand on his thin arm. She meant only to encourage him, but the warmth of that small connection spread through her, and she was the one who felt heartened. "Maybe teaching me will help you remember."

"You're willing to learn? For when you have identification and can fulfill all the fool requirements?"

Not *if, when.* "Do you think I could get my ID?"

"You were born and duly recorded somewhere. The government has everything on computers. We can get copies of your records. I'll ask Pete."

Uncle Max had visited Pete Marshall at his office several times. He'd told his friend that he'd hired help, but had been vague on details. Risking discovery might be the first step toward permanency.

"So what do you say?" he prodded.

"We can't break any laws."

"Of course not. We're not Bonnie and Clyde."

"Who?"

"We'll stay off public roads."

"And you're sure you know what you're doing?" Why was everything that mattered exciting and scary at the same time? Chancy piled more pack-ratted papers into the toss box, which was just about full.

"Do you think I'm one of those senile old people who tromp the accelerator instead of the brake and drive through plate-glass windows?"

"You're the one who brought up brain damage."

"You think I'll get confused and drive the wrong way down a one-way street? Or mow down a crowd of pedestrians on the sidewalk?"

"Stop." She clamped her hands over her ears. That was why she lived in an imagined world. Reality was too alarming. "I don't need those pictures in my head when we get in the car."

Chapter 20

The next morning Chancy and Uncle Max rose early so they could practice driving while most of the neighborhood slept. Alfie didn't mind the hour and bounded into the backseat, eager for a ride. Chancy clutched the steering wheel with damp palms, but Uncle Max assured her it was normal to be nervous. He was a born teacher, patient and thorough, and made the bewildering process seem almost simple by breaking it into small tasks, each of which she would master before moving on.

"Today, the basics." Slipping easily into professor mode, he cautioned her to respect the vehicle's power, to avoid being a danger to herself and others. *Curiosity doesn't kill all the cats; recklessness takes out its share.* He introduced combustion engines and explained what happened when she turned the key in the ignition. After outlining the function of each gear and how it worked in the automatic transmission system, as well as the mechanics of the accelerator and brakes, he wrapped up by allowing her to shift gears and brake.

"Be alert every moment you're behind the wheel," he told her. "When you back up, don't use the rearview mirror. Turn and look behind you."

She backed the car down the driveway, then shifted gears and pulled forward. Back and forth, many times, until she had mastered the first skill level. After two hours of meticulous instruction, Uncle Max declared she'd had enough for the first day.

"I never knew driving was so . . . complicated." She hoped her brain held on to some of the information until the next lesson.

"Driving is a responsibility," he said. "You have to be vigilant at all times. One lapse could mean disaster. Don't look so worried. I won't let you rush out half-cocked. Stick with me, kid; I'll make sure you're safe out there."

Chancy relaxed. She could depend on Uncle Max. Not just to teach her the rules of the road, but how to be safe in the world. She opened the car door so Alfie could jump out. He'd offered moral support in the backseat, panting out the rear window the whole time. Obviously thrilled to be on the move again, he didn't seem to mind that the Lincoln had never left the driveway.

After the intensity of Intro to Automotives 101, Chancy was relieved to tackle a less demanding task. While Uncle Max puttered around the house, she helped Jenny lay tile in her war-zone kitchen. She'd been a little apprehensive when Jenny first asked for her assistance, praising her cleverness and skill in refurbishing Uncle Max's house. Jenny's kitchen was large and would require more calculations and tile cuts, but Chancy had finally accepted the challenge when she'd realized for the first time that she felt competent and clever and deserving of others' respect.

Six hours of intense work later, the Hamiltons' new kitchen floor was down. Except for the last square, which Jenny handed to Chancy.

"I think you should do the honors. You're the brains behind this operation."

"Adam helped." Chancy could accept praise now. And share it. Each time she accomplished a difficult task, B.J.'s belittling taunts became a little fainter.

Adam's nonexistent-muscle-flexing routine made everyone laugh. "I'm the brawn."

But maybe things were getting better. Yesterday Adam had rushed over to borrow the chess set because his father had challenged him to a game. Uncle Max had taught them both to play, but Adam was much more skilled than Chancy. He had paused before running out the door. "I didn't think Dad even knew what a chessboard was."

Since their talk after the movie, he'd spent less time at Uncle Max's and more time at home, trying to offer his father the understanding his mother had requested. He'd told Chancy he was just doing it for his mom, since his dad probably didn't care if his son understood him or not.

"Both brawn and brains are important in home renovations," Jenny said with a laugh. "But if Chancy hadn't set such a good example of initiative, I would never have undertaken this job. Thanks to her, we finally have a floor."

"But still no sink or stove," Adam reminded her. "Or cabinets."

"All in good time. I can't learn plumbing and wiring in free classes at the home center, but who knows? If I get that part-time job I applied for, I can hire someone to do the tricky stuff." Jenny held up both hands with fingers crossed.

While Adam supplied the requisite drumroll, Chancy stripped the protective backing from the last tile with a dramatic flourish. She placed it firmly in the space their careful calculations had ensured would be a perfect fit and patted it down. While Jenny and Adam cheered, she stood for a comic bow. Completing the work felt good, but not nearly as good as making Jenny happy. Her kitchen, like her life, had needed fixing up for far too long.

"Are you sure you like this floor?" Chancy had seen the original kitchen plans. Everything Jenny selected had been luxurious and probably expensive.

"I think it's beautiful."

"It's not exactly what you wanted."

"You're right. Peel-and-stick vinyl is definitely not Italian travertine stone. But I like it. We did it ourselves. We had fun. And best of all, it's paid for." She smiled. "Compromise is a good thing."

"So maybe everything doesn't have to be perfect around here?" Adam jostled his mother playfully. Chancy envied the easy teasing the two shared.

"Oh, I think it's pretty darned perfect." Jenny admired the new floor.

Adam, glad the job was over, ran across the street to work on the wall shelf Uncle Max was helping him make for his action-figure collection. Chancy stayed behind to help Jenny clean up.

"I brought you something." She handed Jenny the large envelope she'd stashed in the living room earlier.

"What's this?" Jenny opened the clasp and pulled out the paper heart Chancy had constructed using Corliss's fancy paper. "Oh, my! This is lovely. Did you make it?"

"For you. If you hang it in the kitchen window, the sun will make the foil sparkle."

Jenny looped the fishing line hanger over the window lock. The green-and-gold heart seemed to glow in the sunlight. "Every time I look at it, I'll think of you. Thank you."

"You're welcome." Chancy told her how she and a friend had made a stack of hearts to deliver to the nursing home the next day.

"That's a sweet gesture. I know the residents will love their hearts as much as I love mine."

They scooped up the discarded backing paper from the tiles they'd laid. After a few quiet moments, Jenny spoke. "Remember what I said about compromising? I didn't want to say anything in front of Adam, but Tom and I reached a compromise, too. He's taking medication again but was bullheaded about therapy."

"Doing new things is hard."

"I know. That's why I promised Tom if he'd go to therapy, I'd get a part-time job to earn the money needed to make the kitchen functional. He doesn't think I can do it, but he agreed. He's been to therapy twice now. And I've been to three interviews. All a bust. I'm overqualified for some and lack experience for others."

"But you've worked at a job before, right?"

"Selling books at the campus bookstore during college. Never had a real job. I've always depended on Tom for everything."

"Nobody can give everything," Chancy said softly. She thought of B.J., who couldn't seem to give anything. For the first time she wasn't flooded with the fear and rage her mother had once inspired. Her mom spot felt empty.

"How did you get to be so wise?" Jenny fetched the broom and Chancy held the dustpan. "Your parents are lucky to have you. I hope I do half as good a job with Adam as they've done with you."

Chancy stared at the floor and the dust Jenny swept into the pan. Lying to Jenny had become a physical pain, worse than the slaps and burns and cuts she'd endured. Lying hurt her heart, which wasn't as strong as her body.

"Maybe what people are is inside them, from the very beginning," she said. "Maybe it doesn't matter what others, even parents, do for them." *Or to them.* Chancy thought of Eddie and his drug problem. Corliss had been a good mother. Chancy had seen the way Eddie's face softened when he talked about her that day outside the bank. For a moment, he wasn't a former addict who had stolen his mother's television for drug money. He was a son who had known that no matter what he did, his mother would still love him.

"Thank you, Chancy Deel."

"You don't have to thank me. You could have done the floor yourself."

"Thanks for being you. I'm glad we met. I'll miss you when you go home in a few weeks." Jenny sniffed and swept the last dust into the pan. She replaced the broom in the closet and returned with the sponge mop and pail.

"Home?"

"Back to Pennsylvania with your parents. They'll be here to get you before school starts, won't they?" Jenny filled the bucket with soapy water and mopped until the black-and-white tiles sparkled, then joined Chancy in the dining room doorway to admire their work.

"I don't know."

"I know you miss them, but I'm selfish enough to want you to stay a little longer." Jenny gave her a quick hug, and the old cold feelings that usually swamped Chancy when she was touched gave way to something new: a tide of warmth that replaced the need for words. She hugged Jenny back.

At first she'd been cautious around the Hamiltons, afraid to let the cat out of the bag, as Uncle Max called it. Now there were days when she almost forgot she was living a lie. A normal girl with normal parents. More and more of her real self showed through the fakery she'd hidden behind. Or was she finally reflecting the light around her, like the heart in the window?

As she'd done with Corliss, she had tried not to lie to Jenny and Adam when possible. She had attempted to share—honestly—the life she'd created in Wenonah. Nothing bad had happened. Sometimes she believed Uncle Max and Jenny and Adam might like the real Chancy. The new Chancy she'd become. To hide her unexpected feelings from Jenny, she carried the bucket into the utility room and dumped it, then helped Jenny move the breakfast set into the spot by the window where the heart hung.

"Cabinets are next," Jenny said. "A huge expense. Forget the custom job. Even manufactured ones are out of my price range unless I get that job."

"So what kind of job is it?"

"Receptionist at a trucking company. Problem is, the girl who interviewed me was young enough to be my daughter."

"Uncle Max says children are running the world. I thought that was just because he was old."

Jenny laughed. "No, I think he's onto something. This girl couldn't have been more than twenty. And if I get the job, she'll be my supervisor. I'm not very hopeful. She wants someone closer to her own age. I also applied for a 'document processing position' at the hospital. Know what that turned out to be? Sitting in the basement for five hours at night shredding medical records. They told me I was overqualified."

"You graduated college. You'll find something."

"An undergrad degree in psychology is actually a liability. Who knew? Interesting jobs require a full-time commitment, and I prefer to work thirty hours a week. It's probably asking too much to expect decent wages doing something that's actually meaningful." She fetched cans of cola from the refrigerator in the dining room and they sat at the breakfast table to drink them. "All these years, I thought I was putting my family first. Now I realize I was too focused on myself."

"Uncle Max says anyone who's wrapped up in himself makes a pretty small package."

Jenny laughed again. "You and Max have been better for me than therapy! You inspire me to make a difference with others—the way you've made a difference with Max. And now he wants to drive again."

"Driving is independence." Chancy quoted Uncle Max all the time.

"Independence sounds good. Maybe it's time for me to branch out. Adam's growing up. Tom's doing better. I know it doesn't seem like he is because he's still in his room most of the time, but I can see progress. Change the mind and the spirit will follow. Did I tell you he offered to take money out of his retirement fund to finish the kitchen?"

"That's good, isn't it?"

"I won't endanger our future for a side-by-side ice-in-the-door refrigerator and convection oven. I'll earn the money myself and do as much of the work as I can. Cut corners. Make compromises. Perfect things don't make a perfect life."

"Family love is messy."

"More words of wisdom from Max Boyle?"

"No. Nietzsche." Chancy had read a quote of his in Hanna's journals: *Family love is messy, clinging, and of an annoying and repetitive pattern, like bad wallpaper.*

Jenny looked at her with wonder. "You know Nietzsche?"

"Doesn't everyone?"

"I'm sorry. Am I interrupting?" Tom Hamilton stood in the doorway. He was dressed in old jeans and a dark T-shirt. Barefoot. His dark hair, silvered at the temples, was too long but neatly combed.

Jenny's attention immediately shifted to her husband and there was no mistaking the relief and joy in her eyes when she looked at him. "Hey, honey, what do you think of the floor?"

"Nice. You did this?"

Jenny smiled across the table at Chancy. "I had help."

"Good job. Looks like a ballroom in here," he said. And it did. Without appliances or cabinets or counters, the kitchen seemed immense.

"Why, Tom Hamilton, are you asking me to dance?" Jenny adopted a Southern plantation belle accent and batted her lashes.

"Sorry, babe. Standing up is the extent of my ability today." He swallowed hard and Chancy saw relief in his eyes too. "But I'll take a rain check on that dance."

"You shaved." Jenny crossed the space between them and ran a slender finger along his jaw.

When Tom grinned, his thin face no longer looked hopeless. He was handsome, and he and Jenny made a striking couple. Both tall. Strong. Devoted enough to endure the difficulties life threw at them.

"Dr. Yuan gave me a list of things to do. He claims shaving is the first step back into the land of the living."

Jenny threw her arms around his neck. "Welcome back, sweetheart!"

The couple clung to each other as Chancy said her good-byes. She hurried across the street, knowing Adam would have another chance with his father. There would be no divorce. Jenny wouldn't be alone. Chancy had never cared so much about the happiness of others. Her heart felt as whole and sparkly as the one in Jenny's kitchen window.

The next morning Chancy waited for Corliss to arrive for their outing to Dogwood Manor. The hearts she'd made were packed carefully in a big shoe box in her lap. Alfie sat by the door. "Why don't you come, too, Uncle Max?"

"No, no! Not me. You're not getting me into one of those places." He settled in the recliner with a box of photographs to sort. He'd spent a lot of time lately looking through them, sharing memories with Chancy. Uncle Max's past was worth remembering, and he'd shaped long-ago days into words to give meaning to the years.

"What places?" She glanced out the window. Corliss was running late.

"Hellholes, that's what!"

"Corliss doesn't think Dogwood Manor is a hellhole."

"She doesn't have to live there. Look, I found another picture of Bunsen."

"He's cute." Chancy looked over his shoulder. In the photo the dog he and Hanna had raised from a puppy had been caught in midair catching a ball. She knew about Bunsen, named after Robert Wilhelm Bunsen, a famous chemist, and his equally famous acrobatic skills.

"Jack Russell terrier. Crazy as a bedbug, but boy, was he lively." Alfie gave a soft yip. "I know, you were probably lively too, in your day."

One of their favorite rainy-day projects had been organizing the many pictures stuffed in drawers and hidden in boxes on closet shelves. They had spent hours poring over them together. Uncle Max had identified the people in the shots, and she'd painstakingly recorded all the names and dates and places he could remember on the back. Chancy had seen Uncle Max grow old in the pictures. Grinning soldier in uniform, his arms thrown over the shoulders of buddies in front of the Roman Coliseum. Handsome groom with a radiant bride. Pictures of Uncle Max in his classroom. Young and energetic. Middle-aged and going gray. Receiving teaching awards. Speaking at his retirement party. He'd grown older, but his students had remained young, only their clothing and hairdos marking the years.

"We're wasting our time with all this labeling."

"No, we're not!" When he was gone, his past wouldn't be lost. But Chancy couldn't say those words aloud. She couldn't even think of a life without him. "We need to make a record."

"For who? No one will care. First thing estate sale planners do is toss out photographs. Bargain hunters don't buy other people's memories."

"I'd never let that happen."

He raised his gaze to hers, maybe to see if she was serious. "Well, okay, then. We should make it official. I, Maxwell Boyle, being of sound mind and scrawny body, do hereby bequeath all my worldly snapshots to Chancy Deel."

She smiled. "Really?" Now she had a past. Many of the pictures they'd sorted had been shot on the spoon-collection trips. At the beach. In the mountains. The desert. Standing in front of monuments Chancy had seen only in books. Max leaning proudly on a new car. Eating cake on his sixty-fifth birthday. Dancing with Hanna at their fortieth-anniversary celebration.

She reached into the box. "Where was this taken?"

"At a dance competition. Hanna was beautiful in that gown. The picture is black-and-white, but the dress was aquamarine. And don't I look jaunty?"

"You won the contest."

"They don't give trophies that big to runners-up."

Uncle Max's childhood photos had been lost over the years, but Chancy had seen plenty of Hanna. As a pretty teenager. Young Hanna in the garden, leaning on a shovel. Laughing at a dinner party, her hair teased high in a bubble on her head. Middle-aged Hanna posed in front of an Indian totem pole, mimicking the carved image's gory smile. Standing at the edge of the ocean, her flat palm positioned perfectly under a sailboat on the horizon, her lips puckered to blow wind into the sails.

Two lives, connected. Linked from childhood to adulthood to old age by pictures that Chancy could roll through her mind like a movie to fill up the black, blank space in her own life.

"I don't understand why you're so interested in memories that aren't your own, dear." He set aside the box of pictures.

"I don't have any good memories of my own."

"Do you want to talk about that?"

She nodded. "I think I do. When we have more time."

"I'll be here." He patted her hand.

"What time is it?" she asked. "Corliss is really late."

"Call her. See if there's a problem."

She made the call, then returned to the living room and glanced out the window. Still no Corliss. "No one answered."

"Maybe something came up."

Eddie. Corliss said he attracted misfortune like a bad-luck magnet. She picked up the box of pictures. In many of them the Boyles were together, and she wondered who had snapped them. A friendly stranger? Fellow tourist? She could almost believe she'd been there too. Not invisible, but standing off to the side, out of the frame. Living a life in grainy black-and-white photographs. Reflected in the eyes of happy people, floating like a mote in their laughter.

She imagined recording the events in their long lives, felt the old-fashioned camera in her hands, solid and heavy.

Let me take a picture. Stand over there. Closer together. Say cheese!

She looked up and caught Uncle Max wiping what he called a "happy tear" from his eye. She'd known him only a few stolen weeks, but she knew his whole life. The orphan boy he'd been. The soldier. The teacher. The dancing fool. The girl he'd loved. The children who'd died. He had shown her his life in pictures and had given her stories to make them real. Words had opened a window into a stranger's heart, and for the first time Chancy understood another human being and knew what it meant not to be alone.

He had shown her there was more to the world than today. Yesterday was important. So was tomorrow. Chancy wanted tomorrow.

Eddie was not the reason Corliss arrived late. When the old car's battery died and couldn't be jumped back to life, he had walked to the Lube Place on his day off, purchased a new battery with his own money and store discount and installed it himself. All the way to Dogwood Manor, Corliss had sat sideways in the passenger seat and bragged to Chancy about what a good mechanic her son had become.

"So what time do you want me to pick you up?" he asked as Corliss and Chancy and Alfie climbed out of the car.

"Come back about one o'clock. The fun should be over by then and the old folks down for naps. So, are you going to talk to my boss about the dishwashing job?"

"Headed there right now." Eddie looked nice, dressed in regular clothes and not his mechanic's uniform.

Corliss leaned in the window and kissed his cheek and he let her. "I'll see you all later. Have a nice visit." And he was gone.

"He's really buckling down, that boy," Corliss said proudly. "He's been working steady. When I told him our morning dishwasher was sick, he volunteered to fill in for a while. He's saving his money for a car. Staying clean too. Couple of idiots from his past tried to suck him back into the life, but he swears he won't have anything to do with them. I believe him. My boy's on the right road now. He's going to be fine. Know what he told me?"

"What?"

"That if he hadn't met you that day at the bank, he would've quit his job and given up. He said you reminded him there were still plenty of good people in the world."

Dogwood Manor didn't seem like a hellhole to Chancy, and she'd actually been in some of those. Corliss spoke to the elderly people she passed on their way to the administrator's office.

"Chancy Deel, meet Barbara Shannon." Corliss introduced the trim, well-dressed woman who ran Dogwood Manor. "Barb's the trail boss around here. If you need anything or have a problem, she's your go-to gal."

The woman extended her hand. "Administrator. And chief bedpan washer, when necessary. Call me Barb."

Chancy trusted her instincts these days and liked Barb immediately. The woman's kind brown eyes reminded her of Alfie's, the way they seemed to say, *You can depend on me.* The dog hadn't made it to the office. He'd been waylaid by eager residents in the dayroom and was patiently walking from one trembling outstretched hand to the next, accepting all the pats and hugs the old people could bestow. Normally gentle, Alfie had been extra subdued since walking into the Manor. No sudden movements or unwarranted noise. Just a big furry ambassador, spreading the love.

They strolled back to the dayroom, and Barb Shannon watched his slow progress around the room. "Alfie's a natural-born therapy dog. So quiet and perceptive. Thank you for bringing him to meet my folks, Corliss."

"Oh, that was Chancy's idea. Just like the hearts. We've been working like Santa's elves on these. You want to see what we made?"

Barb oohed and aahed over the decorations. With the special paper and Corliss's help, they had turned out better than Chancy could have imagined.

"These are lovely," Barb said. "People need visitors and art and warm dogs to pet."

"The hearts aren't exactly art," Chancy protested.

"Of course they are. They're nice enough to sell in gift shops. If you two are ready to start visiting, I'll stay out here with Alfie. There's a big bingo game later in the rec room, but I have to warn you: Don't let our tranquil appearance fool you. Things get pretty cutthroat around here on bingo day."

Five long halls fanned out from the nurses' station in the center of the building, like the spokes of a wheel. Corliss, who seemed to know all the nurses and aides and residents, led Chancy down the first corridor. The facility was clean and modern, not at all like the hospital where Chancy had visited B.J. that fateful Mother's Day. The mental hospital had been a grim holding pen for people whose lives were off the track. The Manor, as Corliss called the nursing home, was a bridge for people waiting to cross from one life to another.

A few Manor residents sat in wheelchairs, but most came and went as they pleased, many leaning on aluminum walkers or canes. They called to one another and to the staff. If they knew pain, they hid it behind smiles and laughter. Chancy didn't understand what Max thought was so bad about retirement homes. Maybe it wasn't the building that made a place grim and depressing, but the people who worked and lived there.

The sunroom was similar to the one in Max's house, with wicker furniture and plants and a big aquarium with colorful fish at eye level for the residents in wheelchairs. A realistic wallpaper mural of a lush flower garden covered one wall. The make-believe gate was open, the make-believe path inviting. Other scenes had been hand-painted on the walls. A fake window with a realistic cat napping on the sill. A fountain so vivid Chancy could hear the water splash. Birds took flight on the walls, and ivy and roses twined on a lattice painted on the ceiling. Someone who understood imagining had given the housebound residents a way to walk outdoors, even if they couldn't leave their chairs.

"What do you think of our trompe l'oeil?" asked an aide pushing an old man in a wheelchair into the room. The staff didn't wear nursing scrubs. They dressed in tan pants and polo shirts with the Manor's logo. According to Barb, treating the residents like patients made them feel sick.

"The what?"

"The artwork." The aide joined Chancy and Corliss in front of the cat window. "Barb says trompe l'oeil is French for 'fool the eye.'"

"Something fake that's realer than real." Chancy touched the cat, expecting it to purr.

"Exactly!" The aide hurried away to help someone else, but turned at the door and spoke to Chancy. "Don't forget the bingo game. There's a prize waiting with your name on it."

Chancy had not known what to expect, but everything about the Manor was a pleasant surprise. As she walked down one of the halls, an old woman reached out and grabbed her hand. Her eyes were unseeing, pale and clouded by what Corliss explained were severe cataracts. Her thin white hair was pinned back with a plastic daisy barrette. She held out her arms for a hug, and Chancy folded the birdlike woman into a gentle embrace. Touching didn't have to hurt. It could heal, too.

"Thank you, honey," the little woman chirped. "Come back and see me again." Then she toddled down the hall guided by the handrail.

The next two hours sped by. Alfie joined Corliss and Chancy on their goodwill tour. He clicked confidently down the hall, as though he knew which residents needed him most. Even the bedridden wanted to pet the dog, and Alfie obliged by standing on his hind legs next to their beds, front paws resting close enough for them to shake if they wanted.

Chancy and Corliss chatted with the residents and hung paper hearts in the windows, suspended on fishing line from Eddie's tackle box. The bright colors caught the sun and reflected light into the residents' rooms, but Alfie was the one who put the light in their eyes.

"What's the deal with them hearts?" an old black man asked Corliss. "Is it Valentine's Day or something? I thought it was summer."

"It *is* summer, Magnus," Corliss said. "It doesn't have to be Valentine's Day to heart somebody."

"So does that mean we're sweethearts, Corliss Briggs?" he asked when Chancy finished hanging a shimmering purple foil token in his window.

"You know I won't sit under the apple tree with anyone else but you." She gave him a hug as she sang the words Chancy recognized from the Andrews Sisters album.

Corliss knew all the residents by name and shared tidbits of their lives during introductions, calculated to make the old people laugh.

"Mina was a WAC in World War Two. She's sneaky, so I think she might have been a government spy.

"Gus used to be an oilman. Folks called him Gusher Gus because he really knew how to sink a well.

"Addy just celebrated her hundredth birthday. Forty-seven of her great-great-grandchildren came to eat cake.

"Mary used to teach in a one-room schoolhouse. Had a former state governor as one of her students.

"Bill flew a barnstorming plane back in the day. Watch out for him. He's still pulling stunts.

"John once sat next to that gangster Pretty Boy Floyd in a movie theater. Takes one to know one, I always say."

On and on. Every room held one or two elderly residents, and every resident had a story. A life. Memories to share. Before Chancy left, they all asked the same thing: "When will you come back?"

"So what do you think?" Corliss asked as they walked to the rec room for bingo. Alfie trotted between them.

"I like this place."

"Me too."

"It's nothing like I thought it would be."

"Some people figure nursing homes are depressing places, like an elephant graveyard where people go to die."

"That's what Max thinks."

"Max Boyle is a brilliant man, but he don't know everything. He's done a lot for you, honey, but you need to form your own opinions about things."

"The residents like you." Probably because Corliss didn't see them as sick old people, but as friends.

"I like them too."

"You feel at home here, don't you?"

"I'd better. I may be living here one of these days. Maybe not too far in the future either."

"Why?"

"You know that cough I thought was a summer cold? Well, it's not. It's emphysema, and my lungs are a mess. Doctor says it's probably from working around greasy grills most of my life. And smoke. Never touched a single cigarette, but I breathed plenty of smoke. Before all the smoke-free whoop-de-do, customers thought nothing of lighting up after a meal. Sometimes during."

Chancy didn't know what emphysema was, but it sounded bad. A million times worse than when her own healthy lungs clenched in a panic attack. "I'm sorry you're sick."

"Oh, I'm not sick. Don't let these lousy lungs worry you. A person is only as sick as they let themselves be. I learned that from Hanna Boyle. Far as I can tell, she never felt sorry for herself, not even for a day. She worried about Max. How he'd make out after she was gone. But she wasn't afraid. And neither am I. I'm gonna roll with the punches. And if my lungs let me down, like Hanna's did, well, I can say I lived right when I meet my maker."

"When will you move here?"

"I don't know. When I can't work any longer, I reckon. Or when I get to where I can't take care of myself. Soon. Three months, maybe six. The lung doctor thinks I'll be toting an oxygen tank before Christmas."

How could Corliss, who was so full of life, be so sick? The unfairness of her friend's illness made Chancy angry. "How can you accept this so calmly?"

She smiled. "I look forward to coming home to the Manor. All my friends are here. Barb is good people. So are the nurses and aides she hires. She doesn't cotton to slackers."

"What about your trailer?"

"Oh, land, that rickety old heap doesn't belong to me. Thank God. I paid rent sixteen years, but I never liked that place. They'll take care of me here. I don't have any money. No insurance or assets. Medicaid will foot the bill, once I get too stove-up to work. Guess that makes me a charity case, but I'm not ashamed of that. I worked hard my whole life. I'm not too proud to accept help. That's what social agencies and government programs are for, you know, to help them that need it."

Corliss painted a far different picture than Max. He considered Adult Protective Services and other "do-gooder" agencies a threat to his freedom. Knowing she had a safety net *gave* Corliss freedom. She didn't have to worry about her future. Maybe Max didn't know everything. Or maybe he'd forgotten some of the crucial facts.

"Can't you stay with Eddie?"

"I don't want to be a burden to him. He's young. Got his whole life to live. I wouldn't dream of asking him to give up his future for me."

"What if he wants to take care of you?"

She laughed. "In that case, he can be a diligent son and visit me regular."

In the rec room, residents sat around a large table with bingo cards in front of them. Corliss led Chancy to a chair beside the little bird lady, whose name was Fern. When the game started, Chancy helped Fern find the numbers. During the blackout round, Fern was the first to cover all the squares. Chancy urged her to yell, "Bingo!" The other players applauded, and Barb delivered the winner's prize: a small teddy bear clutching a red velvet heart.

"You take this, honey." Fern pressed the toy into Chancy's hands. "It'll mean more to you than it does to me."

Chancy understood. She would come back. She liked the wrinkly, cranky, funny old people. She enjoyed making the sad ones smile and wanted to hear more of the stories they'd accumulated during their rich lives. She wanted to connect with a past she could remember and never have to forget.

When the bingo game was over and the residents were taken to the dining room for lunch, Corliss and Barbara and Chancy chatted in Barb's office while they waited for Eddie.

"So how's the learning center coming along?" Corliss asked. She'd already told Chancy about the new program that would soon be launched at the Manor. A deceased former resident had left the proceeds of her estate to build a morning preschool as part of the elder-care structure. A place where the very young and the very old could be together. Any resident who wanted to help out or visit the preschool rooms could do so at certain times.

Barb explained that the guiding philosophy behind the program was to compensate for scattered families. Many children did not know their great-grandparents. Older people often had no opportunity to play with youngsters. The mixed program had proven successful elsewhere, and Barb was looking forward to offering it to the citizens of Wenonah.

"Construction of the addition is complete," Barb said. "We're done with the interior decor, and shipments of fixtures and toys are arriving daily. We have room for thirty three- and four-year-olds, and enrollment is almost full."

"Mark my words," Corliss said. "This project will take off like the space shuttle."

Barb laughed. "There's only one small problem. We still haven't found a director. I've interviewed several candidates, but no one has been right for the job. Maybe I'm being too picky, but I want someone special who can connect with both preschoolers and seniors. Biggest problem is, it's a part-time job. Starting out, we'll only have a morning program. Eventually we may expand, but for now, I can't offer a full-time position or benefits."

"I can see how it might be hard to find a qualified person agreeable to the terms," Corliss said.

"I've talked to a few with the right credentials, but this job isn't about education. Compassion is more important than diplomas."

"You got that right," Corliss put in. "You can train people how to take care of people, but you can't teach them to care. That has to come from here." Corliss pressed her hand on her chest.

"I know someone." Chancy's excitement spilled into her words. "I have a friend who would be perfect for that job."

"I'm all ears," Barb said. "I've been watching you, and you're a natural too, just like Alfie. I trust your recommendation."

Barb's words reinforced the teddy bear's message. As soon as she had mentioned compassion, Chancy knew why she was here. Jenny wanted a part-time job that would make a difference. She hadn't gotten the receptionist job because that was not where she was meant to be.

"Personality is important," Barb clarified. "But due to guidelines and state regs and all that, the candidate must meet educational requirements."

"Will a degree in psychology work?" Chancy asked.

"Sounds perfect. That's what we need around here, someone who understands people." Barb pulled a business card from her pocket. "Tell your friend to call me."

They walked out to the dayroom to see if their ride had arrived. "There's Eddie!" Chancy spotted him in the adjoining dining room. Most of the residents had finished their lunch and gone to their rooms for naps. One skeletal-looking old man sat alone at a table in the back of the room. Eddie sat beside him.

When Corliss started to join them, Barb placed her hand on Corliss's arm. "Let's see what happens. That's Mr. Magruder. He gives the aides holy heck at mealtimes. Won't eat. Insists on sitting alone. We've tried every approach we know."

"He looks really old. Can he feed himself?" Chancy asked.

"Oh, sure. If the doctor threatens to insert a feeding tube, he'll eat for a while, so we know he can. Food is a power struggle. He's stubborn. Hated coming here."

Chancy looked at the old man slumped over his plate of cooling food. Felt his hopelessness. Fear chipped away at the happiness the day had given her. Uncle Max was stubborn. Would he go on a hunger strike if Ms. Wooten forced him into Grayson House?

"What's Eddie doing?" Corliss asked.

"I don't know," Barb said. "I can't hear what he's saying."

They watched as Eddie scooted his chair closer. Mr. Magruder listened for a few moments, then threw back his head and laughed. He was still chuckling when he picked up his fork and ate a bite of meat loaf. Then mashed potatoes. Then peas.

"I don't know what's more amazing," Barb said, "hearing Mr. M. laugh or seeing him eat so much food."

Later, as Eddie drove home, Chancy asked what he'd said to the old man.

He grinned. "Can't really say in mixed company, but I kinda told him a dirty joke."

"Son! I can't believe you'd do that."

"Old men like dirty jokes too, you know. Besides, it worked, didn't it?"

"Men!" Corliss shook her head. "He ate all that food for one of your stories?"

"Not really." The banter went out of Eddie's voice. "I told him I'd sit and keep him company as long as he was eating."

"That was a nice thing to do, son."

"Yeah, well, the old guy looked lonesome."

Chancy sat quietly in the backseat while Eddie and Corliss chatted in the front. Eddie made light of his unexpectedly tender behavior, but Chancy saw it as a sign that he really would be a good son and visit his mother in the nursing home. Corliss had been strong when he needed her. Eddie would be strong for Corliss now. Jenny and Adam had supported Tom when he couldn't stand alone. One day he would be well again, and their family would be closer for having weathered the storm.

But what of her and Uncle Max? For weeks now they'd lived a lie. They'd been dishonest, even to each other, by ignoring reality and pretending everything would be all right. Their time together had been so good, but summer would end. Life, with all its realities, would go on. As much as Chancy wanted to believe Uncle Max would live forever, she knew the truth. The nursing home, clean and cheerful and well maintained, was full of truth. Frail, failing bodies. Minds that had dimmed. Uncle Max had given her memories that would live forever, but the gentle old man would not.

Chapter 21

Every morning for a week Chancy practiced driving with Uncle Max. Each night they studied the driving manual together. Chancy wouldn't be taking the test, not yet anyway, but the drills helped Uncle Max remember the rules for the written exam. Someday, maybe she would be able to sit for the exam herself.

On the day of the big test, Jenny drove him to the Department of Public Safety. They planned to stop at the bank and shop for groceries on the way home. Uncle Max acted as if the test were no big deal, but Chancy knew how badly he wanted to have his license reinstated. How badly he *needed* to pass.

Chancy stayed home and Adam kept her company. Rain the day before made it too wet to work in the garden, so they enjoyed the respite by listening to music. "Mack the Knife." "Woodchoppers Ball." "Shanghai Shuffle."

"Can you believe how big these dudes are?" Holding the album carefully between his palms, Adam positioned another record on the turntable, as Uncle Max had taught them. "Hard to believe people had dozens of records. You can get more music on an iPod and it doesn't take up nearly as much space."

He improvised a spastic jitterbug and pulled Chancy into the dance, but his horseplay didn't make her stop worrying about the tests Uncle Max had to pass. Vision. Written. Driving. If he got flustered and made mistakes . . . No, she wouldn't think about that.

"I think I'll go home and see if Dad's up yet," Adam said after a while. "Do you want to come? We could watch a movie or something."

"No, thanks. I haven't organized all the drawers in the kitchen yet. I'll do that while I'm waiting for them to get back."

"The changes around here are pretty cool. Like it's not even the same house anymore. You and Uncle Max could start your own cleanup business." Adam sang in a comically eerie voice. "When the crap piles up, and the wallpaper sucks, who you gonna call? *Junk*-busters!"

"Remember the day we met, and you said you were good for a laugh?"

"Yeah?"

"You were right."

His attention flitted to another subject. "Can I borrow Scrabble? Maybe Dad will play with me."

She gave him the game from the newly organized hall closet. "I'm glad he's feeling better."

"Me too. He's okay, you know."

"Your mom said the new medicine is working wonders."

"No. I'm not talking about that. I mean, he's really okay. Like, a good guy. I didn't know that before." He hugged the game box to his chest. "Can I ask you something?"

"You know you can."

His chin trembled. "Am I a bad person for being glad my dad got sick?"

"What do you mean?"

"If he hadn't gotten sick, he would have kept working like always. We'd have a big fancy kitchen instead of an empty room, but he never would have had time for me. That's selfish, right?"

"No. Wanting your parent to care is normal." She knew that now.

"When he first got sick, I even wished he would die. He made Mom cry. I thought he was mean to her and we'd be better off if he just went away forever. I didn't know she was crying because he was the one suffering. That's love, right? When someone else's pain hurts as bad as your own?"

She nodded. "Your parents are lucky to have you for a son." She'd often wished B.J. were dead. Then, when she'd had a chance to make her own wish come true, she didn't want it anymore. She used to think a bad parent was better than none, but since coming to Wenonah, she'd changed her mind.

"Do you think God will punish me for wishing Dad was dead?" Adam's voice cracked, and he sniffed loudly.

"God knows you didn't mean it."

"Did He make Dad sick?"

"Maybe." Chancy recalled a line from Hanna's journal. "Everything happens for a reason."

"Thanks." He cleared his throat and was back to the old, teasing Adam again. "If you hadn't spent the summer here, I might not have ever known how cool girls could be."

She laughed. "I'm sure you would have figured that out sooner or later." Adam was a gawky, too-tall adolescent boy, but someday he would be a very nice man. And a good father. Someday maybe a nice boy her own age would think she was cool.

"Call me when they get back," he said at the door. "I want to help celebrate Uncle Max getting his license."

"What if he fails?"

"What? Our uncle Max fail?" Adam scoffed. "That man doesn't know the meaning of the word."

Chancy filled a small trash bag with empty bread ties and loose screws and expired coupons from what Uncle Max called the Everything Drawer. She clipped the unexpired coupons together and placed them back in the drawer. She lifted a stack of embroidered dish towels from a little-used bottom drawer that was sticky and hard to open. Beneath the towels, she found a large yellow envelope like the one Uncle Max had given her for the heart she'd made Jenny. She recognized the manila envelope from her first morning in the house. Uncle Max had snatched it from the middle of the table and tucked it away, out of sight. She hadn't thought about it since. He must have forgotten it too.

His memory lapses were frequent but had not posed a problem. She was usually around to remind him of important things, like taking his medicine. Recently he'd seemed more tired than usual, and when she asked him why, he'd dismissed her concern by reminding her that he'd done more chores around the house in the past couple of months than in the last twenty years combined. Then he'd laughed. *I bet I'm the only man in recorded history who hired a helper and ended up working harder than ever.*

She started to leave the envelope on the kitchen table for him, then recognized the handwriting on the front—Max's, and the name Pete. The flap wasn't sealed, just closed with a little clasp. The same strong feelings that had led her to this house in the beginning urged her to open it. She pulled out a letter written in a thin scrawl with flowing letters and curvy tails. The hard-to-decipher words ran together. Opening a letter that didn't belong to her was a shadowy, old-Chancy thing to do. A survival instinct that might never completely die, no matter how peaceful her life became. And yet she couldn't deny the need to read what Uncle Max had written.

She carried the letter to the table and smoothed the creases, reading the words several times to tease them apart. Outside the open window, chimes tinkled in the breeze. She swallowed hard and scanned the words again and again, quickly, then slowly. With each pass, they rose up bigger, thicker.

> *Dear Pete,*
>
> *I have seen plenty of sunrises in my eighty-three years. Plenty of sunsets, too. I have watched storm clouds darken the sun and chain lightning heat up the sky. I have lived through the Depression, Prohibition and the Dust Bowl. I've seen war and what passes for peace. I have marveled over the gifts of each new season and worried about the fate of mankind for a long time now.*
>
> *I guess what I'm trying to say is, I've lived a lifetime. I've had enough. The best part of me died with Hanna. It's hard to make a final farewell cheerful, but I would appreciate it if you didn't grieve. The doctors and social workers think I should stick around until the bitter end. They are wrong.*

Death should not be bitter. The end should be as sweet as life for those of us who make our own choices.

I'm not crazy. I'm not demented. I'm not even desperate. I'm simply tired. I miss my girl. I know she's waiting for me. With Hanna in my arms for eternity, I will dance circles around all the angels in heaven.

I can't ask you to forgive what I'm about to do, but I beg you to understand. Good-bye, my friend. We will meet again. The next drink is on you.

Max

Chancy's heart slammed against her ribs. A suicide note. It took several minutes for the words to make sense. Max had planned to kill himself. She stumbled to the puppy calendar next to the sink and flipped the pages back to May. She had carefully X'ed off all the days she'd spent in the house. The date on the note was the same as the first X. Max had planned to die the day he found her hiding in his garage. Had he planned to die in the Lincoln?

The implications were stunning and almost more than she could bear. *Everything happens for a reason.* The universe had led her from a miserable life in Pittsburgh to a place in Wenonah's sun for the express purpose of finding a certain garage on a certain street at a certain time. Without knowing what she had done, she had saved Maxwell Boyle's life. In return he had given her a life worth living.

Their connection was deep and true and could not be broken, no matter what happened. She read the words again. It was hard to reconcile the scrappy fighter she had come to know with the man who had written the note, but she understood despair better than most. Certainly better than Ms. Wooten, whose good intentions had driven Uncle Max to want to die. Chancy knew how being alone destroyed the will to live. She'd lost her will to live that night by the river in St. Louis. B.J. had lost hers more than once. Why? Her mother didn't have to be alone. For years Chancy had forgiven everything. She'd tried to be a daughter worth living for. Her mother had never explained why she had felt so alone. Why hadn't she put her pain into words instead of actions that hurt them both?

Feeling light-headed with fear and certainty, Chancy slipped the note back into the envelope and pressed down the metal clasp. She returned the envelope to its hiding place and shut the drawer firmly. Uncle Max would never know she had stolen his secret. She would let him keep it, just as he had let her keep hers.

When Chancy heard the Lincoln purr into the drive, she quickly called Adam's number and told him they were back. By the time she stepped out on the porch, he was already running across the street.

"Uncle Max is climbing out of the driver's side," he whispered when he skidded to a stop beside Chancy. "That's a good sign, right?"

She crossed her fingers and called out. "Well?"

Uncle Max waved. "I did it!"

"Woo-hoo! Way to go!" Adam danced in a victory circle, and Max said he was turning into a regular Donald O'Connor.

"I didn't squeak by either." Max wore pride like a new suit.

"Tell them your score, Max," Jenny urged.

"This old duffer racked up one hundred percent on the written test."

Chancy smiled. "I knew you could do it."

"Then you knew more than me." Max was being modest. He had been confident and determined when he left.

Feelings Chancy had tamped down and buried for so long struggled into the bright afternoon light. She needed to hug Uncle Max. He had overcome his fears about passing the test. She could overcome hers too. When she rushed into his arms, they closed around her. He sighed and his breath warmed her ear. She knew why Hanna had loved Uncle Max. He had made her feel safe.

"I'm proud of you," she whispered. Whatever had made him want to die once couldn't touch him now. He would be around for a long, long time. So would she. And they would be together.

"I couldn't have done any of this without your help." His voice shook and his embrace tightened. "We make a good team."

Something cracked inside Chancy, loosening like an icebound river in spring, and the feelings flowed. She hadn't been able to explain to Corliss how she felt about Uncle Max, but she knew the name of the emotion now: love. She loved him. He was her family. Even if she spent the rest of her life alone, she would be content because she had once found a home in the heart of another person.

"Group hug!" Adam threw himself into the huddle, pulling his mother in as well. Alfie danced in delirious circles. They all laughed, and Chancy couldn't remember ever feeling so happy.

"Mom! I almost forgot." Adam slapped his forehead. "That lady, Barbara, called. About the job."

"What about it?"

"I don't know. She said to call her back because she had good news."

Jenny squealed and pulled out her cell phone. She paced back and forth in the yard as she talked. After a few minutes, she snapped the phone shut.

"I got the job!"

And Chancy was even happier. They did another crazy dance, and Jenny shared the details. "I owe you a big thanks, Chancy. If you hadn't told me about the opening, I never would have known to apply. Barb hadn't filed the position with employment agencies yet. She says she gets the best people through word of mouth."

"The Beatles were right," Adam said.

They all looked at him to explain. "You know, that *Sergeant Pepper* record of Uncle Max's? I guess we all get by with a little help from our friends."

"So tell us about the job," Uncle Max urged as they sat on the porch to escape the heat.

"Barb took me on a tour of the Manor when I was there. I was impressed by the standard of care she enforces. The staff seems genuinely fond of the residents. She explained my duties and what would be expected of me, then showed me the preschool facility. They're calling it Moppet Manor, by the way. Isn't that clever?"

"What the heck is a moppet?" Adam asked. "Something like a Muppet?"

"A moppet is another name for a small child," Uncle Max told him.

"Okay, then it's not so dumb, I guess."

Chancy gave him a little shove. "When do you start?"

"First thing in the morning. Barb wants me to learn the administrative policies and programs before the children come. I told her my computer skills aren't exactly stellar, and she said it doesn't matter. That stuff can be learned. And you know what? I think I can do it."

"Sure you can, Mom." Adam beamed. "You're Supermom, remember?"

"The salary is better than I hoped for. It really is the perfect job for me. I feel blessed to have a chance to work for a dedicated woman like Barb, doing something fulfilling. Things are finally looking up for the Hamilton family."

"A driver's license and a new job! That's a lot of good news for one day," said Uncle Max.

"I could make lasagna for dinner," Chancy suggested. "Jenny gave me her recipe."

"And chocolate cake for dessert?" Adam asked.

"Why not?" Uncle Max ruffled Adam's messy hair. "We have plenty to celebrate."

After the Hamiltons left, Max pulled out his wallet and removed his license. "Read it and weep, my dear."

Chancy admired Uncle Max's picture on the plastic square. No restrictions. He could go anywhere, anytime, with anyone he chose. And she had helped him. She thought about the sad note folded away in the drawer and realized she had made his situation better. For once, she hadn't been a burden. Then, unexpectedly, the fizzy, happy feeling congealed into sick regret. Uncle Max was doing well. His house was neat and organized. Ms. Wooten had backed off. The driver's license meant he didn't need Chancy as much as before. In fact, he might not need her at all.

She felt like crying, but it was selfish to be sad when Uncle Max was so happy. He had hope again. And all because of a little plastic square that said he was competent to operate a motor vehicle. Jenny was happy too.

She had a job. Her husband was on his way back. Adam had a new relationship with his father. They wouldn't need her as much, either. How could she be happy and sad at the same time?

"So, young lady, where would you like to go for your first ride?" Uncle Max asked.

Max awakened in the middle of the night to an elephant standing on his chest. He sat on the edge of the bed with his head in his hands. Lasagna induced heartburn. He pushed off the mattress to find an antacid in the bathroom. Too damned dizzy. He panted like a dog in August. Not enough oxygen in the room. The air conditioner was blasting, so why was he so warm? He tried to open the window but couldn't figure out the lock. Trapped. Wormlike paranoia slithered through him. He pressed his fist to his chest. He wasn't having another heart attack. He'd eaten too much of Chancy's lasagna, was all. He flipped on the bathroom light and searched the medicine cabinet. Chewed three antacids and reached for the bottle of pain reliever. Swallowed two. Just needed to take care of his bladder and fall back into bed. Either he'd be better by morning, or there wouldn't be a morning for him. Either way, nothing else he could do.

Max leaned against the jamb and stared down the hall to his open door. Was his room farther away than it had been before? The elephant that had been performing the Argentine tango on his chest had eased off to a soft-shoe routine. The panic and paranoia faded. His room was closer now. Maybe he should take a couple of those sleeping pills the doctor had given him after Hanna died. A few hours of sound sleep wouldn't hurt. His nights had been restless and filled with old dreams for weeks. He stumbled back into the bathroom and found the pills. Two should do it. Maybe three.

Somehow he made it to his pillow before the medication kicked in.

"He stole it, Sister! I know he did."

"I'm sorry you lost your Saint Jude's medal, Maxwell." Sister Justina sat behind her desk, prepared to give both accused and accuser a fair hearing. Young Sister Blessida stood by the door, her hands tucked into the sleeves of her habit. Max had gone to her first, and she'd taken the matter to her superior.

"I didn't lose my medal! Bob took it!"

"What makes you think Robert is guilty?"

"He's a thief, that's what I *know!* The food going missing from the kitchen? Bob stole it! I saw him eating a whole loaf of bread!" The skinny boys had gone without toast for breakfast, but Bob Mapo was plumper than ever. A pig-eyed bully who took his meanness out on those too small to fight back.

"*Is* this true, Robert? Have you been stealing from the pantry?"

"*Course not, Sister. Max don't know nothin'. Lying little Mick. I ain't never done nothin' wrong. You know me better'n that, right, Sister?*"

"Ain't never been caught, you mean!" Max leaned forward and charged into the bigger boy, head-butting him so hard in the stomach that he slammed backward into the wall. Max, unable to see anything but red fury, fell on his tormentor and pummeled him with his fists. Before Sister Blessida and Sister Justina could pull them apart, Max had made his point several times on Bob's face. His nose was streaming blood and his right eye was already swelling shut.

"Get the little bastard off me!" Bob screamed. "He's killin' me!"

"I wish I could kill ya!" Max was barely twelve and small for his age. "I wish I had a rusty knife to stick in your sorry gizzard!"

As punishment Max was forced to kneel on the rough wood floor in the chapel for eight hours and pray for forgiveness. No water. No trips to the outhouse. He missed dinner and supper, while fat Bob Mapo was escorted to the infirmary, where Sister Dauphine was probably feeding him pudding for his pain.

Max knelt as instructed, because the sisters took turns checking on him to make sure he obeyed. Last time Sister Blessida looked in, she had whispered that she'd saved an apple and a biscuit for him to eat before bed. *Just say your prayers,* she'd begged. But he didn't say any prayers. Didn't ask for forgiveness or anything else. Instead Maxwell Boyle hatched a plot to escape the orphanage. He only wished he could take back his property before he left. A priest had given his mother the Saint Jude medal while she was in the tuberculosis hospital. The priest told her Saint Jude was the patron saint of desperate situations and lost causes. At his mother's funeral service, the same priest had given the little medal on a chain to Max.

That old saint hadn't saved his sick mother. Probably wouldn't save him either. Max had wiped his tears and snotty nose on his sleeve. He didn't need the medal. And he wouldn't depend on anyone's help. Ever. Not even a saint's. He would help himself. Or die trying.

When Max awoke, the room was full of shadows. Hard rain pounded the roof. He glanced at the clock. After eleven. He never slept that late. So why did he feel drained and exhausted? His knees ached, more the memory of pain than pain itself. His head hurt too. No man's skull should throb that hard unless he'd been on a weekend bender. He remembered the elephant that had tap-danced on his chest. Thank God it was gone. The house was dark and quiet. He went to the bathroom, but became disoriented and had to retrace his steps. Where was Alfie? And Chancy?

He returned to his room to get dressed, but couldn't shake the confused feeling that something bad had happened. Had it? Everything was blank after he took those antacids last night. He sat on the side of the bed, trying to put the night's events back together. Then he remembered. He'd been robbed. He went to the dresser where Hanna kept her jewelry and pulled the teakwood box from the drawer. Inside he found only a few pieces of costume jewelry. Where were Hanna's nice things? Her rings? Her ruby earrings? Her butterfly brooch?

He wouldn't be bullied and robbed again. He stumbled into a red fog and charged down the hall to Chancy's room.

Chapter 22

Chancy sat cross-legged in the middle of her bed listening to the rain patter on the window. Before Wenonah, she had hated the rain, but now she saw it for what it was: a nurturing life force essential to the growth and well-being of the planet. The garden she'd tended was looking more like the pictures in Hanna's journals every day. The sunny areas were almost complete. Jenny had taken her to the garden center and they'd poked among the lush rows, looking for specific plants to replace the ones that had died.

The shady corner under the trees still had bare spots. Maybe if it stopped raining later, Uncle Max would drive her to the big garden center in the next town. It might have the particular variety of hosta they'd been looking for, for several weeks now, with no luck.

She glanced at the bedside lamp. It was getting late and Uncle Max was still sleeping, which wasn't like him at all. He always called her a slugabed if she slept past eight thirty. The kitchen had been dark this morning when she went down for breakfast. Dreading what she might find, she'd dashed upstairs and knocked on his door. No answer. She'd peeked in and been both relieved and surprised to find him curled up on his side, sleeping soundly. She'd tiptoed in and had stood by his bed until the reassuring rumble of his snore assured her he was just tired. The impromptu celebration party last night had probably worn him out.

Everyone had said the lasagna she'd made was delicious. Uncle Max and Adam had driven to the bakery to buy a chocolate cake. Adam was thrilled when his mother showed up with his father, who had agreed to join them. Tom had sat quietly while they toasted Jenny's and Uncle Max's achievements. Adam had happily nudged Chancy under the table when his father accepted a second slice of cake.

This morning, Chancy had slipped out of Uncle Max's room and returned to the kitchen, where she'd fried herself an egg and fed Alfie. She'd spread papers on the back porch for him, promising a walk later. Since she couldn't work in the garden, she would start on another project equally dear to her heart.

She filled an old cookie tin with Uncle Max's favorite photographs and returned to her room, where she set out supplies on the bed. She planned to create a memory book for Uncle Max by placing the treasured photos in the beautiful fake-leather album she'd purchased. She stroked the cover. Deep blue, embossed with a simple gold border. She'd also bought special labeling pens with ink that wouldn't fade and had secretly made tiny hearts out of the prettiest paper she could find to decorate the pages.

She was sticking a heart in place with the archival glue the craft store lady had recommended when her bedroom door flew open. Startled, she looked up to find Uncle Max standing there in his pajamas. His feet were bare. White whiskers prickled his cheeks and his hair stood out from his head in spiky disarray. Alfie clambered to his feet and stood between Chancy and his master.

"Have you been snooping through my things?" Uncle Max's sharp words jabbed with a hurtful, serrated edge.

"No." Why was he upset?

"So what are you doing?" he demanded.

"Nothing." Unwilling to spoil his surprise, she slid the memory book behind the pillow sham. "Just looking at pictures." She indicated the tin box containing the photos she'd culled.

"So you *have* been snooping?"

"No." Then she remembered the yellow envelope under the tea towels and her stomach flipped. Yes, she was guilty. Was that why he was angry? Because she knew his secret?

"What else have you been prowling through?" He blinked furiously, and his words spewed out on sharp little gasps.

"Nothing." Chancy's heart hammered and her muscles tensed. She had to lie. Again. Even if doing so made her feel like a traitor. The room that had wrapped around her like a warm cocoon had turned into a trap. The grizzled old man glowering in the doorway didn't look or sound like the gentle Uncle Max she'd come to love. His wrinkled face, collapsed in fury, was that of a demented stranger. Clenched fists shook at his sides. For as long as she'd known him Maxwell Boyle had been kind. This accuser was not.

"I know you're an accomplished liar, but now I need the truth."

What did he want to know? She didn't understand. "About the note?"

"No! About the brooch!"

What brooch? Her brain skittered. He didn't know she'd read his suicide note. So what other bad thing could she have done? Old feelings of desperation and fear that she'd thought were locked away forever boiled to the surface to drown her in a fresh wave of panic. *What did I do?* she'd often beseeched her mother right before the blows rained down. She'd screamed the question at her mother's back as she'd walked away, leaving her behind.

What did I do? She couldn't ask aloud. Her throat was too tight. She searched her memory. She and Adam had washed the dishes after dinner, while Uncle Max and Jenny and Tom talked in the living room. They'd listened to records. Tom liked Glenn Miller, and he and Uncle Max had discussed music. Tom had smiled, and Uncle Max had been his jovial self. Everyone had been happy.

"Don't sit there and stare at me, Chancy! I need an answer!" A flash of lightning outside pumped its own electricity into the air.

"I'm sorry," she whispered. Yelling back had never worked with B.J. and it wouldn't work with the old man blocking the doorway. In order to escape, she would have to push him aside. Could she do that? She climbed off the bed and extended the box. "They're just pictures. I didn't think you'd mind."

"I don't care about the pictures." He didn't take the box, and she clutched it to her chest. "Tell me. Did you go in my room?"

"Yes."

"Why?"

"To clean."

"You sneaked in there to clean?"

"I didn't sneak. I was running the vacuum cleaner in the hall. Your door was open, so I went in to sweep the rug."

"What else did you do in there?" His words sounded slurred again, as they had months ago.

Chancy's thoughts raced back to that day. How long ago had it been? A week? Longer? She sorted the scene in her mind. Ivy-patterned rug prickly with dog hair. She'd moved a chair to plug in the sweeper. The motor had roared, shattering the silence. *Then what happened?* She ran the vacuum over the rug. Back and forth. Then over the wood floor. Under the bed. In the corners. She was proud of the clean floor. When she turned to leave, she noticed the dust. Everywhere.

"Yes, I did something else." She snatched at the answer. "I dusted."

"Did you mess with Hanna's things?"

Uncle Max's accusation struck her like a punch in the stomach. "No!" Her muscles burned. *Move. Run. Hide.*

"I don't believe you."

"I'm telling the truth."

"I wonder if you even know what is true. What is the truth of you, Chancy Deel?"

Without knowing how it happened, Chancy had somehow broken the wondrous connection with Uncle Max. She'd believed he was different. That he could see what was in her heart. She was wrong.

"Hanna's brooch is missing." Uncle Max's words vibrated between them as though they'd been slapped out of his mouth.

"I didn't take it." Chancy backed away, gaze downcast. She was so wounded by his accusations that she could think of nothing else to do. She was bad. B.J. always said so. All the bad things that happened to her mother had been Chancy's fault.

"Well, somebody took it!"

She backed up a few more steps, and Alfie stood firmly beside her. As hard as she tried, she couldn't imagine Uncle Max striking her, but the worst monsters were the ones who didn't look scary on the outside. Alfie gave a worried growl, low in his throat.

The old man railing at her wasn't the same one who'd told her to call him Uncle Max. She didn't know this frail-looking stranger. Could she ever really know anyone? "You forget things sometimes," she reminded him gently. "Maybe you lost it."

"I'm not senile! Is that what you're saying!"

"No. That's not what I meant."

"You think you can steal from me? Take advantage? After all I've done for you? I thought I could trust you." The last words fell on the floor between them, choked on a strangled sob.

"You *can* trust me. Please." Or maybe he couldn't. Shouldn't. B.J. had told her so many times, in so many ways, how worthless she was. She had let her mother down, run out on her. Now she wanted to run from Uncle Max. And she would if she could have moved. She'd felt safe, even happy here, but good feelings never lasted. She didn't deserve anything good. That was what the marks on her arms meant.

"I know you took Hanna's diamond butterfly brooch." Max's accusation clamored into Chancy's head.

"No." Did she take something? She couldn't remember. Maybe. But why? She didn't steal from people. Just from stores. Only food. *Brooch.* She tried to untangle the word in her mind but couldn't find the picture. All she could see was a roach. A coach.

"Before you came, it was in my room. In the jewelry box. Top dresser drawer!" Max's words swarmed like bees and flew, stinging, into Chancy's face. "Now it's gone."

Images flooded back, but all she remembered was sweeping. Dusting. What about the dresser? Had she opened the drawers? No. She'd looked at the picture on top of the dresser. A photo in a silver frame. She had picked it up. Cold metal. A little girl in a big chair with a back like a fan. Wearing a pale dress and tiny slippers and a big bow in her bobbed hair.

She held a small black dog. Chancy had imagined being the girl. Holding the dog. Having a reason to smile for the camera. She had known the child was Hanna, and the dog and bow and tiny slippers meant her mother had loved her very much. Good girls had happy lives. Loving husbands. Bad girls, B.J. had told her, were entitled to nothing.

"No. No. I never opened the drawer." Chancy continued to stare at the floor, focusing on a knot in the wood that looked like a leprechaun's head. Hearing the censure in Uncle Max's voice was hard enough. She didn't want to see the disappointment and disgust in his eyes again. She rubbed her arms. Felt the scars. She'd been careful to hide them, just as she'd been careful to conceal who she really was. Uncle Max had glimpsed them only once, briefly, but he knew the marks were there. And what they meant.

"I have to know," he pleaded. "I haven't asked a lot of you, but I expected so much. I had hoped you would trust me with who you really are. I know what it means to be small and lost." His voice broke. "I thought you were Hanna's angel."

"Uncle Max. You have to believe me. I didn't take the . . . brooch. I'm not even sure what a brooch is."

He crossed the room, and she continued to step away from him until the wall pressed into her back. Alfie moved with her, tense and alert. "Look at me, for God's sake, Chancy. I want to understand whatever trouble you're in. All I want is honesty."

Honesty? He'd laughed at the pack-of-lies story she'd fed Ms. Wooten. He'd encouraged her to lie to Jenny and Adam. Now he wanted honesty? She could no longer separate truth from the fiction she'd created.

"What happened to you? You can tell me. Anything. Let me help you."

Chancy flashed back to the last time she'd seen B.J., choking but still breathing. Her blue lips moving without sound. Her eyes wide without seeing. Another few minutes and the life light that burned everything it touched would go out like a wind-snuffed candle. Chancy had contemplated that darkness. Now the memory hurt as much as the moment. Afraid to remember, she reached for the deep place inside, skidded, slipped down, until she no longer felt anything. She entered a place where nothing mattered.

"Look at me, Chancy." He grabbed her arm. Past wounds made her scream.

"No!" The tin box fell from her numb hands and hit the floor hard, spilling the photos. She wanted to gather them, keep them safe, but her hands wouldn't move. The bones in her legs dissolved and she slid down, down, crumpling on the floor amid snapshots of someone else's life.

"My God! Are you okay?"

Sound rushed into her face, but she couldn't hear the words. Couldn't see Uncle Max. She was too far away, in the dark place.

"Come on, now. Get up." His voice was frightened now. "Let me help you."

She jerked from his touch but allowed herself to be guided to the bed. Her feet moved, but she couldn't think. Didn't dare feel.

"Lie down." A soft pat on the shoulder. A blanket settled over her. "I'm so sorry. Look at me, Chancy." The words rattled as though shaken and thrown like dice. "Open your eyes. Please."

Her eyes *were* open, weren't they? She had tumbled down a hole and shadows from the past thronged and settled, weighing heavily on her. Pressing her into nothing.

"So how long has she been out?" Jenny stood in the doorway of Chancy's room. Her arms were folded across her chest and she nibbled the cuticle on her thumb. Helpless in the face of Chancy's collapse, Max had watched for Jenny to return from work and had called as soon as she arrived home. She was the only person he trusted with this disaster.

"An hour now. Maybe a little longer." He'd dressed. Combed down his Albert Einstein hair. Tried not to look as crazy as he felt. When Jenny arrived, he'd told her only that Chancy had passed out.

"Do you want to call an ambulance?"

"No. Whatever is hurting her is not physical." Alfie lay beside Chancy's bed, alert but calm. If she were in danger, the dog—her protector—would sense it and let him know. After Max had helped Chancy to bed, Alfie had sat at his feet, condemning him like he'd just bitten the head off an inno-cent baby bird. Or maybe he just felt like he had.

"What's wrong with her then?"

"I'm guessing emotional stress. We'll keep an eye on her. Let her sleep it off. Back in the war, I saw boys who'd been through too much collapse like that. They used to call it battle fatigue." Max closed the door and Jenny followed him downstairs and into the kitchen.

"I don't understand. Chancy is such a bright, levelheaded girl. More grounded than most kids her age. Good parents. Good home. What could have happened to suddenly make her flip out?"

"I don't think it was sudden." Max sighed. How to begin? "Can you stay until she wakes up? She'll feel better knowing you're here." If he had to confess every detail, Chancy would need Jenny's maternal tenderness more than ever.

"I'm here for *both* of you." Jenny touched his arm. "You look pale; are you all right?"

A sudden quake of pain cracked Max's composure. He clutched his chest and tears welled in his eyes.

"Max!" Jenny wrapped her arm around his shoulders and helped him into a chair. "I think I need to call an ambulance for *you*."

"No, please! Don't take me to that hospital. I need a cup of coffee."

Jenny was aghast. "You *need* medical attention."

"No. I know what's happening to me. There's nothing medical doc-tors can do that I want done."

"You're confusing me, Max. What's wrong?"

He drew a deep, calming breath. He wasn't worried about himself. He was concerned about the little girl lying upstairs. He was living on bor-rowed time and knew it. What would happen to her?

"Ever hear of mitral valve prolapse?" he asked. "Valvular regurgita-tion?"

"Aren't those heart conditions?"

"Yep. I have a valve with a slow leak. Like a car tire."

"Max, I had no idea. Can't those conditions be treated?"

"Have been, for a while now. Medication's not doing the job. The heart doctor told me four months ago that I need surgery. Open-heart. I won't do that."

"But if that's the only solution . . ."

"It's not really a solution, Jenny. Major surgery. At my age? The doctor warned me of the risks. My old heart could shred under the scalpel. Even if the surgery were successful, I'd require lengthy rehabilitation. Assisted living or a nursing home after that. Nope. Not for me. I've done my bit for medical science. I want to live the time I have left right here. In this house. When the bell rings, I'll join Hanna. I'm not afraid to die."

Tears overflowed Jenny's eyes. "Surely there's something else you can do. Some compromise that could be reached?"

"I know what I want. Hell, I'm halfway prepared for the end. So let's don't talk about me. Chancy's situation *can* be fixed, and you have to help me fix it."

"All right. But what about her parents? Shouldn't you try to contact them?"

"I can't."

"I know they're out of touch right now, but they'll be home soon, right?"

"No." Max wanted to bawl when he thought of how cruel he'd been to Chancy. And the guilt! When had he ever been so unkind? He needed a minute to get his scattered thoughts together. The fog had lifted a little, but he felt like he was waking up from a long coma. The doctor had warned him that impaired heart function could reduce oxygen flow to his brain. Cause muddled thinking. Did this mean the end was near? "Would you make a pot of strong coffee, Jenny?"

"Certainly." She patted his shoulder and opened the cupboard door. She knew her way around his kitchen. She had become a good friend. How could he make her understand the deception he'd perpetrated on her?

Could she forgive him for treating a child so badly that she collapsed? Would Chancy? She may have grown up without love, but Chancy had made the last months some of the happiest of his life. Why had those awful accusations frothed out of his mouth, bitter as bile, like a moment in a nightmare? He had no idea what had spurred such despicable behavior.

Jenny bustled around, setting out mugs and placing some of Chancy's homemade cookies on a plate. Little Red Riding Hood's smiling face broke his heart. Ever since he'd told Chancy about Hanna's baking, she'd kept the cookie jar full. Jenny knew that. How could he explain to her that he'd thought the worst of Chancy because he thought the worst of himself? For a furious red moment, he had believed that Chancy had turned on him because she considered him old and easily hoodwinked. Vulnerable. A sitting duck. She was young and wily and street-smart. He'd heard her fabulous lies, seen her chameleon-like behavior.

Robert Mapo. Why had that bully's name popped into his head? Chancy was nothing like the boy who had terrorized his youth. Mapo had singled Max out because he was fresh meat. A new orphan unaccustomed to being utterly alone. He'd made Max's life a misery for three long years. And the nuns, who were supposed to care for their charges, had not stopped the abuse.

Max flashed to one of Shevaun Wooten's assisted-living pep talks, in which she'd said that after self-neglect, the most common form of elder abuse her agency investigated was caregiver exploitation. Normally he liked to think the young social worker was full of crap, but when he woke feeling unduly wronged for some damn reason, he'd become an instant believer. If he wasn't the victim of exploitation, then he was simply a feeble old man.

What do you call senior citizens who trust total strangers? Victims.

Before calling Jenny, he'd checked the jewelry box again. That was when he'd found the key. In his sock drawer where he had put it the day he'd brought it home. How could he have forgotten that after the burglary, Pete had convinced him to store Hanna's valuables at the bank? Clutching the safe-deposit-box key, he'd felt like an old fool who was losing his grip.

"Here you go." Jenny set a mug in front of him. "Eat something. You seem a little shaky."

"Thank you, Jenny. You've been a true friend to me these past few months."

She patted his hand. "That door swings both ways, you know."

"How's the new job working out?"

"It's wonderful. I love it."

"You probably need to get home."

"I have all the time in the world."

Maybe if he got a few things off his chest, the elephant would retreat for a while. "I'd like to tell you a story, Jenny. Two stories, as a matter of fact."

Chapter 23

"Feeling any better?" a raspy male voice asked from far away.

Chancy stumbled out of sleep. When she opened her eyes, the room was dim, and light pooled under the frilly bedside lamp. Outside the window, the rain had stopped, but clouds covered the low-riding sun. "What?"

"You slept a long time." A gentle female voice spoke. "Do you feel okay?"

She sat up and hugged the blanket to her chest. It took a moment for memory to swim clear of the undertow. A golden paw stretched out, pulling her back. Alfie. Her room. Uncle Max's house. Max. Jenny.

Uncle Max sat in a chair beside the bed, Jenny perched at the foot. Both looked scared and relieved, like they'd just climbed out of a wreck and realized everyone was alive.

"What happened?" She recalled sitting on the bed, making the memory book, Alfie wheezing on the floor, and the rain falling outside. The rest was a blur. "I did something bad, but I can't remember what."

"No, Chancy. You didn't do anything wrong." Uncle Max leaned forward and clasped her hands in his. "This is all my fault. I . . . I said some hateful things. I should be horsewhipped for a fool. I'm sorry."

She blinked and a diamond-encrusted butterfly fluttered past, the light sparkling on its misty wings. "Hanna's brooch. I stole it."

"No! You didn't." Max choked. "Can you forgive me?"

The butterfly drifted out the window, taking her security with it. "What?"

"Oh, God. Chancy, I'm sorry I flew off the handle."

He flew? Behind her closed lids she saw Max rise from the chair and try his wings. He had no wings. Couldn't fly. What did the words mean? She was confused, not thinking right. Her brain was cold and stiff from her time in the nowhere place.

"I'm sorry. I never should have blamed you," Max said. "You didn't take the brooch."

"The butterfly is lost. It flew away."

"No. I forgot. Slipped my mind." He told her how Pete Marshall had convinced him to place Hanna's jewelry in a safe-deposit box. "While you were sleeping, I found the key. That's when I remembered." Uncle Max cleared his throat, unable to go on.

"A safe box?" She didn't know there were such things.

"At the bank." Jenny smiled. "Do you understand?"

"I didn't take the butterfly?" Any relief Chancy felt immediately gave way to worry. How much had Uncle Max told Jenny? What about their secrets?

"No. It's safe," Jenny assured her.

"In a box? With a key?"

"That's right." Uncle Max leaned forward. "I don't know why I doubted you. Guess I just . . . Well, no matter how decrepit a man gets, he can always leap to conclusions."

Jack be nimble. A picture of Uncle Max jumping over a candle flashed through Chancy's mind.

"I'm an old fool." Uncle Max's choked words quavered between them. "Maybe Wooten's right about me needing to be in a home."

"I thought . . ."

"What did you think, dear?" That was real concern on Jenny's face. Whatever Uncle Max had told Jenny had not driven her away.

"You can tell us, Chancy." Uncle Max's voice shook. "Jenny knows everything. I told her all about you, all about our deal."

She knew about the lies? Why did she look so concerned? "Aren't you mad that we lied to you?"

Jenny scooted up on the bed and stroked Chancy's hair. "No! Of course not."

"You don't feel tricked?"

Jenny considered that. "A little, but not in a bad way. I understand. I'm just sorry I was so wrapped up in my own problems that I had no idea everything wasn't what it seemed. You two are actually pretty amazing."

"We're good at improvising, right, Uncle Max?"

"A regular Laurel and Hardy." He pulled out his handkerchief and blew his nose.

Chancy rubbed her arms under the covers. The scars reminded her of everything she couldn't be. Maybe they thrived in the dark, like other bad things. If she showed them to her friends, she might steal their power.

"Uncle Max didn't tell you everything, Jenny. Some things no one knows." She pushed up her sleeves and stared at the welts and scars that had been part of her for so long. Jenny gasped. Uncle Max sighed. Chancy tried to see the marks as others might. Ugly, hurtful things.

"My God! I caught a glimpse of something a long time ago," Uncle Max said, "but I had no idea the scars were so bad."

"Is this why you wear long sleeves, dear? To hide them?" Jenny stroked the marks gently. Chancy had never wanted to touch them, not unless they were covered with fabric, but Jenny's cool fingertips were like a salve that took away the sting of confession.

"Chancy, what in heaven's name happened to you?" Uncle Max's voice was thick with tears.

Keep your mouth shut and your sleeves down. Nobody's business but ours. B.J. had been furious, but Uncle Max and Jenny just looked sad. "I'm not supposed to tell."

"Hurt like this is too much to carry inside." Jenny patted Uncle Max's heaving shoulder, and Chancy was glad she was there to comfort him. "Whatever happened, you will feel better if you share it with people who love you."

They loved her? How could they when she was so hard to love? When she made her mother do bad things? When she was . . . unlovable? She'd staggered under the unbearable weight of the past for as long as she could remember. She needed to let it go.

"Who did that to you?" Uncle Max breathed hard, as though he were angry. Just not at Chancy.

"Me."

Jenny didn't gasp this time. She seemed to understand. Uncle Max just looked more hurt and confused. "Why?"

Could she explain? Did she know? She'd spent most of her life in the cold vacuum her mother had created. She'd never felt strong enough to do anything but hide. She didn't want to disappear this time. She wanted to stay in this warm place with Uncle Max. With friends who didn't have to be the faraway kind.

"Take your time, honey." Jenny's soft hand soothed as much as her touch. "Don't be afraid."

If she opened her heart, good feelings would fill it. But first she had to empty it of doubt and fear and pain. The way they'd cleared clutter from this old house. She started slowly, recounting a few early memories. The night her refuge in the closet had become a prison. Being left alone in cockroach-infested apartments for days at a time. Wetting the bed and being punished. She told them how she never had anything to cling to because her mother's fear kept them constantly on the move.

Uncle Max and Jenny listened as she told about her life with B.J. The ridicule and slaps. Broken bones. She had lived in the dark. A blind albino cave fish, afraid to talk. Unwilling to ask for anything. Unable to feel. She had trusted only the make-believe world she had invented. The dollhouse and the hiding place it offered. She recalled past kindnesses. Teachers. Therapists. People who wanted to help but couldn't because B.J. never stayed in one place long enough for Chancy to form a connection with anyone.

"What about family?" Jenny's voice nearly broke on the word, as though a family was the only certainty anyone could have.

"B.J. was the only one. She hated her mother. I don't know her name." She told them how B.J.'s mother had bartered her daughter for drugs at a truck stop.

"My God!" Uncle Max gripped the arms of the chair. Jenny's horrified silence was too much to bear.

"No. B.J. never did that to me. I had the red alert to help me keep away from men." She told them about the long-ago night B.J. had brought a scary-looking man home. He had looked at her mother as he would a wounded animal he had to put out of its misery. Not with compassion, but with eyes that saw something already dead. Chancy had curled up on the ragged sofa, shrouded in stillness like a frightened fawn in the forest. Her mother screamed and the man stumbled out of the bedroom. B.J. flew at him, beating her fists on his back, demanding the drugs he'd promised.

The man sat beside Chancy and asked B.J. how bad she wanted a fix. *Gonna-die bad.* She would do anything. Chancy had tried to run, but the man had grabbed her. Held her tightly while he lit a cigarette. *How old are you?* he asked. When she couldn't speak, B.J. had screamed, *She's eight, dammit!*

Well, eight is your lucky number. Holding Chancy's thin arms, he'd burned four perfect holes in each forearm. Her mother, twitching with need, had watched Chancy's skin sizzle. The more they both cried, the more the man laughed. B.J. had begged, not for him to stop, but for the drugs he'd withheld.

"I didn't want to cry or feel anything," Chancy said softly. "I fell into the quiet place. When I woke up, B.J. was passed out on the floor with fresh needle tracks in her arms."

A teacher who'd glimpsed the oozing burns had reported B.J. They'd moved in the middle of the night, and Chancy had taken the worst beating of her life. She hadn't told the story since, not even in group therapy. But purging the horrible memories made her feel better, just as throwing up with a sick stomach offered relief.

Jenny cried and gathered Chancy close. "I am so sorry terrible things happened to you. Hearing this breaks my heart. My God, Chancy, you've been through hell. How did your spirit survive? How did you turn out so beautiful and sweet?"

"I'm beautiful?" Chancy didn't see pity in Jenny's eyes. Or disgust. She saw the connection they'd created. Felt it in Jenny's trembling embrace. Chancy's pain hurt Jenny.

Tears streamed down Uncle Max's face. "You are beautiful inside and out, Chancy Deel. Anyone tells you otherwise, he answers to me!"

She smiled at the thought of Uncle Max defending her honor with the clenched fists that rested on his knees.

"You're the daughter Hanna would have loved, Chancy Deel. And *I* love you. The affection of an old man with one foot in the grave can't make up for the tenderness you've been cheated of, but I want to try."

He loved her? The real her? Even though she'd come to him wrapped in ugliness and hate and fear? She'd risked everything to stop running and hiding. She'd dared to hope someone could accept her just as she was. Uncle Max *loved* her? Was the universe rewarding that hope at last?

"Uncle Max, do you think I was meant to come to Wenonah, of all the places in the whole big world?"

"I'm sure of it. Hanna always said there's no such thing as a coincidence."

Jenny wiped her tears. "Chancy, do you have any idea how strong a heart must be to endure what you've been through without breaking?"

She felt that strength growing inside her, pushing her out into the world, like a pale shoot reaching for the sun.

"I still don't understand why you hurt yourself," Uncle Max said gently.

"When I got older, I tried to cut off the burn scars. I just made them worse." She didn't dare close her eyes. If she did she would see the box cutter. The blood.

"But why?" Uncle Max asked. "You'd already been hurt so badly by other people."

"They were ugly. Not only the scars, but what they meant."

"Your mother's betrayal," Jenny said on a long sigh, "etched into your skin."

"I didn't want anyone to see them. I thought maybe if the burns weren't there, B.J. wouldn't get in trouble."

Uncle Max frowned. "You did that to yourself to protect your mother?"

"No. Myself. She hated being reminded of what she'd done. I thought if the scars were gone, she'd stop being angry."

"Cutting must have hurt," Jenny said.

"Everything hurts," Chancy replied.

"Even though that was a hurt you could control, you can't take away one pain by slashing it with another."

"I know."

"Where's your mother now?" Uncle Max looked like he wanted to punish B.J. for what she'd done.

"I'm not sure. She was in the hospital when I ran away from the group home. She's probably out by now." There was more to her mother's story, but she wasn't ready to share that. Yet.

Chancy had once believed B.J. had stolen her from her real family. That somewhere a loving mother cried every night over her little girl who'd been kidnapped. A real mother wouldn't hurt her child. One of the earliest fairy tales Chancy remembered was about little goat boys and girls. Mother Goat had to go out and she told the kids not to open the door, no matter what. When the Wolf came to their house disguised as Mother Goat, the brothers and sisters disobeyed and opened the door. The Wolf, dressed in their mother's clothing, ate all the goats but one.

Chancy often wondered if B.J. was a wolf dressed in her real mother's clothes. She had called Chancy a "bag full of crazy," saying she cut herself as a bid for attention. Her mother, always at the dead center of the emotional hurricanes she created, was wrong. Chancy had never wanted to be noticed. She had wanted to hide in the clock case like the smart boy goat and wait for her real mother to return.

Therapists had different names for what she'd done to her arms. They called it Repetitive Self-Mutilation Syndrome, a sign of self-destructive behavior. Or self-loathing. Or sensory impairment. One indifferent therapist had even called them a way for Chancy to fit in with the other throwaway kids. As if she'd shed her blood for a fashion statement.

"We're going to help you, Chancy." Uncle Max's tears were gone. He had that no-nonsense look she knew well. "There's got to be a legal means out of this. Some way to keep you safe. I'll talk to Pete Marshall. He's a damn good attorney. If anyone can help us, he can."

"No!" Chancy sat up in bed. "If the authorities find me, they'll send me back to Pittsburgh. I can't go back to B.J. Not ever!"

Uncle Max hugged her. "You won't go back. We'll figure out something. Together."

She let him tuck her arms under the blanket. "Uncle Max, I don't like the girl I was in B.J.'s world. I like the Wenonah me better."

"We all love the Wenonah you." Jenny kissed her cheek, and Chancy marveled at how uncomplicated touching could be. "Please understand something. What happened was not your fault. None of it. Do you believe me?"

Would it take a million kind words to tip the scale of B.J.'s spirit-crushing taunts? "I'm trying to."

"Good." Uncle Max pulled the blanket up to her chin. "Just rest."

"Will you stay?"

"As long as you need me."

Jenny patted Uncle Max's shoulder. "We won't leave you."

Chancy closed her eyes, suddenly exhausted. She extended her left hand from under the blanket. Uncle Max's two gnarled hands enveloped hers.

Chancy almost believed she had finally found her own safety box.

But B.J. had a key. She came to Chancy in the night to remind her that she was only kidding herself if she thought Maxwell Boyle would be taken in by her sorry little sob story.

You've let the cat out of the bag now, missy. You had to go and blab about family business. How many times have I told you to keep your damn mouth shut? What goes on at home stays at home. Making me out to be a bad mother. I can't believe you were boo-hooing about your pitiful childhood. Little Miss Cream-filled Cupcake. Bleeding hearts do love big, sad eyes, don't they?

You got me in trouble plenty of times. If you'd kept your lip zipped and your sleeves down like I told you, no one would have been the wiser. Those agency bitches wouldn't have come poking around and I wouldn't have had to run. You made me look bad. Might as well have voted me Loser Mom of the Year. I'll never forgive you for that.

You think you have it good now? How long do you think you can keep pulling the wool over that old man's eyes? The neighbor, Supermommy, seems sharp. Think she really bought your crap? Conning for a roof over your head. Good work if you can get it, I guess. The old fool's half-senile. Are you planning to wait for him to go completely off his skids? What happens when he's gone for good? Still want to burn your bridges?

Life sucks and there's only one door out of the building.

When Chancy awoke in the night, shaking from B.J.'s dream visit, Uncle Max had returned to his room and Jenny had gone home. But even in the dark, Chancy knew bad dreams couldn't hurt her. Only her living, breathing mother had that much power.

She went down for breakfast the next morning and paused at the foot of the stairs. Whenever B.J. slipped into her thoughts, she left doubts behind. Chancy rubbed her arms through her sleeves. For years the scars had been constant reminders that no one loved her. Not her mother. Not even herself. It had been nearly three years since she'd made the last cut. The wounds had healed. And in Wenonah, she had healed too. Sometimes she had trouble separating what was real from what wasn't, but she hadn't imagined the love Uncle Max and Jenny had offered. That was real.

Uncle Max sat at the table reading the newspaper. Same as any regular day. Didn't he know the whole world had changed?

"I made oatmeal," he said. "Help yourself."

"Thanks." She dished up a bowl of cereal, poured a glass of milk. Breakfast looked the same too, but the girl about to eat it was different.

"How do you feel?" He didn't lower the paper. Was he afraid to look at her? She tensed.

She sprinkled sugar on the oatmeal. "Like I fell under a freight train and ninety-seven cars ran over me."

"Guess I win." He laughed behind the paper. "I feel like an even hundred ran over me. But if life was easy, what would be the point?"

She ate silently.

"You know," he said, "I've been thinking."

Thinking he'd said too much? Made promises he no longer wanted to keep?

He cleared his throat. "The kitchen curtains look a little sad. What do you think?"

"Curtains?" They were talking about curtains?

"Let's buy some new ones."

"Okay."

Uncle Max turned the newspaper page but still didn't look around it at her. "We're in for a beautiful day. Rain really cooled things off."

"Yes." She spooned up the last bite of oatmeal.

"Didn't you say you wanted to look for a couple of shade plants for the garden?"

"*Pulmonaria saccharata,* 'Mrs. Moon.' And a hosta called 'Dancing in the Rain.' Those are the only two we haven't replaced."

"Let's try the big greenhouse over in Valley View. Maybe we can find them there."

"Really?"

"You need them to complete the garden, don't you?"

"Yes."

"So, we'll find them."

She could wait no longer. Tiptoeing around yesterday's events was as nerve-racking as juggling knives. "Uncle Max? Are you upset with me about yesterday?"

"No, of course not." He folded the paper and set it aside. "But I understand if you are." Gone was the angry stranger. The gentle Max was back. Shaved. Tidy. Worried. "You have a right to hard feelings, you know."

"I don't have any bad feelings." And amazingly, she didn't. "I'm good at forgetting."

He reached across the table and held her hand. "I'm sorry, Chancy. If only you can forgive all the hurtful things I said."

"Things? What things?" She smiled to remind him that forgiving and forgetting went together.

"You won't hold an old man's mistakes against him?" The hope in his eyes was stronger than the plea in his words. Had he really thought *she* might be mad at *him*?

She lifted the lid off the sugar bowl and pretended to drop something in. "That's my mistakes. Now you."

"Bitter mistakes made sweet?" He swallowed hard and played along.

She clamped on the lid. "Forgotten and forgiven. Okay?"

"Okay."

Chancy pushed up her sleeves with the confidence that came from knowing scars weren't important to the people who mattered.

Uncle Max nodded his approval and smacked the table lightly with both palms. "All righty! I need to run to the bank first, so be ready when I get home. We want to hit the road early, before it gets too hot. Alfie? You ready for a ride in the country?"

Alfie jumped up, his big tail wagging. He seemed relieved too, and happy things were back to normal.

"Can I invite Adam?"

"He's a little busy. Look across the street."

Chancy peered out the window. Adam was pushing the lawn mower, cutting straight swaths across the Hamilton yard. "Is that Tom helping him?"

"Sure is. The other night when they came to dinner, Tom said our yard looked so good, it put the neighborhood to shame."

She watched Tom run the edger along the walkway. Jenny would be pleased when she returned from work. "I'm glad he's feeling better."

"Sometimes it takes getting hit by that freight train to set us on the right path." Uncle Max grabbed the car keys from the hook by the door. "From here on out, no looking back. We live each day to the fullest."

"How can I if I'm not open about who I really am? Not just with you and Jenny and Adam, but with Wenonah?"

"I called Pete last night. Talked to him a good long time. Did I mention he's a damn fine attorney?" When she nodded, he said, "We've come up with a plan."

"What kind of plan?"

Uncle Max tossed his keys in the air and caught them with a jaunty snap. "Ever hear of a little thing called emancipation?"

Chapter 24

Chancy walked Alfie around the block while Uncle Max drove downtown to the bank. He'd told her to be ready to go no later than nine thirty, but wouldn't say why such a tight schedule was necessary.

He made the drive to the greenhouse fun by pointing out interesting landmarks along the way. Not historically significant sights, but those only a longtime resident would know about. The unmarked gravel road turnoff that led to the best swimming hole in the county. The barn atop which the lightning rod had been snapped off by a low-flying crop duster in 1963. The tree to which local Sasquatch enthusiasts had tacked a sign reading BIGFOOT CROSSING. Just as Chancy had found intriguing surprises as she cleared Hanna's garden, Uncle Max shared surprises in the surrounding countryside.

The Lincoln's air conditioner blasted cool air into the front seat, but Uncle Max kept the back window open enough to give Alfie the full canine-nose-in-the-wind road trip experience. The farther they drove out of town, the more space opened up between houses. Acres of cornstalks waved in the sun, and emerald green soybeans blanketed fields on either side of the road.

"So what do you know about the emancipation of minors?" Uncle Max flipped on the turn signal and cautiously changed lanes as they approached their destination.

"Not much." Stories of kids seeking to legally separate from their parents had long circulated in the knockabout underworld of group homes and juvenile shelters. Most states had some kind of provision to allow emancipation, but Chancy had never actually met anyone whose petition had been granted.

"When we get back to town we'll stop for lunch at the diner and say hello to your friend Corliss. I've been craving a Tip-Top burger with smokehouse sauce."

"What about Alfie?"

"We can drop him off at home first. That way, when we're finished eating, we can go to Pete's office. He cleared time to talk to you this afternoon."

"So soon?" Everything was moving so fast!

"Do you feel up to it?"

"Why wouldn't I be?" Uncle Max didn't have to know how scared she was that going public would only bring her old life flooding back.

"Well, taking legal action is a big step. A permanent step. I think we need to act fast, but I don't want to push you into something you're not ready for."

"I'm ready." She'd never seriously considered emancipation before. B.J. always said she was too crazy and screwed-up to dress herself, much less live on her own. B.J. claimed *she* was the only one who cared whether Chancy lived or died. Even the authorities didn't believe Chancy was worth saving. That was why they always sent her home to her mother.

Since she'd been in Wenonah, and far away from B.J.'s poisonous words, Chancy had formed her own picture of what family should be, and B.J. Deel was not it.

"The way I understand the law"—Uncle Max stopped at a red light on Valley View's main street—"procedures are different in each state. Oklahoma doesn't have a statute on the books, so judges make determinations on a case-by-case basis. There's a lot of legal mumbo jumbo to digest, but Pete's a patient man. He'll explain everything."

"Aren't lawyers expensive?"

"Don't worry. We'll work out something."

"I want to pay."

"No need. Pete's been my attorney for years. He'll just put the new charges on my bill."

This was the first step to building a new life. She had to do it for herself. "No, then. Not unless I pay with my own money."

Uncle Max shook his head, an accepting half smile on his lips. "I could argue and try to be rational, but what's the point? When you make up your mind about a thing, you're as stubborn as Hanna ever was."

Chancy just smiled. Being compared to Hanna was the best kind of compliment. Uncle Max was letting her know he trusted her to make good decisions about her life.

"Hey! I think we have arrived." Uncle Max navigated the big Lincoln into the nursery's parking lot.

The Valley View Greenhouse offered more plants than Chancy ever knew existed. She didn't want to miss a thing, but it would take hours to investigate each intriguing row. "It's like an enchanted jungle in here." Their shoes crunched on the gravel paths that connected the buildings, winding among splashing waterfalls and serene lily pools. They paused to watch sleek koi glide through green water. Rows and rows of containerized plants filled the shade house, along with large tables of seedling flats.

According to the gardening books Chancy had studied, shade plants did not produce showy flowers. Their beauty was in the foliage, which came in all shapes and textures, from feathery to swordlike. All sizes too. Some had leaves like great elfin umbrellas and others were as tiny as pearls. And so many shades of green! People were a lot like plants. Some, like Adam, dazzled with all the flash and color of the exuberant trays of annuals in the flat house. Others, like herself, stayed out of the sun and grew in their own quiet way.

They had managed to track down replacements for all the lost plants and shrubs except for the two special shade plants. Surely they would find what they were searching for among such abundance. After Chancy's hard work and many blisters, the garden was almost restored. The nursery attendant directed them to a row at the back. Chancy opened Hanna's journal to the appropriate page and compared the name on her planting chart to the label on the plant candidate.

"That the one you need?" Uncle Max asked.

"Yes! *Pulmonaria saccharata*." Hanna had written about being enchanted by the way the plant's rosy buds opened pink, then slowly turned to a deep blue. "We need five to fill the space." Chancy hoisted the gallon-sized plant buckets onto the little green plant wagon the attendant had provided. She held one at eye level. "Hello, Mrs. Moon. Nice to meet you at last." It was late in the planting season, and extra care would be required while transplanting.

"One down and one to go. How many hostas do you need?" Uncle Max helped her pull the wagon to the checkout area.

"Three. That's a lucky number, you know."

But it wasn't lucky this time. The nursery was the largest in the tri-county area but did not sell the elusive hosta variety. They'd come close to success but would have to leave without Dancing in the Rain. The cashier offered to check the online catalog.

"Sorry, that one is temporarily out of stock. Not just here, but with the supplier." The young man looked up from the computer screen. "I can order it, if you like, and let you know when it comes in. In fact, if you pay in advance, I can have the merchandise shipped directly to your home."

"What do you think, Chancy? We can keep looking if you want."

They'd already exhausted local resources. She was impatient to complete the garden, but she could wait. Waiting had always paid off in the past. "We'll order them. That way they're sure to arrive. Eventually."

"Just think." She let Alfie in the backseat and set the Mrs. Moons on the floor, admonishing the dog not to trample them. "Before long the garden will be just the way it used to be!"

Uncle Max eased the Lincoln into the street. "Hanna would be proud of your hard work."

Chancy collected his words and pressed them into the memory book in her mind. "Do you think she knows?"

"I'm sure of it." When Uncle Max smiled, Chancy knew he was remembering his wife. He looked as he had in his wedding picture. Happy.

· · ·

"So how was that burger?" Corliss stopped by their table to refill their water glasses. The lunch rush was in full swing, but the conscientious waitress didn't skimp on service.

"Best I ever ate," Max said. "And worth every minute of the heartburn I'll suffer later." At his last appointment, the heart doctor had climbed all over his case about his diet, warning him to cut back on red meat and cheese. The very ingredients that made a juicy hamburger worth eating.

"I'm glad y'all dropped by. Sure is good to see you again, Max. I was sorry to hear about Hanna. She was a lovely person."

"Yes, she was."

"You look well, though. I guess our little Chancy is taking good care of you."

"Couldn't ask for a better caregiver." The wary girl had blossomed like the plants she'd lovingly tended. "She's just about got Hanna's garden fixed up. You'll have to come and see it sometime."

"You bet I will." Corliss chatted with Chancy for a moment about mutual acquaintances at the nursing home, and the topic naturally turned to Jenny Hamilton.

"I hear good things about your friend." Corliss patted Chancy's shoulder. "Barb Shannon is so impressed with the job she's doing in the preschool program that she's talking about sending you a fruit basket for pointing Jenny in her direction."

Corliss moved on to the next table but was back in a few minutes with two plates of lemon meringue pie. Dessert was on the house. Max figured the cost would come out of her wages and made a mental note to leave a healthy tip. A young man joined them from the kitchen, and Corliss introduced her son to Max.

Eddie Briggs seemed like a hardworking young man, washing dishes in the morning and servicing cars in the afternoon. He told his mother he would be back to drive her home at the end of her shift and excused himself with a polite "Nice to meet you" for Max and a wide smile for Chancy.

When Max remarked on Eddie's ambition, Corliss beamed. It was clear that if he'd been an astrophysicist or a millionaire rock star, his mother could not have been more proud.

"I would have been satisfied with him working one job," she said. "Now he has three!"

"What else is he doing?" Chancy asked.

"Helping out at a builder's salvage place on weekends. Tyree's brother-in-law hooked him up. Eddie says you wouldn't believe what-all perfectly good stuff people throw away."

Max believed. He was well aware that new owners of old houses loved nothing more than to rip out all the things that had charmed them in the first place.

Corliss offered to pick Chancy up for their next nursing home visit. They set a time, and she scurried back to work. Waiting tables was not an easy job for a woman her age. Eddie had come by his work ethic honestly.

"What does builder's salvage mean, anyway?" Chancy forked up a bite of pie and made a yum-yum face.

He offered an objective explanation, trying not to taint it with his own prejudice.

"Do you think Jenny could find kitchen cabinets there?"

"Maybe. Depends on the job. Salvagers never know what'll turn up. Architectural columns, banisters, mantels. Kitchen cabinets, too, I suppose. Old houses yield surprises." He tried the pie, which merited an *extra* healthy tip. "I thought she wanted new cabinets."

"She changed her mind. Now she wants to make her house look like yours. Vintage, she says."

He chuckled. "That's another word for old, you know."

"I'll give her Eddie's number." Not only was Chancy always thinking; she was always thinking of others. An unusual gift in someone whose childhood had been so tortured. "Maybe he can let her know if any good cabinets get salvaged."

Max was satisfied with his life. He had believed he'd done everything he ever wanted to do. Now he was pierced by an unexpected regret: He wouldn't get to see Chancy grow into a woman. But he didn't have to worry about her. She would be all right.

"You know, kid, you're turning out to be an excellent problem solver."

. . .

"So, Chancy, Max tells me you need some legal advice." Pete Marshall folded his hands on top of his shiny desk.

"Yes. And I can pay. I've been saving my money. I have enough."

"Are you sure? My fees are pretty steep."

"How steep?" She looked at the wall behind Mr. Marshall's head. Anyone who'd earned that many diplomas probably charged a lot.

Pete glanced at Max and a look passed between them. "I charge minors twenty dollars an hour, and I could put, oh, I don't know, ten billable hours in on a case of this magnitude."

"I can cover two hundred dollars. Do I pay you first?"

"No, we can settle the bill later. So you want to be emancipated. Is that right?"

"Yes." Chancy appreciated that Pete Marshall was talking to her like a real client.

"Do you know what that means?"

"It's like divorcing your parent."

"In effect." Pete explained Oklahoma law and how the state's emancipation process worked. "A lot of teens rebel. They don't like their curfew or their parents don't approve of their friends. Most kids believe they can manage by themselves, when in reality they don't have a clue how to live in the real world. What makes you think you would be better off on your own than with your parents?"

Hadn't Uncle Max explained that already? He gave her an encouraging nod. "What do you want to know?"

"I want you to tell me your side of the story, Chancy."

So she did. And this time the words weren't so hard to say. She didn't hold back or trim off the worst bits. She recounted the facts in good faith, no longer believing she had deserved B.J.'s harsh treatment. When she finished, she pushed up her sleeves. Her mother was the one who should be ashamed.

Pete leaned forward. "Sounds like you have an excellent case. Of course, I need to do a little investigation to verify the details. If you haven't satisfied the residency requirement, I may have to double-file in

Pennsylvania, but that's doable. The first thing we need to do is get your documentation in order. Do you have a Social Security card or birth certificate?"

"No."

"No problem. We can obtain copies. I'll see how many of your records I can access. Attorney privilege will come in handy." He spoke into the phone and a few minutes later a young woman joined them.

"This is Leah Perkins, Chancy. She's a lawyer too. I want you to go with her and give her as much information as you can. She'll ask you questions, and you just tell her everything you remember about your mother. Can you do that?"

She nodded.

The junior partner opened the folder Mr. Marshall had handed her. She scanned the top page and smiled. "You live on Poplar Avenue? My favorite street! My husband and I would love to buy into that neighborhood."

"So it's really possible for me to be on my own?" Chancy needed to clarify that "on her own" wasn't the same as "alone." "Legally?"

"Anything is possible," Pete said. "That's what I love about the legal system. Sometimes judicial red tape bogs the process down, but I'll do my best. I know you're working against the clock."

Uncle Max frowned, and the lawyer added, "I assume you want to attend high school this fall?"

High school? She wasn't sure she was ready to blend in for real. How could she help Uncle Max if she was in school all day? "I don't know. Maybe I should get a GED."

"The Wenonah school system sponsors an alternative program. Self-paced. I think you'll qualify, but you'll have to look into it. No matter what you decide, time is a consideration. In order to expedite the matter, we'll go the simple route first."

"What's that?" Max asked.

"Draw up papers for relinquishment of parental rights and try to get Chancy's mother to sign them."

"What does relinquishment mean?" Chancy asked.

Leah spoke up for the first time. "That's when a parent voluntarily consents to the termination of parental rights."

Hope took a nosedive, and the old panic edged back. "You mean ask my mother if she would agree to let me go?"

"Exactly," said Leah. "If she signs away her rights, it's a relatively simple matter to get a judge to grant emancipation."

Chancy's stomach clenched around the undigested burger. She had faith in Pete's legal skills, and Leah seemed like a smart lawyer, but they didn't know B.J. Nothing was simple when it came to her mother. Mr. Marshall and Leah were accustomed to probating wills and settling estates and filing what Uncle Max had called civil cases. They worked with civilized people, not undermedicated hurricanes. No way could they understand that any project depending on B.J. Deel's cooperation was doomed before it started.

On the way home, Chancy mulled over what Leah Perkins had discussed. The young lawyer seemed confident that she and Mr. Marshall could help, but Chancy wasn't about to get her hopes high. Not yet.

"It's been a long day." Uncle Max unlocked the back door. "But I think we made a lot of progress. You've been awfully quiet. Having second thoughts?"

"Not exactly." Chancy set the last of the plants on the back porch, out of the sun. "I'm afraid B.J. won't sign the papers. And what if she would? How will they even find her? I told Leah everything I knew, but it wasn't much."

"We can trust Pete to do whatever it takes. Things may get rough. When you start turning over rocks, you never know what'll crawl out."

"I know." She'd turned over plenty of stones in the garden. All the pale, blind, squirming things that lived in the dark couldn't survive the sun.

"You'll have to appear in front of a judge. Talk to authorities," Max said.

"I know it's risky. I know I could be forced to go back to Pennsylvania. But I want to try. You made me want to try by encouraging me to trust people and do the right thing."

He laughed. "Let's see. I believe I encouraged you to tell a decent public servant a king-size whopper by lying through your teeth."

"That story we made up was just words. The truth will let me belong." She could do anything as long as she had Uncle Max to guide the way.

"I want you to talk to me anytime you need to, but right now I'm pooped. Too much excitement. I believe I'll take a nap. Maybe lie down upstairs for a while."

Uncle Max usually napped in the recliner. Said he liked to be where the action was, not stuck away in his bedroom like an invalid. He really was exhausted if he was willing to retreat to his room during the day. His words were more slurred than usual. That happened only when he was upset or exhausted. She stood at the bottom of the stairs and watched his slow ascent. Alfie walked beside him. Uncle Max gripped the banister with one gnarled hand and dragged his feet slowly up the risers. He'd walked tall in his fancy sneakers, but he was slumping again. Simple fatigue, or something more ominous? Despite arthritic joints, Alfie made it to the landing before his master. Uncle Max wasn't the same empty, hollow old man she'd met that first day in the park, but moments like this reminded her that he was still old.

Chancy decided to work on the memory book until the sun was low enough to make it safe to garden. Couldn't risk shocking Mrs. Moon. She had just arranged her supplies on the dining room table when the phone rang.

Adam. "Good, you're home! Where've you been all day?" As usual, he didn't pause long enough for her to answer one question before barreling on with another. "Want to come over and see what Dad and I did today?"

"Does it have anything to do with the grass catcher?"

"*After* we worked in the yard! How does it look, by the way?"

"Green."

"Yeah, cool, huh? We painted the kitchen. Dad knows how to texture drywall. Who knew? Boy, is Mom going to be surprised."

"That's great. How about I come over later? I'd like to stick around here until Uncle Max gets up."

"Okay. Don't forget! See ya! Bye!"

Adam was a good kind of whirlwind. He sucked people up in his enthusiasm. How could she ever tell him about her real life? She'd ask Jenny how to handle things. Adam didn't need to know everything. He could learn the truth in baby steps. She noticed the blinking red message light on the answering machine. Expecting to hear Adam's happy breathlessness on the other end, she grinned and pushed the button. Her legs went weak when a familiar voice jumped out of the speaker. It did not sound happy.

"Mr. Boyle, this is Shevaun Wooten with Adult Protective Services. I'm sorry I missed you when I dropped by this morning for our scheduled home visit. Please call me at 311-5555 to set up another appointment."

Odd. Max hadn't said anything about a home visit. As far as Chancy knew, he hadn't seen the social worker for a month. During her last "spying mission" she'd been blown away by the changes the old house had undergone and said he would have no trouble finding a buyer now. She'd called twice since then, and both times Max had insisted Chancy tell her he was indisposed, which meant anything from a coma to a bathroom problem.

Chancy had hoped maybe Ms. Wooten would see that Uncle Max had changed too, but she had a one-track mind. Was she still pressing him to visit Grayson House? They'd managed to stall her this long, but what would they do once summer was over? How would they explain Chancy's continued presence?

Before she had time to consider this new problem, the answering machine spewed a second message.

"This is Patty, patient coordinator for Dr. Whittaker's office. I'm calling for Maxwell Boyle. Please phone at your earliest convenience to reschedule your missed appointment."

The tape rewound. Chancy pushed the button and listened to the messages again. Two missed appointments? It wasn't like Uncle Max to forget things like that. Maybe he hadn't forgotten. He'd been adamant about leaving the house before nine thirty. Had he been in a rush to avoid Ms. Wooten? Understandable. She had long been a threat. A thorn in his side, he called her some days, a fly in the ointment, others. But who was

Dr. Whittaker? She didn't recognize the name and hadn't heard Uncle Max mention him before.

He had been tired lately. He tried to pretend he wasn't, but she could tell. Could he be sick? No. If he'd made a doctor's appointment, he would have told her. It was her job to make sure he didn't forget anything important. She checked the calendar in the kitchen. No appointments. Probably it was a routine visit for what Uncle Max called a hundred-thousand-mile checkup. Those were scheduled months in advance.

Chancy removed the Wenonah telephone directory from a compartment in the sideboard and flipped open the yellow pages, scanning for the doctor's name. When she found it, she had more questions than answers.

Dr. Robert Whittaker was a board-certified cardiac surgeon.

Chapter 25

Adam called again, begging Chancy to come see what he and his father had done. His mother was home from work and was thrilled. Chancy put away the nearly finished memory book. She peeked in Uncle Max's room and found him huddled under his favorite afghan. Three hours was a long time to sleep, even for him, but he'd had a busy day and needed rest. With Alfie at her side, she crossed the street, niggling worry following her all the way.

"Can you believe it? I go to work for a few hours and come home to a whole new world." Jenny was dressed in her "uniform." She said the comfort of tan pants and a Moppet Manor T-shirt was an unexpected perk. "Hooray! No more bare-naked drywall!"

"We work fast, right, Dad?" Adam scratched Alfie's ears and tried to act casual but couldn't hide the affectionate spin placed on the word *Dad*.

Tom smiled at his son, then at his wife. A knowing look passed between the adults. "All it takes is the right motivation."

"I just picked out the color swatch last week," Jenny said. "I never expected to see results so soon." Bronzy-gold paint, paired with the black-and-white floor tile, gave the high-ceilinged room an old-world feel.

"It's starting to look like a real kitchen in here," Jenny said. "My next paycheck goes for an electrician to reinstall the old stove. Thank God we saved it. Not exactly the six-burner restaurant range in the plans, but it still has some life in it."

"If we move Ugly Fridge back in"—Adam stepped off the space the old refrigerator would occupy—"we'll almost have a kitchen that works. Maybe even real food! Yay!" He frowned at the bare walls and the wooden planks on sawhorses that would serve as temporary counter space. "I guess we'll have to keep using our cardboard-box cupboards for a while, huh?"

"All in good time, son." Tom ruffled his hair, and Adam didn't complain about him messing it up. "C'mon, let's clean up."

"Tom thinks I'm a little nuts to want to pay for everything myself," Jenny told Chancy. "Do you think that's crazy?"

"Nothing is really yours unless you earn it."

They carried boxes used for food storage into the kitchen. "Did you tell Adam about me?"

Chancy's chest tightened when Jenny nodded. "How much?"

"Not all the gruesome details, but enough. He's not a child anymore. He can handle the truth." She noticed Chancy unconsciously rubbing her arms. "He knows about the scars. Tom too. You don't have to hide them from us. We're your friends."

"Was Adam mad at me for lying?"

Jenny grinned. "Does he act mad? He took the news well. Said he was glad, because now you won't have to leave when summer's over."

Chancy arranged cereal boxes on the plank counter to hide her mounting unease. Too easy. First Uncle Max and Jenny. Now Adam. Pete Marshall seemed to think emancipation would be a legal snap. But she was worried. Nothing was free. Everything had a price. The universe did not give so many gifts without expecting payment. What would she have to barter for her happiness?

"I thought of a way for you to maybe get vintage cabinets. I know this guy who does builder salvage work on the weekends." Chancy marveled at the ease with which she discussed subjects that had been totally unfamiliar to her a few short months ago. "They recycle stuff that comes out of old buildings and houses."

"Great idea!" Jenny clearly had a why-didn't-I-think-of-that moment. "Can you get me the number?"

Chancy provided Corliss's phone number and explained how she knew

Eddie Briggs. If she counted all the residents of Dogwood Manor, she knew a lot of people now. She'd arrived alone, her heart as small and hard as a pebble. Once dropped in the sparkling pool that was Wenonah, the pebble had created an ever-widening ripple of friends around her.

"They may not have what you want right now, but if you don't mind waiting . . ."

Jenny glanced into the utility room where Tom and Adam were cleaning paintbrushes. They stood shoulder-to-shoulder, Adam's noisy laughter mingling with his father's deep chuckles. She smiled in a count-your-blessings way. "I'm in no hurry."

Chancy settled dirt around the loosened roots of the last transplanted *Pulmonaria*. After watering them with a gentle trickle from the hose, she stepped back to admire the arrangement. Hanna's original plants had died of thirst in the hot Oklahoma sun. Lungwort, as the perennial was commonly called, thrived in damp soil. The green leaves were spattered with silvery spots that lit up shady corners. Hanna had chosen Mrs. Moon as an underplanting for hostas and spring-flowering bulbs, creating the "luminous tapestry" effect she'd described in her journal.

Chancy was suddenly impatient for next spring and the surprises it would bring—in the garden, and in her life. Just as Mary Lennox's secret garden had thrived, so had Chancy's. Tender care, hard work, and plenty of fertilizer had spurred the surviving plants to new growth. She and Adam had dug out marauding trumpet vine runners, thus controlling the spread of new shoots and forcing the willowy vines to explode in clusters of orange flowers. In exchange for their blisters and backache, the hummingbirds had returned. They hovered, ruby-throated, their tiny wings invisible, their nectar-seeking beaks thrust deep into blooms shaped like angel trumpets.

Hanna had planned carefully, thoughtfully placing each plant in a particular place, creating a garden that flowed gently with a grace and rhythm more idealized than any found in nature. Hanna had written that a garden was a perfect world in which every plant had a reason and a purpose, and only those who knew how to look would notice the hand of the gardener.

Dusk gathered and Chancy stripped off her gloves to sit on the marble bench. According to Hanna's notes, when the other hostas had appeared under the oaks during the last spring of her illness, one spot had remained bare. *Gobbled up as gopher grub.* She'd sketched a cross-eyed rodent with devilish horns in the margin next to the note. Chancy opened the journal. Hanna had pasted a picture of Alfie on the page too, to remind her of how the plants had looked. She had captured him with his nose buried deep in the brilliant-green-and-creamy-white leafy fountain of the Dancing in the Rain hostas.

Soon, Hanna. Before long you will have your perfect world back.

Relief flooded Chancy when Uncle Max let himself in through the creaky gate. He looked rested, his step a little livelier than before. He joined her on the bench, as he had the first day they met. Only three months had passed, but she'd lived a lifetime worth of feelings in that time.

He surveyed the recent planting and nodded with approval. "I never thought much about this garden before. But now it does my old heart good to see it looking so fine. Like a peaceful snapshot of the way things used to be. Thank you for giving Hanna back to me, Chancy."

"The garden gave me something, too." The leaves rustled in the breeze, as though reciting the lessons she'd learned. How to work hard and be patient. How to plant seeds of faith and wait for the wonder. "Mostly it proved to me that if a ruined garden can be nurtured into something peaceful, so can a person."

"I don't imagine you had much peace in your life."

"There was always noise where we lived. Yelling or blasting music. The molecules were always raging around B.J. I was always on red alert."

"Worried about what ax would fall next?"

"Yes. An ax."

"That kind of existence must be similar to running a minefield, day in and day out." Uncle Max stared at the horizon, seeing the past. "Jenny said when all of one's energy is expended just to survive, the person lives in a constant state of stress. I felt that way myself during the war. It's impossible to think when you're afraid. We called it shell shock. After Vietnam, the military gave the condition a proper name: post-traumatic stress syndrome."

Living with B.J. was like being constantly under fire. "Maybe that's why I had to fall into the quiet place. To escape. I had trouble paying attention in school. It's hard to learn when you're hiding or worrying about what will happen next. I don't feel foggy here. I want to go to high school and graduate."

"I know you will."

"College too?" she whispered, afraid to say the words aloud. The universe might think she was greedy.

"Don't see why not. A smart cookie like you can do just about anything."

"Let's find out about the alternative school. I want to study at my own pace. I don't want to waste time trying to fit in."

Uncle Max's arms opened to embrace the garden. "If your horticultural achievements are any indication of your dedication to learning, you'll rocket through school."

"What's Alfie looking at?" The dog stood frozen a few feet away, his unwavering gaze intent.

"I believe he's staring down a firefly." Uncle Max's laughter was indulgent. "The old boy is too lazy to get up and investigate."

Chancy shrugged. "Maybe he already knows everything he wants to know about fireflies."

"Could be."

The garden world was quiet and still. Within its magic circle, the impossible seemed possible. "Mr. Marshall said I will have to convince the judge I can live on my own, but I don't want to. I want to stay here. With you."

"But, Chancy"—a sad shadow crept across his face—"I won't be around forever."

"No! Please don't say that!"

When he sighed, Uncle Max sounded like Alfie waiting patiently to go out. "We have to say it. We have to talk about it too."

She covered her ears. "I won't. I can't even think it! It's bad luck to tempt the universe."

"Mortality isn't bad luck, my dear." He patted her arm. "It's a fact of life."

She thought about that, then said, "Leah Perkins told me some emancipated teens go into an independent-living program."

"Pete mentioned that too. He said the organization provides an apartment to qualified, legally emancipated teens. Not a handout, but a leg *up*. Under the terms of their emancipation agreements, they have to prove that they are mature and capable of supporting themselves. Pete says they are required to work while completing their education and pay rent on a sliding scale based on earnings. As you've told me many times, nothing good is ever free."

"I don't need a program. I have you."

"We need to think of the future." His arm encircled her shoulder, and he held her close. "And make plans for you when I'm gone."

"You're scaring me!" She couldn't imagine a world without him in it. "I told you my truth. Tell me yours. Are you sick?"

"I'm old, Chancy." He paused, staring down a firefly for a moment himself. "And I have a bad heart."

"No, you have the best heart of anyone I ever knew." Uncle Max's heart was big and full and generous. How could it be bad?

"But it's not working very well right now," he said gently. "You know how we had to buy a new hose because the old one was leaking? Well, the valves in my heart leak a little. Not a lot yet, but enough to be a nuisance."

The doctor whose assistant had called was a heart surgeon. "But Dr. Whittaker can fix it, right?"

Uncle Max frowned. "How do you know about him?"

She relayed the messages. "Can the surgeon repair the problem?"

"No."

The word was more than she could bear. "But doctors perform transplants and put in artificial hearts. I've heard about stuff like that."

"I know. The wonders of medical science are many. But it's my choice not to go under the knife."

"Why not?"

He made a face like the comedian in the old movies they'd watched and pretended to be Stan Laurel doffing an imaginary hat. "My new motto is, 'Just say no to invasive chest-cracking.' Hmmph!"

Frustration made her snap, "How can you joke?" He couldn't make her laugh when tears were so close to the surface. "This is serious."

"Yes. It is. But when you're my age, you will understand that the more serious the matter, the more important it is to maintain your sense of humor. Surgery can be miraculous. But in my case it's no guarantee. Sometimes the heart muscle falls apart like wet toilet paper. When that happens, the doctor says, 'Oopsie,' and closes you up."

"So you wouldn't be any worse off than you already are."

"If you don't count the eighteen-inch hole in my chest." He chuckled. "And the fact that I'd probably be dead."

She jerked away from him. "How can you laugh and say 'dead' at the same time?"

He looked like he wanted to pull her back into a hug. "You think I want to check out now? When I have you and life is so grand?"

She hadn't forgotten the suicide note in the drawer, even if he had. "Did you want to check out before?" She held her breath, waiting for the truth. If he could be honest about that, then she could tell him anything.

"Only one time." He swatted at an insect buzzing about his head. "Before I met you, I was ready to pack it in."

"But you didn't."

"Nope. You gave me a reason to go on."

"B.J. attempted suicide more than once." She told him about the overdoses, from both medication and drugs. The hospitalizations. How Chancy had been shuffled from one place to another while B.J. recovered.

"Your mother is a troubled soul. I hope you can forgive her someday," Uncle Max said.

She could never do that. Could she? "I didn't tell you why I ran away from Pittsburgh the last time. I ran because of her."

"I figured that."

"No, you don't understand. It wasn't what *she* did. It was what I did ... or almost ... well ... She tried to hang herself with a clothesline cord tied to the closet rod. When I found her she was alive, barely. I ran and got a knife to cut the cord but then I froze. Just stood there. Watching her die."

She held her breath, waiting for Uncle Max to look at her differently. To see the bad that had welled up in her that day. When he encouraged her with a look, she went on. "I knew it would only take a few more seconds, one or two, and she would be gone. Forever. I hated her and I hated all the bad things she'd done. A dark, smoky gladness welled up in me. I wanted her to suffer." The truth left her shaking. She rubbed her arms, trying to erase the memory.

"You didn't let her die."

"No! Because I was afraid to be like her. Cruel. Uncaring. Empty inside. If I didn't cut the cord, I would grow up to do horrible things too. Like B.J. and like her mother before her."

"You could never do horrible things," Uncle Max said. "You saved her."

"No. I didn't care about her. I cut the cord and called nine-one-one, but I didn't do it for her. I was trying to save myself!" She had refused to ride with her mother in the ambulance. She had not been able to spend another minute with her and had waited for the social worker to take her back to the group home. Chancy never wanted to feel that heartless again. She cried quietly on Uncle Max's shoulder.

He tipped up her face and wiped away the tears. "Listen to me, Chancy. You let go of all that or it will eat up your dreams. You know how Hanna believed that a weed is a flower growing in the wrong place?"

"Yes."

"You were just growing in the wrong place. This is where you belong. You've bloomed here." He gently tugged up her shirtsleeves. "And these marks? Medals of courage and nothing to be ashamed of. A reminder of what you overcame. A mark of strength."

She wanted to believe him, but she didn't feel courageous. "When I found out B.J. would live, I ran away from the group home. If I stayed, I might not save my mother next time. Worse, I might have had to keep saving her over and over and never have a life of my own."

"How ironic that you came all this way and ended up saving me."

"I think that's what I was supposed to do," she said softly.

The sun dropped behind the trees and a breeze stirred the wind chimes. It was still summer, but autumn was more than a dream. In a few months it would be time to prepare the garden for its long winter sleep. A stillness had settled. The mouse babies had grown up and left the burrow to make their way as grown-up mice. The fledgling birds had flown the nest and were nabbing their own insect snacks. Next season there would be a new clutch of baby mice, and the birds would fill another nest with eggs. Life would go on, and Chancy wanted to stay here to see it.

More than that, she wanted Uncle Max to see it too.

"Won't you talk to the doctor again? For me? Maybe you'll change your mind. Maybe he has a better plan."

"Oh, doctors always have a better plan. Unfortunately, they're not necessarily what's best for patients."

He was willing to die? For what? Stubbornness? Pride? For the first time since they'd met, anger at her old friend pressed its smothering weight on Chancy. She hadn't even been angry when he'd accused her of stealing Hannah's brooch, just hurt. But now fury scalded her. "You're being selfish!"

"I understand why you might think that. But selfishness is why I've hung on all summer. I wanted to spend this time with you. And, of course, I want to spend whatever remaining days God gives me. But I also want to die on my own terms. Do you understand?"

"No! You're afraid to have surgery. You're more afraid of living in a nursing home than you are of dying. That's it, isn't it?" She'd visited the residents at Dogwood Manor. Some of them were sad, but others could still find small joys. She tried a new tack. Maybe he would respond better to a challenge. "Or are you afraid to let Ms. Wooten win?"

A long breath cascaded from him. "I believe the term for that would be cutting off your nose to spite your face."

"Don't change the subject. Did you have an appointment with her this morning?"

"She had an appointment with me. That young woman is more annoying than a festering boil." Uncle Max called to Alfie, who had tired of firefly surveillance and was digging a hole near the fence. "She's trying to complicate everything again."

"Does *she* think you should have the surgery?" Uncle Max was contrary enough not to want to do anything that might make Ms. Wooten happy.

"She thinks I'm senile *not* to want it. But that's just her uninformed opinion. We don't have to listen to her. Don't worry, Chancy. I mean to do everything I can to ensure you're taken care of," he promised.

Except for the one thing that might let him stay with her longer. Sadness slowly replaced anger. She loved him as he was. She couldn't ask him to change for her, but it hurt that he was willing to abandon her as B.J. had, even though their choices of self-destruction were very different.

"I never realized what a burden possessions could be," Max said to Corliss as he set out a few choice items. Hanna's souvenir spoons. The bear cub shakers. Those were for Chancy. It was late afternoon and she and Adam had left to accompany Jenny to a reuse center to look at cabinets, freeing him from having to tell the history of every item he discarded. Pete's wife worked with a group of volunteers who collected furniture and household items for independent-living participants. Pete had told him that when a teen turned eighteen and left the program, he or she was given the furnishings from their apartment to start their new adult life. Max wanted Chancy to have a few meaningful things to remind her of how far she'd come.

"Everyone should sweep the crowded corners of their lives regularly," Corliss said as she ripped packing tape from a large roll.

"I feel lighter already," Max said. "Like one of those fat man 'after' pictures in magazines." With Corliss Briggs's help, he'd made one last critical sweep through the house. This time he'd placed more items in the discard boxes than in the ones marked SAVE. For the first time in forty years, closets were clean and drawers were empty. Surfaces were clear of the knickknacks he hoped someone else would enjoy dusting. Books, clothes, platters, fondue pots and unnecessary small appliances. All were on their way to new homes. He couldn't help but be smug about cheating future estate sale bargain hunters.

"So, Max, tell me again why you're doing all this anyway?" Corliss looked up from the box she was labeling with a marker. At his insistence, Chancy had called her friend for advice in distributing usable items to the deserving tchotchke-impaired. If anyone knew who needed what in Wenonah, it was Corliss Briggs.

"Surely cleaning house is a concept you're familiar with." He kept his tone light and avoided her steely gaze.

"I don't clean house. I just tip my trailer sideways and shovel it out."

He laughed. No one, not even a man tying up the loose ends of his cluttered life, could be down or depressed around Corliss. She was human Prozac. "I appreciate your help. It's past time I got rid of things."

"What kind of house are you putting in order exactly?" Hard to put anything over on the wily lady. "Don't get me wrong. I don't fault your generosity. The ladies down at the women's shelter will appreciate having Hanna's clothes. They need nice outfits and shoes to wear to job interviews. What they don't use, someone else will. Plenty of folks without."

He taped shut a box of books. They were harder to part with than clothes he didn't wear and dishes he didn't need. But it was fact-facing time. If he lived to be a hundred, he could never read all the books he'd hoarded over the years. They were headed for a small-town library in southern Oklahoma that had lost much of its collection to a tornado.

"I had an ulterior motive asking you here today, Corliss."

"Funny, you never struck me as the sneaky type."

He chuckled. "Getting sneakier every day. First, I want to thank you for everything you've done for Chancy."

"Pshaw! She's a joy to know. One of the little Manor ladies calls Alfie a big ray of sunshine. Chancy? Well, she's every star in the sky."

"You're a good friend, and she's going to need all the friends she can get. I know you and Jenny will keep an eye on her. Make sure she's not alone."

"Of course, but—"

"Now for the other favor I want to ask. I guess you know Chancy's turning sixteen soon. I want to celebrate but never planned a girl's birthday party in my life. I was hoping you'd help me out. I figure you and Jenny can give the shindig an appropriately feminine touch."

Corliss beamed, clearly pleased to be asked. "I'm no hostess with the mostest, like Hanna was, but, by golly, I do know how to have fun."

"That's what I'm counting on, Corliss. I want Chancy to have a day she'll never forget."

Chapter 26

"So, birthday girl, you're sixteen now." Jenny helped herself to the breadbasket between them. She'd insisted on treating Chancy to a special lunch at Oklahoma City's finest Italian restaurant. "Do you feel any older?"

"I've always been old." Chancy, more comfortable at the Tip-Top's counter than at a table with a snowy cloth and real flowers, was determined not to embarrass Jenny. She'd picked up etiquette cues in a subtle observation of her friend, the way she was learning proper female behavior.

Jenny's willingness to spend a precious Saturday orchestrating a girls' day out more than made up for the times B.J. had forgotten Chancy's birthday. The afternoon agenda included clothes shopping, hairstyling and Chancy's first-ever manicure.

"Being wise for your age is one thing, but no one should feel old at sixteen. You need to meet kids your own age and have fun."

Chancy's hands tensed in her lap. How would she explain her pre-Wenonah past to teens who were more concerned about lip gloss than survival? She was at ease among the elderly residents of Dogwood Manor, but wouldn't know how to talk to her peers.

The server set salads in front of them. Jenny thanked him and then described the sweet-sixteen party her mother had thrown for her. "Best birthday I ever had."

"This is a good birthday too."

"Foraging for kitchen cabinets?" Jenny chuckled. "Seriously. You need to learn how to have fun." A hot tip from Eddie Briggs had prompted their trip. *Two birds with one stone,* Jenny had called it. Eddie had phoned Jenny with news of recent restoration projects in a historic neighborhood of Oklahoma City. He'd provided the names of the re-use centers where the salvaged materials had been delivered. They'd made two stops and would visit the last one after lunch. Jenny hadn't found the kind of cabinets she wanted but was optimistic. *Third time's a charm.*

Chancy had once believed in charms and lucky numbers. As Uncle Max pointed out, she was still superstitious and sometimes caught herself counting up points or looking for signs, but she wasn't adrift in the universe now. Her own actions were the most powerful force in her life.

Jenny dribbled salad dressing sparingly over the greens in her bowl. "I think we should hit a couple of malls before we leave town. Are you up for serious shopping?"

"If that's what you want to do." Chancy wasn't keen on spending her birthday trailing Jenny from store to store. She'd rather be at home with Uncle Max, who was teaching Tom and Adam to play poker. When Jenny described a hairstyle from a popular magazine, Chancy recalled their encounter at the convenience store. With no place to go and no one to turn to, she had stalled for time by reading magazines just like the one Jenny mentioned.

"What are you smiling about?" Jenny sipped her water. "You think girlie stuff is silly, right?"

"No. I like girlie stuff." She'd managed to shed the too-tight make-believe skin she'd lived in but was not at home in her femininity. "I was remembering something." She told Jenny how she, a polite perfect stranger, had offered hope when Chancy had first arrived in town.

"That was you? But I didn't do anything." She unconsciously toyed with the silver heart locket. Adam had recently suggested she place a picture of Tom on the opposite side.

"I first saw you and Adam on Mother's Day. Then I saw you again at the store, and that time you saw me too. The necklace told me I wasn't invisible, because you believed in hearts, same as me. Then you said, 'Sorry, dear, I wasn't paying attention,' and I knew Wenonah was different."

"Wow. You really know how to blow a person away." Jenny's smile quivered as she fingered a single tear from her eye. "What if I hadn't stopped at the store that day? What if I'd been rude or in a bad mood? I guess we can't always know how seemingly inconsequential acts impact others."

The server returned with their entrées. Jenny had ordered tortellini in white clam sauce. Chancy had chosen plain spaghetti. They chatted as they ate.

"What did you decide about school?"

"The alternative program suits me better than Wenonah High. I like moving at my own pace."

"But alternative school is for kids who might not otherwise have a chance to graduate. Juvenile offenders. Pregnant girls. Students with illnesses that keep them out of full-time classes. You need the social and intellectual stimulation of a real high school."

"I don't like stimulation, and I don't need the drama of a 'real' high school. I can move through the program as fast as I want. I could graduate in a year."

"Is Max the reason you want to go the alternative route? You're worried about being away all day, aren't you?"

"Maybe." Uncle Max paid for her housekeeping services. The house was clean and organized. She would get behind if she sat in a classroom thirty hours a week.

"But think of all the fun you'll miss."

Chancy imitated one of Adam's wry faces and borrowed a phrase she'd heard him use. "I was raised by wolves. Can you really see me at a football game pep rally or decorating the gym for Spring Fling? Really?"

Jenny laughed. "Okay, maybe you are too 'old' for that stuff."

She'd had a rotten childhood, but she was ready to move on to a happy adulthood. She didn't want to waste three years in the limbo world of high school when she could study on her own, without distractions, and prepare for real life.

"Any word from the law office?" Jenny asked.

"Leah Perkins calls twice a week, even when there's no news to report. Uncle Max says I'm her new favorite project."

"I'm glad they're taking such an interest."

"Mr. Marshall got copies of my birth certificate and Social Security card. We're waiting on school records, but the way we moved around so much, it might take a while."

"So when are you planning to take your driving test?"

Uncle Max had asked her the same thing. He said his bum ticker might cost him his license again. *And then where will we be? Back to investing in the blankety-blank cab company, that's where!*

"Your brows are scrunched together," Jenny observed with a good mom eye. "You look worried. You're not allowed to worry on your birthday."

"Mr. Marshall hired an investigator to find B.J. I'm afraid they won't find her. And I'm afraid that if they do, she won't sign the papers." Chancy didn't want to spoil the birthday lunch, but she'd lost her appetite.

"Why wouldn't she? She hasn't exactly been a devoted mother," Jenny said gently.

"You don't know her. She would refuse just to hurt me."

"If she can't be a parent, giving up the responsibility would make things easier for her. Why wouldn't she do something to her advantage?"

"It's called cutting off your nose to spite your face." Chancy was always surprised when Uncle Max's phrases slipped into her conversations. "B.J. might say no because she found a tiny piece of shell in her scrambled eggs that morning. Or because the shower took too long to warm up or because the day was sunny instead of cloudy or cloudy instead of sunny. I stopped trying to make sense of her a long time ago."

"That kind of perversity is typical of people with mood disorders. Don't let your mother make you sad today. Don't give her that power." Jenny believed good was always rewarded and justice was always served. Nice ideals. But not at all like the real world.

"You know a lot about things." Jenny had managed to put Chancy's fears into words she could understand, which made them less fearsome. "You should have been a counselor."

"I like being a preschool director. Especially at Moppet Manor, working with the very young and the very old. The little ones don't know how to be anything but what they are, and the old ones don't have time to be anything else. Do me a favor? Don't worry for the rest of today. Tomorrow if you want to worry, we'll worry together. We'll gnash our teeth and wring our hands. But not today. Today you're not allowed to be unhappy."

Chancy smiled. Jenny made happiness sound simple. Just another decision that anyone could make.

It was after seven o'clock when they got home. Jenny dropped Chancy off and pulled the minivan into her garage. The house was silent. Uncle Max had probably gone across the street to the Hamiltons'. A spark of disappointment flashed. She'd hoped to have a quiet birthday celebration, just the two of them. She carried her purchases up to her room, pausing on the landing to ask Hanna's opinion of her new hairstyle. The layered, shoulder-length cut made her look mature, which would be a big advantage when she talked to the judge. Maybe good hair would help convince him she could take care of herself. She'd spent some of her precious money on a yellow dress to wear to court. A new dress. With short sleeves. Secondhand ragamuffins needed to be in someone's custody. Stylish, independent women did not.

She was hanging the dress in the closet when a loud sigh made her turn around to find Alfie in the doorway. "Hi, buddy, did you miss me today?"

Instead of demanding his daily ear scratch, he ambled into the hallway and gave a low summoning yip.

"What? You want to go for a walk? We'll have to make it short. I've already walked a million mall miles today." She followed Alfie down the stairs and through the quiet house to the back porch to attach the leash. When they stepped outside, the dog did not take to the sidewalk. Instead he headed straight for Hanna's garden.

Chancy thought she heard a faint ripple of laughter but didn't see anyone in the shadows. "Uncle Max? Are you out here?" She unlatched the gate and stepped inside. A thousand white fairy lights, strung around the garden fence, twinkled into brightness. Many voices yelled in unison, "Surprise!"

Chancy gasped and Alfie barked. Uncle Max was the first to step into view at the end of the garden path. "Happy birthday, Chancy!" Then Corliss and Eddie walked out from behind the lilacs. Adam and Tom rose up from behind two picnic tables, turned end to end and covered with Hanna's embroidered tablecloths and food. In the center a tall cake dotted with unlit candles towered over brightly wrapped gifts. More people stepped out of the shadows. Barb Shannon. Mr. Marshall. Leah Perkins and her husband. Two nursing assistants from Dogwood Manor with whom she'd become friends. Three Manor residents. Everyone was laughing and wishing her a happy birthday and asking her if she was really surprised.

Uncle Max wrapped her in his trembling arms. "I love you, Chancy." His voice was thick with emotion.

"Was this your idea?"

"I couldn't have pulled it off without everyone's help."

"Party time!" Adam punched a button on his portable CD player and soft music from the 1940s filled the night.

"Do you forgive me for dragging you around Oklahoma City all day?" Jenny's hands on her shoulders reminded Chancy that the magical scene before her—the friends and family—was real.

"You knew about this?"

"Of course. Max said to get you out of town for the whole day."

"You're the princess tonight." Adam awkwardly placed a rhinestone tiara on her head. "You have to wear the crown."

"Happy sweet sixteen!" Corliss gave her a bear hug and then turned to the guests. "Plenty of food, folks. We don't stand on ceremony around here. Help yourselves. Are you surprised, honey?"

Surprise didn't begin to describe what Chancy felt. All these people had come together to help her celebrate. She was left speechless by wonder. Awe. Joy. Gratitude. Love.

The cake-eating-joke-telling-song-singing-health-toasting-gift-opening party went on for hours. Corliss had baked the cake and a glazed ham. Guests had contributed to the potluck. Adam claimed credit for the twinkle lights, a very good idea indeed. Chancy mingled, talking easily to everyone who'd made her first birthday party so special. How was it possible that she knew so many people who cared about her?

Leah Perkins introduced her husband and they raved about what Max and Chancy had done in the house.

"Such a lovely old home. Just beautiful. And the garden! Incredible. Tim and I are in the market for our first home and would love to find a place like this. Chancy, will you and Max show me around the garden?"

Once they were out of earshot, Leah shared what she seemed to think was good news. "The investigator found your mother, Chancy."

The night air raised a chill on her bare arms. She rubbed the scars that would always be there to remind her who she really was. "And?"

"Following her discharge from the hospital, she underwent court-ordered drug treatment."

"Does that mean she might be more . . . reasonable?" Uncle Max asked.

"Reasonable isn't what she's about," Chancy said dully. Where had the magic gone? How could her mother kill the joy in everything, even when she was far away? "My mother fools people into thinking she's better, but she never is. Not really."

"She's living in a halfway house in Pittsburgh. I wanted you to know we're serving her with termination-of-parental-rights papers on Monday."

"What if she won't sign? What if the authorities make me go back?"

Uncle Max wrapped a protective arm around her. "We won't let that happen."

"I'm sorry, Chancy," Leah said. "I thought you'd be glad to know we're making progress."

"I *am* glad. Thank you. When will we . . . find out if she signed?"

"The process server will advise her to consult an attorney. The deadline gives her time to fully understand her rights."

"She could run away. She moves around a lot."

"In that case, we post a notice in the Pittsburgh papers, and after a certain amount of time we can go to court and request that her rights be legally terminated."

"Even if she doesn't sign the papers?"

"It will just take longer, but yes."

Chancy sighed. There was still a chance.

Later, after the other guests had departed, the Briggses helped clean up. "Eddie has something to celebrate." Corliss gave her son a sly smile as she wrapped the leftover ham in aluminum foil.

"Mom, it's no big deal." He tied up a trash bag filled with paper plates and cups.

"It is too! He got promoted to assistant manager at the Lube Place."

"Congratulations, Eddie."

"I'm just one of several assistant managers. But it's something, I guess."

"Work your way up in the business," Uncle Max advised. "Men who start at the bottom and learn everything on their way to the top make the most effective managers."

"Good advice, Max. Thanks." Eddie nudged his mother. "You told on me; now I get to tell on you. Mom had a good checkup last time. Her emphysema isn't progressing as fast as the doctor expected."

Corliss shrugged and pooh-poohed their excitement. "Yeah, looks like I still have a few hash-slinging days in my future."

"Best darn party I ever gave." After saying good-bye to Corliss and Eddie, Max wanted to have one more look at the garden.

They sat on the picnic bench. "I know the garden looks good, but I wish the hostas would come," Chancy said. She had received a notice from the grower saying shipment would be delayed until early spring because of the season.

"They go dormant in the winter anyway," he reminded her. "Come spring, we'll get 'em in the ground. Did you like your party?"

"It was wonderful! Thank you so much."

"I have a gift for you."

"But you already gave me my gift. *The Secret Garden* movie."

"That was a decoy present. I wanted to give you this after everyone was gone." He placed a small, foil-wrapped box in her hand. "I could say I want you to have this, but the truth is, it was Hanna's idea."

Inside the box was the diamond butterfly. The fairy lights made its pavé wings glitter. The real butterfly was more beautiful than any she could have imagined. "Uncle Max!"

"Girls nowadays don't wear brooches. I had the jewelry store take off the clasp and make it into a necklace. Here, let me put it around your neck."

She lifted her hair and he fastened the catch on the silver chain. The weight grounded her, and the symbolism set her free.

"Uncle Max." She could never own anything so precious. "I can't keep it."

"Of course you can. It's yours now."

"I'm afraid I might lose it."

"Oh, I have something else for you." He folded her trembling hand around a key.

"What's this?"

"A key to my safe-deposit box. The rest of Hanna's jewelry belongs to you now. It's no fortune, but there's plenty of sentimental value. I know she'd be happy to know you have it."

Too much. His love and trust were enough. "I can't take this. Or Hanna's jewelry. It doesn't belong to me."

"Legally it does. I told Pete what I was doing, and I put your name on the box at the bank. Everything in it belongs to you."

Chancy could scarcely absorb what Uncle Max was saying.

"I never had a daughter or a granddaughter to give these things to. We don't share the same blood, but what we do have is more important than a few strands of DNA."

"A heart connection," she said. His features relaxed in relief. "Thank you, Uncle Max. You've given me something worth more than diamonds." They sat in peaceful camaraderie for long moments. "Are you ready to go in?"

"You go ahead. I want to stay out here with Hanna for a few more minutes."

When Chancy leaned down to kiss his cheek, the shiny butterfly fluttered between them. "When you come in, I have something for you."

"It's not my birthday."

"I know, but I've been making you something special. So don't stay out here too long."

Chancy carried her gifts up to her room. She opened the bottom drawer of her bureau and removed the memory book. She'd been close to finishing it several times but always found a few more pictures to include. She'd had to return to the craft store twice to buy additional pages. It was ready now. What better time to give him a gift than on her birthday? He'd made her life worth celebrating.

She held the heavy book close to her chest and pushed open the gate. He wasn't on the bench where she'd left him. Alfie raced ahead of her and barked. Chancy found Uncle Max lying at the back of the garden, crumpled on the ground next to Mrs. Moon.

Chapter 27

Chancy rode to the hospital in the ambulance with Uncle Max. She wasn't allowed in the back, where two paramedics worked over him. The only thing she could give him now was her strength. That strength had enabled her to call 911 and answer the dispatcher's questions coherently. It had held panic at bay while she waited at his side for help. Even though he was unconscious, she had continued to talk to him, to encourage him with words. Their heart connection. *I love you. Help is on the way. Hang on. Don't leave me. I love you.*

Tom and Jenny followed the ambulance in their car. Chancy had managed to comfort her friend when Jenny raced across the street, fearing the worst when she saw the flashing ambulance lights outside Max's house. They'd held each other while the medics worked to stabilize Uncle Max. It was past midnight now as the ambulance careened down Wenonah's dark streets, flying through red lights with siren screeching.

"I know you're worried about your grandpa." The driver's eyes never left the road, but his concern was genuine. "We're taking good care of him."

"Thank you." She was grateful for the man's honesty. He didn't make empty promises, didn't say everything would be all right. She trusted the dedicated medics to do what they could for Uncle Max. When the driver pulled into the ambulance bay, Chancy and the Hamiltons were directed to the waiting room while Uncle Max was rushed into an emergency examination room. Jenny provided the information admitting needed while Tom led Chancy to the chairs.

"It will probably be a while before we know anything," Tom said. "Hard to believe this happened. Max looked fine at the party. Did he say he was having problems?"

"No." Her hand closed on the diamond butterfly necklace. Maybe if she held it tightly, it wouldn't fly away again and take Uncle Max.

"Jenny told me about his heart condition. Sometimes it's better to go quickly than to suffer."

"Do you think he'll die?" Chancy was filled with a strange tranquillity. Her mind was clear, free of chaos. It was almost as if she were watching events unfold on a television screen.

"I couldn't say. We'll just have to wait and see what the doctor says."

"I can wait." Jenny joined them and sat next to her. She and Tom murmured across Chancy, but she didn't listen. She closed her eyes, not to slip into the dark place, but to see all the memories and pictures Uncle Max had given her. She didn't sleep. She remembered.

"Boyle?"

Chancy opened her eyes. A tall doctor in blue scrubs stood with his hands stuffed in the pockets of his white lab coat. He explained how the leaky valve in Uncle Max's heart was allowing blood to seep into the chambers and reducing oxygen flow to his brain. Medication had helped, but surgery was the only real fix.

"Problem is, there's not much we can do. Mr. Boyle has a DNR order on file."

"What's that?" If it kept Uncle Max from getting help, it couldn't be good.

"Do not resuscitate. That means we can't operate or perform any other lifesaving procedures. We can only make him comfortable."

"What's the date on the order?" Chancy asked.

"I don't have his chart with me, but I believe it was signed and filed just a few weeks ago."

"Is he awake?" She wanted to see him again. One more time.

"No. But he's stable. We're moving him to CCU. You won't be able to visit until tomorrow. I'll know more in a few hours. If he didn't suffer too much hypoxia, he'll probably regain consciousness."

Chancy didn't understand the medical terms. She asked the only question she could: "Will he live?"

"He might. He's pretty tough. I've treated him in the ER before. Spirited, isn't he?" Everyone laughed. Who knew you could laugh when life was so serious? The doctor said, "Attitude is probably the best thing Mr. Boyle has going for him right now. If he fights back and continues to respond to medication and hasn't suffered brain damage . . . he could live awhile longer."

"How much longer?" Chancy was afraid of the answer. More afraid not to know.

"Three months? Six? Hard to say. He'll need a considerable level of care, so I'll have someone talk to you. Who's his next of kin?"

"Max doesn't have any living relatives," Jenny said. "I'm his legal medical power of attorney." The doctor directed the rest of his comments to her.

After he left, Chancy turned to her friend. "What does that mean? Power of attorney?"

"Max asked me to be legally responsible to make medical decisions for him, in case he wasn't able to make them himself. Pete Marshall drew up the papers and Max and I filed the DNR."

"You signed a paper saying the doctors aren't allowed to save him?" Chancy was drowning in confusion. She didn't want to believe Jenny could be that heartless.

"It's what Max wanted. I was opposed at first. I tried to talk him into having the surgery. Then he explained why this was the best way. I respect his decision. I hope you will too."

"You don't love him like I do," she accused.

"Maybe not in the same way, but just as much. Everything happens for a reason, remember? Even if the worst happens, you're not alone."

Chancy trembled with a million tears, but she couldn't cry. Crying was pointless. She stared at the shiny green floor, subtly shifting away from Jenny's embrace. Maybe loving people was pointless too. Everyone left eventually.

. . .

Uncle Max surprised everyone by slowly regaining strength and showing some of the attitude the doctor had mentioned. The nurses and therapists who were in and out of his room kept Chancy updated on his progress. Even though Chancy had no legal or blood ties to Uncle Max, Jenny encouraged her to attend the discharge planning meeting. They sat in the hospital social worker's small office waiting for her to join them.

"Max looks good today, don't you think?" Jenny was trying to distract Chancy. She'd insisted Chancy and Alfie stay at her house while Max was in the hospital, but Chancy had moved back across the street that morning to get it ready for his homecoming.

"Yes." Uncle Max had regained consciousness the morning after his collapse. The heart specialist said that was a good sign, and Chancy trusted any doctor who believed in signs. Medication had slowed the leakage. He was almost back to his old self. For now. He had to avoid exertion, but the occupational therapist had okayed him to do most activities of daily living.

"Sorry I'm late." A middle-aged woman in a purple suit bustled in and settled noisily behind her desk. She didn't shake hands with Jenny or introduce herself, a breach of etiquette that Chancy understood now that she had observed the social skills of good role models. Maybe the woman expected them to read her name on the small wooden plaque on her desk: SHEILA MYERSON.

She perched a narrow pair of reading glasses on the end of her nose and glanced through the file she'd carried in. She spoke without looking up. "This won't take long. Mr. Boyle is ready to be discharged to skilled care. Do you have a choice of facilities?"

"Shouldn't he help decide?" Chancy asked.

"No. That's for the family—or in this case, the medical power of attorney—to do."

"Why does he have to go to skilled nursing if he doesn't need that much care right now?" Jenny asked. She seemed almost as confused as Chancy.

"Medicare pays for him to have a skilled level of care after a hospital stay of this nature. Any other questions?"

Jenny and Chancy exchanged uneasy looks. "Just because Medicare will pay doesn't mean he has to go, does it?"

"He doesn't *have* to do anything. But that's our usual procedure. Any more questions?"

"That's it?" Jenny asked.

"Unless there's something you need to know." If Sheila Myerson's voice were a thermometer, it would have just plunged several degrees. She removed her glasses and set them on top of the closed file.

"The doctor said Max didn't suffer brain damage," Jenny said. "He can eat and walk and breathe on his own. He's fully cognizant and can participate in his own care."

"Maybe for the time being. But his heart is going to kill him. As his condition deteriorates, he will require increasing levels of care."

"What about hospice?" Chancy remembered that Hanna had had hospice at the end.

"What about it?" Sheila Myerson didn't seem to like answering questions.

"Doesn't he qualify?"

She consulted the file again. "His prognosis is less than six months, so yes, he would qualify, but I understand he lives alone. Hospice doesn't provide round-the-clock care, you know."

"He does not live alone! I live with him."

"You're a child. You can't supply the kind of care he needs. Any other questions? No? Let the discharge nurse know when you decide where you want Mr. Boyle transferred and she'll make the arrangements. Have a nice day." She dropped Max's file in a plastic out-box and picked up another.

"Isn't this kind of fast?" Jenny's voice thermometer heated up a few degrees.

"I have more than one case to attend to. Now if you'll excuse me."

"I thought a social worker's job was to help people," Jenny said. "I think you need to be in a different line of work! Like scraping the trays in the cafeteria downstairs! Come on, Chancy. Let's get out of here."

Jenny swept out the door. Chancy turned for another glimpse of

Sheila Myerson's shocked expression. Wait until she told Uncle Max that his medical power of attorney had stuck up for his rights.

Uncle Max did laugh when they told him, but he quickly sobered, and his response dismayed Chancy. "You know, maybe she's right. I can't ask you to take on that kind of responsibility. Call Dogwood Manor, Jenny. See if you can get me in."

"Wait a minute!" Chancy knew how long and hard he had fought this step. He couldn't just throw in the towel. Not to protect her. "I *want* the responsibility. Unless you don't think I'm qualified to take care of you."

"Honey, I'm going to get worse."

"And I'm going to get more experienced. Jenny will be right across the street. Corliss will want to help too."

"As long as she can draw a breath, I'm sure she will be helping somebody. Somewhere."

"So? What do you say? I don't know exactly what we have to do, but we can manage. If you're willing to give it a shot."

"Are you sure? I don't expect you to give up your life to take care of me."

She stood by his bed and leaned in close. She wanted to stay with Uncle Max for the precious minutes and hours and days he had left. "I wouldn't have a life if you hadn't taken care of me, so no more arguments!"

She convinced Jenny to hold off calling Barb Shannon about a room at the Manor until she talked to Leah Perkins. She might be aware of options the hospital staff had been too insensitive and disinterested to offer.

Leah called Chancy the next day with some promising information. The state had recently received a $50 million grant called the Oklahoma Long-term Living Choice Project from the federal Centers for Medicare and Medicaid Services. She didn't want to bog Chancy down in all the details but assured her that the purpose of the grant was to give older state residents a choice of whether to receive medical and social assistance in an institution or in their own home.

"Ask the hospital's social worker to look into this option. But she'll need to hurry so plans can be put in place before he leaves the hospital."

"She won't." Chancy knew Sheila Myerson would not be amenable to extending herself on Uncle Max's behalf. Especially not after Jenny had encouraged her to downgrade her employment expectations.

"What about Max's caseworker at APS? She might be able to help."

Wooten the Relentless? Chancy wasn't optimistic, given the woman's track record, but she was desperate to see that Uncle Max lived out his days at home. That had always been his goal. She wasn't about to let him give up because he thought she couldn't handle being his caregiver.

Chancy and Jenny met with Ms. Wooten to relay the info Leah had provided.

"Of course, I'm well aware of the new funds," the social worker said when she'd heard them out. "State agency and community organization leaders developed the application for the Money Follows the Person grant. I just don't think that changes anything for Mr. Boyle."

Chancy had seen the women's skepticism before, but this time it didn't frighten her. It made her more determined. "So why can't Uncle Max receive care at home?"

"Because he lives alone, without family. I know you want to help him, Chancy, but you'll be leaving soon. Mrs. Hamilton, you have your own family and a job. This isn't what you want to hear, but he will soon require twenty-four-hour care that can best be provided by an institution."

Chancy looked at Jenny. Time for more truth. "About me leaving..."

It took a long time to reveal the whole story. Ms. Wooten's professional demeanor gradually gave way to disbelief. When she asked questions, her tone softened. Not much, but enough to give Chancy hope.

"So," Ms. Wooten said finally, "everything that happened at 639 Poplar Avenue was a lie?"

"No!" Chancy would make her understand. "Maybe the story we told was fiction, but aren't good stories always true? At the heart? You saw the changes—in Uncle Max and in the house. Those are real. The garden is real. I'm real."

"Yes, you definitely are."

"So will you help?" Jenny spoke up. "Ms. Wooten? Can we count on you? Can Max?"

She nodded, slow and knowing. "I became a social worker to help others. Never thought I'd develop do-gooder's astigmatism, unable to see the people for the cases."

"If it makes you feel any better"—Chancy crossed her fingers in her lap—"you weren't easy to fool."

Ms. Wooten laughed. "I guess there's always more than one side to any story. Give me until tomorrow. I'll see what I can do."

The next day Shevaun Wooten dropped by Uncle Max's room. She stood in the door and nodded. "Okay."

"Okay?" Chancy and Uncle Max asked together.

"I should have slowed down, preached less and listened more. Thanks for teaching me something about myself."

"Does that mean I can go home?" Uncle Max was clearly confused that his enemy had come over to his side.

"I'll expedite the paperwork. You should be able to leave in a couple of days."

Chapter 28

The hospice aide plumped Max's pillow and angled his hospital bed so that he could enjoy the late-March sun through the sunroom window. Chancy had hung some of her hearts in the window and they winked in the light. She was in the garden, but she must have felt him thinking about her. She looked up from the flat of pansies she was transplanting and waved. He couldn't lift his arms these days, but she knew he was waving from his heart. Seemed he slept most of the time, like an old dog whose senses were failing. Alfie, curled up on the rug in the corner, was never far away.

I might be an old dog, Hanna, but I beat the odds that fancy doctor gave me. Doubled my ninety-day prognosis.

You always were a show-off, Professor.

Fools thought I'd be history by Thanksgiving, but there I was, head of the table. I was truly blessed. Had seven people around our table board. Remember those puny Cornish game hens we used to fix for our lonely holiday meals? This year I carved the biggest damned turkey you ever saw. And it took Jenny and Chancy two days to cook all the trimmings. Corliss was feeling poorly. Suffered a setback, bless her heart.

Hope you helped with the dishes. Terminal illness is no excuse to slack off, you know.

Chancy and I spent a quiet Christmas. Just the two of us. While she was visiting poor Corliss at the Manor, my old teacher, Sister Blessida, dropped by to see me.

Sister Blessida really gets around for a woman who is a hundred and seventeen years old.

All right, that afternoon is a little fuzzy, but this part is crystal-clear. Tom went back to work after Labor Day. Jenny doesn't have to stay on at the preschool now, but she won't give up her new career. Why, she's blossomed damn near as much as Chancy. She's all the time creating some new program for the Moppets and their "adopted" grandparents. Chancy volunteers at Moppet Manor two mornings a week.

She's almost a Moppet herself.

She's growing up! Did I mention she's driving the Lincoln now?

Don't forget to tell her to let it run a few minutes to warm up the engine on cold mornings. It can be temperamental.

School has been like brain fertilizer for that girl. I bought her a computer to use at home for distance learning. She only has to go to the alternative school for reviews and tests. She'll graduate by the end of the summer. And she's making mostly As.

Because you're helping her study. Old teachers never die, you know. They just grade away.

Notice how nice the place looks? Chancy and I fixed it up, and I hired a lady to come in once a week to clean and wash laundry. That way Chancy can spend more time with her books.

With you, you mean.

So what if I like her company? She doesn't give me a hard time like you always do. She loves me.

Oh, I love you, Professor. I love you more than sunshine.

"Mr. Boyle? Are you awake?"

"Huh? Just resting my eyes." Now when he spoke, his words sounded like they were leaking out of a balloon. He didn't recognize the woman beside his bed. Must be someone new from hospice.

"Ms. Wooten's here to see you. Are you up to a visit?"

Well, I was going to reshingle the roof, but if she's already here . . . "Yeah."

Max had come to look forward to Shevaun Wooten's visits. She checked in more often than case-management duties required, and had been a valuable resource for both him and Chancy. In the beginning, they had agreed that if their start-over-forgive-and-forget-white-flag arrangement was going to work, they would have to clear the air about their mutual misconceptions. They admitted they had both been wrong in their previous dealings.

Shevaun Wooten wasn't a completely officious and zealous bureaucrat, and Maxwell Boyle wasn't a totally prideful, pigheaded curmudgeon.

"I can't stay long," she said. "I just wanted to check up on you."

"'Kay."

"I spoke to Chancy earlier. She said you've been eating more."

I'm nowhere near up to my starving orphan days, but I do my bit. "A little."

She stood by the window admiring the garden. "Every day is a wonder, isn't it? Max?"

Sorry. I dozed off for a second. Did you say something? "Huh?"

She patted his arm. "You rest. I'll see you next week."

Don't hold it against me if I stand you up. "Bye."

Chancy finished planting the pansies. Green shoots were popping up all over the garden. The hostas had appeared, but the back-ordered Dancing in the Rain was still AWOL. She'd check local greenhouse stock in a few weeks. Maybe she would find it this year.

Shevaun Wooten looked over the fence. She'd been instrumental in making arrangements for Uncle Max's in-home care. The hospice agency had handled all the details, stepping up the care level as his condition worsened.

"Did he talk to you?" Chancy asked.

"He tried."

"It won't be long now, will it?"

Shevaun patted her shoulder. "Soon. Will you be okay?"

"I'll be fine. We've had some good months together."

"Together. That's the important thing. You and Max have taught me how to be a better advocate. Thank you. Call if you need anything."

Chancy couldn't think of anything she needed. Except maybe more time. Her emancipation had been granted shortly before the holidays. She would never forget the day Leah Perkins had called to tell her B.J. had left the halfway house less than twenty-four hours after the papers had been served. She'd left them stuffed in the wastebasket in her room. No forwarding address.

Fortunately, the investigator was smarter than B.J. He tracked her down again and served a new set of documents. That time he told her that if she didn't sign or respond to the request for a legal hearing within thirty days, Chancy's attorneys would proceed with the termination of rights anyway.

A few days later, Leah stopped by the house to talk because Max could no longer leave it, and Chancy didn't want to leave *him*.

Leah had pulled a stack of papers from her briefcase, which she had handed to Chancy. "The signed termination agreement arrived by special courier this afternoon from the process server. Pete wanted me to explain what will happen next."

Chancy flipped to the last page. On the line over the words *natural mother*, B.J.'s scrawled signature was notarized and affixed with an official-looking seal. *Betty J. Deel.*

A single word was typed on the line over the words *natural father*: Un-known.

"You can read the document later," Leah said. "I made a copy for you."

"Thanks." Maybe Chancy could forgive. After all, her mother had finally given her a paper heart.

"You won't understand the legalese, so if you have any questions, I'll try to answer them."

"I understand." She hadn't been surprised when B.J. ran from the half-way house. She was good at that. She hadn't been surprised when her mother had thrown Chancy's opportunity for happiness in the trash. She'd been doing that for years. What was surprising was that Chancy was finally holding the signed papers in her hand.

"This means my mother doesn't want me. I already knew that, but I'm glad it's finally official." She had expected this moment to make her new inner peace complete. She hated that B.J.'s final gesture twisted in her heart like a knife. Despite all that she'd accomplished, her mother had managed to hurt her one last time.

Leah's demeanor had shifted from that of attorney to friend. "Chancy, don't read too much into this. Legal forms have nothing to do with human emotion. I'm sure this decision was difficult for your mother. Parents often terminate their rights for good reasons."

"Did she say anything? Include a note?" Chancy wasn't sad. So why did she feel like crying?

"No. This is good news, you know. We can set up the hearing now. I've never handled one of these cases, but no judge in the land can read my petition and deny you legal emancipation."

"Did she sign the papers on the spot and throw them back at the messenger? Screaming the whole time he put the notary stamp on them?"

Leah's silence had told her that she'd become expert at predicting her mother's behavior. But now she would never have to deal with her again.

Her mother's signature had marked a turning point for Chancy. Once the worry was behind her, she had made steady progress through school. She was free to enjoy her volunteer work with Jenny. She fulfilled the terms of her emancipation agreement by working for Uncle Max, her duties cut back to those of night nurse. She had moved one of the recliners into the sunroom and that was where she slept. Next to his bed.

She had decided to go into the independent-living program once Uncle Max was gone. Jenny had tried to change her mind, had said the Hamiltons would be happy to give her a home. Chancy had finally convinced her that living on her own and being alone were not the same things. She still wanted to be part of the family of friends she'd made in Wenonah. She just wanted to take responsibility for herself now. Jenny relented and encouraged her to talk to Barb Shannon about a paid position at the Manor. She would need an income to fulfill the independent-living program requirements.

Chancy washed her hands in the kitchen and checked on Uncle Max. His breathing was as noisy as his snoring used to be, so it was hard to tell when he was awake. The hospice nurse checked his vitals and gave Chancy a silent no-change look. He still had a few alert moments, but this week they'd been farther apart. The price paid for palliative care. He wasn't in pain, but she missed his voice. His laughter. And his stories. She would miss him.

That night around midnight, Alfie's cold nose nudged Chancy's hand until she roused.

"What is it, boy?" When she looked over at Uncle Max, she saw that he was awake. He tried to speak, and she leaned over the bed. She thought he said, "Book," and asked if he wanted her to read to him. No, that wasn't it. Book. Oh, the memory book? Yes, that was what he wanted. She switched on the bedside light and removed the album from the drawer. Raising the head of his bed to a comfortable position, she propped the book in his lap. They started at the beginning and she told him the stories behind each picture.

When they reached the end of the album, he wanted to start over, as though he were memorizing his life. It was after two a.m. when he finally tired. She kissed him good night, and he whispered something that sounded like "love."

She pulled up the covers and lowered the bed. "I love you too, Uncle Max." Curled in the chair under her own blanket, she soon fell asleep.

Outside the window the wind chimes tinkled.

Chapter 29

"Are you sure you can do this?" Jenny asked.

Chancy stood in the living room she'd helped redecorate, Alfie at her side. The old dog had been subdued since Max's death six days ago. He wandered from room to room as though looking for his longtime companion. The house was quiet, and the heavy stillness weighed on all of them.

"Do you think Uncle Max would have been surprised by the size of the crowd at his memorial service?"

"I don't think he had any idea how many lives he touched over the years. There were former students in attendance from thirty years ago."

"I like to think he was sitting in the back row, counting heads." She laughed, then sobered. "It's so empty without him." Not just the house. Her life.

"If you need me, I can stay with you tonight," Jenny offered.

"No, you go home to Tom and Adam. I'll be fine. I don't know how I would have gotten through the last couple weeks without you."

"I'll be over first thing in the morning to help you pack. By this time tomorrow, you'll be settling into your new apartment."

"My own place. Feels like a dream."

"It's real. You have an advantage over most independent-living teens. Eventually, you really will be independent because of the inheritance Max left you." Jenny smoothed a stray lock of Chancy's hair. "Pete will take care of the money you'll get from Max's insurance policy."

"Did you know he'd made me the beneficiary?"

"We discussed it, yes. He wanted to ensure that you had the funds to pursue your education."

"I'm glad having money in trust from Uncle Max won't disqualify me for the program." According to Leah, who was handling the probate of the estate, when Chancy turned eighteen she would receive the first payment to cover college expenses. She would receive another sum at age twenty-five to help her buy a house or start a business. The last payment at age thirty could be used however she chose. In the meantime, she would receive a small monthly stipend for living expenses based on the portfolio's earnings.

"Leah wants to buy Uncle Max's house," Chancy said. "She loves the garden!"

"She'll take care of it for you." Jenny looked around. "You know, it's a good thing you and Max did so much work. It'll make clearing out the house easier."

"I think Max knew that too." That day at the furniture store, he'd told her to choose what *she* wanted. "Once I take a few pieces for my apartment, I want to give the rest to the independent-living program."

"When do you start your new job?"

"Monday. Just a few hours in the afternoon, so I can prove my 'willingness to be self-supporting' and still keep up with my schoolwork." Barb Shannon had gladly agreed to hire Chancy. At first, she would help the activity director. Be an extra pair of hands. A ready hugger. Later, when she was older, she could train as a nurse's aide. The best part of the job was being able to bring Alfie to work.

"Barb thinks a lot of you," Jenny said. "She believes you should consider becoming a geriatrician."

"That's a doctor, right?" High school was hard enough, but medical school? "Why would she think I could be a doctor?"

"Why not? There're always going to be older people who need specialized care. And you'd be good at it . . . because you have such a caring heart. It's something to think about."

Yes. Everyone needed something to think about. Something to care about. Something to love. She liked old folks. Maybe she *should* go to medical school. Someday.

She walked to the sideboard and picked up Max and Hanna's wedding picture. At sixteen, she was already planning her future. This time last year, she hadn't even had one. Now anything was possible.

Uncle Max had given her another dream to hold.

Jenny looked over her shoulder. "Gorgeous couple, weren't they?"

If Chancy did only one thing in her life, she wanted to have a love like theirs. "Dancing fools. Crazy in love. A perfect couple."

"It'll be wonderful having you at the Manor. Quite a coincidence the way things worked out."

Chancy smiled and set the portrait back in its place. "Oh, haven't you heard? There are no coincidences."

The next morning Chancy awoke early to a knock at the door. By the time she made it downstairs the postman was walking away. At her call, he turned and waved. "Left a package for you, miss."

She found the small box on the rocker. Greenheart Nursery. Portland, Oregon. After all these months, the elusive hosta had arrived. She'd expected containerized plants like the Mrs. Moon, but this package felt incredibly light, as though there were nothing inside. She carried it into the kitchen and cut through the packing tape. Inside, wrapped in plastic and sphagnum moss, she found three clusters of brown roots. Hanna's journal notes had warned not to be misled by bare root plants. They didn't look like much, but a little water, a little sunshine and a lot of faith would create a miracle.

Clouds had gathered by the time Chancy dressed and retrieved the spade from the garage. Before she moved out, she would plant the hostas in the spot reserved for them. Leah had assured her she could come and visit the garden anytime she wanted. She welcomed Chancy's plant-care expertise. Chancy couldn't wait to return in a couple of months to see if the spidery roots had warmed in the soil and transformed into the beautiful plants in Hanna's picture.

"C'mon, boy." She opened the gate and Alfie ran in. He snuffled around in the daylilies, while she dug the holes. A first gentle raindrop struck her face as she sprinkled crushed eggshells in the bottom, layered in a bed of peat moss, and gently arranged the roots. She filled the hole and patted the dirt, in a hurry now because the sprinkle had become more determined. She poked into the ground the plant stake on which she'd written the plant's name.

Dancing in the Rain.

The wind kicked up and the wind chimes tinkled. *Crazy pixie marching band.* Chancy heard Max's laughter on the breeze and what sounded like a woman's laughter too. She would miss him, but she would not mourn him. He'd lived his life the way he wanted.

Now she would live hers.

The soft drops splashed down, but Chancy didn't mind. She'd weathered the storm her life had been. She'd cleared away the strangling weeds and reached for the sun. Max had nurtured her spirit, just as the gentle rain would bring new life to the garden.

A time and a season.

Chancy stood, picked up the spade and walked to the gate in the misty rain. She called her companion. "Okay, boy. That's enough poking about. We have work to do. Let's go."

When Alfie did not bound to her side, Chancy turned and found him staring at the spot where she'd just planted the hosta. He stood frozen, focused and intent. His body quivered, and he tipped his head from side to side, as though seeing something he didn't understand.

The rain came down, a shimmering, silver sheet. Chancy followed the line of Alfie's determined gaze, and for a brief moment she glimpsed something that made her heart pound with joyous disbelief.

Beside the beautiful blooming plant, Hanna and Max, young and strong, dancing together in the rain.

About the Author

Debrah Williamson has written professionally for twenty years and is the author or coauthor of nearly thirty novels. A native Oklahoman, she lives in Norman. Visit her on the Web at www.debrahwilliamson.com.

Paper Hearts

Debrah Williamson

A CONVERSATION WITH
DEBRAH WILLIAMSON

Q. Paper Hearts *is narrated primarily by a teenage runaway and an old man contemplating the end of his life. On the surface, the novel doesn't seem to have much in common with your own life. So, what inspired you to write it?*

A. As a speech/language pathologist, I worked with the elderly and at-risk children, two populations rarely given a voice in fiction. During college I worked in a residential treatment facility for severely emotionally disturbed older children and teens, where I met several Chancys. I have certainly drawn upon my experience with these populations in writing *Paper Hearts*, but then, I think everything writers do eventually becomes assimilated into their work. I wanted to create characters who could put a face on seemingly "invisible" members of society and show that they, too, have contributions to make.

Q. *Can you elaborate on what you consider the most important themes of* Paper Hearts?

A. If I had to sum up the book's theme in two words it would be *Love heals*. I try to write about people who are larger than life because they have been tested by bad experiences. The characters in *Paper Hearts* are heroic simply because they do not let adversity destroy their hearts and spirits. The book's message—I hope—is that the individual can make a difference in the lives of others, and that is the only way to truly change the world.

Q. Paper Hearts *is set in a small Oklahoma town, and you live in Norman, Oklahoma. Are the two places similar?*

A. Not at all. Norman is the third-largest city in Oklahoma, a university town offering many social and cultural opportunities in an urban setting. Fictional Wenonah is a composite of several small Oklahoma towns, one of which I grew up in.

Q. *In* Paper Hearts *you show ordinary people struggling with major problems—emotional and physical abuse, neglect, depression, addiction, self-mutilation and the threatened loss of independence due to failing physical health. Why did you decide to explore so many tough subjects all in one novel?*

A. I enjoy a challenge? Suffer delusions of grandeur? Seriously, author Stanley Elkin once said he would never write about a character who was not at the end of his rope. Sounds like good advice. One purpose of fiction is to illuminate a character's journey. As a reader, I find the reading experience more satisfying if that journey is long and difficult and truly tests the characters. The more challenges characters overcome, the stronger the message of hope. In *Paper Hearts*, several characters must move beyond their own problems to connect with others.

Q. *You seem to have an affinity for the very old and the very young. Your first novel under the name Debrah Williamson,* Singing with the Top Down, *is narrated by a thirteen-year-old girl and features a cranky, elderly secondary character named Tyb. In* Paper Hearts *we have not only*

Chancy and Max but also twelve-year-old Adam. Why do you think you're particularly drawn to characters of these ages?

A. Maybe because in my previous writing life I wrote romance novels in which the protagonists were young men and women between the ages of twenty and thirty who were focused on finding mates. With the move into women's fiction, I was eager to explore different sensibilities, experiences, goals and motivations. Jenny, in *Paper Hearts*, says she likes to work with children because they don't try to be anything but what they are, and the elderly because they don't have time to play games. Maybe that's it for me too.

Q. Can you tell us a little bit about your writing career—how long you've been writing, what kind of books you wrote early in your career, and how you came to be published?

A. I've been writing all my life, but it wasn't until the mid-1980s that I seriously pursued publication. A collaborator and I sold our first category romance novel and went on to cowrite twenty-plus more—and a couple of historical romances—under a variety of pseudonyms. After establishing a solo career, I wrote five short contemporary romances under my married name. I chose to use my maiden name for women's fiction as a way to honor my family, since many of my stories focus on family issues.

Q. I don't know how you find the time, but I understand that you read widely in recently published women's fiction. What novels have you especially enjoyed in recent months?

A. I'm a compulsive and eclectic reader, have been since second grade. I don't only read women's fiction. I also read historical and literary fiction and memoir. I'm especially fond of Southern fiction and am always on the lookout for debut novels by new writers. Recent novels I have enjoyed are *Water for Elephants* by Sara Gruen, *The Memory Keeper's Daughter* by Kim Edwards, *The Observations* by Jane Harris, *The Madonnas of Leningrad* by Debra Dean, *Any Bitter Thing* by Monica Wood and *Once upon a Day* by Lisa Tucker. That list gives the impression that I only read female authors, but I read male writers too, such as Michael Chabon, John Irving, Mark Haddon, Charles Frazier, Robert Morgan and Silas House.

Q. *What's your writing schedule like? How hard is it to keep writing, despite the demands of work and family?*

A. Hard doesn't begin to describe the challenge of staying focused on my writing. In a perfect world, I would have a schedule, but life is messy and demanding, so I don't. Since writers who finish books and meet deadlines are those who say no to other things, I carve out writing time by forgoing activities many people consider essential: social engagements, travel and hobbies. I don't require much sleep and often write when the rest of the world is quiet. My prime writing time is on weekends, and I take advantage of those uninterrupted hours when I'm wide-awake and not tired from my day job. Luckily I have a supportive family who understands my need to be a hermit.

Q. *Since you published* Singing with the Top Down, *what has most surprised you about reader response to your book?*

A. Probably the demographic diversity of readers who've taken time to write and say how much they enjoyed the "uplifting spirit" of the book. I've heard from readers as young as thirteen and as old as eighty-four, both male and female. Many ask if I will please write a sequel so they can spend more time with the characters. For a writer, that is the ultimate compliment.

Q. *If you could ask your readers anything, what would it be?*

A. People have so many demands on their time these days. I would like to ask readers, "How do you choose the books you read? What determines how you will spend your reading time?"

Q. *What do you ultimately hope to achieve in your writing career?*

A. I've been at this for over twenty years. Since it's too late to become an overnight sensation, my goal is to simply endure.

QUESTIONS
FOR DISCUSSION

1. What is the author's goal or intention for this book? In your mind, does she achieve it?

2. Who is your favorite, or the most effective, character, and why?

3. Even though the author tackles tough subjects in the novel—teen runaways, the plight of senior citizens, depression, addiction—the overall message is one of hope. How do you think the author accomplished this?

4. The story is told through the viewpoints of two characters—Chancy and Max. Does having both viewpoints enhance the reading experience? Which of the voices did you identify with most? Why? How would the story change if told from only one character's point of view? Would that make the story more enjoyable, or less?

5. Chancy Deel is a damaged child. Was her transformation from troubled loner to confident young woman believable? Why, or why not?

6. Have you known people like Max Boyle? What experiences have you had with elderly individuals? Do you consider those experiences

positive or negative? How does Max represent the problems faced by the aging in our society today?

7. What themes are represented in the story? How do the characters deal with these themes?

8. Chancy is a magical thinker when the story begins. Why do you think she developed this style of thinking? How does her thinking change and adapt as she grows?

9. How does the setting influence the characters' lives and decisions? Have you ever lived in a small town? Is Wenonah a fair representation of small town life? In what ways are Chancy's perceptions of the town idealized or romanticized?

10. Two important characters—both story catalysts—never appear onstage. How well do you feel you understand Hanna Boyle and B.J. Deel? How does the author use these two "absent" characters to represent good and bad memories?

11. Chancy starts out believing in luck and the influence of the universe but eventually learns that actions determine fate. How do you feel about fortune or fate? How do your beliefs guide your decisions?

12. It has been said the true test of society is how it treats its most vulnerable citizens. In your opinion, does the author's fictional world treat the story's vulnerable characters believably? Realistically? Fairly? Does the fictional world's treatment of the elderly and at-risk children mirror real-life experiences you've had? How is it the same? Is it better, or worse?

13. In the story bad things happen to good people. How does this reflect real life?

14. *Paper Hearts* is about unrelated people coming together to form a family. Do you know people like Chancy, Max, Jenny and Corliss who don't have a real family and yet have cultivated a network of friends who act much like a family in their lives?

15. In what ways might contemporary culture isolate people from their families, so that they're compelled to seek out other families?

16. If you had to name a villain in the book, it might be the authority figures who work for Child and Adult Protective Services, who pose a threat to Chancy's freedom and to Max's independence. Do you believe it serves the public good for government agencies to step into people's lives and demand that they make changes? When does that right end, and the individual's right to make his or her own decisions take precedence? In *Paper Hearts*, in what specific ways are the people who work for government agencies both helpful and hurtful?

17. What do you think will happen to Chancy after the book ends? What will happen to Corliss, Jenny, Adam and Eddie?

18. Discuss the significance of the title *Paper Hearts*.